Closer to Indigo
Maria Koropecky

Ebook ISBN: 978-0-9739283-4-1
Paperback ISBN: 978-0-9739283-5-8

Designed and produced in Canada

I dedicate this story to all of the spiritual singles, writers, artists, introverts, energy healers, coaches, nature lovers, crystal lovers, late bloomers and pilgrims of the world. May you find your voice, feel your feelings, let go of your past, be more authentic, and foster worthiness from within, and be free to live and love as your like.

~ Maria

Closer to Indigo
Maria Koropecky

Part 1

white • caps

Contrary to Maria's wishful thinking, many people scoffed and said, "A cruise to Alaska is not a pilgrimage!" And even though a cruise conjures up images of people sitting poolside with their fruity cocktails by day, and dancing to a live band under sparkling disco balls by night, and eating lavish meals prepared by talented chefs in the formal dining rooms in between, Maria still experiences some moments of spiritual depth during her sailing.

Maria's mother, Lubomyra Ponomarenko, is a seasoned world traveller and for this tour, she has invited her daughter. To help take things up to the next level, three Ukrainian Catholic Bishops, along with several priests from distant cities, are also onboard.

On the second day of the cruise, one of the travelling priests gives an inspiring lecture on the "Symbolism in Icons" and talks about how the colours, composition, angels, Greek initials, halos and so on, relate to the significance and meaning of the icon overall.

"Icons are written, not painted and they are the windows into heaven. Icons are sacred, visual expressions of our faith and are intended to illustrate the holy figures of the Bible to anyone who contemplates them, whether they are literate or not," he says as he advances the slides. "Let's look at the eye motif in particular. It represents the omnipresent and omniscient Eye of God."

The next day at sea, the cruiseship makes its way further north along the British Columbia coastline to the amazing and awesome Hubbard Glacier (which is actually featured on one of the episodes of the "Love Boat," circa 1980, and it is sobering to see how much it has receded since then).

As the ship pivots for an hour in the icy waters that lap up against the foot of the glacier and the bilge of the ship, a naturalist narrates the scene over a loud speaker, describing the circling wildlife as well as pointing to the caving chunks of ice that resonantly plummet into the thick, frigid, steel blue and somber ocean below.

As Maria makes her way to the bow of the ship and braves the cold and misty terrane, her jaw drops when she notices the big, blue eye opening from the compressed layers of snow and ice at Hubbard's waterline.

"It's the Eye of God!" she beams! "This is where art imitates life, life imitates art, and art imitates life! That's what the priest was talking about yesterday!" She stares into the deep, blue, crystalline wall and composes a poem on the spot.

God is the present moment and the present moment is God.
The potent present moment is where all of the power and energy is.
The vast, present moment is the realm of possibilities, the spark of
creation.
The ethereal present moment is the womb of God.

God is the music playing within us and around us.
Having peace is living, being and dancing in the present moment.
We are all unfolding, blossoming like flowers, exploding like stars,
forever expanding.
Let God's creative spirit come through.

God is the alpha and the omega, the beginning and the end.
The present moment is the question and the answer.
The present moment is where infinity and eternity meet,
beyond space and time, just like God.

Satisfied with her mystical experience, Maria carries on with the cruise with a new spring in her step.

She is not bothered too much that the cool weather is not ideal for a summer cruise on the best of days and turns into a epic storm on the worst, and is grateful she has inherited her father's constitution of not being prone to seasickness while sailing in choppy waters.

She remembers her father, Yaromyr Ponomarenko, saying how relieved he was during his first commission on an HMCS Destroyer, after having completed two years at RMC in Kingston and two years at Royal Roads in Victoria, that he did not suffer from the dreaded and swift career-ending affliction of nausea on the high seas.

If, on the rare occasion the word "nausea" comes up in conversation, Maria likes to add, "Did you know "nausea" is a word from the 1500s that comes from naûs which means ship? Plus it has the word "sea" built right in!" She thinks she is being clever; everyone else changes the subject.

During the heaviest hours of the billowing storm that starts brewing during their second to last day at sea, and with swells of white wine rolling through her own head, Maria is trying to fall asleep in her top bunk, (beggars cannot be choosers after all). She peers out of the porthole and sees the whirling whitecaps whizzing by the ship, frosting the tips of the black ocean beneath, and she gasps at their speed and energy.

Lucky for her on this particular night, she does not have to jump out of bed in a quick hurry and race for the head. Instead, the philosopher in her chimes in.

"This is what my father saw."

Maria catches a glimpse into her father's life on the high seas as an officer in the Canadian Navy. Her late father would have weathered many storms like this at sea during his 33-year career, and in that moment, she is able to see through his eyes. She feels connected to him in a new way, even years after his passing.

"His career was one big adventure" and she pictures sailors singing, "Farewell to Nova Scotia" while climbing the ropes of the tall ships of yesteryear and secretly admires their brazen foolhardiness.

Then it occurs to her that this mighty cruise ship is just a mere toothpick precariously floating in the expanse of the ocean, with the possibility of one rogue wave snapping it in pieces. Somehow though, the crew manages to keep the ship going, and eventually, they make their way back home to the Port of Vancouver, safe and sound.

you • knee • verse • all

Maria Ponomarenko wonders what may exist beyond the rim sometimes. If she catches the right current, she can enter the space where navy blue ends and royal purple begins, and lets herself hover there for a while.

She reaches for the infinite midnight sky in her sleep, floating, drifting in the great cosmic sea, but forgets her questions and lands back down on earth swiftly and with a bit of a thud, to Victoria, British Columbia, Canada, remembering that she's pushing 50, has never been married or has had any kids, and is still living with her mother.

"It's not fair to be a late bloomer everywhere else in life and have a midlife crisis right on time," she thinks, bursting into tears, not aware of who else is with her in spirit.

It finally dawns on her that unless she wants to continue life as a struggling single woman indefinitely or definitely, she needs to make some drastic changes, including getting in shape and going outside, and venturing far beyond the comforts of home.

"Maybe tomorrow," she says as she pulls her comforter to her chin.

For her, it is much easier to spend her time in her own imagination, the indigo spaces of the Universe, reading, writing, and dabbling in the energy of crystals, and quietly venturing beyond her traditional, Ukrainian Catholic upbringing, to her deeper Pagan roots.

"You can stay here all swaddled up for as long as you like, Maria, but your story is bigger than this. Now get up and start your day."

* * *

The name Maria comes with heavy baggage. As the Latin form of Mary, which is derived from the Hebrew Miryām, Maria is Biblical, following in the footsteps of the Virgin Mother of Jesus, of all people.

Besides Mother Mary, there are three other Maria's in the New Testament: Maria Magdalena and Maria Salomé, who are considered to be disciples of Jesus, and Maria Betânia, who is the sister of Lazarus, the man who Jesus restored to life, four days after his death.

As a melodic sounding name, Maria is also the inspiration behind many songs that ring out in churches, theatres, and from radios. Our Maria likes it when people sing her name to her and when they roll their "r's" in their pronunciation.

On the flip side, she does not like being called, "a problem." She prefers the song, "Beautiful Maria Of My Soul," as sung by Los Lobos, even though it breaks her heart every time she hears about the ever-expanding distance between the lovers. How she wishes they would be reunited for good because he obviously loves her. "Why can't they just be together?" she wonders.

Maria also knows that her name means, "bitter," a piece of trivia she once shared in Spanish class that amused her teacher for the duration of the semester. Had Maria known that her name also means "of the sea," she would have liked it more, even if "sea of bitterness" or "sea of sorrow" are included in the meaning. "Lady of the sea" works much better though and so do the other interpretations of rebellion and wished-for child.

Her Ukrainian parents had given her the name "Maria" because they considered it "universal" and figured it would take her far in the modern world.

True enough, variations of her name occur in many languages including: Basque, Bulgarian, Catalan, Corsican, Danish, Dutch, English, Faroese, Finnish, Frisian, German, Greek, Icelandic, Italian, Lithuanian, Norwegian, Occitan, Old Church Slavic, Polish, Portuguese, Romanian, Russian, Sardinian, Spanish, Swedish, and of course, Ukrainian.

On the "Most Popular Given Names in the Past 100 Years List," a list that ranks "James" and "Mary" at the top, "Maria" currently comes in as number 51, next to "Tyler" for boys, with 527,601 occurrences in a pool of 170,337,487 female babies born between 1919 and 2018.

Even though most of her Canadian friends do not know this, Maria also selectively goes by her Ukrainian nickname, "Marichka." While her mother insists on keeping the name in play, Maria feels it is a little too cute and familiar for a middle-aged woman to wear in public. She wishes her mother would just keep the name in the family and not share it with everyone she meets.

As for a middle name, "Alexandra" was an easy choice. Her parents lucked in with naming their daughter "Maria Alexandra" (and not offending either side of the family) because Maria Alexandra and Alexandra Maria are also her paternal grandmother's name and maternal grandmother's name, respectively. So Maria is in good company.

Her family name, "Ponomarenko," on the other hand, is not so common. It is not a noble name; it is not a *Kozak* name, but it does have a certain ring to it – literally. Ponomarenko is an occupational Ukrainian surname that means, "church bell ringer."

For better or for worse, she believes her resonant surname gives her what she secretly calls, "bionic hearing" which allows her to pick up on the faintest sounds off in the distance, even with earplugs or earphones in, and especially while she is trying to fall asleep. She is equally sensitive to sudden loud noises (as everyone is because crashing and banging are hardly ever good news) and soft sounds, (like crinkling candy wrappers) and would have been a talented Foley Artist, if that had been available to her.

Even though being sensitive to sounds comes at a price, she still prides herself on her listening ears and conversational skills. Friends say, "You're such a good listener!" every once in a while, which makes her happy.

Coming from Slavic, Pagan, and possibly even Scandinavian or Amazonian roots, she has a heavy-set, thick-boned, and curvy body – which is ideal for farming in the fields of "the breadbasket of Europe" but not so good for horseback riding, archery or sprinting. She likes her thick, straight, dyed-blonde hair, her average height, her left-handedness, and that she has an inny bellybutton.

Her complexion is reddish from sun damage, her nose has no bump, and she has a faint beauty mark, (read mole) on her right cheek which she had reduced considerably after riskily applying a Ukrainian herbal preparation called, *Chysto Til.*

"Burned like a disco inferno, but it was worth it!"

Maria's eye colour, (which she inherited from her mother and a mystery ancestor) is a relatively rare shade of forest green with gold flecks that are encircled by a grey ring. Her eye shape is hooded, framed by bushy and unruly eyebrows that she has threaded on occasion, and long, thick, feminine lashes. Her eyes are so deep-set that they recede into obscurity whenever she smiles.

Although her teeth are straight, the braces she wore in her early teens were not set quite right, which left her with an overbite anyway. Even so, she has one of those authentic, full-face *Duchenne* smiles, like Julia Roberts, that makes her more likeable than she knows, something she also shares in common with her father.

land • fill

Victoria, British Columbia is jokingly referred to as, "the city for the newlyweds and the nearly deads," of which Maria is neither – yet. Named after the notorious Queen Victoria in 1868, Victoria is a city on an island in the northern Pacific Ocean, on the western edge of Canada.

Victoria maintains its strong English roots with its High Tea at the Empress, ever-blooming gardens, manicured lawns, double-decker busses, and not one, but two, castles to visit. British accents are often heard spoken on the streets.

Maria's brother, Krystiyan, who goes by "Krys," is a director of photography in the movie business. He lives on the mainland with his wife, Olivia, their two children, Maxim and Zoryanna, and dog, Jasper.

Krys' exhale, whenever he drives off the ferry to visit, carries like waves of wind over the island. Compared to sheer and booming Vancouver, life in Victoria is so much calmer and slower.

Day in and day out, not much ever happens in Victoria even though it is the capital of the province. More of a town with old-fashioned sensibilities than a modern city, Victoria purposely thwarted expansion for the longest time, and up until a decade into the 21st Century, the city had a strict policy against constructing any buildings taller than four storeys.

Even to this day, Victorians think going to their one and only Costco is a field trip – "Good thing they have snacks there!" The most significant intersection in the whole city is on Government and Belleville, where the Parliament Buildings, the Royal BC Museum, the Empress Hotel, and the inner harbour converge.

Built on a landfill that sags a little bit more each year, this picture-postcard cross-section is the hub of politics, tourism, and commerce, and will tell you everything you need to know about supernatural British Columbia and its people.

Living on an island, however, also comes at a premium. It takes extra effort to get on and off any island, so after a few years and a story or two about being the last car to get on the ferry with a brick placed behind your tire, or sitting in your vehicle through a two- or even three-sailing wait, most people on Vancouver Island choose to stay close to home.

"But don't get them started on building a bridge!"

Victorians like to go about their business locally and do not travel far unless they have caught island fever, need to go somewhere else for work, or have their own boat. Sailing is a beloved tradition in these waters and Her Majesty's Navy is the biggest fish. Everyone has a relative in the navy and you would be hard-pressed to find anyone who does not have a military connection.

Maria's family is no exception. You can even find Maria's father's name on a brick near the *Homecoming Statue*, an endearing portrait of a father and daughter reuniting, which was commissioned to commemorate the 100th Anniversary of the Canadian Navy, in 2010, if you look hard enough.

* * *

Maria is startled by the slam of the front gate. It is the newspaper carrier delivering the latest edition of the *Saanich News*. She gets up from the dining room table, opens the front door, and retrieves the newspaper from the mailbox. The headline reads, "OPEN: New Johnson Street Bridge Unveiled Today in Victoria."

"I guess that's that for the blue bridge – out with the old and in with the new," she says, drifting back in time to her toddler years when the Ponomarenko's lived on the other side of the bridge in Esquimalt in the early 1970s.

She can see their grey, split-level house perched on a steep hill up the street from the skating rink, with a blue Marlin parked in the driveway. Her memory takes her to the day a rare blanket of snow covered their front lawn. Her mother, Lubomyra, had bundled her up in a sky blue snowsuit and red scarf and plunked her down in the middle of the powder, while she ran back inside the house to get something.

Even though the Gary Oaks kept watch and her Uncle Borys took photographs, little Marichka shrieked with terror for all of the neighbours to hear, releasing burning tears down her cold, chubby cheeks, as she looked in every direction for signs of her mother's return. It was a trauma of "my mama left me and is not coming back and I am going to die" that slowly dripped like an icicle down Maria's spine for decades.

Coming back to the present moment feeling a little bit sadder than she did a minute ago, she tosses the intact newspaper on the coffee table for her mother to read at her leisure. She does not like the feeling of having the "shipping news," as she calls the ink smudges on her fingers, so she rinses her hands before returning to her makeshift desk at the dining room table.

She looks around the room at all of her mother's things. "These aren't mine. None of these things are mine. I'm pushing 50 and I'm still living in my mother's house."

Maria only came back to Victoria in 1997 after her father, Yaromyr, (who had just retired from the Navy after a stellar, 33-year career), had flown to Toronto to pick her up, knowing she was not ship-shape. Together, they drove across country in the over-wintered, past its prime, black Chrysler New Yorker, with its burgundy leather seats, faulty heater and iffy speedometer, through the States and over the Rockies, and on the ferry, to Victoria.

Maria intended to only stay a short while, get her bearings, and then move to Vancouver but... "I just couldn't get myself off the island. The future seemed so fuzzy with the Y2K question in the air. Would the computers be able to handle the jump from 11:59pm on 12/31/99 to 12:00am on 01/01/00?"

At that time, Maria drank wine to feel better — white wine for day drinking and weddings; red wine for warmth on rainy nights.

At 29, she made another break from living with her parents and found her own little apartment on Stanley Street for $450/month. Other than the mysterious, dark, thick, gooey stain the size of a tire on the brown carpet in the living room, she liked her place because it had a balcony and was just a two-kilometre walk to downtown and to work.

One evening in December, 2000, Maria went out for drinks with her friends in a trendy bar with exposed brick (unusual for the area) and heavy, dense, negative energy (not so unusual for that street). Drunk and miserable, Maria's dark side reared its ugly head. She blurted out to her soon to be ex-friend, Laura: "Nobody likes you and nobody wants to hear what you have to say."

She had only learned of her somewhat out-of-character meanness days later and had no memory of the attack other than the preceding racing thoughts, sharp like cracks in a mirror. But her insult scared her enough about her drinking and with that, she went to her doctor, started taking anti-depressants, and went off the sauce for four and a half years, until she met Rocco, the dilettante chef. Good thing she did not end up with him but still, she threw away her sobriety for a guy who did not have the slightest interest in her.

(On a positive note, Maria has since resumed her path of sobriety and has not had a glass of alcohol in over three years).

Lubomyra had been so mortified when she heard her daughter had fallen so hard and brought shame to the family name, that she took it upon herself to not let anything remotely similar happen again. She noticed her daughter was feeling awful about her disrespectful behaviour towards her friend, so to lighten Maria's spirits, she invited her daughter to a party and said, (perhaps as a reference to the open bar) "stay close to me and my friends and you'll be fine."

As comforting as her mother's gesture was at the time, it sent Maria, whose self-worth was non-existent for so many years already, on a lonely path towards dependency on her mother and the ever-dreaded spinsterhood.

Just a few short weeks into her sobriety in March of 2001, Maria's father passed away suddenly at age 61 from cancer that had gone undiagnosed until his last days.

Needless to say, the event interrupted and impacted her life immeasurably. She felt tied to staying close and loyal to her family and not even think about straying too far away, ever since.

* * *

A grey cloud passes over the skylight at the top of the stairs and dims the timbre in the dining room. Fast forward to 2018, Maria has reached the tail end of her forties and it dawns on her that her hopes and dreams of getting married and having a family of her own and a career as a writer did not show up wrapped in a bow like she assumed it would.

After 22 years of being a resident of Victoria, with one prospecting week in Calgary, Alberta in the year, 2000, and one failed escape to Brampton, Ontario in the winter of 2012-2013, Maria has finally figured out that this island paradise is not working out for her as she had wanted.

"Especially by now... Something about Victoria, with its snobby, who-you-know mentality... It never delivered on being my town, a writer's town, or place for me to meet good men... But where else would I go?"

un • wave • ring

In Ukrainian, "lubov" means "love" and "myr" means "peace" so Lubomyra's name literally means, "lover of peace." Meanwhile, Maria's father's name, Yaromyr, also includes the word for "peace" within it, which makes them a well-matched couple and has contributed to their harmonious marriage.

Their wedding anniversary is in August and by now in 2018, many of their friends are celebrating 50 years together. Maria's parents made it to 36 years and if Lubomyra is bothered that she had been widowed in her late fifties, she does not show it.

Maria admires her mother for how many places she has travelled in her lifetime. She was the ideal Navy wife and had joined her husband on many exotic postings across Canada and beyond, including, Honolulu, Hawaii, Washington DC, and Brussels, Belgium.

To her mother's credit, she mastered the art of throwing elegant dinner parties and attending cocktail receptions and somehow always managed to find a Ukrainian church and community in the haystack.

In addition to taking Maria on a cruise to Alaska, Lubomyra has also taken her family to Mexico where they visited pyramids at Chichén Itzá. She also spent summers in the South of France, visited Turkey and Greece, and got her Church Anthology blessed by Pope Benedict XVI in Italy. In one year alone, she went to Whitehorse, Yukon with the newly appointed Bishop Leo on the first of several "pilgrimages" and then she set off to Brazil for an ecclesiastical conference on the Bishop's request.

Of course, Lubomyra also went back to Ukraine to visit cousins and to study church music at a monastery and she thoroughly enjoyed sampling the spring soup, *Zeleniy Borsch,* or green *borsch,* made from sorrel instead of beets, every chance she had.

* * *

Lubomyra steps out of her bedroom wearing an authentic Ukrainian costume, complete with an embroidered shirt (*vyshyvana sorochka*), a heavy, woven wrap skirt (*plakhta*), an apron (*fartukh*), orange coral beads (*korali*) and bright red boots (*chervoni choboty*). She is getting ready to go to a summer song festival where she will be performing with her acapella group. She is the soprano.

Lubomyra loves to sing and has instilled in her daughter an appreciation of music, starting with Ukrainian and contemporary folk songs. As a child, Maria would plunk herself on the living room floor in one of the circles of the modern, orange, yellow and white shag rug, and listened to her mother's records, singing along to songs like Nana Mouskouri's almost prophetic,

I never will marry
I'll be no man's wife
I will remain single
for the rest of my life.

Maria would study the album covers as if they had hidden messages. She especially liked a Ukrainian record with a photograph of a young girl with long brown hair, wearing a floral dress, twirling in a field of wildflowers, under a blue sky, with a butterfly approaching her extended hand.

Maria hears her mother's voice calling her back to earth from her daydream, "Can you please pull this sash tighter for me?"

"Yeah, sure," says Maria, trying to tie it as tight as she can but feeling uncomfortable herself in the process.

"Pull it really tight and don't let the sash twist." "Okay, okay, I got it. There."

"I'll be home around six," says Lubomyra. "Would you be so kind and put the roast in the oven at 5:00pm at 375 degrees? The broccoli is already to go on the stove and there's some leftover smashed potatoes in the fridge for dinner tonight."

"Sure, no problem."

"Mary-Jo is picking me up, so I'm not taking my purse or my keys or my phone… I'll just wait for her outside. See you, love you."

"Love you," says Maria as her mother closes the front door. "Oh my gosh, Mama's birthday is coming up in a couple of days. I should do something nice for her. I guess I can start by making her a card. It won't top last year's solar eclipse and taco salad, but I hope she likes it anyway."

As it happened last year, Lubomyra's 75th birthday was divinely timed with a solar eclipse that partially darkened the skies over Vancouver Island as it headed South East across the United States. In that pivotal moment of planetary, lunar and solar alignment, Maria realized how far her mother had come from such humble beginnings in Ukraine during WWII. Who would have predicted or even thought that Lubomyra would be alive to witness such a spectacular moment in history, on a milestone birthday no less, both in person and through the lens of technology beaming in from space on a television screen?

Eclipses are references to specific times and places in history and the Gospel of Luke account states, "and the sun was darkened" during the event of Jesus' crucifixion. On this occasion, Maria's philosophical side surfaced again and she saw the eclipse as a lesson in faith. It was faith in motion because it was just a matter of divine timing that the sun would shine again and everything would return to normal.

"Faith is knowledge without proof. It's believing in the invisible and the intangible and even though the sun, with all of its life affirming light, seems to vanish from the sky entirely, it's simply an optical illusion... Deep down everyone observing the spectacle –

without looking directly at it, of course – knows the sunlight will soon return and sure enough, it does."

Still, there was that looming pause in Maria's mind, "maybe this is it, maybe it won't come back this time?" But as Maria bounced between optimism and pessimism, she reminded herself, "Don't be fooled by appearances because the sun has been there all along."

Meanwhile, Lubomyra, with her strong soprano voice and Leo astrological sign, had unwavering faith. She had faith in life itself and in God, the Almighty. Maria suddenly understood in the muted sunlight that her mother trusted with full faith that everything would eventually work out, even if there was no concrete evidence showing up on the horizon…yet.

In that moment of clarity, as the television announcers described the solar event from different vantage points across the North American continent in real time, putting everyone who cared on the same page, Maria saw her mother's whole journey in one arc – child, teenager, student, teacher, wife, mother, baba.

She saw how much the world had changed over the decades – borders between countries, political affiliations, cultural mores. Communications technology alone had changed from radio, to television, to cable, to wireless Internet, and who knows what else, all in her mother's lifetime.

While the sun and moon crossed paths and the eclipse receded, Maria began to see her mother in a new light. She knew they were divinely connected rain or shine, but alas, there was still so much work to be done on their mother-daughter relationship, which arguably for everyone, was the most complicated relationship in the Universe.

land • turn

If job-hopping was an Olympic sport, Maria would have won the gold for sure. Over the course of 30 years, Maria worked at Chesapeake Bay Seafood House, the Ukraina Country Club, Michelin Tires, an integrative wellness centre, a B&B, a high-end spa, and a grocery store deli.

On top of those entry level jobs, she also worked at Canada Post, Canada Trust, the National Archives of Canada, Bell Sigma, Cineplex Odeon, Ogilvy & Mather, *the Peninsula News Review, Focus on Women Magazine,* and the BC Ministry of Forests. Most notably, she can also put the NATO Visits Section in Brussels, Belgium on her resume – that was her favourite.

Somehow though, none of those panned out for her in the long run and did not turn into the illustrious careers that could have followed. But even before she turned 30, Maria could see the writing on the wall, that she was not cut-out for 9 to 5, and so, in the months following her father's death, she made her first attempt at becoming an entrepreneur and working for herself.

"Me…Creative? Yes. Smart?...Yes. Business head?...No."

Her first business was about teaching people how to make their own homemade cosmetics using natural ingredients. She spent months researching the healing properties of herbs, flowers, fruits and vegetables and eventually self-published a book of spa and skincare recipes.

Although her creative idea was not a commercial success, she learned a ton and could also add website design to her box of tools. Still fascinated with all things spa almost a decade later, Maria took the chance to apply to esthetics school after being laid off from the BC government. After graduating with perfect attendance, she turned her initial idea of recipes for sleep and beauty to a mobile spa where she could actually provide spa services like manicures, pedicures, massages and facials to real people, rather than just talking about the treatments and their benefits.

However, now, by late August of 2018, Maria's mobile spa business is running on fumes and she needs to find another job yesterday. After having many, many doors slamming shut in her face, she has an intuition to call her old employer, Louise at the Lantern Inn, first to ask an unrelated question and second to sniff around to see if they are hiring again.

The phone rings and rings. She has a feeling they recognize her number and are letting it go to voice mail.

"Hi Louise, it's Maria. It sounds like you're busy. Just wondering if I could talk with you briefly about using one of your photos for a blog post I'm writing. Please call me back. Thanks."

Two days later, "Sorry, for not calling you back sooner, Maria," says Louise sounding out of breath.

"That's OK."

"It's still our busy season and Stefan quit last week and we've been trying to cover his shifts and find someone else…"

"Sorry to hear that," says Maria with her ears perking up.

"You said you wanted to use a photo?"

"Yes, I'm writing a blog post about how to turn your bathroom into a spa – you know me – and I remembered the photo of the Amethyst Room on your website and thought it would be perfect."

"Yes, sure you can use it."

"Thanks, and if you're looking for a new Breakfast Cook, maybe I can help. I'm looking for work anyway – just had an interview at the Senior's Residence near Elk Lake – you know, the one that's like a cruise ship."

"Yeah, I know the one – fancy! Well, if you'd like, why don't you pop by the Inn this afternoon… say 4pm?"

"Sure, I'll be there – thanks Louise!"

* * *

HOW TO TURN YOUR BATHROOM INTO A HOME SPA RETREAT

by Maria Ponomarenko, Spa Therapist

Spas have a certain aesthetic. Whenever you walk into a spa, you probably exhale and say to yourself something like, "I feel more relaxed already."

What is it about the design of a spa that helps us feel better upon entering and can we re-create those spa touches in our own home bathrooms?

Since September is Self-Care Awareness Month and since we're heading into the cooler months of autumn, I thought it would be a nice idea to show how to add spa elements to a bathroom and turn any space into more of a home spa retreat.

I'm taking my inspiration from the Amethyst Room bathroom at the Lantern Inn, a Bed & Breakfast property, in Sidney-by-the-Sea, BC, a place I'm very familiar with.

Spa Features of this Bathroom:

* Calming Lavender paint colour * Lights on a dimmer switch * Separate shower and tub * Fancy mirror * Plush towels * Spa robes and a place to hang them * Live plants * Hardwood floor * Selection of body care products like soaps, spa salts, moisturizers, shampoos, mouthwash, etc. * A window with a third story view of the street below and optional blinds * Clean and clear of clutter * Housekeeper to clean up afterwards

Spa Features I'd Add if I Could:

* Heated floors * Massaging shower head * Jetted whirlpool tub * Towel warmer * More counter space around the sink * Essential oil diffuser with a selection of synergistic blends * Portable waterproof music speaker that plays an assortment of spa music, waves on the beach, rain and white noise * A folding table next to the tub to hold things like candles, drinking glasses, spa salts, clay masques, sugar scrubs, books, etc. * A place to drape your clothes * Slippers * Artwork * Rocks, crystals and sea shells

I hope this list inspires you to add some spa touches to your own bathroom, whether you live in a big house or a tiny apartment or even an RV. I also hope that you take some time out for yourself, at least an hour every week, to relax and practice self-care, in your newish, lovely, spa bathroom.

* * *

Driving down the Pat Bay Highway towards Sidney to meet with her former manager, Louise, Maria catches a glimpse of Mt. Baker off in the distance. "Oh, there's another 'fairy bubble,' travelling down the other side of the highway," she says, remembering a term her father coined to describe the pockets of traffic coming off the docked ships.

Maria marvels at her own intuition and wonders, "How did I know Stefan-with-an-f (as he says) quit his Breakfast Cook job?

He started when I left – how many years ago was that, 2011, 2012?" she recalls while trying to do the math in her head.

The stately inn, which borrowed its design from a B&B somewhere in Europe, had been built in the Edwardian Style, now 20 years ago. In the autumn or winter months, it is a cozy little chalet of sorts, even with the piped-in muzak playing in the background, but in summer, the aesthetic feels a little heavy-handed, especially in a beach town.

Maria parks across the street and gazes up at the building. Upon entering the front courtyard with the gurgling fountain, she notices the cushions on the benches have faded, but otherwise, the place look the same.

"Come on in, Maria" says Louise opening the door. "Nice to see you again. This is Martha – she has been working with us for two years now. Have a seat in the lounge."

Maria takes the winged-back chair between the fireplace and the front window. "I've actually never sat here before – just always vacuumed around it!"

"It's almost Sherry time – would you like a glass?"

"No thanks, but I always thought it was a nice touch – Sherry always seems so civilized to me."

"Yes, the guests sure do enjoy it!"

The mansion with the inviting staircase at the entrance, has nine guest rooms in total, all with their own complementary colour schemes and all named after crystals. The high quality hardwood floors are well-worn after having been walked on by countless travellers over the years, including a Canadian celebrity or two, and the paint colours are dark and rich to match the jewell theme.

"You said, you interviewed at the retirement home?"

"Yes, I had done some mobile spa treatments there over the years and thought maybe I could pick up some shifts in their dining room a few days a week. The guy who interviewed me was dripping with clichés – with his slicked back hair, expensive suit, gold watch, and heavy cologne – and he cracked his knuckles and leaned over, looked me straight in the eye and said, 'I'd like to offer you a job for $12/hour' – as if he was being generous! I couldn't believe it! And no chance of tips on top of that…"

"No tips?" repeats Martha who is listening in from the front desk.

"I asked him, 'is there any room for negotiation?' and he said leaning back, 'I can't do better than that.' I said I'd think about it and left and then you called me back."

"Sounds like a charmer. So, just to bring you up to speed, Stefan quit last week at the height of our busy season and we've been scrambling to cover his shifts and to find a replacement. We need someone to take on a few breakfast and front desk shifts and help April with housekeeping when needed."

"Oh is she still here?"

"Yes, going on 8 years I think – anyway, would you be up for coming back at least until we find someone more permanent?"

"Yes, I'd be happy to pitch in."

"Can you come in on Friday to work the front desk – I know it's the long weekend."

"Yes, I can do that, but just so you know, I prefer the breakfast cook job."

"OK, well, let's start here and see how it goes. See you back here for training on Friday at 3pm?"

"I'll be here with bells on."

* * *

Maria feels at home at the Inn. The place is busy, the shifts go by quickly and the tips are generous. She is enjoying working with her hands and being creative and then serving delicious breakfasts to travellers from far-away lands.

"I think this is good practice for me if I ever do get married – it's like running a household in its own way."

She also finds it thrilling to have people from all corners of the world including Australia, Germany, England, the United States and from the rest of Canada, all descending to this one tight dining room in this small town on an island, and chatting with each other, sharing their stories and getting along. She often thinks the United Nations should seriously consider adopting a breakfast program!

As a gesture of thanks for welcoming her back, Maria feels inspired to donate a framed photograph that she had taken years earlier of a fig leaf and a few unplucked figs that were still barely hanging on. The lavender mat and silver frame are a perfect match for the Amethyst Room and now her art hangs over the toilet. (Not Maria's first choice but it has a captive audience from time to time).

During one of her shifts, a local reporter for the *Peninsula News Review* – a newspaper Maria once worked for back in the '90's – drops by to take a photo of Maria and Louise for winning an award from 5-star reviews on a popular hospitality website. Unfortunately, staff members do not get to meet the guy on their ads – who Maria secretly calls, "Brad's stand-in" – but they do receive a plaque and a pizza party, which is always nice.

But all is not fig trees, lavender walls, awards, free pizza, and international guests. As the winter season edges up the coast like a rising tide and things start to slow down at the Inn, Martha's true nature starts to show and she increasingly becomes more hostile towards Maria.

Martha is like fire and moves through life very quickly. She is sharp-as-a-tac and has tremendous energy. But get fire mad and you get burned.

Martha is an all-rounder as an employee. She does all of the jobs at the Inn well and quickly, including working the front desk, cooking breakfast, and cleaning the rooms. Maria appreciates that Martha has standards and has the ability to see the details of the Inn from a guests' perspective, but her loud and fast talking style and her fiery energy is just too overbearing for Maria's soft, quiet, gentle and nurturing nature. Both cannot meet in the middle and it would be just as futile to ask Martha to slow down as it would for Maria to speed up.

At first, Maria shrugs off Martha's antics, like insisting on keeping the 'staff in training' sign up for at least six weeks in the dining room during Maria's shifts, or re-posting a note in the kitchen to turn the stereo on before breakfast, as immature pettiness. She tries to chalk up the questionable moments to high-maintenance guests wherever possible, but the incidents have a certain creativity and craftiness to them and somehow Martha always has a quick answer locked and loaded in her holster, whenever asked a pointy question.

Maria gets her first clue about Martha's dark side within the first month when sweet and savoury Blueberry pancakes and sausages are on the menu. Two women travelling together from Vancouver on a cycling holiday have requested the 9:15 breakfast and not one guest has been scheduled for the 8am.

You would think that serving only breakfast to up to 18 guests over two sittings (and only two people this particular morning) would be fairly straightforward, but with the vegans, vegetarians, dairy-frees, gluten-frees, allergies, aversions, and coffee or tea drinkers, breakfast can often become awfully complicated.

"Come in tomorrow at 8am instead of 7," says Martha's email. On the surface, giving a staff member an extra hour of sleep may seem like a nice gesture, but Martha takes every chance she can to shave off hours from Maria's shifts, so she can get more hours and more tips from the pool (each pay period) herself.

To her surprise, when Maria shows up to work at 7:50, she sees two guests in the dining room all ready to eat. They are sitting on the high-back, upholstered chairs at the most popular table, which has a nice view of the Maple Tree out front, and are dressed in their cycling gear. The women insist they are scheduled for the early breakfast and are seriously annoyed at the miscommunication.

Flustered, Maria does her best to accommodate the ladies, but in protest, they decide to skip breakfast altogether and check out early. "Martha, about this morning's guests..." she asks later. "I confirmed with them three times and they wanted the 9:15 breakfast!"

* * *

Maria's philosophy of life is based on the Universal Law of Hospitality. She likes to greet people with a warm welcome, offer them a safe place to rest, give nourishing food and drinks, have an amazing conversation, and then send her new friends off with encouraging words as they continue on their journey.

There is a chapter in "Book XIV" in "the Odyssey" by Homer called, "Hospitality in the Forest," that captures the spirit of the relationship between the host and the guest,

Come to the cabin.
You're a wanderer too.
You must eat something, drink some wine,
and tell me where you are from
and the hard times you've seen.

Under the code of the ancient Law of Hospitality, whether the travellers are rich, poor, or weary, the host cannot refuse guests or make them leave. In return for a safe place to hang their hats, the guests cannot act inappropriately towards a fellow traveller or member of the household, nor can they overstay their welcome.

The Law of Hospitality also comes into play in the Bible when Mary and Joseph travel to Bethlehem to be counted in the Census while Mary is with child. "There is no room at the Inn" so the out-of-towners have to find some sort of alternative arrangements, which happens to be with barn animals. Quietly, Jesus is born in a manger among oxen and lambs. In order for guests like Mary and Joseph, who seek shelter from the elements to feel safe enough to let down their guard for a while and rest, everybody concerned has to agree to trust each other and get along.

Unfortunately, Maria's co-worker, Martha, does not seem familiar with this concept. She really hates it when Maria gets too chatty with the guests. "Clearly, there is more important work to be done!"

Each day, Louise (or anyone else who would listen) would get an earful about how Maria does nothing productive at work, and while she is wasting time in idle conversation, everyone else – especially Martha – has to pick up the slack.

"Why do I have to do all of the work around here?" Martha mutters while lugging the vacuum cleaner, spare towels, dust wand, and cordless phone up to the third floor for the fifth time that day. "And how did Maria get her picture in the newspaper when clearly, I was the one who got us that best B&B award?"

* * *

When Saturday rolls around, the staff-in-training sign is up again in full view. This time, however, Maria is the one training a new part-time staff member, Joyce, who, just like her name, is a very bubbly, positive and upbeat soul.

The dining room is packed for both breakfast sittings and the spirit in the room is jovial. Maria and Joyce are getting along well. After the last of the coffee is poured, Joyce suggests to Maria, "How about you finish cleaning up the dining room and the kitchen, and I'll go upstairs and start cleaning the rooms."

The compact disc on the stereo switches to one that Maria does not care for and suddenly Martha blasts through the front doors, slightly too early for the beginning of her shift. She turns her head in Maria's direction and hisses like a cat! Martha then bolts up the stairs like a rod of lightening on a mission to strike her next target!

"Joyce! You should be cleaning the dining room and Maria should be cleaning the suites!" shrieks Martha's nasal voice from roof to basement.

Later as Maria and Joyce pass each other on the servant's stairwell, they giggle like kids in the playground over Martha's outburst.

man • hat • tan

Thanksgiving is Maria's favourite holiday. Her Thanksgiving long weekend fantasy involves visiting a log cabin on a lake that is tucked in among tall coniferous trees. She is wearing soft, plaid, flannel pajamas and is cozying up to the fire with a smooth cup of hot chocolate, a kitty cat, and the love of her life.

The Lantern Inn is also a perfect setting for a Thanksgiving retreat and Maria does not miss the opportunity to serve a few holiday-themed dishes for breakfast that weekend. First, she makes an apple crisp from local, organic apples using her mother's recipe and then she prepares the best ever individual, crustless, pumpkin pies she would ever make from the recipe off the label on the pumpkin purée can.

Adam and Dinah, a couple from New York City, are particularly enamoured with her creations, and while they are savouring every spoonful, they ask her, "What's your best New York story? We've already asked everyone else, but we haven't asked you yet."

"Well, I've got a good one," Maria begins. "When I was going to high school in the '80's, my family lived in Virginia just outside of Washington DC because my father was in the navy and worked at the Embassy. While we lived there, we belonged to the Ukrainian community also. Part of that included going to Ukrainian school every Saturday morning which was a real drag — my weekends were always spoken for.

"Anyway, on Columbus Day weekend — otherwise known as Canadian Thanksgiving — all of the kids in our school piled on a tour bus on the Friday night and headed North to visit New York and New Jersey. We had just spent a couple of hours visiting the Ukrainian Museum…" "Oh yeah, on the Lower East Side," says Adam. "And while we were sitting on the bus for 10 or 15 minutes waiting to go to our next stop on the tour, I noticed a taxi cab pull up to the corner up ahead. Someone got out and dumped a mannequin against a street post and then quickly jumped back into the cab and tire-screeched away!"

"Hmm," Adam nods. "So far, so good."

"I thought to myself, 'wouldn't it be cool if I went to New York and came home with a real mannequin as a souvenir?'"

Adam's and Dinah's eyes pop open like saucers.

"As I sat there in my cushy seat, I pictured myself getting off the bus, crossing the street, walking up to the corner, picking up the mannequin and hauling it back onto the bus."

They both flag their arms wide, mouthing, "Noooo!"

"I was trying to figure out if I had enough time to do this little side trip before the bus left, and as I debated whether or not I was actually going to go ahead with this hair-brained idea, another taxi pulled up to the corner, someone got out, picked up the mannequin, threw it into the back seat, and drove away in a matter of seconds!"

Theories form in the minds of the hardened New Yorkers. They look at each other and then look back at Maria.

"For all of my humming and hawing, I missed my chance, but then I realized later, that what I saw was probably a drug deal going down right there in front of my eyes!"

"Sounds like it!" says Dinah.

"Yeah," Maria agrees. "I figure they probably got the mannequin from the fashion district and stuffed it with drugs and if I had stepped into that mess, and picked up the mannequin myself, could you imagine what would have followed?"

"A car chase!" exclaims Dinah.

"With a bus carrying a bunch of Ukrainian school kids," adds Maria.

"I don't think it would have ended well for you," says Adam.

"Yeah, so that's my New York story."

They clap.

Maria curtsies.

"I can see that happening in the '80's, especially in that neighbourhood, but that probably wouldn't happen these days.

We've really cleaned things up in the last while," says Adam as he drinks his last drop of coffee.

"But good thing you didn't grab the mannequin," adds Dinah.

"I know," says Maria smiling. "Can I take your plates?"

Up until then, Maria has never had the chance to tell that story to real New Yorkers before. Why they would spend five days in Sidney, Canada is beyond her, though they may have appreciated knowing that the area from Sooke to Sidney is roughly the same size as Manhattan, though one is covered by skyscrapers, while the other, tall trees.

"I guess New Yorkers like to travel and go on vacations too."

* * *

FEELING STUCK IN THE MUD? TRY THE KNEELING, STANDING & SITTING METHOD
by Maria Ponomarenko, Spa Therapist

My mother likes for me to go to church with her on Sundays. Sometimes I'd rather watch "SuperSoul Sundays" on television instead, but I've been going to church more often these days.

When I'm at church, I mostly sit in contemplation. Last Sunday, I was reminded of a conversation I had with my friend when I was a kid. We were comparing notes about our churches — I'm Ukrainian and she's Irish — and I was saying something like, "We do a lot of kneeling, standing and sitting —sit, stand, kneel/

stand, kneel, sit/ stand, sit/ stand, sit, stand, kneel/ stand, sit... oh brother."

These days, I still prefer to sit. After a long sermon, hauling myself out of my pew to stand for what feels like hours without relief, seems like a lot of effort. And getting back up from kneeling is a different ballgame altogether when you're in your forties.

So while I was thinking about this, it occurred to me that there's actually a rhyme and reason behind these postures. And since it's Thanksgiving weekend in Canada, I'm going to use a metaphor of a farmer couple, Fred and Frinta, to illustrate my theory.

Kneeling

It all starts with a prayer. Prayer lets you get centered. It's the "asking" side of the equation. Basically, you're just having a conversation with yourself and with God (if you're so inclined) to get clear about what you want. Praying helps strengthen your faith that whatever you're asking for, you'll eventually have, even if you haven't noticed any physical evidence yet.

Farmers Fred & Frinta

Our farmers, Fred and Frinta, have just acquired a plot of land in a community garden. They want to start growing vegetables for their family and maybe sell the surplus at markets. First, they have to figure out what sorts of vegetables they'd like to plant and they have lots of options to choose from. They figure it wouldn't hurt to pray about it so in their own way, they each take a few moments to gather their thoughts and ask for:

* ideas

* good weather for the crops

* good health for themselves so they can do the labour, and

* the knowledge to solve any challenges that will come up.

They're also able to visualize what their garden will look like in full bloom and how they're feeling as they share their bounty with friends, family and neighbours.

Meanwhile, the land and the seeds of the plants represent pure potential. Prayer is what's inside the acorn (the code inside the seed) before it cracks open and becomes the grand oak tree.

But it doesn't stop there. Praying by itself isn't enough. If you want results, you also need to take action — thoughtful, consistent and repeated action.

Standing

There's an African proverb that says, "When you pray, move your feet."

Everybody knows that you can't get anywhere without taking some sort of action steps along the way. Getting up on your feet is about taking a stand for what you believe in, showing others that you mean business, declaring out loud what you want and taking action. Also, many times, action is about reaching out, giving and being of service.

Farmers Fred & Frinta

By now, Fred and Frinta have procured their seeds and have designed the layout of their garden. They've come to the community garden prepared and are wearing the proper clothes for the job and have brought all of the equipment they'll need for planting. '

The kale will go here, the zucchini will go there, the tomatoes over there near the basil.'

They've rolled up their sleeves and are working hard all day. They come back to their garden rain or shine, day after day, week after week, and make sure the plants are getting enough nourishment and care.

At first, the soil looks pretty much the same as it did in the beginning, but all of a sudden, there's colour and little green leaves are starting to break through.

Fred and Frinta are excited about their progress and they're motivated to keep going. Eventually, after all of their hard work, the vegetables are awesome and the garden is ready to be harvested. The growing part may be over but there's still a lot of work to do so that these vegetables and all of that effort don't go to waste.

Sitting

After kneeling (praying) and standing (taking action), the next step is sitting (receiving). Sitting is deceptively simple, but some people skip this step. Sitting is about relaxing, resting and receiving. You can't just give, give, give all of the time. You also have to be able to receive the gifts that others are trying to give you.

Farmers Fred & Frinta

Fred and Frinta are grateful they have had a good growing season. They have plenty of healthy vegetables for their family meals and like to share the best veggies and recipes with their friends. They've also opened a stand at the local farmers' market and are receiving compliments and cash for their quality produce and they plan to expand their plots next year.

I think, all in all, Fred and Frinta are successful because they've prayed, worked hard and accepted the blessings that came their way.

So, if you're feeling stuck in the mud of life and are ready for a positive change, try the kneeling, standing and sitting method.

Thanksgiving

But you may be thinking to yourself, "I don't know how to pray," or "I can't remember the last time I prayed and I don't know what to say." Well here's a good place to start: "There's nothing greater that you can say to God than thank you, thank you," – wise words from Maya Angelou.

And then you'll be able to know which steps you'll need to take that will yield the best results.

So, I'd like to take this moment and say "thank you" for all of the blessings of my life, and for all of my clients I've met over the years, and all of the readers of my blog. That's what I'm most grateful for.

Happy Thanksgiving.

Now have a seat at the table and pass the turkey and the stuffing, and the mashed potatoes, and the gravy, and the Brussels sprouts, and the cranberry sauce, and the pumpkin pie, and ENJOY the fruits of your labours with your loved ones.

* * *

During the short week following Thanksgiving 2018, three stellar events converge on the streets of good ol' Sidney-by-the-Sea, earning it a little pushpin on the world map.

The sleepy town wakes up to the Town Crier's bell ringing which clamours with more fervour than the Sidney Classical Orchestra's opening concerto. First, from October 11th to 14th, Sidney hosts the 2018 World Rowing Coastal Championships, an extreme sport that appreciates windy and wavy conditions.

The patch between Tulista and Lochside Parks makes for the first ever beach start in the history of the competition, and the Salish Sea creates a spectacular ocean playground and backdrop.

Meanwhile, the Sidney Fine Art Show, which attracts artists from far and wide, who splash colours onto their canvasses of choice to create new worlds, is being held at the Mary Winspear Centre from October 12th to 14th and Maria discovers that one of the award-winning artists of the event is actually staying at the Lantern Inn that weekend. As a perk, Louise has given Maria two free tickets to attend the show, so she takes her mom on Sunday afternoon.

On top of all of that, quaint little Sidney also turns into "Hollywood North" for a day on October 11th! Movie crews magically transform Beacon Avenue into a winter wonderland for a "Hallmark Channel" love story called, "Christmas Bells Are Ringing."

The joke is, in reality, the town is actually enjoying unseasonably warm and sunny autumnal weather, with temperatures hovering around 13 degrees Celsius – which is great for the rowers, but not so ideal for a Christmas-themed movie set.

While leaves on the trees are turning amber, pumpkin, saffron, crimson and aubergine, all of the actors in the movie have to stretch to pretend it is a stereotypical, snowy, Canadian Christmas.

To help everyone get into the holiday spirit, the producers festoon the storefronts with glitzy-golden garlands and flashing lights. Meanwhile, extras have to wear scarves, coats, mittens and hats and it is hard not to trip over all of the wrapped gift boxes that are nestled here, there, and everywhere.

The crew even procures twenty cartloads of ice from the Satellite Fish Co. to create real snow on the Sidney Pier and after they yell, "Action" for the last time, both actors and locals revel in a real, old-fashioned snowball fight.

From the sky, the locations of the three coincidental events in Sidney form a perfect triangle across the town, with the art show near the Pat Bay Highway at the top point, the filming at the pier at the bottom right corner, and the rowing competition on the shore at the bottom left. The Lantern Inn, where Maria works, is about midway down the line.

All of this extra activity is attracting thousands of bustling tourists to the island, and that means, the Inn is booked solid. Both breakfast sittings are full and Maria is flying from the kitchen to the dining room, carrying plates of the crowd-pleasing

Eggstravaganza Casserole, that is jam-packed with hashbrowns, cheeses, bacon bits, and eggs.

The sleepy little town of Sidney cannot press the snooze button anymore.

holy • day

Hark how the bells,
Sweet silver bells,
All seem to say,
Throw cares away
Christmas is here,
Bringing good cheer,
To young and old,
Meek and the bold.
Ding dong ding dong…

If the Ponomarenko's had a family theme song, "the Carol of the Bells" would be it. Lubomyra has a special place in her heart for the song because it was originally composed in 1914 by Mykola Leontovych, a Ukrainian, who was also a dear friend's uncle, and was therefore related.

"To nash (то наш)," Lubomyra says every time she hears the song chiming over CBC Radio Victoria, reinforcing the Ukrainian tradition of claiming anyone who has Ukrainian roots and who makes it big in the world, as "one of ours."

The carol is based on the Ukrainian folk chant *Shchedryk* and Lubomyra's a cappella group performs the complex arrangement (that nostalgically echoes the sound of bells in its musicality) numerous times in churches, folk festivals, and Christmas concerts to adoring crowds.

Hearing the "Carol of the Bells" always announces the beginning of the Christmas season for Maria, which is not her favourite time of year, mostly because it interrupts the calendar for six to eight weeks, if it starts from American Thanksgiving in November (or Diwali even earlier) and lasts to mid-January on the old Ukrainian calendar.

It is a long haul and Maria does not look forward to travelling on the 9am ferry on Christmas Day to the mainland to visit Krys' family and his in-laws, especially after eating the traditional Ukrainian, 12-course, vegetarian, Christmas Eve feast the night before, plus going to an eight o'clock version of midnight mass.

Actually, that excuse is not entirely true. Maria does not enjoy Christmas because the season reminds her that she is still single and does not have anyone to call her own.

"I have to learn to accept that I'm a 49-year-old spinster...an old maid... an ugly old crone... a hag... I wouldn't be surprised if a Crazy Cat Lady Starter Kit shows up on my doorstep. Might as well start wearing wide-rimmed hats and pointy boots."

On Christmas morning, Lubomyra and Maria pack the green car with leftover meatless *borsch, vushka,* potato and cheese *varenyky,* sauerkraut *varenyky, holobtsi,* Turkish fish, salmon, *kutya,* and torte, plus presents for the kids from Saint Nicholas (who somehow always drops off the wrapped gifts at the wrong house) and board the scant ferry sailing.

Lubomyra and Maria arrive after eleven o'clock in time to catch the 'opening of the presents' tradition with Krys, Maxim, Zoryanna, Olivia, Krys' in-laws, including Olivia's three siblings, plus their partners, and their kids, and dogs.

"There's something about holding a baby that gives me hope for the future," Maria thinks while everyone else buzzes around the living room, commenting on each other's gifts, taking videos on their phones, and re-filling their glasses with either beer, wine, or spiked coffee.

She admires the gigantic, live Christmas tree that proudly stands near the stairs that they cut down and haul back home themselves, and she enjoys watching the wrapping paper and ribbons cascade to the floor while Jasper, the family dog, sniffs out morsels of food.

She is also impressed that her 11-year-old niece, Zoryanna, has baked the most perfect shortbread cookies Maria has ever tasted!

After the Christmas Day whirlwind passes through the living room, everyone in the family goes to their own spaces to do whatever they want for the afternoon. For Maria, there is nothing else to do but watch movies with Olivia's brother Carlos and his son all day.

After scrolling through the holiday listings in the kids section, they settle on, "A Wrinkle in Time" and "Gnome Alone," which in their own way tell a story about a young girl, who is different from her classmates, who travels into an alternate, supernatural dimension of the Universe, and saves the day.

Maria does not dare to offer any help in the kitchen because there are already three very dominant women juggling knives, pots, and pans in there, and Maria does not want to get in the way, nor does she want to be bossed around, or told she is doing her job wrong.

"Better to just lay low and let them take care of the food like they always do," she thinks. "And come to think of it, it is a nice change of pace to just sit around and watch movies all day."

Soon, dinner is ready and the family sits around the modern, heavy, glass table in the dining room. Turkey and all of the fixings are served in addition to the Ukrainian dishes that Lubomyra has brought over from Victoria. Everybody has their fill.

* * *

After enjoying the Christmas Day potluck feast, the family moves into the living room to play a new-to-them word game. They divide into two teams and arrange the cards on the coffee table according to the instructions.

To make things fair, Zoryanna calls the clues for Maria's team while Maxim calls the clues for Krys' side. The goal is to link two or more cards together under a matching category like, 'four seasons,' 'types of transportation,' and 'things that are yellow,' and it is the clue caller's job to help their team members connect the dots and name the category as written on the card.

It involves thought and Zoryanna is trying to come up with a winning strategy.

To add confusion to the mix, the other team is allowed to be as distracting and obnoxious as they want. Tension is mounting and the stakes are high. Everyone's eyes jet from the cards to Zoryanna and back again to the cards, in anticipation of her next clue.

"Did someone remember to flip over the hour glass?" asks Lubomyra.

Zoryanna continues to think.

And then from stage left, Lada, who is on Maxim's team, flies over to the game board like a seagull and scatters the cards into an unruly clump! The game screeches to a halt and everyone looks at Lada in horror!

"We needed a timer," Lada says flatly, satisfied with her work. "It was taking too long."

"Bitch!" thinks Maria in her head, though they probably could read her thoughts loud and clear. "How dare she ruin our game like that?"

"Leave it to Lada to wreck the game," says Olivia in her mom voice and then everybody bursts out laughing.

Just as quickly as the house of cards topple, the tension clears, everyone hugs it out, and the drama is exactly what they needed to bond the family closer together.

"But will this game ever see the light of day again?" says Olivia as she puts the cards back into the box.

It is time to say good night and call it a merry Christmas. The royal blue lights on the Christmas tree continue to glow softly.

As Maria tries to fall asleep on the slippery, black leather couch with the dog at her feet, she thinks about how the game went down. At first, she thinks it was about egos and how games have a way of bringing out the worst in people – especially "Monopoly" for some reason – and maybe Lada's outburst is a window into her childhood.

But after a while, Maria realizes that what Lada did was actually a rather refreshing and wonderful life lesson.

"She did a reset! Of course!" Maria says in a low whisper as she opens her eyes in the dark. "In the bin and start again' as Chef Gordon Ramsey would say. Why keep on playing the same game and run around the same track if it's not fun anymore?"

For the first time in her life, Maria realizes she can scrap the old and create something new for herself. She does not have to hang on to old things, ideas, relationships, habits, or what might have been – just for the sake of longevity and tradition. How freeing is that?

"If you don't like the game you're playing, you can always reset and play again – or do something else entirely – even midstream! Thanks, Lada! It was just a game after all."

road • trip

Although not quite as epic as the Blizzard of '96, the winter of 2018-19 is becoming considerably stormy in its own right.

In February, while the rest of the country is experiencing beyond nippy, well past chilly, minus 50 degrees below Celsius temperatures, Vancouver Islanders are witnessing powerful winds gusting from 60 to 80 kilometres per hour – strong enough to use the word hurricane.

"The word *shumka* comes to mind for me." "Shumka" is the Ukrainian word that describes the kind of wind that whips up everything within reach, pulling whatever it can, swirling, twirling, and whirling, around and around, like berries in a blender.

Throughout Victoria, these ferocious winds are making the tall, coniferous trees bend like licorice sticks – even snapping their branches like toothpicks and tossing them across roads and power lines, creating a life-sized game of Pick-Up Sticks.

"The wind picked up my mobile home with me and my husband still in it and then dropped us a few feet over with a thud," said one of the Lantern's guests to Maria as part of their breakfast conversation a few weeks later.

On top of the howling winds and power outages, snow decides to join the party. With traffic lights out on the highway and cars spinning in the middle of intersections, driving conditions are treacherous and not worth the risk for a seven in the morning, barely-above-minimum-wage shift, so Maria makes arrangements to stay home.

"Martha can cover my shifts this weekend – she just has to walk three blocks to get to work anyway – and I'll figure out how to get there for Tuesday morning, as usual."

Turns out, Maria cannot drive the 22 kilometres at all in her car even if she wants to because the private cul-de-sac where she and her mother live is still yet to be ploughed. Snow tires or not, the snow is just too deep.

"Snow plows are like the old man's teeth," she thinks. "Few and far apart."

The strata did hire a snow plough guy on retainer, but so far, he has not showed up.

Eventually the truth surfaces: he is currently in jail and is not available.

* * *

So, on Monday afternoon, Maria decides to brave the busses. All decked out in her warm, three-quarter length leather coat that her mother had given her, a pair of orange *Cougar* boots from 1977, and a purple hat knitted by her friend Vasylyna from church, she hikes through snow-covered streets for 25 minutes to the bus stop to take the #6 then #70 busses to Sidney.

As she leaps over greying, slushy puddles and steep snow banks, it occurs to her that it would have been nice to have a backpack in this situation.

The busses are running better than expected and Maria makes her connections without much waiting. As her bus passes "the Roost," a local favourite farm-to-table restaurant, vineyard, and bakery on East Saanich Road, where chickens wander free around the parking lot most days, she remembers a clever sign that had been posted many years ago across the street, which said, "Why did the chicken cross the road? Because it was poultry in motion."

Walking to the Inn from the bus stop, Maria notices how the headquarters of the National Green Party is just a stone's throw away from where she works. It is a blessing to live and work in Elizabeth May's strategically-chosen riding. Maria scans the street and sees the silver lining of taking the bus.

"It's a good thing I didn't attempt to drive to work today because there's nowhere to park – not out front, not in the back. And all this snow pushed along the sides of the roads looks like icing piped on a wedding cake."

When she steps through the front doors of the cozy inn, knocking the snow off her boots, Martha is sitting at the front desk and does not look up. Weary from her journey, Maria gently shuts the door behind her and admires how the fireplace casts a golden light into the lounge.

She is expecting to stay downstairs in the staff quarters and although Martha does not welcome her warmly, she does give Maria the option to stay in the Amethyst Room on the third floor.

"Here's the key to Amethyst," Martha says without a smile, the keys jangling from the colour-coordinated tag. "It's nicer than the basement and has a TV."

"Are you sure?" "Yes, Louise insisted – but you have to clean it before you leave."

Maria loops the key ring through her finger to keep from dropping it, grabs her sports bag and then braces the curly-cue base of the wooden railing with her right hand, and pulls herself up the stairs.

A life-like, white orchid amid a sea of creamy crystals greets her at the top of the stairs on the first landing. She keeps going up another two sets of eight stairs to the second floor and glances at the credenza which works double duty as a place to store extra linens and as a water serving station.

She climbs another eight stairs and peers over the railing to take in a bird's eye view of the lobby, and then crests the last eight stairs to the third floor.

* * *

The door to Amethyst is open and the room has been turned down. Maria walks in like a guest and raises the blinds to look out into an expansive, northern view of the town of Sidney.

"The porch lights and the snowy streets look so nice at dusk."

Even with no fireplace, Amethyst, with its lavender walls and white-trimmed windows, is arguably Maria's favourite room in the whole inn.

Work-related or not, she is treating her stay as if she is on a retreat. To start things off, she takes a peek to see if her fig photograph is still there, "Yup, there it is."

Then she calls her closest friend, Samantha, who lives in Alberta, just outside of Edmonton.

"I'm in the Amethyst Room!" she exclaims, showing Samantha a quick panoramic view from her laptop.

"At the Inn?"

"Yes, I made it through the snow today! I've got my road trip chips, my Pomegranate juice in a wine glass—I'm all set for the night!"

To Maria, who dresses much too casually (even by Victoria's standards) when she is out and about among people, Samantha always looks so put together – even when her long, auburn hair is tied up in a ponytail. Samantha is a very attractive, recently separated, single mom of three, and her bright, green eyes shine from behind her big, butterfly eyelashes.

Samantha also likes to change the colour of her nails frequently. She and Maria met online through the Walker Coaching Academy and on that day, Samantha's nails were bright blue like the prairie sky. Today, they are peach like a Himalayan salt lamp. Not staying single for long, Samantha is currently in a serious relationship with Ed. He got his coaching certification first through the Walker Academy and then introduced Samantha to the online school later.

As much as Maria hates to admit this, "If it wasn't for Ed, Samantha and I would never have met. I guess that's something to be grateful to him for." But how Ed managed to stumble upon the school at all is anybody's guess.

"Have you made plans for Valentine's Day with Ed tomorrow?" Maria asks her friend.

"Still, up in the air," Samantha replies while unloading her dishwasher. "It doesn't look like it."

"I don't get it. Valentine's Day is such easy points in a relationship – not that you're keeping score or anything – but just a little something would be nice."

"Yeah, well, it's not his thing. He's not big on greeting card holidays," she says using her guy voice.

"Speaking of disappointments, have you talked to Nick recently?"

"No, I'm still mad at him for not telling me he was getting married last year and I had to find out about it at the same time as everybody else. I thought we were closer than that."

"I'm more mad at him for getting married in the first place. I thought she was going to be me. Remember when you brought your kids to Victoria last summer and we spent the day together and I took you to Island View Beach…"

"And you made Taco Salad for us…"

"And we called him? And then she came on the phone?"

"Yeah."

"I felt sick after that."

"I keep on trying to tell you that if he liked you, you'd know. Has he done anything to show any interest?"

"Well no, not lately. But in the beginning he seemed to."

"I think you just have to accept this and move on."

"I know, but I can't. I still have some hope that he'll come around."

"What's his hold on you, anyway?"

"You know what it is?" Maria takes a deep breath to collect her thoughts.

"What?"

"He listened."

"Oh, I get that…yeah, you're right, he was a good listener…"

"Well," says Maria, reading 12:12 on the clock radio. "It's getting late."

"Yeah, I have two houses to clean tomorrow."

"What? On Valentine's Day?"

Samantha laughs.

"Well, if it helps, I have to work, too," Maria adds.

"One of these days, we have to get our coaching businesses going, so we don't have to do these other jobs anymore," says Samantha.

"Yes, but that's a whole 'nother conversation."

"You're right, good night, Maria, and enjoy your retreat."

"Thanks, I will, and happy Valentine's Day."

As Maria shuts down her laptop, she realizes how much Samantha has helped her these last couple of years.

"Even though Samantha is as petite as they come, she has a really big heart! I don't know what I would have done if I couldn't talk to her about Nick – and when my cat *Panchyk* died last year, she was my shoulder. I know that if I stuffed that pain down any deeper, it would've killed me."

She fluffs up her pillows, bunching them from the sides, and climbs into the fancy bed with the crisp, clean, white sheets.

"Ah… I can get used to this."

* * *

Five hours later, Maria's phone alarm goes off. It's time for her to get ready for work. The shower pressure on the top floor is a little shoddy and Maria has to crank the taps to feel warm. Unfortunately, blasting the hot water scalds her already sensitive scalp.

"That's it. I'm going to stop colouring my hair blonde altogether and just go grey!"

From that day, Maria starts growing her hair out – and her hair grows longer than it has ever been in her entire lifetime – and amazingly, her hair also starts growing in white and not drabby grey at all! It blends in seamlessly with her bleachy blonde colour from before and you can hardly tell where one colour starts and the other colour ends!

"Come to think of it, now my hair is silver and gold – much like our Canadian Toonie – without any effort or expense on my part!"

Feeling a little groggy after staying up past midnight talking with Samantha, Maria is almost late for work, even though all she has to do is go down two flights of stairs!

Regardless, the Valentine's Day breakfast shift goes by uneventfully and Maria has the rest of the afternoon to explore the charming, Sidney-by-the-Sea.

"Can't forget my hat," she reminds herself before she canters down the stairs.

Once again, she gets to wear the plummy coloured hat her friend Vasylyna had knit for her.

"Usually, the winters around here are just too mild."

But this day is a different story. Although the sun is shining, there is still so much snow on the ground and it is perfect hat weather. Soon, Maria heads down Bevan Avenue towards the ocean where there is a pier that jets out over the water.

The cold, clear waters around Vancouver Island are popular among divers, fishermen, and boaters, and the pier is a great place to catch crabs!

Before she can step on the pier, a woman stops her. "I just love your purple hat," she says as she raises her hand to block the sun from her eyes. "The fine threads are dancing in the sunlight and it looks like you're an angel with a purple halo! May I take your picture?"

The next person she meets on her walk is just as friendly and chatty and as she continues five blocks towards the Pat Bay Highway and stops in shops along the way, many people nod and smile, each new person friendlier than the last, and asking questions like, "Was the hat a gift?" or "Did you knit the hat yourself?" and then saying, "I wish I was that talented" or "I wish I knew someone who could make me a hat like that."

Even the manager at Mark's admires her hat and flirts with her while she is shopping for underwear!

"What a great Valentine's Day!" she thinks as she smiles from ear to ear!

* * *

Two days later, the snow had melted enough and Lubomyra drives out to Sidney to pick her daughter up from work. Instead of going back home though, they jump on the ferry to the Mainland to help celebrate her niece, Zoryanna's, 12th birthday.

"It's hard to believe Krys has a 12 year-old daughter," she thinks in the car.

Although Maria is happy for him that he has such a nice family life, she is also disappointed that she does not have her own kids to guide and nurture.

As Maria, Lubomyra, Krys, Olivia, and Olivia's sister-in-law Lada sit around the glass dining room table eating *Empanadas*, the doorbell rings. It is Olivia's friend Jewel who has just driven all the way from Sicamous, where she lives in a hundred-year-old farmhouse with her two daughters, seven dogs, and two cats.

Jewel is saying how her older daughter has a talent for Badminton and how she, as her mom, would never stand in the way of something her daughter wants to do.

"Well…" Maria chimes in. "When I was in junior high school, my friend Philippa wanted us to join the school wrestling team together so I asked my father and he expressly said, 'NO! – No daughter of mine is going to be on a wrestling team…'"

"Why, what's wrong with that?" they all ask.

"Different times, I guess, and something about 'I'd be 'barking up the wrong tree'… and then when I was in high school, I wanted to learn how to play the accordion for a reason I don't remember and this time my brother was the one who said, 'absolutely not, no sister of mine is going to play the accordion!'

"Krys," they all say in two syllables.

And Lubomyra chimes in and says, "Yes, he was very much against her playing the accordion – that I remember."

"Could you imagine how I would have turned out if I had wrestled by day and played the accordion by night?"

In a flash, they all had the same thought – Maria wearing a revealing wrestler's suit while playing a Polka on her accordion. They all burst out laughing!

cue • wake

If the fear of being left behind by her family and having to fend for herself like an orphan was not enough, Maria's other fears from childhood included being haunted by Bluenose Ghosts and having to run from exploding volcanos.

Bluenose Ghosts blew into her life during her Dartmouth years. After watching a movie about the classic ghost stories in class when she was 8, (presumably on Halloween) she saw the figments of ghosts lurking and scratching in the bare branches of a tree outside her window at night from her bed.

To be fair, with the long and sordid history of sailors and pirates circling Nova Scotia's shores in their lofty Schooners, as depicted on the Canadian dime, being surrounded by Bluenose Ghosts may have been a remote possibility – but having to escape from volcanos, was not – until the Ponomarenko's moved to Hawaii a few years later, that is.

As far as witnessing real life ghost sightings after childhood, Maria saw a ghost once when she was living in Brussels, Belgium in 1993, after a night of drinking the hard stuff. She woke up to see a man wearing a black suit from the 1800s, stooping at the side of her bed. He was wearing a top hat and when spotted, he quickly faded away.

Later that morning, before she could tell her friend and neighbour, Sorcha, what she had seen, Sorcha said, "I saw a ghost with a top hat in my kitchen this morning – he was stooping over my father's kneeling chair, you know, the one he was using after his back operation."

Maria suspects that the Lantern Inn may also be haunted. She and the housekeeper, April, whose First Nations ancestors came from Haida Gwaii, had both seen things out of the corner of their eye and felt energy in the shadows.

But if there were any resident ghosts at the inn, nobody complained about them until two couples, who did not know each other previously, decided to push their tables together for an extended conversation after breakfast.

Somehow, while Maria is cleaning up the kitchen, the guests in the dining room erupt, swearing up and down that the sugar bowl suddenly tipped over by itself with no one touching it, spilling sugar all over the white table cloth.

Did the sugar bowl topple over on its own because it was precariously perched on the crack between two unevenly matched and tippy tables, or did the guests accidently knock it over while they were talking and did not want to admit it, or was there an invisible hand in play?

Maria thinks the spilled sugar has something to do with the new construction next door. After 18 years of only having a woman in her senior years living in a one-story bungalow as a next door neighbour – which gave the dining room lots of light and the Jade Suite a view of a charming church steeple, a gentle hillside, and a small patch of ocean – a developer started building a four-story, million-dollar condo complex, and it was a pounding headache for Louise and the Lantern Inn's owner, from the get go.

Maria suspects that since the Town of Sidney was originally the sacred home of the WSÁNEĆ People, who have lived on the Saanich Peninsula for thousands of years, the digging into the earth and the booming construction is disturbing the peace. The spilled bowl of sugar is just a little admonition of sorts.

Maria does not appreciate the loud activity next door either. The big trucks, the grinding of heavy machinery, and the incessant though intermittent hammering and yelling interrupts the tranquility without mercy.

"I'm not sure if I can cope with this noise pollution much longer."

On this overcast February morning, after cleaning up the sugar, Maria starts on the task of re-filling the jam pots. It is not her favourite job as the Breakfast Cook because she never has time for it in her shift and the gloppy jam goes everywhere but in the bowls, as she intends.

"Surely, I was cut out for more than feeding travellers fancy scrambled eggs and toast with jam each morning," she sighs to herself, tears welling up in her eyes, feeling like she has wasted her whole life playing way too small, feeling like she is missing out, and it is too late for her to live the life of her dreams.

As she stands at the kitchen counter with six clean porcelain pots, a big spoon, and a brand new jar of blackberry preserves, the energy in the room hushes, as if it is on a dimmer switch.

Although the kitchen looks the same as it always has, the clock stops ticking and the space becomes quiet. Maria feels like she is in a silent bubble. She feels like she is being observed. She feels the density of an invisible stare from someone hovering nearby.

It is unclear whether this energy is benevolent or not. She does not dare move her body, other than her eyes, and her breath becomes shallow as if a doctor is looking into her ear with a light.

"What could possibly be so interesting?" she always thinks in that situation.

"Is this what you want?" she asks herself, though the question does not come from her normal thinking voice.

"No," she sobs. "I want love, I want a man in my life, I want a booming business of my own, I want to travel and see the world... I'm tired of watching everyone else be in relationships and having meaningful careers and going on adventures in far-away places. When is it going to be my turn?"

"It's your choice, Babe," she hears.

"Well... in that case... game on," she says with the gravity of an earthquake.

in • to • it

Chantal, a former flight attendant from Edmonton, sits at the table by the stairs in the dining room of the Lantern Inn. She has just flown in from Nepal after climbing to base camp at Mount Everest and has come to the Inn, of all places, to recover for a couple of days.

Without her intrepid guest, Maria would never have met anyone who has Everest on their belt, nor known about the Psychic Fair taking place in Sidney that day. Meanwhile, Maria and Martha are not on speaking terms, so Maria does not think to mention that she is leaving promptly at noon to attend the fair.

"Never mind. Martha will figure it out. If she doesn't say 'hi' to me when she walks into the kitchen to punch her timecard while I'm standing right there at the sink for the last three Saturdays, I'm not going to say 'bye' to her."

With forty dollars of cash in hand, Maria heads towards the Mary Winspear Centre thinking about what she most wants to know about her life. Her mind goes straight to Nick.

"Do I dare ask about him?"

Psychic fairs are not for everyone and Maria is well aware that she has to be careful about mentioning this topic in certain company. However, at the end of the day, she likes that she can travel in between the Catholic and New Age worlds easily and is able to speak both languages.

To her, the Church is more masculine in its structure and tradition, while the "spiritual but not religious" camp is more feminine and fluid, and both are needed to make the world go round.

After circling the buzzing room and scouting out her options from among Angel Card Readers, Tarot Readers, Energy Healers, and Psychic Mediums, she is drawn to Lorenzo, a Face Reader.

Lorenzo is a gentle soul who speaks with a pleasing accent. "Please sit down," he invites her as he sits across from her, knee to knee. His eyes pour over her face for a long moment. "You hear what people say to you in your left ear."

"Oh good, he's talking about listening," thinks Maria to herself, unable to say her thoughts out loud. "Does he know I'm left-handed just from my face?"

"All of the negative and critical things people have been saying to you have been going into you through this ear, making you doubt yourself," he continues. "And then after they stopped years ago, you took over with your own words where they left off, repeating the same negative sayings over and over again all of your life…" he continues.

Hearing the truth, tears have no choice but to spring from her eyes. "…The messages cross over from your left ear to the right side of your face, making everything, especially your smile, droop on this side. You're tired…tired of being beat up."

Maria recalls being constantly corrected by her grandparents, parents, and teachers, never feeling like she quite measured up to their invisible and unattainable standards. "This is how you pronounce words in Ukrainian," or "Here's a big, red X next to your pop quiz answer," and "Wrong, Wrong, Wrong!"

Most of these people are long gone now but she keeps replaying the same refrains, feeling the same shame and struggle she did when she was a kid.

"Your eyebrows are furrowed and it looks like you're trying to figure out if you can trust people," says Lorenzo. "Like when you came to my table, I asked myself, 'Why doesn't she trust me? I'm a nice guy… she doesn't know me… what's not to trust?'"

"I had to see who else was in the room first before I could make my decision," thinks Maria silently, not realizing how she comes across to the intuitives in the room.

"Your face is saying, 'Can I trust you?' and so people are wondering if you're trustworthy as well. That's why you're getting mixed results in your relationships. You don't trust that people like you, but if you want to know how someone feels about you, just ask them."

"Oh, I just couldn't ask someone how they feel about me because maybe I don't want to know the truth," Maria thinks inside her head.

"Where are you feeling this in your body?"

After pausing for a moment and tuning in, she says out loud, "I feel it in the corner of my right jaw."

"Yes, that's the strongest muscle in the body."

"And in my shoulders."

Lorenzo gets up from his chair and walks behind her. Some of Maria's hair has escaped from the elastic in her hair and has fallen out of her ponytail. As he gently moves it aside, he touches her shoulders that are carrying all of the 'shoulds' of her life and feels the tension with alarm. He sits back down again. "You're also hiding behind your hair – not letting people to see you, trying not to let them see what you don't want them to see."

Fighting the feeling of being exposed like an upside-down ladybug, Maria is aware that looky-loos are hovering on the other side of the table, listening to their hushed conversation. She has all but tuned out the whole room and is focusing on Lorenzo's eyes. She has never had the chance to look so intimately into a man's eyes before and does not realize how much she longs for that experience.

Now they are both speaking without words. She studies his face, his eyebrows, his nose, his mouth. So many worlds come forth as she travels deeper, beyond space and time, into his dark brown eyes. She sees colours – yellow, orange, violet, green – splashed on his face like paint on a canvass. Lorenzo is an artist, he is a healer, and in his eyes, that are as dark brown as the depths of the earth, she feels kindness and love without an agenda. Maria feels seen.

* * *

Maria wishes Samantha could have come with her to the Psychic Fair. "She loves this stuff. If only we lived in the same city. I'm going to give her a call now to see if she's free to chat… 'Hey Samantha, do you have a minute?'"

"I was just about to jump in the shower and get ready for tonight but yeah, I have a few minutes."

"Oh, Okay, I won't keep you. I just wanted to say I went to a psychic fair today and got a face reading."

"Oh my goodness… that's amazing. How did it go?"

"I cried the whole time. I was very emotional. It's like he just opened up the tap and everything I've been hanging on to rushed out in buckets."

"Sounds like you needed it. Do you think I should get a face reading, too?"

"Yes, sure, if you can find somewhere nearby. It may be healing for you. I can give you his website if you're stuck. I think you'd like him. He's very gentle. I was hoping to find out more about Nick but was too afraid to ask."

"Speaking of Nick…"

"Have you talked to him?"

"No, but I had an intuition to check out his profile. It's not like I stalk him or anything but something told me to look and I don't want you to get your hopes up but…"

"But what?"

"Well, he changed his relationship status to "separated."

"What?" Maria looks from side to side as if she was speaking on a payphone in a dark alley. "Are you sure? They've only been married for like a year and a half. I wonder what happened?"

"I don't know – just wanted to pass that along."

"Thanks, Samantha. That changes everything!"

pile • on

Unexpectedly, Maria decides to try her hand at losing weight again to drop the pounds she has packed on over the last couple of years. Her weight has climbed up to 191.5 pounds recently, mostly as a result of trying to comfort her heartache with food.

It is the beginning of March, 2019 and some of her casual friends are talking about what they are giving up for Lent. "No interest at all to me," so she keeps scrolling past their posts.

But on Pancake Tuesday, after having been invited to Petrovna's birthday dinner party with her mom and after eating four pieces of pizza and birthday cake and drinking sugary soda, the tables have turned: Maria gets the download to give up snacks and desserts for Lent.

At the dinner party, Maria meets Brett, who is writing a book about his Camino adventures, his wife Jean, and another couple who had met each other more than 30 years ago at a bus stop – just like the song by The Hollies.

Maria asks the guests the question, "Which country would you live in if you could live anywhere in the world?"

Lubomyra and Petrovna both say, "France;" Luke says, "somewhere in Montana;" Brett says, "Salt Lake City;" and Maria says, "Spain or Sweden."

Surprised by her own answers and without knowing how or when, Maria thinks to herself, "there's travel in my future."

"We'd better say goodnight now," says Lubomyra. "Marichka has to get up at 5:30 to go to work tomorrow."

"Thanks so much for the lovely evening – good luck with your book, Brett! Good night everyone," adds Maria.

"I'll drive. I only had one glass of wine," says Lubomyra as they walk toward her green sports car.

"It's no trouble. I can drive home. I didn't drink at all."

"Next time."

"Fine," Maria says as she climbs into the passenger seat. She takes a deep breath and quickly states before she can change her mind, "I'm going on a diet. I've decided I'm only going to be eating three square meals a day. I guess you can say I'm giving up snacks and desserts for Lent!"

"That's nice, dear."

Maria does not realize that by fasting, she would be embarking on a spiritual quest, and was heading for days, weeks, and months filled with emotional upheaval. Yes, she would often feel hungry, cranky, and tired, but she decides to stick with her eating plan because she realizes she no longer wants to stuff down her feelings and numb herself with food.

With a history of turning to food and wine to anesthetize herself, Maria is not going to let emotional eating be her coping strategy anymore. She wants to face her feelings and demons head on. In her mind, as hard as it is to get through the rough patches, the intense emotions actually mean she is dredging up a lot of old emotional junk that she has been hanging onto for decades.

Each day as she fasts for five to 12 hours between meals and loosely sticks to 1500 calories a day or so (the calories required to maintain her ideal weight), she is releasing and clearing tons of emotional baggage! If she can only see the wake behind her of debris that is no longer weighing her down and keeping her from living the life of her dreams. Being emotional is actually a good sign, but do not tell her brother that!

The next day presents the first challenge. There are certain occupational hazards associated with working with food and one of them is gaining weight.

"Never trust a skinny chef," her mother's friend Zoya would say. Following the natural rhythms of day and night, the word "breakfast" comes from 'breaking the fast' from the previous day's last meal.

On top of serving hot breakfasts to the guests, Maria is also expected to bake cookies as an added homemade treat at the self-serve coffee station. Maria is a good cook and her talent for baking comes from both sides of her Ukrainian family. On her father's side, her Aunt Lida is known for baking spectacular nut and chocolate tortes and her Great Aunt Stefa ran a restaurant at her motel in upstate New York.

On her mother's side, her grandmother worked as a cook at Aetna Insurance and their family recipe for a Napoleon Torte, made with creamed butter, eggs, evaporated milk and vanilla bean, sandwiched between several layers of crispy, buttery and flaky pastry, is out-of-this-world delicious!

To avoid temptation, Maria tosses a cloth napkin over the tray of cookies that always sits in the corner of the kitchen overnight. By 10:30, after managing to get through breakfast without eating a morsel of food, not even a single strawberry, the hunger pangs kick in. It is time for a pep talk.

"Marichka, I know we're hungry but don't worry, I'll make sure we eat when we come home from work today. We'll have a really nice lunch. Just hang on a little longer. I promise I'll make sure that we always eat plenty of food each and every day but from now on, we just can't eat absent-mindedly every few minutes. I'm doing this for us so we can be healthier and look better and enjoy our life more. Are you onboard with that? Yes. Super. We can do this!"

* * *

Three days into her Lenten fast and partway through a slow breakfast shift, Maria runs smack into a roadblock. She suddenly starts feeling the symptoms of a cold coming on. Her eyes are watery, her nose is running, and she is going through countless tissues from sneezing every few minutes.

"Good thing there are only three guests staying here today and none of them want breakfast."

Lucky for her, Louise always keeps packets of Emergen-C powder for staff (another one of Stefan-with-an-f's ideas) and so she quickly mixes up a glass as a one-time exception and carries on with her baking duties.

She finds a recipe for "Skinny Cranberry Bliss Bars" and goes to work, washing her hands every few minutes, hoping not to transfer her cold to anyone else. She already has all of the ingredients on hand, other than the white chocolate chips, but true to staying on top of groceries, Louise makes sure there are plenty of semi-sweet chocolate chips she can use instead.

The batter is calling to her at every stir, "Go ahead and take a nibble. Try me. Taste me. Here's a spoon. Take a bite. No one will know…" Yet, with steadfast determination to not give in, Maria ploughs through every step and layer of the recipe without entertaining the temptation of sneaking a taste, not even the dark chocolate drizzle she clumsily pours over top. "I'm going to count this as a win!" she says as she marvels over her creation.

"I know this tastes good, so I don't need to try it to make sure."

Maria wins that battle and even though everyone raves about how heavenly the bliss bars are, (she even brought some home to her mom), she never did sample a square herself.

As for the sudden flu that has descended upon her out of nowhere, it does not hang around for long. In fact, by the next day, the cold and flu symptoms completely disappear as if they never showed up in the first place.

"How strange," Maria thinks. "I've never heard of a 24-hour cold before."

She gets the idea to look up "Spiritual Cold" on the Internet and sure enough, having short-lived cold symptoms, also known as "Ascension Flu," is a thing. It is a way of clearing and processing deep, unresolved emotional junk from the physical body in a quick hurry, and although it looks like the flu, it is not. How long the symptoms last depend on the awareness of the individual and somehow Maria manages to clear that particular hurdle in good time.

* * *

As the month of March progresses and the Cherry Blossoms adorn the streets of Victoria, shedding their petals in soft pink flurries and blessing everyone graciously, Maria is starting to shed herself.

Here is a page from her journal showing her progress:

Day 22: Thursday, March 28, 2019 – 183.5 lbs! -8 lbs from Day 1 @ beginning of week 4!

Day 23: Friday, March 29, 2019 – 184 lbs (+.5 lbs). Went on a wellness walk.

Day 24: Saturday, March 30, 2019 – 183.5 lbs (-.5 lbs). Went on a wellness walk.

Day 25: Sunday, March 31, 2019 – 184 lbs (+.5 lbs). Went on a wellness walk.

Day 26: Monday, April 1, 2019 – 183.5 lbs (-.5 lbs).

Day 27: Tuesday, April 2, 2019 – 182.5 lbs (-1 lbs). Ran for 8 minutes. Worked out with Angie.

Maria's father, Yaromyr, was an athlete. While attending Bloor Street Collegiate in Toronto in the 1950s, he held an impressive record for swimming the Butterfly stroke faster than anyone at the time. He was also recruited by the Argonauts Football team to play for them but declined the opportunity in order to pursue a career in the Canadian Navy instead.

Even though her father's eyesight was poor and he could barely see without his thick, black-rimmed glasses, his hand-eye coordination was astonishing. He was a fisherman, sailor, rugby player, and pool player, and he taught Maria how to play squash and tennis.

During a friendly game of squash between Maria and her heavy-set father when he was fifty and she was half his age, she hit the ball into a corner and turned to walk away, thinking she won the point.

Suddenly, she heard his running shoes squeak as he picked up speed and vaulted cross-corner over the shiny, painted wooden floor of the echoing room. He caught the bouncing ball on the upswing and slammed it into the wall for the game!

Now approaching fifty herself, Maria thinks about her own health and fitness levels.

"Should I call Angie and workout with her again?"

To Maria, Angie is on the top five list of the most influential people of her life, after her immediate family of origin. As yet another lefty, Maria believes she and Angie are from the same soul family and are meant to stay connected on this journey.

They first met 20 years ago when Maria signed up for Angie's dance class on the suggestion of Montana, her co-worker at the *Peninsula News Review*. Maria won a free pass after her first class and she and Angie have been friends ever since.

Once Maria watched Angie carry, not one, but two, hefty barrels of drinking water across a gym! Without a doubt, Angie is the strongest person Maria knows, both physically and emotionally. Angie's own personal trials of life have been massive and she has suffered many heart-breaking losses, including the sudden disappearance of her orange cat, Stanley, who got lost immediately following the breakup of her second marriage.

Somehow, in spite of all her anguish and trials, Angie still manages to shine her light every day, being a force for good for so many people in this crazy, crazy mixed up world.

As a way to motivate Maria to run five kilometres in the "CIBC Run for the Cure for breast cancer" in October, 2009, Angie found a picture of a dashing man with short, dark brown hair, blue eyes and six-pack abs, and with three of his fingers just barely reaching south, just past his waistline. Angie printed his photo off on a sheet of glossy paper and taped it to the console of the treadmill as Maria was training, and said, "There... this will help!" and walked away.

They named him "Jackson Starley" – "Jackson" in honour of Michael Jackson who had just died that past summer and because they liked his dance moves, and "Starley" was a cross between Angie's cat's name, "Stanley" and Maria's cat's name, "Charlie."

On the day of the Run on the University of Victoria campus, "Team Bosum" (sic) was in fine form. On top of their Hope t-shirts, they each wore hot pink tutus, sparkling tiaras, and feathery boas. Maria had her iPod strapped to her right arm with a playlist that started with, "I Believe" by Nikki Yanofsky, written to get Canadians excited about the Vancouver Winter Olympics of 2010; "Today is Your Day" by Shania Twain; "The Climb" by Miley Cyrus; and the theme song to the "Laverne & Shirley" television show: "One, two, three, four, five, six, seven, eight, *Schlemiel, Schlemazel, Hasenpfeffer* Incorporated... We're gonna do it!"

Each of the runners and walkers who wove their way through the leafy streets of the University campus on that crisp and sunny autumnal day, had their own stories and reasons to participate. She recognized many familiar faces as she navigated through the crowds of thousands, including her friend Svitlana from church, and she loved the high-fives and cheers of encouragement they exchanged along the way.

When Maria forgot she was running for her Great Aunt Stefa who had died from breast cancer and complications to her surgery, and her mother's friend, Theodosia, who beat breast cancer but would die of Esophageal cancer in 2013, she could barely keep running up the long hill that merged on to the ring road about halfway through the course.

Suddenly, out of the sea of pink ahead and jogging against the current, Angie emerged out of the crowd, wearing a big smile and that photo of Jackson Starley taped to her chest. "Come, follow us, Maria!" cheered Angie. "You can do this! Keep going, keep going!"

Much like a Border Collie tends to their flock and rounds everyone up, especially the most reluctant ones, Angie had been running circles around everybody on Team Bosum, keeping everyone inspired and on track. Running back and forth and up and down the road, she must have covered 15 kilometres that day herself!

With that extra boost of encouragement, Maria dug deep to the bottom of her heels and crested the hill and kept going to the finish line!

* * *

5K ALL THE WAY!

By Maria Ponomarenko

On Sunday, October 4th, 2009, I reached a new milestone in my life. I participated in the CIBC Run for the Cure for breast cancer with huge trepidation and managed to run the whole 5-kilometre course non-stop.

It was quite an accomplishment for me and I'm so glad I did it!

If you're curious to know what it's like for a first-timer to run 5K — that's 3.107 miles for those of you on the Imperial system — here's a rundown of my day.

I've learned that distance running is just as much of a mind game as it is a physical challenge. In this post, I'm trying to recall the types of thoughts I was thinking throughout the morning as I got closer and closer to the finish line and beyond.

Breakfast of Champions

I woke up long before 6am and by 7am, I ate a big breakfast. Eating a healthy and nutritious breakfast is important every day of the week and on Sunday-Runday, mine consisted of a glass of orange juice and a toasted plain bagel topped with unsweetened, smooth peanut butter, honey and a banana. I also drank a cup of green tea instead of my regular coffee. I haven't had a bagel in a long time and it was a nice change of pace for me. I think it was a good choice because the meal gave me the energy I needed for the run. In this case, carbs are recommended.

Suiting Up

Gemma, my Team Bosum Captain, suggested I wear a long-sleeve shirt under my event t-shirt because the morning air would probably be chilly. (Thank God it didn't rain or worse, snow, like it did in Calgary! We had brilliant weather!)

When I unfolded this year's Run for the Cure official t-shirt and saw the word "Hope" splashed across the front for the first time, a tear came to my eye and I had to take a deep breath.

Everyone knows that having the right shoes makes a big difference when running and I'm so happy that the cross-trainers I bought 6-weeks ago fit me like a glove and presented no issues for me. What a relief! Oh and how can I forget the pink tiara and the fuchsia tutu? More on those embellishments later.

Getting to the start line I left my house at 7:30 to give myself lots of time to get to the University of Victoria and to find a decent parking space. It took me longer to get there than it should have because I completely missed my exit onto MacKenzie. I just drove right past it. And it didn't occur to me for at least 5 minutes.

I guess I was more nervous than I realized. My excuse was, I was listening to Coldplay's "Now My Feet Won't Touch the Ground [Prospekt's March Edition]" on the radio, a song I had never heard before, and thought, wouldn't that be a fun way to run this race, running so fast and effortlessly like I was running on air. That's not exactly what happened though.

In spite of my detour, I was the first to arrive from my team. It took a while for all of the team members to find each other in the crowd. Gemma asked if anyone else wanted to wear a tutu. I was going to pass — the pink foam crown was goofy enough for me, but Angie, my trainer, insisted.

Warm Up

Local Jazzercise instructors, including Angie, lead us through the warm up. I'm so glad they picked the 9-1-1 song — "Fire Burning" by Sean Kingston — because that's one of my faves these days.

I heard 4000 of us registered in Victoria! We managed to raise over $500,000 for breast cancer research. Over $5000 of that was raised by Team Bosum and of that, I raised $300 (200% of my initial fundraising goal).

Angie, who inspired me to sign up for the run in the first place, made a deal with me and another Team Bosum runner, Goldie. She promised to tag team between us and motivate us throughout the whole 5K course, which meant she ended up running way more than anyone else did that day.

So, the three of us had to start together and there was a bit of a delay because they both had to check their bags and use the facilities right before embarking on the run. I was losing patience. I just wanted to get this thing over with. Angie said to me,

"You're panicking; I can feel it." I would not have used the word "panic." But now I know what "Chomping at the bit" means.

And then she said, "I do this every year. Trust me, we'll fly by everyone anyway. Just follow me. First we're going to walk for a few minutes to warm up and then we'll run. And it's not a race."

Challenge #1

I was surprised by the amount of people who were participating. Angie, Goldie and I walked briskly along the grassy median past all of the walkers on the road. Within a few short minutes we started running. Keep in mind that I trained on a treadmill for the past several months and running outside with people was a totally different experience.

The first challenge was to keep up with Angie and Goldie (Goldie is a grandmother by the way) and dodge past all of the people. There were women, men, and kids of all ages walking and running at various speeds, shoulder to shoulder, along the campus road. We had to maneuver around dogs too. It was an obstacle course!

We mostly ran along the outside edge of the circuit which also meant we had to occasionally jump over the odd, orange pylon. Later Angie said she prefers weaving in and out and forging her own path because it distracts her. I think in this case, distraction is a good idea.

Soon enough, Angie and Goldie started pulling further and further ahead of me. I just clipped along at my own pace, which was pretty slow. Slowest runner in the West, I think. I enjoyed meeting my other team members at various moments along the way. The pink tutus were easy enough to spot and the spontaneous high-fives were a huge boost.

Challenge #2

I barely noticed running downhill which apparently can be hard on the knees. Running up hill was a completely different story. It wasn't a steep hill — it was just long. That's when I really slowed down. I simply chugged and chugged and plowed my way up.

I realized when I finally crested the top, my heart rate escalated too. Angie caught up to me at that point and I was breathing heavily. A little too heavily for my liking — somewhere in the 170-plus beats per minute I'm sure and I was having trouble catching my breath.

I told her I was at the top of my zone and she agreed. And then an interesting thing happened. Angie said to pick up the pace.

I thought about that afterward and I realized it was a make or break moment. Most times when you think you've hit your physical and psychological limit, you slow down and maybe even stop things altogether. The natural tendency is not to increase your effort or over exert yourself.

Although counter-intuitive, pushing myself that much harder at that critical moment did the trick and I was able to continue. I applaud Angie for reading my situation and for catching that. She felt confident enough to leave me and find Goldie who was out of my sight by that time.

I rounded a corner and one of the volunteers yelled, "Less than two kilometres to go."

"Whaaattt???" I thought I was so much farther along than that. Ironically, that's when I started to actually add a little stride to my run.

The Home Stretch

Somewhere in the last kilometre, I had a thought. It occurred to me that this whole thing was a given. It was a given that I would finish this run. It was already *a fait accompli*, a done deal. It was just a matter of a few more minutes. I also remembered hearing someone else say, "Never slowdown in the home stretch." And those thoughts somehow made the last steps so much easier.

Out of the corner of my eye, I spotted my friend Danielle running out to meet me. She and I have been sharing Angie's treadmill for months and she knows the journey I've been on better than most. Grabbing my hand, she said, "I'll run in with you."

And then Angie came out of the crowd and grabbed my other hand.

Danielle said, "I know you don't think you can do this, but you can. I want you to sprint to the finish." Somehow, I gave it everything I had and ran all the way home. Our feet didn't touch the ground!

All in all, I'm guessing it took me about 50 minutes. And remarkably, my body bounced back well afterward. I felt my quads for a couple of days and that was about it.

Bonus

In the midst of all of this, a photographer [Adrian Lam] from the *Victoria Times Colonist* newspaper was on hand at the finish line too. I was tickled to learn that a professional photographer captured this intense moment, one of the greatest victories of my life, for posterity and posted the photos online for all to see.

pep • talk

The cement slope in the crawlspace beneath Lubomyra's house is too steep and rough to climb without shoes. Maria hardly goes into that room because it is just too overwhelming. There are too many things in there she does not know what to do with, and so they sit in boxes, untouched, year after year.

The clutter also keeps Lubomyra awake at night. In the basement, you will find everything from old Barbies, to photo CD's, to handwritten letters, to paper shopping bags from fancy stores, to tennis rackets...

"On this floor we have housewares and appliances... here we have luggage and baggage... and over here we have toys, books, magazines, and records. Keep going up and on this floor we have our seasonal department with ornamental wreaths for 50% off till Sunday."

In an effort to clear the clutter on her day off, Maria shuffles indecisively through boxes, drawers, and hope chests. "Here's that old, crumbled picture of Jackson Starley – that's where it went –

in this suitcase. It must have been sitting here for almost ten years. That's it. I'm calling Angie later."

She keeps digging and finds a navy blue t-shirt she received from the Walker Coaching Academy. "I buried this on Boxing Day 2017, the day Nick told me on the phone, 'I'm getting married in three days.'"

That was a crushing day to say the least. Maria fell hard, summersaulting backwards all the way down the side of a mountain, hitting every jagged rock that was remotely on her path. Her heart hurt from smashing around so much.

Even with Nick's gutting news, she still cannot let him go. They continue to have deep conversations every once in a while. Like the time he asked her, (though he is not a religious man or church-goer himself), "Have you ever heard the Bible verse, "Pick up your bed and walk?"

"No, can't say that I have," she replied.

"Jesus said, 'Pick up your bed and walk.' Look it up on the Internet and see what it's about."

So after their phone conversation ended, Maria typed in the verse on the search bar and found some websites that brought everything to light.

Then Jesus said to him, "Get up! Pick up your mat and walk."

John 5:8.

In this story, Jesus comes across a crippled man who is lying near a healing pool but cannot bring himself close enough to the pool to touch the water. As an outcast, all this man can do is sit next to the spa of Jesus' day and beg for handouts from the people who flock there from neighbouring places, for their own healing.

By taking a moment to talk to him, Jesus shows the man compassion. He is saying, "You do not have to be a victim, anymore. You do not need that mat. You do not need to rely on the capricious kindness of strangers to bring you to the water, and you can now walk on your own two feet."

And in that moment, the man is healed. For years, the mat was the crippled man's whole world – he rested on it day and night, suffering, begging, and worrying, while watching the world go by without him. But after Jesus' pep talk, he no longer needed that crutch that had become a burden rather than a lifeline. The time had come to chuck the old raggedy mat for good.

Maria felt Jesus himself had spoken directly to her that Friday. Nick was only the messenger. She had never received such a communiqué from Jesus before and was humbled by the encounter.

As a way to bring the point home, Maria heard a variation of "Pick up your mat and walk" two more times that weekend. First, the message dawned on her again as she was folding up the Murphy bed into the wall on Sunday morning while visiting her brother's family for her nephew's birthday.

"I'm literally picking up a bed!" she said as she looked up to heaven, smiling. "Ha, ha... very clever."

Then on the following Monday, she heard the author, Miriam Fisher, quote the verse again from out of the blue during a recorded interview online.

Maria can see how playing the 'woe-is-me' victim card is showing up in her life and is now extra motivated to call Angie to explore the possibility of training with her again.

"I've found that old picture of Jackson Starley you gave me and I saw it as a sign to call you!"

"Oh my gosh – I remember him!" Angie says chuckling. "How are you, Sweetheart?"

"Well, I've actually been having a really hard time lately and things aren't going so well. I'm tired of low-paying jobs and my mobile spa isn't going anywhere and I just feel like I need to pick myself up somehow and start working out again to build some confidence."

Working out with Angie is the only way Maria knows to dig herself out from under the heap. She is aware her muscles are not going to grow overnight but regular exercise would be a step in the right direction.

Once again, her intuition guides her well.

"I'm so glad you called, Maria. Your timing is perfect. I'm just putting the finishing touches on a new fitness studio and I'm looking for new clients! I'll be officially opening my doors in one week!"

"Oh, I had no idea!"

"How about you join our Tuesday at 5pm group fitness class – and you get to decide what you can pay each week – if it's $20, $15, $5, $10 or zero, it's OK with me – whatever you can afford – we'll work it out," says Angie.

"Are you sure, sure?"

"Yes, I wouldn't have offered if I didn't mean it."

"Then, yes, I'll come. Thank you from the bottom of my heart, Angie. I'll pay you something, I promise, every week. I really appreciate this," Maria replies emotionally.

"Then it's settled. Bring your water bottle and I'll see you in the new studio on Tuesday!"

Suddenly, the obstacles and excuses have cleared and there is nothing left for Maria to do but walk the path ahead of her. It is up to her to pick up her gym mat, accept the gifts that are being offered, and run with them!

hard • hats

In the weeks leading up to Easter, 2019, Maria bounces between the highs and lows of feeling strong and empowered, to insecure and tormented, and back again, up and down, up and down on a daily basis. Meanwhile, Martha is amping up her bullying.

Maria finds assurance and protection from wearing a silver, (straight from the Holy Land) Jerusalem cross necklace that her world-traveller mother, Lubomyra, had recently given her.

The Jerusalem cross, also known as the 'Five-Fold cross' or as a 'cross-and-crosslets', is a Christian cross, originally designed in the 1280s, and includes a large cross surrounded by four smaller, symmetrically-placed Greek crosses.

Martha is not the only source of vexation for Maria at the Inn. The construction crew, who insist on starting their booming work at 7:20 in the morning on the monstrous property next door, infuriates her beyond measure.

They promised Louise they would respect the residential neighbourhood and start hammering at the designated time of eight o'clock in the morning (which is still too early for hotel guests).

"If word gets out in one bad review that guests can't sleep because it's too noisy – construction or not – all our work from the last twenty years will go straight down the drain," says Louise, rubbing her knee that just started aching for no known reason recently.

"Keep an eye on them and let me know what they're up to."

During the Christmas season, Louise decided against giving the crew a tray of cookies as a gesture of goodwill. She drew the line after the hardhats cleared and ripped out the established vines that were growing along the fence between the properties, which subsequently weakened the foundation of the narrow driveway. Then they built a huge, ominous, grey cement wall – literally right on the edge of the property line – to add insult to injury.

"No cookies for them!" Louise's declaration rings through Maria's ears when she looks out the front door window and sees two pickup trucks blocking the Inn's 15-minute parking space, and of course, one of the guests has ordered a taxi to go to the airport at that moment.

"Enough is enough!" Maria says, clutching her cross necklace.

She runs out the front door and stands in the middle of the street in front of the fenced-in construction site.

"Stop!" she yells to the crew member who is working on the second floor, waving her arms to get his attention. "It's 7:30 in the morning! We had an agreement! You're not supposed to start till eight!"

In that moment, still buckling his jeans, one of the senior crew walks out of the porto-potty. He walks right up to Maria and stands just inches from her face, but she holds her ground and does not back down.

"Stop! Shut up!" she bellows again, her arms pointing left and right as if she is directing traffic. "We had an agreement! We're a place of business – a hotel for God's sake – people are trying to sleep! And you're making that very difficult!"

Hearing an offbeat to the usual commotion, the construction manager makes his way to Maria.

"Don't you understand that you're working next to a bed and breakfast?" she asks him. "Your trucks are blocking our lane, your workers are starting well before they're supposed to. We're a place of business where people pay to get a good night's sleep!"

"We're a place of business, too," he replies. "They're breathing down my neck and we have to get this job done. We're already so far behind because of the stormy winter."

The loud work suddenly hushes. Maria looks into his brown eyes and sees that he is being sincere. She sees he is doing his best to juggle all of the moving parts of this construction project. She does not envy his position and even feels a tiny spoonful of compassion for him.

"Tell you what," he says. "Tomorrow, I'll make sure my crew starts at eight but I can't promise anything after that."

"Fair enough," she says straightening her sweater, and with that she walks back to the kitchen. Miraculously, the next two mornings are quiet and the guests are able to enjoy their breakfast in peace.

"Yes, they've upheld their side of the agreement at least for now," she tells Louise.

"Maria! You must have put the fear of God in them with whatever you said! Thank you!"

art • if • facts

While Maria prefers to think of herself as a "cat holic" rather than a "Catholic," seeing the images of the spire of the Notre Dame Cathedral in Paris, France, fully engulfed with fire on Monday, April 15, 2019, just six days before Easter Sunday, is depressing to say the least.

It is hard to believe that yet another place where Maria had stood in the mid-1980s is being destroyed. She had also visited the Twin Towers in New York during a field trip with her Ukrainian school and had taken a black and white photograph from the observation deck with the skyscrapers eerily shading the metropolis below.

She thinks about "the Pillars of the Earth" by Ken Follett, a book everyone in her family has read, starting with her father, and how generations of families would work on the construction of the immense superstructure over hundreds of years, the first foundation builders never seeing the glorious harvest of their blood, sweat, and tears.

Now, 856 years later, the whole world is witnessing the collapsing of Notre Dame Cathedral back into the ashes.

Remembering the words of Spiritual Teacher and Author, Eckhart Tolle, who once said: "All structures are unstable" she posts that cryptic message on her profile page. Although she shutters to say it out loud, she figures that even religion, with all of its history, rituals, and devoted followers, no matter how close to the Truth it believes it promotes, is also, at the end of the day, not immune to the temporary nature of existence, and may also someday disappear, back into the ethers. Perhaps this is the day.

"The world seems to be going to hell in a handbasket," she says shaking her head.

* * *

"I stand corrected" she says under her breath as she sees a photograph of Notre Dame's solid gold cross still shining brightly on the alter, in spite of the raging fire that consumed the Cathedral the day before.

Her jaw drops as she reads the headlines, "Despite Fire, Notre Dame Cross And Altar Still Standing," and "Notre Dame's Golden Altar Cross Seen Glowing As Images Emerge From Inside, Showing Fire-Ravaged Cathedral," and "Notre Dame Altar And Cross Remain Miraculously Untouched After Fire."

It is amazing to see images of the cross standing strong against the backdrop of the still smoking, charred rubble and debris. Reportedly, even votive candles, lit by visiting tourists as prayers in the hours before the start of the event, still continue to flicker as if in solidarity with the surrounding angel statues, holding space for the preservation of the alter.

"It's as if all of the eyes of all of the many, many, millions and millions of people who have stared at this alter over the centuries, studying the various treasures, the stained glass windows, never seeing the same thing twice, and looking up to the vaulted ceiling with thanks, praying for hope, healing, and answers, have somehow created a force-field around this cross, protecting it from all harm," thinks Maria. "Perhaps there's more Truth here than I thought."

It is equally touching to learn that thanks to a human chain of workers, Jesus' Crown of Thorns, among other significant relics, has also been spared.

"It must have been a surreal experience to handle those amazing artifacts that date back to the earliest days of Christianity, in such an intense moment in history, in the glow of the fire, while everything was burning and crumbling around them," she imagines.

"Miracles are unexpected plot twists," concludes Maria. "I consider this nothing short of an Easter Miracle."

sun • day

Contrary to Maria's theory that "East" is the root word in "Easter" and means the point on the horizon where the sun's light rises and breaks through the darkness, signaling the beginning of a new day, surprisingly, the word "Easter" has ancient pagan origins and is actually named after the goddess, *Eostre*, who is celebrated in England at beginning of spring.

In the Ponomarenko family, Easter means preparing a feast for your nearest and dearest and going to Church on Sunday morning, looking your very best, and carrying brimming baskets of pungent ambrosia in hand.

By mid-Saturday afternoon of the Easter long weekend, Lubomyra has already been to church once and has baked three braided loaves of *Paska*, a sweet, egg-based Ukrainian Easter bread that tastes yummy any day of the week, but even better, toasted.

As the church cantor, Lubomyra is attempting to squeeze in a quick rehearsal of the music for the upcoming Divine Liturgy, when the phone rings and the doorbell chimes at the same time.

"Being Ukrainian is a full time job," Maria says as her sister-in-law, niece, nephew, brother, and their dog enter the home, just having travelled on the one o'clock ferry.

"We have one more joining us for Easter," announces Lubomyra as she greets everyone with open arms. "Roxolana is on a last minute flight from San Francisco and we need to make extra room!"

"Oh, I like her," says Olivia, hugging Lubomyra with one arm, still carrying bags in the other. "We had such a good time when we went to visit her just after we got married… and I didn't have any film left on my camera for the rest of our weekend because I took so many shots of the Bridge from the plane!"

Krys nods as he unpacks the beer into the fridge.

Soon, everyone in the family converges in the kitchen while Lubomyra prepares a pescatarian meal of fish and chips and Maria cuts up broccoli and red onions for the broccoli salad that has to sit overnight. In spite of Krys' protesting that the same old broccoli salad has made far too many appearances on the Easter table over the years, both the broccoli and carrot salads add zing to the pink *kobasa* and ham that dominate the plates, and somehow, this year, the broccoli salad has turned out better than ever – even Krys agrees!

When Lubomyra first downsized into her new home after her dear Yarko passed away, she decided to go rogue and paint the walls of the dining room, a rich, cranberry red. Although the neighbour across the street was overheard saying, "it looks like a brothel" as he peered through the open French doors from his balcony, she stands by her red walls knowing they stimulate hearty appetites and encourage lively conversations.

After dinner, Krys, Maxim, and Maria set the dining room table for Sunday's feast. They pry apart the 40-plus year old, heavy, oak table to insert the two chunky leaves, bring in extra chairs from downstairs, and cover the length of the table with a starched, white table cloth.

They decide to go with the creamy china with the pale blue flower pattern and the newer silverware with the cresting scallop shell motif on the handles. Maria holds one of the silver spoons in her hand for a moment before placing it down on the table. She smiles at the elegant shell as it rests in the palm of her hand.

Of the four kingdoms of earth – mineral, plant, animal and human – rocks and minerals did not register on Maria's radar for the longest time. She only started paying attention to the mineral kingdom recently when she noticed by chance how many rocks, seashells, and lovely pieces of jewellry she had in her collection.

Visitors to the home, especially children, love to sort through the various rocks and figurines that adorn the window sills throughout the house, and Maria likes to hold her earthly treasures in her hand to see if she is able to hear their stories. Aligning the knives, forks, and spoons as straight as possible next to each plate, prompts her to say, "scallop shells are perfect for Easter," to no one in particular.

"Why is that, Tia Maria?" asks Maxim, holding two Czech crystal goblets in his hands, wondering where to put them on the canvass of the table.

"Well, priests have been using big shells as ladles during baptisms, so in essence, they're about rebirth and new beginnings, like springtime."

Eleven guests are coming for Easter brunch but there are not enough matching chairs or china plates to go around, so having been to art school, Krys gives Maria and Maxim a lesson in composition.

"People like symmetry, they like to balance things out," says Krys. "But sometimes there are extra pieces."

"Like this chair," says Maxim. "It doesn't match the rest and it's kind of separate."

"When you have stranglers and leftovers, you have to fit them in somehow. But odd numbers are also good because they mix things up and aren't so predictable. If we arrange the chairs like this, with the similar ones grouped together, it's more pleasing to the eye. In design, it's called 'resolving the elegant remainder.'"

They each grab a chair and move it to another place setting. "I still don't like how one plate is different from the rest," says Maria. "Why don't we pair up the heads of the table with the same plates and chairs?"

"That works," says Krys.

"That's so neat," says Maria, exhaling. "Now I know why I've been matching things up my entire life! I guess it's the artist in me. I've never liked leaving something hanging by itself, and have always tried to pair it up with something similar to keep it company, even inanimate objects. Elegant remainder. Awesome! And now the table seems that much more inviting!"

* * *

The sun is shining on Easter Sunday morning. Lubomyra and her cousin Roxolana rush out the door at 7:20 to sing in the choir, knowing everyone else in the household would arrive hours later, during the sermon.

Usually, late comers are nudged to stand at the back of the church at Christmas and Easter masses but even halfway through this three-hour religious celebration, the Ponomarenko's manage to squeeze themselves into the third pew from the front, their timing most noted by Lubomyra from the choir loft.

Maria thinks of her late father as she steps between the wooden benches to her space in the row. Yaromyr used to sit in this spot and they would often play pinky wars whenever they sat together, while pretending to pay attention to whatever the priest was saying.

She also muses over the early childhood memory of sitting on the floor next to Krys and together they would creatively remove the bolts that held the kneelers together, as if it was their job. She looks over at her brother who is looking respectfully at the altar, now a father of two himself.

Slowly, over the years, Saint Nicholas the Wonderworker Ukrainian Catholic Church, on the corner of Cook and Caledonia, has grown into a vibrant parish, filled with eccentric characters and ecclesiastical artwork.

The icon of the Mother Mary with her arms extended in prayer, known as the *Oranta*, perches above the alter. If you look closely, you can also see a golden figure-eight encircling Mary and Jesus' faces, which means infinity, the ever expanding universe.

Just weeks after the *Oranta* was first installed at St. Nick's five years previously, one of the parishioners, Myroslava, experienced a bona fide miracle herself. She had broken her back after falling off the roof of her farmhouse up island and was rushed to hospital by helicopter. Her chances of ever walking again were slim to none. Still, everyone at church prayed for her recovery. After several weeks of doing her physio therapy and learning to play the violin in hospital, Myroslava was discharged – with "Miracle" literally stamped on her records – which ironically complicated her insurance claim.

When Maria saw Myroslava walking up the aisle to receive Communion after her accident, she knew Mother Mary had a hand in her healing.

Today, as Maria stands in the pew between her brother and niece, her eyes swiftly travel to the ornate, cherubic chandelier that hangs front and centre. She hears her second cousin, Roxolana's voice emanating from the choir loft beside her own mother's, together singing:

Let us who mystically
represent the cherubim
and sing the thrice-holy hymn
to the life-giving Trinity,
now lay aside all cares of life,
that we may receive the King of all,
escorted invisibly by ranks of angels
Alleluia, alleluia, alleluia.

Underneath the melody, in the notes between the notes, Maria also feels the deeper voices of her ancestors coming through, and is comforted knowing her whole extended family is with her in spirit. She also feels the energy in the church rising to the rafters as everyone in attendance is progressively lightening up.

Then Maria has an insight. "We're not meant to suffer…" she thinks in her inside voice. "We didn't come here to live and die as victims…to slog through nothing but untold hardships. Jesus died on the cross so future generations wouldn't have to suffer in life… "And even though the cross was the instrument of torture… it's now a crucial doorway of transcendence…

"By stepping across the threshold, Jesus showed us how to transcend the density of pain, misery and physical death, so we can ultimately experience the intended state of pure love and joy... 'On earth as it is in heaven'... right here, right now... that's what it's all about. It's our choice."

"Alleluia," sings the choir while the church bells ring.

Moments later, Father wraps up the formal part of Easter Sunday. The congregation steps outside to the front of the church and gathers on the green grass for the blessing of the Easter baskets. The parishioners and visitors greet each other with an enthusiastic, "Христос Воскрес!" pronounced (with a hard "h") *Hrystos Voskres*, which means, "Christ has risen!" and reply, "Воїстено Воскрес!" pronounced, *Voyisteno Voskres*, which means, "Indeed He has risen!"

While the children run around the yard looking for chocolate eggs left by the Easter bunny and giggle with delight upon finding their treasures, the adults mill around and chat. Zoryanna is being overly competitive.

The colourful Easter baskets, lined with embroidered cloths and filled with decorative *Pysanky*, as well as edible hard-boiled eggs, and foil-wrapped chocolate eggs, plus a coil of *kobasa*, a square of butter dotted with a cross of cloves, a ramekin of beets mixed with horseradish, a small loaf of *Paska*, and a candle to light during the blessing, are placed side by side along the shrubbery.

In the Ukrainian tradition, *Paska* symbolizes Christ, our Bread of Life; eggs mean, new life and the Resurrection of Christ; butter represents the goodness of Christ; horseradish is for the Passion of Christ; cheese is about the moderation that Christians should show in all things; salt stands for the duty Christians have to others; *kobasa* signifies God's favour and generosity; bacon reminds us of God's Mercy; and Ham epitomizes the great joy and abundance of Easter.

As Father sprinkles holy water with his trusty aspergillum upon the heads and faces of the church family, Lubomyra leads the choir in another bi-lingual round of the hymn:

Christ is risen from the dead,
Trampling death by death,
And to those in the tombs
He is giving life!

Now it is time to go home and eat!

butt • dress

Carrying a big bowl of potato salad and two containers of homemade ice cream, Petrovna and her husband, Luke, arrive for Easter Brunch first. Luke is the actual bell-ringer in their church and each Sunday, it is his job to run up to the choir loft at pivotal moments to hoist the bell's rope, swing the clapper, and wake up the neighbourhood.

Luke is always looking to help around the kitchen whenever he is invited over, so Maria says, "I've got a job for you."

Feeling proud of herself for her brilliant idea, Maria leads Luke (yet another lefty) to the hutch that matches the dining table and hands him a sparkling crystal bell off the glass shelf.

"Ring this to let everyone know we're ready to eat!" she says smiling.

Luke accepts the dinner bell with a puzzled face because he does not want to break anything, but acquiesces and rings it gently while Maria lights the beeswax candles. Upon hearing the call of the bell, each of the guests stop mid conversation, look up, and head toward the dining room. They take their places around the cornucopian table.

Before formally inviting everyone to sit down, Lubomyra shares a piece of hard-boiled egg with each of her guests and individually gives them all a special blessing of health, love, and prosperity.

"Everything looks so delicious," says Roxolana as she arranges her napkin on her lap. "I like how you folded the napkins, Marichka, they're like Pope's hats!"

"I've been doing this for years," replies Maria. "Ever since my mother took me to work with her when she was teaching kids to run a restaurant – before 'bring your kid to work day' was a thing – and one of her students, Gerome, taught me how to do this."

"Start with what's in front of you and pass it to your right," announces Lubomyra. "Does anyone want to top up their wine?"

"I'll have some more red," says Pylyp.

"Send the bottle down this way," echoes Krys.

Pylyp and his wife Kalyna moved to Victoria a year or so earlier. When they called Lubomyra from out of the blue, she happily invited them over for Easter. Pylyp grew up with Krys and Maria's father in Toronto and Lubomyra remembers how handsome he was back in the day. He became an architect, along with three of the four guys in their group, and it made sense to seat him next to Krys.

"What do you think of the Notre Dame fire?" asks Maria to the guests.

"Heartbreaking."

"Surreal."

"Hard to believe."

"Do you think they'll re-build it exactly as it was?"

"No, I don't think they'll rebuild it exactly the same – probably would use more modern technology and materials – maybe even go LEADS if they're smart. It would be amazing to see the original plans though," says Pylyp.

"Written on parchment, no doubt" muses Roxolana.

"And buried in a secret crypt somewhere," adds Olivia.

"In those days it was all about arches and vaulted ceilings," says Krys.

"And flying buttresses!" says Maria, always happy when she can use this phrase in a sentence.

"Yeah, flying buttresses are crucial to the design – without them, the vaulted ceilings wouldn't hold up!"

"One can't exist without the other."

"I remember learning about them when I went to France with my French class – and we visited Notre Dame and I took the photo that is hanging in the family room from the top of the stairs at Montmartre," says Maria.

"It's like you're literally stepping into the staircase," says Krys.

Architects and artists make good couples and Pylyp's wife, Kalyna, is a photographer with an impressive portfolio and collection of prints. In keeping with a certain, Ukrainian rustic esthetic, she too has chosen a vibrant red for their dining room walls, (though hers is slightly more tomato than Lubomyra's) and it is the perfect backdrop for the art and books that are hanging around their townhouse.

Lubomyra's art collection is not so shabby either. She has a good eye and may have been a successful artist herself if she had thought to take that path. Instead, she channels her creativity into her sewing and cooking and takes great care in decorating the family home to be as warm and inviting as possible – displaying a *chachka*, plant, embroidered pillow, or throw rug into every nook and cranny.

The chimes of the tines slow down to a casual clink on the plates. Maria excuses herself briefly from the table and comes back with a framed painting in hand.

"Speaking of art, if the "Antiques Roadshow" ever comes to town, I'm bringing this," says Maria as she passes her 'show-and-tell' around the table. "Recently, a painting by Maude Lewis from Nova Scotia was found by volunteers who were sorting through donations in a thrift shop. The piece of art was appraised at $16,000 and went for $45,000 at auction!"

"It's primitive," says Kalyna studying the painting, "but that's the kind of art I'm drawn to."

"When Mama read the story in the newspaper, she asked me to go downstairs to the crawlspace to find the picture with the green felt frame. There it was, loosely stacked up against some other framed pictures and when I brought it back upstairs, Mama had me read the article."

"Is this the same artist?" asks Olivia, reaching for the painting to get a closer look.

"Yes," says Lubomyra. "Back in the late '60s, when Yarko and I were first married, I was teaching in Halifax while he was off at sea. One day during my lunch, I was shopping at a thrift store and I think I bought this for three dollars and change," says Lubomyra.

"Wow, this might be worth something!" says Olivia.

"I remember this painting," says Krys, as he holds the art in his hands. "It was always in my room in every house we lived in."

"Let me see," says Zoryanna.

"She doesn't blend her colours at all," adds Krys as he studies the painting. "I wonder if it's authentic."

"I can't see why it wouldn't be," says Maria. "Here's her signature and she was known to paint on beaverboards cut by her husband, rather than on canvass. Sometimes she paints on shells and rocks. All of this with crippling arthritis in her hands!"

"It's amazing how this painting has been sitting under your nose all of these years," says Roxolana.

"Yes… come to think of it… I guess it's a lesson in appreciating what you already have," says Maria. "Maude had to be resourceful and use whatever was available to her…"

"That's what artists do!"

"She couldn't just go to the art supply store to pick up more paint whenever she ran out. So, living out in Nova Scotia, her husband would get leftover paint from local fishermen, who used bright colours to paint their boats, so they could be spotted at sea from shore.

"Use what you've got."

"This piece was always in my peripheral vision but I never stopped to look at it, thinking it was too simple," says Maria. "Now, I appreciate how the buck and the doe are approaching the lake, side by side, with their footprints in the snow behind them, and facing a row of houses, a church and rolling hills, being warmed by a gentle setting sun."

"What makes you think they're walking into a sunset and not a sunrise, Marichka?" asks Roxolana.

Thinking for a moment about how there is more orange than yellow in the sunlight and it just feels like a sunset, Maria surprises herself when she says out loud, "Because this scene is the life that's ahead of the couple and East is the past and West is the future. That's how the world moves."

Roxolana thinks about Maria's answer.

"If you get a chance, go and see the movie, "Maudie." Mama and I saw it in the theatre on Mother's Day and I cried all the way through. It's a beautiful story of an artist who triumphed over adversity and I like to feel I'm connected to her since we were both born in Nova Scotia."

"Who wants dessert?" asks Lubomyra.

"I do," says Zoryanna, and on that note, the dishes are cleared to make room for cheesecake, a walnut torte, and a choice of creamy vanilla or rich chocolate ice cream. Three guests want tea and five prefer coffee so Maria puts the kettle on and startles the guests with the loud coffee grinder.

"If you'd like honey in your tea, Kalyna brought a lovely pot of honey for us to share," says Lubomyra.

"I found some local honey at the Red Barn Market," says Kalyna, "and we always try to eat the local honey while we travel and when we move to a new home. It's a way for us to meld with a new place."

"Marichka and I love honey," says Lubomyra.

"Honey is good for seasonal allergies because the bees use pollen from the same flowers and trees that surround us, and when we eat the honey produced by local bees, we're eating some of the regional allergens in small doses, which in turn, builds immunity in a natural way," says Kalyna.

"It's the beauty of the ecosystem," says Roxolana. "It's like the flowers and bees help each other and then the honey extends to us, too! Every element doing its thing, in its own rhythm and then contributing to the greater whole… like voices in a choir."

"Yes, I saw a documentary that mentioned how the honey in New York City, of all places, is amazing because of all of the unique and diverse rooftop patios and window sill gardens that are around for the bees to explore," adds Maria. "Thanks, Kalyna!"

"I'll switch my coffee order to tea with honey," says Roxolana.

"I'll stick with wine for now," says Olivia, and they all laugh.

back • yard

By late afternoon and more than three hours of sitting, eating, drinking, and talking, both Olivia and Roxolana are clamouring for a walk outside. Kalyna, Zoryanna, Maxim, and Jasper are game, too!

Maria suggests they all go to Rithet's Bog which is just a stone's throw away, located behind Emily Carr Drive. The bog has been zoned as a 42-hectare Nature Sanctuary thanks to the generous donation by the Guinness family in 1994, and is a bountiful setting for a family walk.

As the home to several rare plant, bird, and butterfly species, Rithet's Bog is the last of seven large peat bogs on the Saanich Peninsula and on any given day, many birders, dog walkers, scenic strollers, photographers, and hikers come to the bog to walk the easy, gravel trails and get a fresh dose of Vitamin Nature.

Although watching the mothers take care of their baby ducklings in the spring is always endearing, Maria particularly likes to spot the Red Wing Blackbirds because they remind her of the "Blackbird" folk song, written by Paul McCartney.

"Take these broken wings and learn to fly," she always sings when she sees them.

Historically, the *Tsawout* people visited the bog annually to hunt ducks and game and to gather cranberries, Labrador tea leaves, and Sphagnum Moss. The cranberries could be dried and carried easily for food, the fragrant Bog Labrador Tea leaves were used as a beverage and medicine, and the moss was used to fill wood in canoes, to fill pillows and mattresses, to treat infected wounds, for baby and self-care, and in cooking.

Whenever she passes a certain bench on the trail, Maria remembers a day when she was walking home through the bog from the bank, and came across an elderly woman who was sitting on that bench, crying.

Maria stopped to ask her what was wrong and the woman, who spoke with a distinct Nova Scotian accent, said she had fallen. Somehow the woman had managed to pick herself up and make her way to the bench but her hands were cut up and bleeding and she was disoriented.

Maria introduced herself and found out the woman's name was Elaine and yes she was from Nova Scotia. She recently came to Victoria to live with her son and his family.

"Do you by chance have a cell phone on you so we can call your son?"

"I think I do somewhere in here," Elaine said as she rummaged through her purse. "But we don't have to call him. I can just sit here."

To Maria's relief, Elaine did have a phone in her purse with her son's number in her contacts list, and within a half hour, he came by car to pick her up, grateful she was okay.

Fortunately, on this Easter Sunday afternoon, the path is clear and Maria's family is able to walk at their leisure through the budding thicket.

While Olivia and Kalyna run up ahead with the kids and the dog, Maria walks behind with Roxolana at a slower pace. Roxolana is an accomplished choir director who, like Maria, is not married. But unlike Maria, it seems Roxolana prefers it that way.

Even after a long and noteworthy career, owning a house with an average $1,299,000 price tag was beyond her means, so Roxolana decided to move out East to retire and start a new chapter in her life, in just a few short weeks.

This weekend is the last opportunity for Roxolana to visit her Canadian cousins while in their time zone, so she spontaneously sprang into action and bought her tickets at the last minute. All weekend, she was noticing that although Maria was being a gracious host, she could tell there was something else on her mind.

"Tell me about your job," she says in an effort to get some clues.

"Well, I'm a breakfast cook at a B&B and I like how I can be creative with my hands and talk with guests from all over the world. One time, I heard one of the guests speaking in what I consider a Toronto-Ukrainian accent, so I asked her if she was Ukrainian. Her husband said, 'Yes!' Her maiden name is, *Dobriyvechir*!'"

"As in 'good night,'" says Roxolana chuckling.

"And I said, 'do you know Vlad?' and she said, 'Yes! He's my brother!'"

"You're kidding!" Roxolana says. "Small world!"

"And it gets even smaller, their father went on a date with Mama sixty years ago in Toronto and Vlad had a road trip adventure with Krys in the '90s – so somehow, even though I don't know these people at all, they're still oddly connected to my family history and then suddenly, this woman shows up randomly at my work, across the country in BC, years later."

"I love it when that happens! And if you hadn't thought to ask her, you would never have known who she was."

"I guess that was my intuition talking to me. Anyway, these are the kinds of people I meet and I like that, but I'm having a hard time with one of my co-workers."

"In what way?"

"I feel I'm being bullied but I really need this job to keep my head above water, so I'm not sure if I should stay and put up with her taunting, or if I should just quit and try to find another job."

"It's a tough decision."

"'Should I stay or should I go' – remember that song?"

"Yup!"

"We used to sing a Ukrainian version at camp."

"Leave it to Ukrainians…" says Roxolana collecting her thoughts.

"I wasn't going to mention this, and a lot of people don't know this, but that's why I've left my job a few years earlier than planned. There was a change of staff and that person also bullied me and I just couldn't deal with it. It just wasn't worth it."

"I didn't know."

"It was taking a toll on me so I started talking with a counsellor and eventually I came to the decision to leave. Do you have anyone to talk to? What does your mother say?"

"I don't really have anyone to talk to. My mother doesn't understand. She thinks I should just be nice and hope things will get better. I just feel like there has to be more for me than living with my mother and working in a minimum wage job," says Maria as she drops her head in despair.

"I know you have so much more to offer, Marichka. You're perceptive and insightful and the questions you ask are really interesting. I can tell you're deeply listening to what people are saying. It's a real gift. There's so much more for you out there – you just need to break free from your shell."

Tears brim in Maria's eyes. She does not think anyone is noticing what she is doing. "I'm sorry you were being bullied also and you had to leave a position you enjoyed, Roxolana. It seems that workplace bullying is quite common in our day and I'm not the only one who has this problem. I hope you enjoy your new life on the East coast. I feel like you came here for a bigger reason and I appreciate talking with you. I was hoping to make a decision about this job this weekend and now I'm pretty sure I know what I'm going to do. Thank you for showing up for me."

* * *

After a whirlwind weekend in Canada, Roxolana heads back to the States as swiftly as she had arrived. The social part of the day is over and there is not much to do, so Olivia takes her laptop and grabs a seat outside on the deck. Soon, Maria follows suit. As she opens and closes the sliding screen door, she is quietly singing a melody to herself.

"What song are you humming, Maria?" asks Olivia.

"'Right Here, Right Now…'"

"There is no other place I want to be…" says Olivia finishing the lyric.

Maria smiles brightly.

"Right here, right now, watching the world wake up from history," they both chime in together.

"Let's look it up," says Olivia. "Here it is, Jesus Jones."

Before they know it, one song leads to another and soon Olivia finds a Gen-Xer's choice playlist on the Internet. Within a few melodies, the sisters-in-law time-travel and end up singing all kinds of songs including, Air Supply's, "I'm All out of Love" and Queen's, "Bohemian Rhapsody."

They bellow out the tunes one after the other and Olivia is impressed that Maria knows all of those song lyrics and that she can sing to boot. Before long, sitting at the patio table cannot contain them – they jump up out of their seats and sing at the top of their lungs. Together they dance, laugh, and sing until the sun goes down behind the mountains, their voices carrying across the neighbourhood. Maria pretends the tall, swaying, pine trees in the backyard are her audience.

Krys, Lubomyra, Maxim, and Zoryanna each come out one by one to see what the commotion is, standing there at the foot of the deck, shaking their heads as if Olivia and Maria have gone crazy. Maria does not care what the rest of the family is thinking or if the neighbours can hear them. Any inhibitions she may have had are blowing away with the wind!

Later that night, as Maria crawls into bed, she replays the events of the big day. She realizes how strong an influence music and family have had in her life. First with her mother. "I guess she was showing me love every time she sang me a lullaby."

Then with her father. "We used to hold hands and dance in the kitchen."

She even remembers that on one occasion, she and her brother spent an evening together as kids, learning the words to the classic showdown song, "the Devil Went Down to Georgia," written and performed by The Charlie Daniels Band.

Now Maria has the key to her own heart. From this moment on, if she ever needs to raise her spirits, all she has to do is sing and dance. "That's it! That's my love language!" she says to herself. "Singing and dancing is how I know I'm being loved and now that I'm an adult, I don't need to look for that from anyone else! I can just sing and dance anytime I want! Brilliant!"

break • fast

In the joyful post-Easter Sunday tradition known as "Wet Monday" or "Обливаний Понеділок," that is still liberally celebrated in Eastern Europe, Maxim and Zoryanna quietly enter each bedroom first thing in the morning and spiritedly wake up each member of the family with a splash of water.

Spring has sprung and it is a new day. For the first time in a long time, Maria feels good about her future. She has a sense that she would be travelling by car and plane across British Columbia and beyond in the upcoming months. She sees herself going on road trips and giving talks about her success with wellness and weight loss to people in nearby communities, but how that would happen, she does not yet know.

* * *

HOW I LOST 12 POUNDS DURING LENT

by Maria Ponomarenko, Wellness Coach

On Fat Tuesday, I went to a birthday party and ate a few slices of really good pizza along with a piece of fancy birthday cake from a bakery. Two days later on March 7, I spontaneously decided to give up eating snacks and desserts for Lent.

I really like to eat potato chips, cookies and ice cream whenever I have the chance but during the six weeks of Lent, I was only allowing myself to eat three square meals a day, with nothing in between, often for five, six, seven, eight plus hours each day.

I decided to schedule my meals rather than worry about what I was eating. Basically, I ate whatever I wanted during my three meals a day (including bread, potatoes, meats and cheeses) but that was it until the next meal.

By eating full meals rather than grazing, I gave my body a chance to work on digestion and burn stored fats for energy rather than using quick sugars and carbohydrates. Once I started burning fat for fuel, I started losing weight.

Did you know the word "Breakfast" comes from "breaking the fast" from the last meal you had the day before?

To me, snacks and desserts represented too many extra and unnecessary calories and I was trying to run on approximately 1500 calories a day, without actually counting anything. I've learned that we really don't need as many calories as we think we do.

The good news is, as of Easter Monday, I've managed to release 12 pounds in just over six weeks, which is less than two pounds a week, which is a very healthy and sustainable pace. I plan to keep going.

My Guidelines

Of course, there are many approaches you can take but here are the guidelines I personally follow:

* Talk to your doctor before attempting any kind of significant dietary changes.

* Know your big why — I happen to have a big 50th birthday coming up so that's motivation enough for me!

* Weigh yourself and record the weight in a journal. It's not really about the weight and how many pounds you lose, but it's a good idea to know where you started. The real evidence is how you're feeling about yourself.

* If you're going to eat fat, choose your sources wisely. Fat helps you feel full, makes your brain function better and keeps things running smoothly.

* No snacks, no desserts, no alcohol

* Drink lots of water and tea

* Eat three times a day: breakfast, lunch and dinner

* Try not to eat past 7pm

* Eat mindfully and taste each morsel of food you put into your mouth. Food will start tasting better as you go along.

* Take supplements including: Vitamin B, Vitamin C, Vitamin D, Omega 3's, Women's Daily or Men's Daily, and Magnesium

* Go on Wellness Walks 4-5 times a week

* Workout and lift weights at least once a week

* Train to run — I'm up to running 8 minutes!

* Go to an Acupuncture Clinic — they can tailor your treatments to help support your digestion and weight loss efforts and it's really relaxing!

* Do stretches daily

* Reach out to old and new friends and have meaningful conversations each day

* Get a good night's sleep every night

* Crystals that may help include: Amethyst, Angelite, Bloodstone, Blue Apatite, Carnelian, Citrine, Garnet, Labradorite, Jasper, Rhodonite, Rose Quartz, Sunstone, Tiger's Eye, Turquoise

* Good foods for weight loss include: high fiber veggies, fresh fruits, dark chocolate, fish/seafood

* Eat lots of orange foods like carrots, salmon and mango — they're about the Sacral Chakra, which is located below the naval, and our Divine Feminine nature.

* Practice daily self-care, relax and manage stress

* Clear clutter in your environment

* Assure yourself that this isn't starvation and that you're doing this for your long-term health and you will eat lots of good food every day.

* Talk to a Wellness Coach, like me!

Somehow, I managed to get through baking without sampling, cooking breakfasts for crowds, three dinner parties, one restaurant lunch, potato chips in the house and Easter brunch without giving into temptation.

Now, my skin in clearer, my hair is softer, my eyes are brighter, my pants fit better, and I'm living more as my authentic self.

To me, that's worth it and I'm planning to continue to eat like this for the foreseeable future. If you have any questions or would like some Wellness Coaching, please contact me, Maria, by email.

crumb • pet

Feeling rejuvenated and empowered, Maria has a new spring in her step. Working out with Angie every Tuesday at five o'clock, along with sticking with her healthier eating plan, and going on wellness walks in her neighbourhood a few times a week, are really starting to show.

"Is that Maria?" the people nearby would ask.

While most of the guests of the Lantern Inn enjoy Maria's hospitality, Martha seethes and squints at her from behind the tasseled curtains. It does not take long for Martha's smoldering temper to escalate into a full blown rage, and ironically, the tension plays out in real time as a power surge at the Inn, which unfortunately, takes out Louise's desktop computer and the oven with it.

Working with an oven that races to over 500°F is interfering with Maria's breakfast. She has been burning her creations — including the ones that are only supposed to stay warm.

She resolves to prepare the hearty and savoury Eggstravaganza Casserole for Sunday morning anyway. The recipe requires 18 eggs for a large pan that can feed 12, and as she cracks each egg into the ample metal bowl, she counts not one… not two… not three… but four double-yolked eggs!

"Holy jumping!"

It is a thrill to see each pair emerge! Maria enthusiastically shows the eggs to April, the housekeeper, who just happens to come into the kitchen to get a glass of water before cleaning her next room.

"Cool," says April as she fills her glass with ice.

Undaunted, Maria takes a photo for posterity with her phone. Her research tells her the odds of opening one double-yolked egg are one in 1000, so Maria concludes that four in the same bowl must be a miracle.

"The eggs are twins so this must be a sign that my Twin Soul, the love of my life, is on his way to me," she thinks to herself as she looks up to the ceiling.

Soon, after adding the rest of the ingredients into her egg mixture, including bacon bits, hashbrowned potatoes and three different cheeses, she is ready to put the casserole into the oven. But when she opens the pre-heated oven door, a huge blast of smoky, hot air billows out, like fire from a dragon's mouth.

"This isn't right," she coughs and reluctantly goes to tell Martha.

At first, Martha does not believe that the oven is fried, but calls Louise at home to let her know what is going on. They decide to test the temperature of the oven.

After waiting a few minutes to let the oven cool down again, Martha puts a tempered, Pyrex, baking pan filled with water on the middle rack and sets the oven to 350°F to see if the water temperature matches the oven's.

Sure enough, after only a few minutes, the oven's temperature soars again and when Martha puts the turkey thermometer into the water, the needle spins out of control, whipping over the numbers and around the ring, as if caught in the Bermuda Triangle.

Without further hesitation, Martha puts on a pair of heavy-duty oven mitts, takes the pan out of the oven, and drops it into the empty, metal, kitchen sink with a sizzle.

Wanting to contribute, Maria has the brilliant idea to pour water over the pan to cool it off but unfortunately, the shock causes the thick glass to shatter!

"Oops... That's hard to do with Pyrex," says Maria, stunned.

"I guess the oven is broken," says Martha dryly. "Louise is not going to want to pay to fix this – especially on a weekend."

"How am I supposed to pre-bake the casserole now and how is Joyce supposed to warm it up tomorrow? We've got a full house!" says Maria.

"I'll bake the casserole for tomorrow's breakfast even if I have to take it home tonight," says Martha and off she goes back to the front desk.

Maria appreciates Martha's gesture and gives her points for being a team player in this case. Thinking that perhaps she and Martha are starting to get along, Maria lets her guard down ever-so-slightly the following Saturday when she and Martha are scheduled to work together again.

Sadly, the truce between them is short-lived. First, Maria notices that the guests are referring to Martha as "the boss of the place" and wonders how on earth they are making that assumption. Is Martha introducing herself as such? Does Louise know?

Then the laundry list of all of the things Maria does wrong starts growing longer by the day. If she did not restock the coffee sufficiently, or clean the coffee pots properly, or use the "correct" napkins and tablecloths, or take the ties off the bathrobes before putting them in the washing machine, or heaven forbid, not highlighting something on the housekeeping report in bright yellow, there would be an angry note with spelling mistakes waiting for her on the kitchen counter.

Martha is relentless in her quest to wring as much out of Maria as she can and soon Louise starts finding faults with Maria's work, as well.

"More notes, more notes," says Maria as she hides the neon papers out of her sight.

"There's a big spill in the laundry room!" yells Martha as she charges into the kitchen the minute Maria comes back from her lunch break. "Orange juice is everywhere! You have to clean it up because I didn't do it."

Not having a clue what Martha is talking about, Maria looks at her co-worker as if she is from Mars. "How could I miss sticky orange juice in the laundry room?" asks Maria to herself. "I haven't even been downstairs in hours and why would the orange juice be there?"

Eventually, Maria makes her way to the basement with a rag in hand. She finds a dried puddle of orange juice in the doorway between Louise's office and the laundry room. She quickly cleans up the mess and carries on with her shift.

Martha is not satisfied. She also insists that Maria mops the floors in the dining room and lounge that afternoon. Mopping and vacuuming are not in the cards for that day and as Maria opens the front door to start her weekend, Martha asks, "Did you mop the floors?"

"I did what I did," says Maria.

"Two can play that game," says Martha with a chill in her voice.

"I'm not playing games, you are," says Maria closing the door behind her while Martha keeps talking.

"That was the last straw," says Maria to herself as she walks towards her car, tears streaming from her eyes. "I'm done."

* * *

When Maria comes home from work, her mom is in the kitchen.

"Martha was awful today," says Maria, "I'm going to write a letter and give my notice to Louise on Tuesday."

"Are you sure?" asks Lubomyra, worried for her daughter's wellbeing. "What are you going to do instead?"

"I don't know. I guess I'm just going to have to take a leap of faith."

The sun is still shining so Maria changes clothes, grabs her violet sunglasses, and goes for a long walk to sort through her options. She walks down the private driveway, past the blossoming pink flowers and past the mailboxes. Her neighbours from Ukraine wave to her from their deck.

Along her way, Maria watches two squirrels chasing each other around trees and three bunnies holding their poses in the open fields before darting into the bushes. She glimpses a Quayle family scurrying into the blackberry bramble and notices Turkey Vultures, a murder of crows, fat robins, butterflies and dragonflies circling overhead. She sees dogs checking their "pee-mail" and cats basking in the sunlight.

As she crosses the street between two connecting forest paths, she spots two deer grazing on the property with the striking log cabin that belongs on a film set.

At last she makes it to her favourite pond where she has stood innumerable times over the years, thinking about life's big questions. She likes to practice her listening skills by tuning into all of the sounds in the environment, including the rustling of leaves, chirping birds, ducks landing in the water, lapping waves, lawn mowers, cars driving past, and people's voices off in the distance.

She likes how the blue, green, and brown colours from the trees and sky reflect in the water and when she softens her focus, she finds the ripples created by tadpoles, ducks, wind, and sunlight to be mesmerizing as they play together, merging and receding, making fleeting patterns, revealing alternate dimensions.

"Have you seen the wood ducks?" says a woman coming from Maria's left.

"No, no I haven't," says Maria, peeling herself out of her trance.

"Curious things, God bless 'em. They're just a pile of fluff and feathers but each spring, they jump out of the trees, one by one, hoping to fly, with only the pond beneath to catch them."

Maria tries to picture the fuzzy ducklings jumping from the trees.

"They just have to take a leap of faith!" says the woman gleefully.

Astonished, Maria cannot believe how this random woman said, "leap of faith."

"It's the sweetest thing to watch," the woman continues.

"You have no idea how much I needed to hear that," says Maria trying to explain the beauty of that moment. "I've been wrestling with a decision and the answer is 'taking a leap of faith.' Thank you!"

"Anytime," the friendly neighbour says. "Let me take you around the pond and show you where the wood ducks live so you can look for them another day."

* * *

To keep her mother in the loop, Maria shows her the letter she has written to Louise.

"If this is what you want to do," says Lubomyra, sliding the letter back across her cutting table, not pleased.

Although Maria is armed with a new plan, her breakfast shift does not go so smoothly. She is too much in her head, replaying the events of the previous weeks, trying to justify her decision. As a result, she miscounts how many Croque Madames she has to prepare, so one of the guests has to wait extra-long. On top of that, the oven is still wonky, so everyone else's sandwiches are slightly burnt.

After serving breakfast, cleaning up the kitchen, resetting the dining room, and stripping the rooms, Maria preps the next day's breakfast. She makes six mini quiches that just require eggs in the morning. She takes the crumpets out of the freezer and puts them in the breadbasket to thaw overnight.

Also, one of the guests request a gluten-free, vegan muffin because she is Celiac, so Maria sets one aside and puts it in a marked plastic bag on the counter to defrost as well.

At the end of her shift, Maria heads downstairs to talk to Louise.

"Do you have a minute?"

"Yes," Louise says, adding, "Close the door if you need to," after seeing the expression on Maria's face.

"I'm giving you my notice," says Maria, handing her the letter.

"Oh, Maria," Louise complains. "It hasn't even been a year! I gave you a second chance and I picked you over that other cook. Do you know how hard it is to find a good cook in this town?"

"I appreciate how you hired me again. It's all in the letter, but basically, I'm running off my feet every day and it never seems to be enough. And the construction next door is stressing me out, and gas prices have hit a record high, and Martha has been giving me a hard time."

"What do you mean?"

"Well, Martha, doesn't say "hi" to me when she clocks in and I'm standing right there – who does that? And one time, she hissed at me!"

"She hissed at you?" says Louise buckling over in her seat, half laughing, half alarmed.

"Yes," says Maria. "I can't work with someone like that."

"OK," says Louise rubbing her sore knee again. "Go home for today. I'll read the letter and we'll figure something out."

* * *

Dear Louise,   *May 7, 2019*

After careful thought, I've decided to leave my job as Breakfast Cook at the Lantern Inn and am giving you my notice. I'm prepared to work through May 21, 2019 unless you are unable to find someone else to replace my shifts, in which case, I'll work to the last day of May, 2019.

I appreciate that you gave me another chance to work at the Lantern Inn in August, 2018 and although things started off well and I was enjoying the work, things have changed.

I'm finding the work environment to be hostile. Perhaps the construction next door has contributed to raising the stress levels for all of us but in the last several months, I've been feeling overwhelmed by all the tasks that have been piled on top of me and I know I've been making many mistakes. It feels like the Lantern Inn has become a bottomless pit and whatever I do is never enough.

On top of that, Martha has taken it upon herself to give me a hard time. She has been bullying me and yells at me and doesn't even say "hi" when she starts her shifts. This past Saturday, she asked me if I had mopped the floor and I said "no, I did what I did" and then she said, "two can play that game" which I interpreted as a threat. That's not the kind of environment I want to work in.

Furthermore, now that gas prices are up to $1.61/L, it doesn't seem to make economic sense for me to drive 22 klicks one way to work, times two, 5 days a week, at $15/hr plus tips.

I sincerely wish the best for the Lantern Inn and am grateful for the time I spent there but now it's time for me to move on in pursuit of other adventures and opportunities.

Sincerely,

Maria Ponomarenko

* * *

If Maria thinks Martha is hostile now, before she has given her notice to Louise, she is in for a rude awakening in the coming days.

When she unlocks the kitchen door at 6:52am the following morning, she finds two muffins sitting next to each other on the kitchen counter. The marked bag she used has vanished and now she does not remember which muffin she had set aside for her Celiac guest.

She thinks it is the chocolate one, but is not completely sure. Thankfully, Maria finds another gluten-free muffin in the freezer to serve but clearly this is an act of sabotage.

Trying to shake it off and carry-on, it is time to prepare the yogurt parfaits, bake the quiches, and open the packages of accompanying crumpets. Maria never tasted crumpets before working at the Lantern and is sorry she had been missing out on their buttery goodness all of these years.

"Where are the crumpets?" she says out loud, horrified, picking up half a loaf of cinnamon raison bread in the basket instead.

She opens the fridge door, no crumpets there. She opens the freezer drawer and digs around, but cannot find a single crumpet in there either. She runs downstairs to check the deep-freezer and there is not a crumpet to be found. Doubts fly through her mind.

"Didn't I see them in the freezer? Didn't I set some aside?"

All Maria can do is improvise. She is nothing if not resourceful. She decides to go with Texas toast instead. No one is the wiser and Maria feels good about herself that she has managed to meet the challenges without crumbling.

Having the morning to think about the missing ingredients, Maria concludes that Martha returned unseen to the Inn sometime after 8pm last night (after Louise had left and the front desk had closed and the guests had retired for the night). She pictures Martha scheming in the darkened hallway.

"Perhaps playing the shell game with the muffins is too small potatoes? But what else can I do? Think, Martha, think... ah yes, the crumpets... That's perfect! Mwah-ha-ha!"

Maria figures Martha went for the jugular: "I bet she took every remaining crumpet home with her."

She can see it all in her mind's eye – four packages of crumpets strewn casually on Martha's kitchen table while her husband sits idly by, drinking his coffee, and reading his newspaper.

Later that morning, Louise asks Maria, "How did breakfast go?"

"Well, how can I put this? First, there was an extra muffin defrosting on the counter and I wasn't sure which one was gluten-free for our guest up in the Ruby Room."

"What?"

"And all of a sudden, we didn't have any crumpets on hand."

Louise searches her memory. "I'm sure there were at least two packages in the freezer."

"I thought so, too."

Maria follows Louise as she races up the stairs to the kitchen, opening every cupboard and drawer, including the compost and garbage bins. Baffled, Louise is not impressed.

When she asks Martha later whether she knows anything about the missing crumpets, she quickly replies, "Joyce used them up on Sunday morning."

Martha's answer seems plausible and deep down, Louise cannot believe that Martha would go so far out of her way to hide crumpets on Maria, but later that hour, Louise also discovers that Martha has not laundered any of the rags as she usually does, so housekeeping is delayed.

When Maria returns to work the next morning, four packages of crumpets magically appear in the freezer, hours before Louise would have a chance to buy more on her morning run to the grocery store.

Not one whole week later, after giving Maria a dollar an hour raise and taking her off Saturdays with Martha, Louise finds a new cook to replace Maria much sooner than expected. Maria's last day at the Lantern Inn is Friday, June 7th, just a few days shy of a meeting with an unexpected visitor.

Closer to Indigo
Maria Koropecky

PART 2

arm • our

Friday night, hoping to find something good to watch on TV, Maria scrolls through her options. "Let's see… 7pm… "Big Bang Theory," always on… "Friends," makes me feel old…"Vikings," too violent."

Her stopover in Iceland while coming back to Canada from Brussels and studying the obscure topic of Medieval Icelandic Literature in university (which she thoroughly enjoyed!) spring to mind.

"Something about the stark, rocky and volcanic terrain looked oddly familiar when I first landed in Reykjavík," she remembers thinking as she scanned the distance, riding the bus inland from the airport. "Maybe, it was a past life flashback or something."

She also remembers the priest who Christened Maxim saying: (while they were sipping Mimosas to celebrate – also the day she relapsed from her first attempt at sobriety) "With your fair skin and blonde hair, you definitely have Scandinavian genes; your brother, on the other hand, looks more Middle Eastern."

"What did Rocco say again when I mentioned this to him? Oh yeah, 'Who doesn't have a little Viking in 'em?'"

She glances around her bedroom and spots her little collection of Icelandic treasures – a heavy, coffee table book and a piece of porous lava her father had given her that he must have picked up straight off the ground, plus a creamer fired with chunks of lava, glazed in a deep, ocean blue she bought herself as a souvenir.

Maria does not say for sure if she is a firm believer in the notion of past lives or not because she figures people can generate enough trauma from this lifetime alone without having to drag more heavy baggage from history to deal with on top of it.

On the flip side, she can also see evidence to support past life theory. "Things like child prodigies, talents, music, language, memories, and dreams – where do they come from?"

She refolds some rumpled sweaters in her closet as she waits for an answer, starting with the yellow cable knit.

"Quantum Physics is getting so close to explaining how the Universe works – waves, particles dancing around the field of possibilities – who's to say we don't appear, disappear, and re-appear all day long?"

She pulls another sweater off the shelf while accidentally dragging three more with it, sending them to the floor.

"And energy can't be created or destroyed – just like this sweater – it just moves and changes – folds and unfolds, folds and unfolds, folds, left arm, right arm, shove back into closet…"

She picks up one of two red, Chenille sweaters that fell and presses it out on the bed, extending the arms and fixing the shoulders.

"So when the physical body dies, the energy that animates it must eventually regroup itself and wear a similar temporary shell somewhere else, further along on the space-time continuum."

On that note, Maria guesses that Maxim may be the reincarnation of his grandfather, Yaromyr, because they have similar intelligences, temperaments, life challenges, and eyesight.

"Same energy, different sweater? Or different energy same sweater? No, wait, the first one makes more sense. But if that's true, where does Tato's soul exist now? Does his energy as I knew him also float around as a separate sweater somewhere else or has he merged seamlessly into the next one?"

Even if Maria wanders around the field like a lamb on the past life question, perhaps she does have an Icelandic chapter on her inter-stellar orbit. If she were to venture a guess about the other past lives on her earth-bound trajectory, she would recall being a medicine woman who died falling off a cliff, a thief who died robbing a grave during the Black Plague, a banker who died penniless, an herbalist (read witch) with a black cat, a monk who had a secret relationship with a nun that produced a love child, a Jewish prisoner in a concentration camp, and a back-up singer.

With nothing interesting on TV, and rocks, lava and the Universe on her mind, she turns to her crystals.

"Maybe I can do something with these to bring in extra cash?"

She decides to jumpstart her intuition with a little crystal magic. Sometimes, when she wants to know a new answer to a question that has been weighing on her mind, she chooses a few crystals from her stash and puts them inside her pillow case, on the mattress side down, and sleeps on them.

Depending on the crystals, colours and combinations she chooses, her dreams can be quite vivid, even lucid, some nights.

"Tonight, I'll go with flashy Labradorite, cosmic Blue Quartz, tropical Blue Apatite with the orange tip, and one more to make it even – the purple and green triangle, here it is, Charoite. Let's see what the crystals say.

But first I'll watch Father Brown." Soon she falls asleep.

* * *

Standing on the dock, Maria measures the gap between her feet and the deep sea green and navy blue water that swirls like lollipops, tempting, waving, calling her in. Her eyes travel up and follow the star bursts that shimmer like opals on the side of a ship. She sees breadcrumbs floating on the water and watches them melt like raindrops into the depth. She remembers she has not finished packing, so goes back home and tries to cram everything she owns in a trunk, worrying she will not make it back to the ship on time. One more stop at the grocery store to buy orange Thousand Island salad dressing. One more stop to see her friend. Back home because she thinks she forgot something. Will she have time? She hears a doorbell ringing in her cabin.

"Who's texting me at this hour?" she wonders, waking up at 3:33am. "Just a notification telling me my cell phone bill is overdue? – Oh, for the love of…"

wall • king

Now that Maria does not have to go to work for the foreseeable future, you will likely find her sitting at her desk – also known as the dining room table – searching for ideas to write about on her laptop. Her 50th birthday is fast approaching and she thinks it would be interesting to capture her wisdom in writing as a love note to herself.

Meanwhile, her mother has left the house in the pouring rain to clean the church. If Maria has any wisdom to share, it is buried deep, and she is coming up blank.

She thinks listening to Loreena McKennitt's album, "The Visit," may help her relax and focus. For the first time in all of the hundreds of times she has listened to these songs, she is able to hear the accordion weaving its way throughout the melodies.

"Here's someone who managed to turn the accordion into a sexy instrument," she muses.

"The Lady of Shalott," a narrative poem written by Lord Alfred Tennyson in the early 1800s, speaks loudly to Maria from across the pond of time. First written in the prudish Victorian era, "The Lady of

Shalott" is based on the medieval novella, "Donna di Scalotta," and tells the Arthurian legend of the noblewoman, "Elaine of Astolat," who lives in a castle with no less than four great masculine towers, on an island in a river, near bustling Camelot.

As the Lady of Shalott (a young woman with an unknown first name) weaves her colourful tapestries by night and day in the hidden world of the Divine Feminine, she cheerfully sings her song, which carries across the hills and valleys, that will ultimately reach the ears of the dashing, Sir Lancelot.

The mysterious lady (or mythical fairy) has no real world experience to date and is only able to observe the comings and goings of life – from weddings to funerals – through a crystal mirror, which is also a tool of her trade.

One sunny day, Sir Lancelot comes riding into Camelot on his trusty horse. He is all decked out in his best brass armour, which ringingly announces his arrival. Perhaps he is coming especially to meet her?

Catching a glimpse in her mirror of the knight in shining armour as he sings out his own mating call, "tirra lirra," the Lady suddenly drops what she is doing and launches into a full blown fantasy about him.

She left the web,

she left the loom,

She made three paces through the room,

She saw the water-lily bloom,

She saw the helmet and the plume,

She looked down to Camelot.

Having taken her attention off of her weaving, one of the taught strands snaps and flings far and wide with such a force that it shatters her lifeline to the outside world – the mystical mirror – into pieces!

Described as a "curse" in the poem, Maria prefers to call the mirror mishap, "the Lady of Shalott's moment of awakening."

Out flew the web and floated wide;

The mirror cracked from side to side;

"The curse has come upon me," cried

The Lady of Shalott.

In an instant, the world of innocence gives way to the world of experience. There is no turning back for her now. The cracked mirror will never return to its original condition. It is not possible for her to un-know what she now knows, that there is a whole new world out there beyond the confines of these four, grey walls.

She must break out of her prison! She must flee! To her love, she must go!

Now, in a frenzied state, the new Lady of Shalott flies down the spiral staircase, breaks through the front doors, and steps outside! With a quick glance around the property, she spots a boat resting on the shore. This is her getaway ride.

The Lady of Shalott writes her name on the bow and climbs inside.

"Now what do I do?" she probably asks herself as the boat launches and begins drifting down the river.

With tears in her eyes, she thinks the little boat is taking her to Camelot, but instead the current pulls her further out into the open waters. Once she realizes her attempt to escape the confines of her monotonous life is coming up fruitless, she loses her fight and gives up.

As a final act of surrender, she lays herself down flat, which turns the boat into her coffin.

And at the closing of the day
She loosed the chain and down she lay;
The broad stream bore her far away,
The Lady of Shalott.

"If she had only known how to steer her boat towards the future she wanted with Sir Lancelot, or even had the life skill of swimming, this story would have ended so much more joyfully," thinks Maria.

Now, as her body drifts downstream, the townspeople come out of their hilltop houses and line the shores to witness the event. Now, it is the Lady of Shalott's turn to be the spectacle.

"The artist becomes the art," Maria adds.

As one final nail in her coffin, Sir Lancelot steps forward and holds court.

"Excuse me, excuse me, pardon me…" he says pushing back the crowd and clearing his throat as if he is about to say something really deep.

But Lancelot mused a little space
He says, "She has a lovely face;
God in his mercy lend her grace,
The Lady of Shalott."

"She was pretty? That's all he had to say?"

Good ol' Lance is utterly clueless about what this woman has just gone through to be with him. She faced her fears, shed the protective armour of her old self, and naïvely, yet boldly went forth into the unknown, risking everything she held dear.

Perhaps in another day and age, Sir Lancelot and the Lady of Shalott would have been the celebrity couple of Camelot, but in this version of the story, this romance does not blossom.

"I can't let this sad fate happen to me, too," Maria sighs. "I can't die in the boat!"

The Lady of Shalott's story of living cloistered on an island, doing her art, and not participating directly in life, but watching everyone else enjoy prosperity, abundance, and romances second hand, is a running theme in Maria's life as well.

"But maybe the Lady of Shalott triumphs after all?" thinks Maria. "Perhaps she transcends the mundane world, and in her death, the death of her ego, she takes a leap into an entirely new level of being. She surpasses him. He is just the shiny wrapping paper, not the prize."

With that insight, Maria looks at the clock. "11:45am? Where did the time go? I have to take a shower."

* * *

"I'm sorry, I accidently flushed the toilet on you," says Lubomyra almost happily.

Maria is a little miffed and does not hide her attitude.

"But I have a present for you!" her mother continues. "I've been thinking about what to give you for your 50th birthday."

Maria's expression softens.

"Svitlana and Charles showed up to church this morning completely drenched, I mean soaking wet from head to toe from walking in the rain – you know they're going on the Camino this summer!"

"Yes, I knew that."

"Each weekend, they've been going on long hikes to practice for their trip and today they thought it would be a good idea to put on their raincoats and backpacks and walk from home to church, on purpose in the rain, just to see what it would be like."

"Wow, they're serious about this."

"Anyway, while they were drinking coffee to warm up, I asked them if they had any ideas of what I could give you for your birthday, and Svitlana said, 'Why not send her on a Camino?'"

"Go on a Camino? Me?"

"What do you think, Marichka? Is this a good idea? Would you like to go on your own Camino?"

"Well… I… yes?" says Maria as she shuffles through her mind, trying to find what may show up in her way and comes up empty.

"With all of the walking that you already do, I thought you might really enjoy this."

"This is very generous, Мам. Дякую," she says as she hugs her mother.

"Good, then it's settled. Let's have lunch. I'll be going to Costco later if you want to come."

"Sure," says Maria as she quickly messages Svitlana to thank her for the idea.

* * *

Maria hardly ever goes to Costco because the huge warehouse store is too loud and crowded for her sensitive nature and now that she is not snacking in between meals, she no longer makes a beeline for the free samples that dot the aisles.

On this trip, she finds a really cute, navy and white skort with a Hawaiian-like floral pattern and matching navy shirt. She does not yet know why she wants this outfit or on what occasion she would wear it, but she knows she has to buy it.

As she carries the clothes in her arms around the store wondering if they would fit her now slimmer body, she cannot believe her eyes when she sees Svitlana holding two different boxes of cereal, trying to choose one.

"We were just talking about you!" says Maria as she hurries towards her church friend.

"I just saw your mum over there somewhere," says Svitlana as she vaguely points towards the books. "I hear you're going on a Camino!"

"Yes! Thanks to the conversation you had with my mom this morning."

"I'm so happy for you!"

"I'd love to talk with you more about planning my Camino. Are you going to be at church tomorrow?"

"No, we won't come tomorrow because we have to go up Island but we will certainly try to share with you what we've learned so far. When were you thinking of going?"

"I thought maybe end of June?" Svitlana made a face. "That might not give you enough time to get ready but it can be done."

"Hey look. There's Charles," says Maria as he turns the corner towards them with a big shopping cart filled with camping gear.

"I hear there's a Camino in your future," he says. "We're giving a talk at our church in a couple of weeks with the Canadian Company of Pilgrims, if you're interested."

"Yes, that sounds great! When are you going again?" Maria asks them both.

"We're going in July – the hottest month – because of the school year – but if you don't absolutely need to go in the summer, I wouldn't."

"And how long are you going for?"

"We're going to Portugal for two weeks – we don't have time to do the whole thing."

"That answers my next question."

"Do you know which route you're going to take, Maria?"

"I have no idea. This is all so brand new to me."

"Anyway, we have to get going," says Svitlana. "I'm so happy that you're doing the Camino, too. We'll talk more about this soon."

"Thanks for suggesting the idea to my mother. It's the perfect gift for me!"

post • card

Maria's Uncle Borys found love late in life. He married his wife Claire when they were both in their early sixties, after they each retired from teaching in the same high school in New England.

As a couple, they are really big on birthdays and have been thoughtfully sending a constant stream of carefully chosen greeting cards for every holiday and anniversary to friends and family alike.

Cards are their love language and they would thoroughly appreciate any cards in return, but the Ponomarenko side of the family is not so organized, and often forgets to reciprocate, though Lubomyra tries her best.

A few days before Maria's 50th birthday, Lubomyra is shocked to find an empty, red envelope mixed in with the usual mail. It is addressed to Maria and is, of course, from Borys and Claire.

"I'm so sorry," Lubomyra says as she hands the envelope to her daughter.

"What happened?" Maria asks as she accepts the thin paper scrap. She peers inside only to discover an empty pocket, but still tries to shake out any remaining contents in the style of Johnny Carson. "Yup, there's nothing in there."

"It looks like someone tampered with your card..."

"Look how neatly they sliced it open..."

"And took whatever was inside... "

"And sent the envelope through the system anyway... oh my gosh, that's mail theft – I bet it was an inside job. We need to call Vuiko Borys right away. What's his phone number again?"

Lubomyra recites the number by heart and Maria always appreciates how her mother can do that. Not many people can remember phone numbers anymore.

"Hi Vuiko. It's Marichka. Thank you so much for sending me a birthday card but I have some bad news..."

"Yes?"

"Unfortunately, the card that you so carefully picked out for me was stolen and I just received an empty envelope."

"What? Completely empty?"

"Yup, just a flat, hollow shell with your handwriting and a nice stamp."

"Oh dear."

"It's not like it was ripped open in a quick hurry – they used a letter opener and sliced through one of the sides. I'm so sorry."

"It's not for you to be sorry about," says Borys. "I just don't understand why they wouldn't just take the whole thing, envelope and all... I'm going to go to Canada Post and report this. I suggest you talk to the U.S. Postal Service, too."

"I will. There was a cheque in there also."

"Oh no. I appreciate that but I also suggest you talk to your bank."

"Yes, I'll cancel the cheque."

"And perhaps even go so far as change your banking information. Sorry to say but this might be an attempt at identity theft."

"OK. I'll get on it first thing tomorrow. In the meantime, do you have money exchange stores up there in Canada?"

"Yes, we do."

"Well, then I'm going to forward you some money in the next couple of days."

"Thank you but that's not necessary."

"I'm doing it anyway – for your Camino."

"OK. Thanks. That's sweet. Keep me posted on how things go with the post office. Have a good night."

* * *

The following afternoon, Maria calls her Uncle again.

"I opened up a ticket for you with Canada Post. They're looking into this."

"Thanks, Marichka. I've also arranged for a money transfer for you through Western Union. The numbers are: *cim, vicim, odyn, chotyry, chotyry, dva, vicim, dva.* You need to go and pick it up at a money exchange store that isn't your bank. Bring some I.D."

"Aw, thanks." "It's for your Camino and I really hope you have a wonderful trip."

So, Maria heads to the money exchange behind Mayfair Mall in a shady area of town. She does not feel comfortable going there and would have preferred to do this transaction through her regular bank, but that is not possible.

As she stands in the vestibule waiting for her turn, she feels intimidated by the bullet-proof glass that protects the clerk. She wonders what prompted such extreme measures. When she approaches the counter and slides her documents under the window, the clerk checks the numbers but cannot find the order.

"I'm sorry I can't fill this," says the clerk. "You need to check your numbers and come back."

Annoyed, Maria goes home empty handed. She calls her uncle again as soon as she returns home and asks for the numbers again – this time in English. Now she is able to see that she reversed the seven and the eight in her haste to write down the code.

With the correct numbers in hand and cell phone in her purse this time, back she goes to the money store. Parking is also much easier now that she knows where she is going. The clerk gladly gives Maria the cash.

Much to her surprise, Maria finds a treasure tossed in with the coins. It is a commemorative Loonie with the dates 1969 to 2019 embossed on the edge!

"Out of all of the coins and all of the Loonies that are in circulation right now, this is the one that lands in my lap today?

How brilliant! That's why I had to come back here a second time and that's why the mail was stolen – so I could get this birthday wink from the Angels!"

Maria is curious about what this particular coin represents, so she looks up "Commemorative Canadian Loonies" online and finds the Loonie with the face that reminds her of a Roman Sun God.

"There it is: 1 Dollar – 50th Anniversary of the Decriminalization of Homosexuality in Canada."

The reverse image by Canadian artist Joe Average is a celebration of community, equality and inclusion. The intertwined stylization invites a personal interpretation of the design, viewed through the lens of sexual orientation, gender identity, gender expression and sex characteristics. The facial traits intentionally reflect gender fluidity and the spectrum of genders; they may belong to two individuals, or they may represent different aspects of one's identity.

"Not what I was expecting, but I like the spirit."

* * *

Through the grapevine, Maria hears there is a 10K walking and biking path that loops around Victoria's airport. She knows this open patch of land would be the perfect training ground for her upcoming Camino adventure.

Just after lunch on Monday, she grabs her bulky digital SLR, (another gift from Uncle Borys), jumps into her Chevy HHR that looks like an old-fashioned milk truck, and drives North, along the windy, West Saanich Road.

As she catches a glimpse of Salt Spring Island, an island known for its artists, Maria pulls over. She easily finds a parking spot near Saanich Inlet, a charming little picture-postcard, cross-section that includes the green, open fields of the airport in one direction, blue water views in the other, and the historic, Holy Trinity Anglican Church, in between.

"This is new!" she says to herself as she reads the sign, "Welcome to Jubilee Park Play Area."

She is surprised to see cascading green and blue sails sheltering picnic tables and a bright, orangey-red jungle gym, shaped like an airplane, for kids to climb!

"Wow! This is really cool!" says Maria as two siblings race passed her, their dad watching from a distance.

Maria hears a plane coming in for a landing and waves to welcome the visitors.

"I think that's a Twin Otter! she says to herself as she quickly snaps a photo. "Yup. I wonder who's on it?"

Maria turns her attention towards the church to her right, which had been originally built in 1885, following Vancouver Island's own Gold Rush in the 1860s. To add to the church's caché, scenes from the mini-series, "Gracepoint," had been filmed on the premises in 2014.

On a more personal level, Maria originally found out about this church through her mother's friend, Anastasia, who was now resting in peace in the church's graveyard. On the rare occasion when Maria comes to pay her respects to Anastasia, she always takes a spin around the labyrinth that had been painted on the church's parking lot, as well.

* * *

FIND PEACE OF MIND AS YOU WALK A LABYRINTH

by Maria Ponomarenko, Spa Therapist

To travel a circle is to journey over the same ground time and time again. To travel a circle wisely is to journey over the same ground for the first time. In this way, the ordinary becomes extraordinary, and the circle, a path to where you wish to be. And when you notice at last that the path has circled back into itself, you realize that where you wish to be is where you have already been... and always were

~ Neal Donald Walsch

If you are looking to solve a problem using your intuition, or expand your spiritual horizons, or find peace of mind, try walking a labyrinth. Walking a labyrinth is an ancient spiritual practice that can work wonders for your soul.

Recently, I literally stumbled upon a labyrinth that I previously didn't know about. I was attending a friend's funeral at Holy Trinity Anglican Church in North Saanich, BC, a lovely historic church that was consecrated in 1885, and I just happened to notice the markings of a labyrinth in the church's parking lot.

I made a mental note to come back at a later date.

I first heard of labyrinth walking after reading Daniel Pink's book, "A Whole New Mind: Why Right-Brainers Will Rule the Future," several years ago, and have kept my eye out for them ever since.

I didn't think labyrinths could possibly exist in Victoria but as it turns out, there is more than one. There is also one in James Bay behind the Legislature, too.

Contrary to popular beliefs, labyrinths are not mazes. A maze is a complicated and confusing network of paths with many forks and options. Maybe you have walked through a manicured, life-sized maze with high hedges in a garden park before, and had a difficult time finding your way out?

Labyrinths, on the other hand, are not designed to bewilder or puzzle. Labyrinths are not difficult to navigate and have a single path that leads to the center. There is only one way in and one way out and all you have to do is put one foot in front of the other and follow the yellow-brick road, so to speak.

It didn't take long for me to make my way back to my newly discovered labyrinth. I dusted off my copy of "The Artist's Way" by Julia Cameron and decided that the labyrinth would be my first "Artist Date."

I picked a sunny and hot Saturday afternoon and headed off to North Saanich near the airport. When I got there, I made a point to visit my friend's grave in the church's cemetery first.

The classical labyrinth pattern of seven inter-linking circuits has appeared on Cretan coins since 430 BC and labyrinth symbols can be found in many cultures.

I made an effort to walk the Labyrinth because I have had a lot on my mind lately and I'm trying to quiet my mind and tap into my intuition.

To me, walking the labyrinth is a kind of mini pilgrimage to a sacred place.

To me, just following the meandering path helps me lose track of the outside world and get into a contemplative and meditative state.

From there, I get ideas and end up feeling better. I decided to go through the labyrinth twice that day.

When I got back into my car, I decided to take the scenic road home. Out of the corner of my eye, across the street from the church, I noticed a beach. I quickly parked the car again and thought I would explore a little further.

I walked down the stone steps to sea level. The beach was covered with an abundance stones and rocks and pebbles and seashells. I thought to myself, "She sells seashells by the seashore."

I hopped from rock to rock, trying not to step on any seashells but that was not easy. There were just so many of them! And then, there it was. Just sitting there plain as day: a Sand Dollar. The first one I have found in my life — ever.

It made me smile and I thought, maybe this gift was something to do with the labyrinth path I had just walked minutes before.

I like to think it is and although I can't guarantee that you will find some kind of treasure after walking a labyrinth, I invite you to try and to at least keep your eyes and ears open.

Who knows what you will discover!

If you'd like to find a labyrinth in your own city or in a city you're planning to visit anywhere in the world, check out the Labyrinth's Society's web page. They have a world-wide Labyrinth locater tool that just may point you in the right direction.

* * *

With plane after plane coming in for a landing and a cool breeze on her face, Maria repeats her mantra, "As I stand on the bridge of love, I release the past with love, and I welcome the present and future with love."

Memories of previous labyrinth walks come flooding back, like the time she ran through the church parking lot after a wedding ceremony, wearing a short dress and heels and clutching her pearls, as well as that grey day in late December, 2017 after Nick crushingly told her, "I'm getting married tomorrow."

"As I stand on the bridge of love, I release the past with love, and I welcome the present and future with love."

At last, Maria makes it to the centre of the spider's web, the eye of the needle, the vortex into another dimension, the heart of the labyrinth. She feels somewhat lighter and it is time to return to the present day, back to her ordinary life.

"As I stand on the bridge of love, I release the past with love, and I welcome the present and future with love."

When she arrives back home, Maria downloads all of the photos she had taken that afternoon onto her laptop and studies them one by one. In her creative state, she has completely lost track of time, and is startled by a sudden chime on her phone. It takes some effort to pry herself from her photos but she checks her phone anyway. Stunned, she reads this text message from Nick:

> Hi Maria.
> I am in Victoria this week
> and would like to meet you.
> Will you have some time
> to grab a coffee?"

day • dream

Maria feels a very strong connection to Nick even though the Pacific Ocean and the Rocky Mountains are lodged between them. Their worlds are so different. In contrast to Maria's feminine city of Victoria, Nick lives in Calgary – arguably Canada's most masculine city.

"Oh my gosh, I'm going to finally meet him in person!" she says collapsing on her bed, with her cell phone still in hand, breathing purposefully, trying to catch her breath.

"And he's coming here!"

She re-reads his text three times.

"Now's my chance to impress him and make him choose me this time. It's happening. We're going to be together soon and all of this stupidity will be worth it. Maybe he'll come on the Camino with me? Wouldn't that be amazing?"

She thinks about replying to his message.

"Should I wait awhile so I don't look too eager?"

She hugs her purple pillow and thinks about the chain of events that led her to this relationship that she has been dreaming of her entire life. If it was not for their mutual acquaintance, Alice, they would never have met at all.

Alice entered Maria's life in the summer of 2014. She called Maria to book a mobile manicure for her dear, 90-year-old mother, who owned an oil well, who had just moved to Victoria from Calgary. On the following day, Maria packed her gear which included: a folding table, towels, implements, a shell-shaped nail soaking bowl, hand cream, and 24 nail polish colours. She drove through downtown Victoria to the seniors' care home near Mile Zero of the TransCanada Highway.

Maria had no idea how pivotal this day would be for her. The door to the room at the far end of the hallway was ajar and Maria recognized the TV show "Bonanza" blaring from inside. As she knocked, three voices ushered her to enter.

"Come in, come in. I'm Alice, we spoke on the phone, and this is my mother, Ruth, and my husband, Gerry."

Stepping over the cavernous oxygen tank, Maria made her way to Ruth, who was sitting in the far corner of the room near the window facing Beacon Hill Park. Maria quickly set up her make-shift manicure station and proceeded to give Ruth a decent manicure, complete with two coats of pinky-orange and gold-flecked nail polish, while chatting with everyone.

As Maria listened to Alice describing the process of moving her mother to the Island where she would be closer to her children, grandchildren, and great grandchildren, Maria clipped and filed Ruth's nails.

Somewhere between the left hand and the right, Alice had to explain to her mother that she would not be visiting her in the following week because she was going to California to upgrade her coaching training.

"Did you say coaching???" Maria's ears perked up.

As it turned out, Alice was a coach and a facilitator at the Walker Coaching Academy.

"There are courses starting in November and February, if you're interested."

Maria took Alice's card and thought about it long and hard.

* * *

"I'm still really interested in the coaching program," Maria said to Alice when they were making arrangements for Ruth's next manicure, "but I can't start in February because my family is going to Hawaii for March Break."

"Wow, Hawaii, good for you," said Alice. "But you know, you can always call in from anywhere in the world – that's the beauty of online classes."

"Yes, I know, but I don't want to do this with the family nearby – who knows what our plans will be."

"Yes, of course, how about April?"

Maria's excuses to not sign up for the coaching program were running out. Hawaii just bought her time. She wanted to learn the art of coaching so she could add that service to her mobile spa, but the truth was, she did not know how she would pay for it. Her debt was hanging over her head like a cliff.

As it was, her mother and brother were covering her flight and accommodations on this family vacation already. She was hoping a week away in Hawaii would give her the time and space to think things over.

March Break came early in 2015 and like many other families with school-aged kids, Maria (Tia) and Lubomyra (Baba) each packed a suitcase and headed for a change of scene. For their trip, they left one island in the Pacific and headed to another, still in the same ocean, but one was more exotic.

With indigo and gold passports in hand, Maria and her mother made their way to the ferry, picked up Krys, Olivia and the kids on the mainland, and headed across the border to the Bellingham Airport in Washington State.

Taking the evening flight to Honolulu was not Maria's first choice of travelling times but since she was just a side salad on the family's dinner table, she had to go along with the rest of the family's main course.

"Who knew that flight would turn out to be so spectacular?" thinks Maria in hindsight. "That sunset!"

Not only did she witness the beautiful orange sunlight cascading over the chiseled, snow-covered Rocky Mountains from take-off, but she also experienced a perpetual sunset during the flight, as the aircraft continued heading West. For at least the first three hours into the six-hour flight, as the indigo night hovered behind them in the East, and the horizon remained pale yellow, bright orange, and warm pink in the West, the plane flew right in between, creating a trick of time.

Staring out her oval window, Maria experienced what she called a "Champagne Bubble Healing" when all of a sudden, she felt the sensation of effervescence. She felt as if tiny bubbles were floating through her body, like sparkling bubbles rising in a flute glass. She rested in the feeling with her eyes closed as long as she could.

During the snack service, Maria remembers chatting with the guy seated next to her. He was debating about going back to school for biomedical equipment technology.

"Would you like a million dollar idea?"

"Sure," he said, putting down his rum and Coke on the plastic seat tray in front of him.

"I was watching the news a few years ago and they did a story on how a live, beating heart that was heading for emergency transplant surgery, got dropped on the way to the helicopter!"

"Really?"

"The heart was riding in a cooler on wheels – like you take to the beach – and it just tipped over in slow-mo – and the poor heart fell out, right there on the pavement – like a piece of chicken out of the grocery bag – and sat there exposed on the Big H landing pad for however long – just a few feet away from the helicopter!"

"Yikes!"

"So, the two guys who were hired for the delivery job scrambled and scraped the heart off the ground and threw it back in the cooler as quick as they could and then carried on like nothing happened."

"Did the heart make it?"

"Hard to believe, but yes…"

Maria nods to herself while repeating her answer in her head in real time. She marvels over her million dollar idea from this point in the future: "a bulletproof, temperature-controlled, high-tech suitcase for transplant organs on wheels. I wonder if that's a thing yet?"

Her mind swiftly switches scenes to the airplane's descent.

"The far-flung Hawaiian Islands were lit up like a carnival – so the pilots wouldn't miss them entirely. How these islands even exist at all in the middle of the ocean without any neighbours just boggles my mind."

Punchbowl and Diamond Head and the Kalaniana'ole Highway appeared in her vision.

"Thirty-five years since we left," she remembers thinking. "How do the years add up so fast? And now it has been another four. What have I been doing with my life?"

In those days, Maria thought that perhaps returning to Hawaii, a legendary place that may be a link to the hypothetical lost continent of Lemuria, as well as the home of "Pele, the goddess of fire, volcanoes, lightning, wind, dance and transformation," she too would be able to create a better future for herself.

Maria realizes in the midst of her reminiscing, she has not responded to Nick's text yet. She quickly grabs her phone and writes:

> Hi Nick, that's great.
> Welcome to the island.
> Yes, I have time to meet
> for a coffee.
> What day were you thinking?

Maria settles back on her bed. While waiting to finalize the plans that have been too long in coming with Nick, she tries to relax by listening to her Hawaiian playlist, starting from the theme from the original "Hawaii Five-O" TV series.

"Like diving into a crystal blue pool," she says picking up where she left off on her Hawaiian family vacation.

Having landed in the middle of the night, the Ponomarenko's did not waste a single drop of daylight on their first day in paradise. Once they settled into their suites at the Aulani Resort, where the craftsmanship was "solid" according to Krys, they spent the day lounging by the bar.

It was unseasonably cold and windy that day in the tropics and one of the resort servers, who was wearing a coat, explained the high winds were the remnants from a hurricane that was whipping around the rim of the Pacific Ocean for the last couple of weeks.

The next day, they made plans to drive to the outskirts of Honolulu where they used to live. The opportunity to revisit her childhood was not lost on Maria. Seeing the steep, lush, green mountains again, with all of their rolling folds and ripples, like arms reaching to the ocean, brought Maria right back to her 10-year-old self, a bittersweet and lonely chapter of her life.

How many times did young Maria, who always felt like a fish out of water with her sun-kissed blonde hair, fair skin, and fat, curvy body, gaze longingly into the mystical valleys of the mountains of Oahu, wondering what secrets lived inside?

Was it possible for her to rise like these mountains, which were once the floor of the ocean, and touch the sky, too?

Krys drove the mini-van South-East and after they rounded the Hanauma Bay corner of the island, he parked the car at one of his favourite beaches, where he used to surf with his buddies, if they could swing a ride out that way.

Maria had no idea her brother went so far afield – and hitchhiking with his surf board – and having a blast on top of it all – while she was rearranging the furniture for her Barbies and hearing, "Rock With You," on the radio at the same time every afternoon.

Her new knowledge of her brother's adventures stirred up some jealousy.

"Why did he get to do that fun stuff and I didn't?"

After everyone in the family had their fill of playing on the beach and flirting with the crashing waves at high noon, they were ready to move on. They dusted the dry, pale sand off their feet, got back in the van, and headed back toward Hawaii Kai.

Next stop was Hanauma Bay, a relatively young, 32,000 year-old, ocean-flooded crater, whose banks curved somewhat like a banana.

"This is a window into the earth's crust," thought Maria when she stood on the edge of the cliff before making her descent down the steep road to the beach.

Aside from being required to watch an introductory film about respecting all of the marine life and coral in the now designated nature preserve, "Hanauma Bay looks pretty much the same now, in 2015, as it did in 1980," she remembers thinking. "It's like entering a gigantic fish bowl… complete with coral-laced sand… filled with enough salty water for various schools of fish, sea turtles, and snorkelers to swim around to their hearts' delight!"

After spending a few hours in Mother Nature's cradle, watching the gentle waves slowly roll into shore, it was time to make the journey back to their hotel. But while they were here on this end of the island, they still had two stops to make.

First, they had to visit Holy Trinity Catholic Church, which was also Krys and Maria's elementary school. Talk about entering a time warp. Although the Church was still standing, the parking lot was empty. The private Catholic school has long ago been shut down.

Maria imagined children in uniforms playing games in the sunshine at recess.

"Hurry Up!" her classmate's voice echoed in the wind, a call that somehow sounded like, "Ma-rrii-yaah!" to her ears.

It was strange and surreal to see her niece and nephew in this space where she, at their current age, won at tether ball, practiced her volleyball serve, played her flute, learned to hula dance, mastered the game of Jacks, tasted Saimin, and performed a wedding ceremony for her friends.

Future self, past self, and present self all reunited for a moment. In her trip down memory lane, Maria saw herself looking up towards her old classroom windows and wondering if maybe, in some other dimension, the younger version of herself was looking out the window in this moment, too.

"I guess now I am."

Maybe it is better for young Maria not to know how her life would turn out, that she would still be single in her forties and still be living with her mother, her father having passed away at the turn of the century.

"But if I could tell that sweet, scared, lonely, young Maria anything right now, what would I say? What wisdom would I give her?"

"Well, to start, we made it to our forties," thinks Maria from her bedroom in the future. "Some people can't say that. Also, don't worry so much, things will all make sense… And take care of our health… that's what I'd say. Do everything possible to be healthy."

After the current tenants graciously offered a quick tour of one of the classrooms and gave the chance at one more glance of the ocean from the second floor open hallway – Who else can say that about their childhood – that they could see the ocean from their desk? – the Ponomarenko's continued on their journey towards their old house on East Hind Drive, now totally unrecognizable, save for the house number painted on the curb.

Krys parked the minivan and everyone except Maria headed to the beach across the highway. She stayed behind to look at the house. Maria remembers looking for familiar landmarks to make sure she was at the right house. Yes, the bungalow was on a corner lot about three long blocks from the highway, but this house was surrounded by a thick, white fence with a locked gate.

"Where are the Plumeria and the Kukui Nut trees?" she asked while also noticing the roofline had been changed and the carport turned into a garage.

How Maria yearned to knock on the front door and say, 'I used to live here,' to the current residents, but it just did not seem like a good idea. The closed gate clearly meant, 'DO NOT ENTER' and on top of that, a neighbour's watch dog was barking incessantly throughout this stop on the time travel tour, warning Maria not to take the trouble.

Still, she continued to gaze at her old house from across the street. She remembers how a faint sprinkling of rain could come out of nowhere. In her mind's eye, she pictures the limes, bananas, mangoes, and Bougainvilleas that once grew on the property. She thinks about her babysitter who taught her how to play the board game "Pay Day" when they first arrived in 1979, and the neighbours' random "Ahoogah" horn that occasionally billowed down the street.

"I wonder whatever happened to the skateboard ramp that Tato and Krys built?"

She would have to be satisfied with a curbside looky-loo, learning one more time, "You can't go home again – but at least you can see how far you have come."

* * *

A few hours later, Nick responds and suggests they meet on Tuesday afternoon.

> Do you know a good place
> downtown?

> Yes, how about Habit?
> It's where I first met Alice too.

> Great. What time?

> 2:30pm?

> See you then!

Now that their plans are settled, Maria can finally go to bed. She resumes the home movie in her imagination, and picks things up on their surfing day. Krys rented two surfboards and found a non-touristy beach on the North Shore.

Once again, the Ponomarenko's piled into the mini-van, braving the infamous Honolulu traffic.

As Krys was teaching Zoryanna and Maxim how to surf the turquoise waves and Olivia was taking photos of their triumphs, Maria sat on the beach next to her mother, who was reading a book.

The waves were calling Maria, too, so she got up off her red and yellow beach towel and walked toward the water, feeling the tawny sand massaging her feet.

"Ah," she sighed as her feet plunked into the ocean, making a splash.

There she stood on the edge of an island, a speck in the middle of nowhere, in her black, two-piece bathing suit, while her blonde and pink hair whipped around in the wind as if she was the lucky volunteer in a science experiment.

In her daydream, she stares at the great expanse before her and watches the steady parade of waves roll closer and closer to shore after travelling hundreds and hundreds of miles from some unknown place of origin.

Her imagination morphs with her Hawaiian playlist, so the heaving waves sound like a percussion sectional in her imagination. Maria is able to hear the roaring thunder of the Bass Drum, the rhythmic Timpani, and a hint of sparkle from the Chimes and the Triangle.

She tunes her breathing to the rhythm of the waves, exhaling as they rush in and crest... inhaling as they recede into the depths of the unknown universe... breathing in and out... in and out... folding and unfolding... pushing and pulling... in the dance of creation.

"As I stand on the bridge of love, I release the past with love and I welcome the present and future with love," she mumbles.

The waves continue to lap over and beyond her feet, pausing for a moment at the height of the canvass behind her, and smoothing the sand in their wake. She tastes the salt in the wind.

* * *

Throughout the whole trip to Hawaii, Maria remembers being overly pre-occupied with the question, "Should I bite the bullet and sign up for this coaching program?"

The back and forth got so intense that she could not hold it in any longer, so while the family was sitting on the hotel room's balcony, drinking their beverages of choice and listening to more ukulele music wafting up from the courtyard, Maria drummed up the courage and asked the family about her going to coaching school.

At first Olivia seemed to think life coaching would be a good fit for Maria, but Krys put his foot down.

"You are not a coach," he said, that sentence still echoing in her ear to this day. "Coaches wear power suits in the corporate world and that's just not you. Try something else."

Krys was right, of course, and managed to plant huge seeds of doubt in Maria's mind. For the rest of the family vacation, Maria did not say another word about her coaching idea or much of anything else for that matter. Instead, she turned her attention to the faces of the other guests of the resort, hoping to finally meet the love of her life and "make my getaway, as soon as possible."

* * *

Although Maria is "3 sheets to the wind" at this moment in her memory movie, she could not sleep a wink on the red-eye flight back to the mainland. The family vacation was not exactly a picnic for her and this time, there was no spectacular scenery to watch through the oval window.

Meanwhile, Zoryanna was kicking in her sleep and on top of that, Maria's bionic hearing would not let her tune out a muffled conversation between two other passengers, no matter how loud she raised the volume on her iPod.

Bleary-eyed and tired, Maria just wanted to go home and see her cat, Panchyk, but she knew there was still a 2-hour ferry ride to endure that day after their flight. Maria nervously watched the clock, hoping to catch the next ferry.

"There was still time but it was going to be tight." All they needed to do was get through customs, drop Krys' family off, and then head to the Tsawwassen Ferry Terminal.

Unfortunately, Maria did not factor in the duty free liquor store at the U.S. border and she lost it when Olivia and Krys pulled over.

"You've got to be kidding me!" she complained.

On top of resenting her brother and Olivia for living the Vancouver lifestyle and for discouraging her from a career in life coaching, she did not want to miss her ferry because they wanted to buy more alcohol. It was too much and she let them know.

"Well, Maria, what do you expect us to do? We've just spent a week in Hawaii so we can shop duty free and we're not going to pass this up," said Olivia.

"I'm just tired and I want to go home. This is going to take forever and your shopping trips take so long."

"We'll be in and out, promise."

Maria rolled her eyes.

Krys and Olivia were not impressed. As a punishment of sorts for her outburst, Olivia did not invite Maria to Krys' milestone birthday party a few months later, which was the reason why they wanted to stop at the duty free shop in the first place.

Maria started crying in her sleep at the memory of calling her brother on his birthday and hearing partying in the background, knowing she was not invited.

Still on the fence about whether or not to go to coaching school, she crawled in her bed for the night. Soon, Panchyk jumped onboard. Settling on her tummy, he purred loudly and tickled her face with his whiskers.

"I suppose I could just study by night and teach myself coaching," thought Maria, as she worked herself up into a big crying lather. The cat would not have it. He got up and yawned, as if to say, 'Just sign up for the darn coaching school, already — you and I both know you're not going to learn this stuff by yourself,' and then he moved to the lower corner of the bed.

"There's my answer," she said rolling over. "Thanks Panchyk."

The next day, she took the plunge and enrolled in the online coaching program at the Walker Coaching Academy.

"But I'm not telling them about my plans."

And that was when she first met Nick. She remembers not liking his voice or his goatie at first, but soon the salt and pepper beard disappeared and his speaking voice lowered.

"So much water under the bridge since then."

* * *

Soon after starting her coaching program, Maria remembers how she had to balance her mobile spa appointments with her online classes that took place in the middle of the day.

She also remembers how navigating around town was never her strong suit. Every time she got in her car to go to a new mobile spa appointment, chances were she would get lost and take the long way to get there. She always gave herself extra time in case the directions she scratched out on a piece of paper, lead her in circles.

She had yet to personally discover Siri, even though the technology was well established and the voice-over actor who actually played "Siri," followed her mobile spa on Twitter.

Once again, Maria had to rely on her own sense of direction and memory as she drove to another spa appointment. On a sunny Thursday afternoon, just a few short weeks into her coaching training, she had to go to Esquimalt to give a woman a "Pacific Ocean Pedicure," which included a foot soak, nail shaping, cuticle grooming, nail buffing, scrub, seaweed masque, hydrating foot massage, and optional nail polish.

As she turned the corner on Walker Street in Esquimalt, her cell phone rang, which peaked her curiosity, so she stopped the car for a minute at the side of the residential street to check who it was.

It was Nick Walker!

Though she missed answering the call in time to talk to him, that striking coincidence of a phone call and a street name coming together in one moment, cinched it for her. He had her heart. There was something special about this man and they seemed to have some sort of spiritual and telepathic connection, that did not require physical proximity or words spoken out loud.

trap • ease

Maria is dying to meet Nick in person and after four long years of occasional video chats, emails, texts and phone calls… the golden day, Tuesday, June 11, 2019, the day she has been hoping and praying for, has finally come!

In a flurry of texts and a butt dial on his end, Maria suggests they meet at 2:30 at a coffee shop called, "Habit," the place where she had originally met Alice to learn more about the Walker coaching program four years before.

"Nick's single and takes summers off," Maria remembers Alice saying while glancing up and to her left to double-check her facts. "I think you'll like him."

"The day has come! It's finally happening for me! I finally get to meet Nick face to face!"

'Nervous' does not begin to describe how she feels as she scrambles around her bedroom, trying to find something suitable to wear, slowing down only to take another bite of her overly-sweet peanutbutter and banana sandwich.

Looking in her chest of drawers, she finds the blue and white skort with the Hawaiian floral pattern she bought a few weeks back, tags still on.

"Yes, of course. This is what I'll wear. I hope it fits," says Maria as she steps into her new clothes. "And I need a necklace... purple Cat's Eye... that'll be nice."

With all of the thoughts swirling in her head, Maria remembers what her mother's friend, Anastasia, told her about the time she met her husband, whom she married late in life, at the age of 38, which gave Maria hope.

"As he stood behind me to massage my shoulders, I felt a power surge run through my body," said Anastasia caressing her own arm. "In French, they call it a *coup de foudre* or 'lightning bolt.' It was love at first sight and I've been hooked on him ever since."

"I want that, too," says Maria softly to herself, deep down believing that it would never happen for her.

Still, secretly, Maria hopes that once she and Nick touch each other for the first time, there will also be a powerful rush of energy between them, and they would be together from that moment forward.

She races downtown, even runs a late yellow light, almost causing an accident with an ambulance, and parks her car a couple of blocks away from the coffee shop. Maria cannot run fast enough in her sensible shoes from the parkade to the corner of Yates and Blanshard.

When she arrives, Nick is not there yet, so she puts on her purple sunglasses and sits outside in the sunshine to wait for him, her heart beating out of her chest.

"There he is!" she says, as she spots him across the street waiting for the light to change. As he crosses the street towards her, Maria holds her breath. "Who is he with?"

"Maria, Maria, Maria!" he says as he runs toward her.

She does not know what to do with her purse or sunglasses and before she can say anything, he jumps in and says, "This is Arielle. She has been taking photos of me all day for my website."

"Oh, he brought a photographer," thinks Maria, relieved she is not anything more.

"Let's take some photos," says Nick.

"Take one with my phone too, please," says Maria as she hands her device to Arielle. They stand there for a moment on the sidewalk, his arm around Maria's shoulder, hers around his waist. She cannot help but squeeze his side to make sure he is real. She keeps trying to lean her head on his shoulder without much luck.

"Oh, look, you're both wearing blue!" comments Arielle as she looks through the lens. "Your shirt and your jeans are both indigo."

For Maria, wearing the same colour as someone else is actually a code that means they are on the same wavelength. When they were in class together, Maria purposely tried to choose her shirt colour based on what she thought Nick might be wearing that day under his blue suit jacket and most of the time, she was right. (The yellow shirt came from left field though and she only saw it once).

Maria had almost forgotten about her clothes game until Arielle's comment and yet this time they managed to match each other without trying, all the way down to his translucent, pale purple shirt button mirroring her Cat's Eye necklace, resting right over their hearts.

Maria likes Nick's sky blue shirt. For the first Christmas after they met, Maria wanted to buy him a similar blue shirt as a thank you gift for all he had done for her. Having no clue about what was involved in buying clothes for men, she talked with her hairstylist first, whom she figured was about the same size as Nick, and when she went to the Bay to catch a one-day sale, it seemed all of the light blue shirts in what she guessed was his size, were snapped up. She had to go with her intuition and decided on a purple one, oddly similar to the shirt she had given her father thirty years prior.

The three of them enter the coffee shop. Maria orders her standard Mint Tea to help ensure her breath would be fresh and Nick goes with the Lavender Lemonade, an unexpected, though charming, choice.

As they stand around waiting for their orders to come up, Maria feels as if there is a gymnast doing somersaults in her solar plexus.

"I have butterflies," she says out loud.

"You know, you're exactly the same in person as you are online," Nick says leaning into her.

She does not know how to respond to his comment other than to say, "I didn't know your eyes were so blue," and "Thank you for treating us," but makes a face when she does not see him leave a tip.

They find two tables pushed together in the somewhat busy dining area. The women sit next to each other with their backs against the wall, while Nick sits across from Maria. Sitting with one leg crossed over the other, Nick's foot reaches Maria's side of the table, and she thinks, "Oh, he's wearing flip flops." She is not expecting to have such a visceral reaction to his bare feet of all things.

"You know, I was at the airport yesterday afternoon. Maybe I saw your plane come in!" says Maria.

He tilts his head and looks at her like, 'how did you know to do that?' "What were you doing out there?" he asks.

"There's a labyrinth at the edge of the airport that I like to walk."

"Oh, I've been there," says Arielle.

"My mantra is, 'As I stand on the bridge of love, I release the past with love and I welcome the present and future with love.'"

"That's sweet," says Arielle. "Speaking of airports, Nick, if you want, I can drive you there when you're heading back home in a couple of days."

"Darn," Maria thinks to herself. "I wanted to do that. She beat me to it."

"Yes, that will be great."

"How do you two know each other?" Maria asks.

"Arielle is dating my nephew," says Nick, glancing at Arielle to get their story straight.

"He's at work now. He's an amazing guy. I'm really happy with him."

"The three of us were having dinner last night and I thought I would hire Arielle do to some photography for me. She's also starting her own school."

"What a gift," Maria says, "to spend the day with someone who is doing what you want to do. So what brings you to Victoria, Nick?"

"I'm here for the week to attend a conference organized by Alice but I'm not sure if I'll go."

"Why are you hesitating?" asks Arielle.

"I don't know… just not feeling it," says Nick.

"What's the theme of the conference again?"

"Identity."

"Identity…hmm… I think we're far too caught up on labels. I'm this, I'm that. Labels and packaging.. but that's ego. It's like sometimes we care more about the outside than what's inside, and sometimes we need the jaws of life to crack open the case!"

"They have special scissors for that," says Nick jokingly.

"But what if we could let go of those labels and peel them off from our identity, who would we be?" Maria asks.

"I think you should reconsider going to the conference, Nick," says Arielle.

"I'm sure you would add a lot to the conversation," adds Maria. "Besides that, how are things with the Walker Coaching Academy?"

"We're busy. I'm teaching five classes a week and oh, I've been meaning to tell you this for months... you know how we talk about how important focus is?"

"Yes."

"I was noticing that the students weren't fully grasping it..."

"Yes, it always seemed a little unclear."

"It wasn't until one class a couple of months ago when I realized focusing is actually pouring life force energy into something. It's like putting gas in the car to take you where you want to go, and fuel to help you create what you want," says Nick.

"I get it. Energy is palpable, like feeling a heavy stare from across a room. That's why cats sit on your book while you're trying to read – they want to bask in that energy!"

"So what you're focusing on is really important," says Nick.

"We need to put that much focus and energy into whatever we want to create. That's great! I've actually been reading about energy in the 'Celestine Prophecy.'"

"I remember you recommended that book to me before."

Puzzled, Maria asks herself, Why would I recommend a book I never read and how does he even remember that? But outloud she says, "I've been meaning to read that book for at least twenty years but my brother said it wasn't well written and I wouldn't like it, so I kept putting it off. But it's actually pretty good."

"I think they made a movie," says Arielle.

"There's a movie?" ask Maria and Nick together.

"And I also read about the energy of focus in Dr. Oscar Boshon's blog just last week! Have you heard of him?"

"Yes."

"The energy and geology of the land and how it mirrors our brain – that's what he talks about," says Maria.

As they talk, Maria feels like she is in a parallel universe, where an alternate version of herself and what could have been, is playing itself out. Even though Arielle is an unexpected guest at the table, Maria likes her and even thinks that if she and Nick had had a daughter together thirty years ago, she would be Arielle – creative, perceptive, sensitive, and ambitious.

Maria feels like she has briefly stepped into a life where her family is meeting for coffee while on vacation and she is the frumpy mom – which would have been nice – but it is only a peak in the window for now.

To Maria, Nick seems so confident and relaxed – she may even say, 'suave' to describe his manner. There is no sign that his pending divorce is bothering him and it sounds like he wants to be married again as soon as possible.

"I was talking with one of my students, a man from the Middle East. He always dressed in the most impeccable white attire," says Nick as he leans back in his chair, patting his chest. "He says, 'you have to bring your coaching model to my country. We need it here.'"

"Wow, that's great!"

"But I can't go unless I'm married."

"Well, aren't you?" asks Maria playing dumb.

"We're separated."

"Oh, I'm sorry," she says as sincerely as she can.

"It's really okay."

Thinking he probably does not want to talk about it, "Why would you need to be married to travel to the Middle East? Would the women pounce on you?" Maria gestures a little bit too aggressively, startling Nick.

"No, it's the law of the land where a single man from another country can't travel there."

How Maria longs to be his wife and travel with him to distant lands.

"And what's going on in your life, Maria?"

"Well, I was working as a breakfast cook up until last week but I quit because I didn't like how I was being treated there. It had been building up over the last few months until one day I just had it. When I came home from work, I took a walk to my pond and learned about wood ducks and how they have to take a leap of faith. It's such a paradox but, you know flying trapeze artists?"

"Yeah," they both say with curiosity.

"They climb up the ladder to the top of the platform."

"The artists, not the ducks."

"Right," Maria pauses to collect her thoughts.

"The artists grab the trapeze with both hands and take off, knowing that if they fall, there's a net beneath to catch them, and all they have to do is bounce, land, and climb back up the ladder again, and start over. No harm, no foul."

"Same for the ducks. Go on, Maria, this is getting interesting."

"So they take off and swing through the air like monkeys jumping from tree to tree and when the swing goes as far as it can go, another perfectly timed swing shows up and all they have to do is jump forward and grab it to keep going!"

"So far, so good."

"But here's the trick – they have to let go of the old swing before they can grab the new one…"

"You mean they have to let go first?" says Nick with a bit of a chuckle in his voice.

"You can't hang on to both bars at the same time!" adds Maria.

"You can't move forward while holding on to your past," says Nick. "You can't let go unless you feel safe."

"It's about trust," says Arielle.

"And for a split second, the daring trapeze artists are suspended in the space between, flying through mid-air! You might even call it the present moment. That's where the magic is! That's the leap of faith!"

"I like it," says Nick.

"Louis from class told me about that whole concept. You remember him? It's all going in my book!"

"Maria is a writer, too," says Nick to Arielle.

"I'm also writing a book."

"What's it about?"

Nick proceeds to describe his book to Maria and Arielle. It sounds like it is one of those time loop stories, where there are multiple possible scenarios depending on the character's choices, like the movies "Groundhog Day" or "Run Lola Run." Nick is an amazing storyteller and his stories are one of the top two things Maria loves most about him.

"You must be burning the midnight oil," says Maria.

"I'm just playin'," he says with a wink.

"With my heart!" thinks Maria with a sigh then switches the topic to, "Have you made any travel plans for the summer?"

"I was thinking of going to Greece or somewhere in the Mediterranean, but we'll see."

"I'm going to Spain in September to walk the Camino. My mother graciously gave me this trip for my upcoming fiftieth birthday," [hint, hint] "perhaps I'll bump into you somewhere out there."

"Well, I guess it's time for us to go," says Nick getting up from his chair.

"If you have time, I'd love to see you again before you leave. Maybe you can come over for dinner or maybe we can go on a nature walk?"

"Maybe."

"Well, call me before you leave," says Maria.

So after an hour or so of talking, they hug goodbye. Maria soaks up the moment as best she can.

"This was a long time coming," Nick says.

"Don't make it another four years," Maria says into his ear while they hug.

"Where are you going after this?"

"I'm going to work out with my personal trainer and friend, Angie. We have a group class on Tuesday nights. Angie has been one of the most important teachers of my life and oh my, I've lost track of time. I'm running late. I'd better get going."

pot • holes

"**O**h my gosh – Nick is Sir Lancelot – straight from central casting – all the way down to coal-black curls!" says Maria to the steering wheel as she drives in rush hour traffic up MacKenzie for her fitness class.

"Sorry, I'm late," she says pushing through the door of Angie's studio, her arms overflowing with her workout clothes, a water bottle, and pink running shoes.

"It's OK," says Angie. "We're just warming-up. And see, you're not even the last one here. Hi, Rhonda!"

Maria changes clothes in the washroom and just catches the end of the warm up circle. The rest of the workout is a wash. Although Maria is physically going through the motions, the rest of her is in outer space. She feels like she is in some kind of sound-cancelling chamber, as if tumbling underwater.

At the end of the hour, she feels she has to explain herself to Angie.

"I'm sorry I was not present for the workout."

"Yes, I noticed. What happened?"

"Well, you know that guy I told you about a couple of weeks ago?"

"Yeah."

"He's in Victoria this week and I just met him in person."

"And…" she starts brightly, then midword she changes her tone to concern. "And?"

"There was no chemistry," Maria says with tears gushing from her eyes like in a cartoon.

To be fair, that may or may not be true. Maria certainly feels the chemistry for him but she does not believe that he can possibly feel anything for her also.

"Oh, I'm so sorry, Hun," says Angie, giving Maria one of her best hugs. "But it's better you find out now than later, after wasting more of your time. Sometimes there's just no chemistry and there's really nothing you can do about it. Take a day or two to lick your wounds and then move on."

That is not what Maria wants to hear. She wants Angie to say, "How do you know there is no chemistry? Wait and see what happens. Who knows, maybe he'll surprise you."

Maria hopes she will see Nick again before he leaves Victoria but on Thursday morning she receives this text from him:

Hi Maria. It was so great to
meet you Tuesday.
I am in meetings and an
instructor needs me to teach
his class because he is travelling.
I will not be able to take you
up on your offer of dinner or a
walk in nature.
Please go for a walk for me
and I will be back again and
we can go for that walk then.
Have an amazing week. Nick

"Well, at least he contacted me before he left like I asked him to," says Maria to herself.

True to her experience, anytime Maria needs some extra comfort in her life, a cat shows up for her. Most significantly, her first black cat, Charlie, emerged from a dark, rainy night just days before Maria's father died in hospital. Charlie was a God-send. Then Panchyk came along during another dark chapter.

This time it is Morris' turn. His mum, Mary-Jo, the most colourful person Maria knows, has asked Maria to look after her senior, orange cat and stay at her house while she and her husband go for a road trip to Saskatchewan to visit family.

It is a perfect chance for Maria to be in her own space for a few days. It gives her a sense of independence, even if it is just temporary.

In the meantime, Krys and his crew are planning to come to Victoria for the weekend to help Maria celebrate her 50th birthday.

To her surprise, as Maria is watching yet another episode of "Father Brown" on the Knowledge Network and with Morris curled up next to her, her niece, Zoryanna, calls.

"Tia," begins Zoryanna in her haughty, elongated, tween accent that emphasizes all syllables even when there aren't any. "I was wondering if it would be okay if I didn't come for your birthday tomorrow."

"Why?"

"Because I have to go to gymnastics in the morning and we were going to come after that but my friends are going shopping and I really want to go with them."

"It's your choice," says Maria, trying to sound like the cool aunt. "Of course, I'd love for you to come but I know that, if you were here, you'd want to be with your friends and you'd resent me, and I don't want that, and if you went with your friends, you'll feel guilty for not coming over to Victoria to help me celebrate."

"Yeah. You see my problem," she says dryly.

"Is there any way you can still go to gymnastics and go shopping at the mall and come here afterwards?"

"Well, by the time we finish shopping, it'll be too late to catch the ferry. But I'll try."

* * *

The next morning, as Maria pours her coffee, she looks outside Mary-Jo's kitchen window to admire the amazing garden. The backyard is in full bloom with waist-high plants wrapping their way all along the backyard fence. Also, to maximize her space, Mary-Jo has planted more greenery on a little island in the center of the lawn.

Suddenly, one-by-one, a family of three raccoons crawl drunkenly out from the bushes on the botanical island, like clowns from a car.

Too stunned to even take a sip of her coffee, Maria watches the creatures as they cross the lawn towards the house. Then they turn right and shimmy up the wooden banister under the kitchen window and scamper over the deck under the patio table, only to disappear just as quickly as they arrived, into the next door neighbours' yard.

"Thank goodness, Mr. Morris hasn't gone outside yet this morning… but raccoons, is that a bad omen or a good one?"

Upon seeing the trio, Maria is reminded of the evening when she was driving home at night after an unusually awful spa party, where she lost money, and was undervalued for her service, and basically donated her time and talent when she was just scraping by herself.

She saw a raccoon trying to cross the street up ahead and as a way to avoid any kind of heartache, she made eye-contact with the animal and commanded him to turn around and go back into the woods. Thankfully, he received the message and promptly got off the road.

As a spirit animal, the raccoon is a very powerful shapeshifter. With its natural masque, beady eyes, striped costume, dexterous hands, and nocturnal lifestyle, the raccoon has had a bad reputation as 'the bandit of the wilderness.' However, behind the veil, the raccoon is actually a strong protector and generous provider, and would put family first before anything else, much like "Robin Hood."

The raccoon is a noble creature that shares its blessings and bounty with family and the less fortunate, when it has more than enough. Seeing the raccoons is a reminder for Maria – as she is about to step through the threshold into her fifth decade – "I need to be more generous, creative, curious, flexible, and resourceful," and not be so insular and self-involved. Selfishness is a killer of spirit" and the key to living a fulfilling life is giving from your abundance."

Her phone rings and interrupts her thoughts.

"Family plans have changed," says her mom on the other end. "Only Krys and Maxim are coming on the 9am ferry. Zoryanna wants to go shopping with her friends and she and Olivia will come later with Jasper, in time for our dinner reservations."

"Yes, I figured that would happen. She called me last night. Thanks for letting me know. I'll see you in a couple of hours."

Maria is excited to spend the afternoon with just her brother and nephew. They had never actually spent any time together just the three of them before.

As a way to show support for Maria's upcoming Camino and to help her train to walk long distances, Krys suggests they go to the Sooke Potholes for the afternoon.

Of course Lubomyra makes them a big lunch, complete with sandwiches on fresh, Mount Royal bagels and chocolate chip cookies, but she decides to stay home because nature hikes are not her thing.

The trek out to Sooke does not go smoothly, however. As the driver, Maria figures she would be able to just follow her nose along the scenic road into the backcountry but she gets confused and takes an early left turn at Metchosin Road.

They end up driving through farmland where one street name turns into another without any sign or warning. Good thing Krys consults his phone and gets them out of the woods without much delay. Meanwhile, Zoryanna keeps calling Krys every five minutes from the mall to get out of coming to the Island.

"You will be on the 4pm ferry, Zoryanna," he says in his stern fatherly voice.

"Parenting is hard," Maria thinks.

Maxim sits uncomfortably in the backseat shaking his head, knowing full well where this conversation is going. As they approach Edward Milne Community School, Maxim sits up.

"Hey, I recognize that school. They have a really good jazz band!" he says.

Maria turns the car right onto Sooke River Road and drives another five kilometres into the Provincial Park.

The Sooke Potholes are part of the *T'Sou-ke* Nation's territory. The Potholes are roughly 15,000 years younger than Hanauma Bay in Hawaii and had been formed during the most recent Ice Age. As the heavy ice slowly moved across the landscape, millimeter by millimeter for millennia, it carried huge boulders in tow. In time, with the help of fluid meltwater and glacial pressure, the ice and boulders carved the surface of the natural bedrock beneath them, leaving gaping potholes in their wake.

Even though it is a beautiful and sunny day, ideal for being outside, the park is not crowded and they have their choice of parking spots.

They are greeted by a volunteer who is standing behind a table in the shade. She gives them a trail map and suggests that since they are not planning to jump off the cliffs and go swimming, the next three kilometres of trails will give them a really good taste of the natural beauty the park has to offer.

Being full of energy, Maxim scouts ahead and checks out the views first, bringing back news about whether or not it is worth stopping for a moment or going further.

Within a few, short minutes into their hike, the cameras come out. Krys takes a nice photo of Maria standing on the sandy forest path, holding her pale pink purse, and embraced by the lanky, green trees behind her.

Further along the trail, Krys takes another photo of his sister, this time without her awareness. From the vantage point of balancing on a rock in the rushing river, he looks up to see Maria with her camera around her neck, standing on the cliff above him, peering off into the distant future and with the sun illuminating her golden hair.

He captures the moment as her arms are posed in a "marching forth" type of way and it looks as if she is walking with steadfast determination. By luck, she finds a quote from the godfather of all modern nature lovers in Mary-Jo's sewing room where Morris the cat likes to sleep, that reads:

Go confidently in the direction of your dreams!
Live the life you've imagined
~ Henry David Thoreau

With every new photo Maria takes of Krys and Maxim, which include ethereal sun flares, shiny rocks, magnificent trees, inviting mountains, and swirling bubbles in the rejuvenating water under the clear blue sky, she feels her spirit expanding with love and joy.

She particularly loves the pothole that is shaped like a heart and how the sunlight dances and sparkles in the clear, dark, green, aqua pools.

"It's all of this supernatural green energy surrounding me," Maria thinks with a smile.

Having studied chakras and energy healing, Maria knows that green energy is about the heart, love, relationships, emotions, health, nature and new beginnings. She also knows that the colour green is associated with Archangel Raphael, the angel for healing, travel, and romance.

Throughout their hike, Ed Sheeran's song, "Perfect," plays through her head. "Dancing in the dark… with you between my arms… Is Nick singing this to me?" she wonders to herself, briefly forgetting their meeting did not go so well.

As they continue walking along the banks of the river and reach the cliffy, high points of the trail, they hear shrieks of delight through the trees as people jump and take the plunge into the cool, clean, rushing mountain water below them. For a moment, Maria has a vision of returning here someday soon, taking her own leap of faith while holding hands with Nick.

In the wind, she hears, "God is telling you today… I know you've felt passed over by romantic love when you were younger, but now is your second spring and I have a man ready to be with you and I promise, waiting all of these years will be worth it."

The contented hikers take their sweet time heading back to the car. Just one more stop at Skipping Rock Beach (which brings back childhood memories for both Krys and Maria of tossing flat stones into Lake Schenectady, where their Great Aunt Stefa used to live), which caps off their 6-kilometre excursion nicely.

As they drive home along Sooke Road, Maria spontaneously suggests the idea of dekeing into Royal Roads University for a few minutes to show Maxim where his Dido went to school. Maria knows the campus fairly well after having worked in the Registrar's Office as a temp in 2006, where each day, she would spend her lunch hour taking photos of historic roses, strutting peacocks, old-growth trees, and the monumental Hatley Castle.

She still kicks herself to this day for not having taken Kim Basinger's photo as they crossed paths on the grounds one afternoon while the actor was on premises filming the movie, "X-Men," but Maria wanted to respect the celebrity's privacy.

They come up from the beach side from behind the castle and while they are walking around the campus, reading the plaques and studying the extensive stone work on the property, both Maria and Krys are happy they are able to honour their father's memory and include him in the birthday weekend celebrations.

When they reach the front of the castle, they stumble upon a bride and groom posing for a photo shoot. Maria likes how the bridesmaids are wearing purple dresses and hopes this is a preview of her own future wedding.

It is a full afternoon and when they finally arrive back home, Lubomyra says, "Olivia and Zoryanna will not be coming at all because they were not able to get on the ferry at Tsawwassen."

"Oh, that's a shame."

"They did their best but the 4pm ferry was full and there was a three-sailing wait, so with the dog and the heat, they decided to turn around and home."

Disappointed, Maria thinks, "It just goes to show that if you give the Universe mixed messages, like Zoryanna who kept changing her mind about coming – first she was coming, then she wasn't, then she wanted to, then she didn't – you get mixed results."

Maria realizes that if she is not clear about what she wants and keeps changing her mind, the angels, who truly want to deliver her order to her, will be confused. She pictures angels running ragged, back and forth across the cosmos trying to please her, but with all of the commotion, whatever she asks for, does not quite show up as elegantly as it may have. It is as if she presses the 'stop here' button as the angels are heading in the 'not quite what she wanted' direction.

* * *

Lubomyra changes their reservation for the second time that afternoon. She has chosen the Fireside Grill, a fine dining, steakhouse restaurant because it is just a stone's throw away from home and their cuisine is always on point. Also, the Tudor style of architecture, accentuated by the distinctive Hammerbeam roof, provides a somewhat sophisticated yet cozy setting for the Ponomarenko family dinner.

As the party is seated in the dining room near a window, everyone either gazes around the room or at their menu.

"Welcome to the Fireside Grill. My name is Darla. Tonight our chef is delighted to prepare your choice of seafood, pasta, or steak entrées as well as an appetizer and dessert from our tasting menu. In the meantime, please enjoy some freshly baked bread and I'll be back shortly to take your orders."

The bread is still warm, which allows the compound butter to melt easily over top. Maria is happy to see there is cheesecake on the menu. For their entrées, Krys chooses the burger, Maxim picks the salmon, and both Lubomyra and Maria go with the Pecan Mushroom Crusted Chicken.

"And can I have some hot sauce too, please?" asks Maxim.

"I'm going to have to go to the back to get you some," says Darla with a smile. "We have a bottle kicking around for staff, but as you can tell by our mostly senior clientelle," she adds while sweeping her arm around the room, "we don't exactly get that request much around here."

"Well, I guess now that I'm about to turn fifty, I'll fit right in," jokes Maria.

"Are you sure you don't want some Prosecco to celebrate your birthday, Marichka?" asks her mother, who still does not fully recognize Maria's decision to not drink alcohol.

"No thanks," says Maria closing her menu. "I'll have a Shirley Temple for old time's sake."

"Where does that staircase go?" asks Krys before Darla has a chance to scoot away.

"The stairs that are closed off and don't go anywhere behind me? Yeah, the room up there used to be the wine cellar but it was a real pain for the bartenders to climb up the ladder to grab another bottle of wine, as you can imagine, and on top of that, it also gets really hot up there."

"So they couldn't control the temperatures for the wine," adds Krys scratching his chin. "Interesting...You'd think they would have thought of that."

"You'd think. Now it's just a good conversation starter. I'll be back shortly with your drinks and appetizers."

"You know, I went on a date here once," begins Maria. "Back in 2006, I joined a group dating club of sorts and every few weeks they'd send me on a date with five or seven other people to one of the restaurants in town.

"One night we met here. My group date sat at a six-top in the corner, next to our table here. I was sitting in the middle on this side, there was a gentleman sitting to my left and another one to my right. On the other side of the table, there were two women on each end and a vacant seat across from me.

"Just as we were close to finishing eating our meals, another guy comes in the restaurant and sits at our table. He started talking about how he was from Kingston and there was another man with his same name who was a famous inmate in the prison there. He also says he was the youngest in a really big family and everybody had to eat their dinner really fast, otherwise the other siblings would take their food right from under them."

"Aren't you going to order something?" the group date asked. "We can call the waitress over… 'Nope' he answered and then he said to the woman to his right, 'Are you going to finish that?' And she said, 'no, it was pretty good though. Do you want to taste it?'

"'Yes, thanks,' he said with his arms reaching for her plate. We all thought he was just going to steal a cold fry or two but he unrolled his napkin and pulled her plate toward him. He dug right in! 'Mmm… this is really good. Yup, really good,' he said. We all watched in amused horror as he scoffed down his date's remaining dinner. 'Great, thanks,' he said while giving the clean-as-a-whistle plate back to her.

"And then he looked over to the woman to his left. 'Are you going to finish that?' he asked her. 'No,' she said, 'I'm full.' 'Can I have it?' 'Sure, help yourself,' she said sliding the plate over with a mock eyeroll. 'Mmm… this is really good. Yup, really good.'

"He was very charming and we were all thoroughly entertained by him because up until he came, the group date was fairly lackluster. As he finished the second plate of leftovers, he looked across the table at me. 'Here,' I said and he happily took my plate. For some reason, this time he did not say, 'Mmm… this is really good. Yup, really good' but as soon as he finished my scalloped potatoes and before the coffee and desserts came, he stood up and said, 'Well, gotta go,' and then he left, just like that! And then one of us said, 'Who was that masked man?'"

The family chuckles.

"Well, these are the men in your life, now, Marichka," says Lubomyra raising her glass to make a toast. "Maxim, Krys and your Vuiko Borys…"

"And Tato in heaven and my future husband!" Maria adds.

"About that, Marich, "starts Krys. "You need to get on that right away and step up your game."

"I'll get around to it in my fifties, in the next decade or so," says Maria trying to be all cool and casual.

"No, like this year… not in ten years, not in two years, you have to do this now. Go to Spain, meet a guy, move there if you have to. We'll ship your stuff!"

"I already have someone in mind," thinks Maria.

"Cheers," they all say clinking their glasses.

Sir • Prize

Maria's 50th birthday lands on a Sunday, the first day of the week, and her mother is eager to go to church. Maria likes the idea of starting this new, mid-life chapter of her journey on a spiritual note with song and prayer, surrounded by people who care.

Early in the day, she receives spirited texts from Zoryanna and Olivia and an enthusiastic phone message from her priest-friend, Father Odyn, who lives near Vancouver.

It is easy for her to choose which dress to wear for her special day. Lubomyra has sewn a shift dress with splashes of green and blue on a white background that really flatters Maria's now slimmer body. She feels really good!

To close the Liturgy, Lubomyra leads the congregation in every Ukrainian's favourite song, the universal solution for all festive occasions, the words that can play with one hundred different melodies, "Mnohaya Lita" or "Many Happy Years."

Smiling, everyone goes downstairs to the church hall for some coffee and to share in the chocolate birthday cake that Lubomyra has brought.

Maria has long thought mothers are just as important to acknowledge on their children's birthdays 'because they were there, too.' The priest himself takes a jovial photo of mother and daughter together serving the cake.

Going to church is just part one of a lovely, sunny Sunday in June. Lubomyra has invited some close friends over for an afternoon gathering. Before they arrive, however, Samantha calls.

"Happy Birthday, Maria! I hope you're enjoying your day so far!"

"Thanks, Samantha!"

"I'm sorry I wasn't able to fly out for your party – with the last week of school and sitting in legal meetings about my divorce, I just couldn't go."

"I understand."

"I really have a strong feeling you're going to have a great year with your Camino and maybe you'll meet someone new!"

"I hope so."

"Thanks for sending that photo of you and Nick earlier this week."

"Yeah, I wanted to talk to you about that."

"How did it go? What was he like in person?"

"He seemed very relaxed and charming. He even winked once."

"He's a winker?" Samantha says with mock horror.

"Yeah," Maria says hearing the humour for a second and then losing it to the breeze. "He was talking about the book he's writing and said he was 'just playin'' and then winked at me. I didn't know what to do with that. And he also brought a photographer, who was lovely, but it threw me right off."

"Sounds like there was a lot going on. Do you think you'll see him again soon?"

"I'd really like that. Oh, it sounds like the guests are here. Let's talk again soon."

"Yes, for sure. Happy Birthday, Maria. Love you!"

"Love you!"

* * *

Guests bearing gift certificates and flowers help Maria celebrate her milestone birthday. The conversations are light and lively as they sit outside in the sunshine on the deck, eating the Napoleon Torte Lubomyra had been baking in stages for the last three days. Everyone always marvels at how deliciously rich the Napoleon is and Maria always likes to eat the pastry from the bottom, layer by layer, saving the most gooey top layer for last.

Hidden beneath her own coatings of cheer and celebration, in the midst of all of the family phone calls, photos, hugs and well-wishes, Maria quietly waits for Nick to call as well, or even say,

"Happy Birthday" on her social page, but her hope diminishes by the hour.

Still, she smiles all day and is grateful to all of the wonderful people who do show up for her to help her celebrate her life. Soon, it is time for Krys and Maxim to leave to catch the ferry back to the mainland.

The party guests have given Maria donations toward her Camino along with colourful bouquets of flowers that now sit bunched in the living room, their faces leaning towards the sunlight coming through the windows.

"Thank you, Mam, for all that you've done for me, on this day and over the last fifty years," and with a hug, she goes back to Mary-Jo's to take care of Morris the cat.

* * *

The next day, Maria plans to return Father Odyn's call before lunch but her tears keep getting in the way. She is devastated that Nick has not made an effort to acknowledge her milestone birthday at all.

Even so, she misses the big, neon clue on the front of the building; she misses the push to forget him and move on and comes up short once again. Even with Nick being such a jerk, she continues to hold on to hope that he will eventually come around.

Maria is grateful for Father Odyn. He entered Maria's life in August of 2012 when he showed up for Lubomyra's Hawaiian-themed, birthday party. Soon into their first conversation, he mentioned, "a psychic told me she saw three angels hovering over my shoulders, here, here and here," he said pointing above his head.

"The fact that he even spoke with a psychic at all and did not run screaming from her in judgement and condemnation, speaks volumes about him," thinks Maria as she scrolls through her contact list on her phone to find his name.

"Of course, being connected to angels and wearing a Hawaiian shirt also helps."

Father Odyn is one of the good guys, a "Salt of the Earth," kind of person, as they say, and Maria trusts him. Having grown up on a farm in the Prairies, he speaks plainly, and seamlessly jumps between English and Ukrainian mid-sentence, peppering his stories with his own made-up words.

But underneath his kooky and jovial manner, he is devoutly committed to his calling and makes it his life's mission to comfort the lonely, the poor, the orphaned, the homeless, the addicted, and the imprisoned members of his community, and is known to walk through Vancouver's toughest neighbourhoods, late at night, where the term, "skid row" was first coined, offering his own style of non-preachy, pastoral care.

Father Odyn has known about Maria's feelings for Nick from the very beginning. They have had several conversations over the years thanks to Lubomyra always making sure to invite him over for her famously ambrosial, home-cooked meals, whenever he comes to Victoria.

He is particularly impressed with Borsch Fest Victoria, a charity event which was held for three consecutive years in collaboration with their church and the Ukrainian Cultural Centre.

"It's like a chili cook-off but with borsch," she told him one evening at the dinner table. "As you know, no two borsch batches are the same and you can never have the same borsch twice, even if it's made by the same person – and we thought it would be fun to taste other people's borsch recipes all in one place like they do in the Ukrainian city of Borshchiv every year."

"It sounds like a community event that will bring people together – especially now with the *Maidan* going on in Ukraina. Good for you, Marichka," Father Odyn said.

Borsch Fest's volunteer committee members, which included Maria, Kataryna, Kvitka, Vasylyna and Arthur, got together each August, to plan this annual charity fundraising event from the idea stage, to marketing, to clean up. They coordinated contestants, judges, volunteers, venues and prizes, and drummed up interest on social media. Maria also emceed the judging portion of the event and in three years, they raised over $3000 for humanitarian aid in Ukraine.

Father Odyn loves hearing the story that on the event's last hurrah, Lubomyra, along with her teammates, Petrovna and Luke, won the "Best Meat-Based Borsch" title from the judges, a notable victory, which came with a burgundy apron and some cash prizes.

On the flip side, he does not like hearing about Nick. He has been trying to tell Maria all along that perhaps she is dodging a bullet with this bozo.

"It's better you find out now than going so far as being left at the alter or something like that. What did you say to him when he told you his news that he was getting married?"

"I wished him all the best."

"That shows your character, Marichka. It shows your heart. Many people wouldn't do that. You deserve better than this guy."

Her priest-friend's good intentions fall on deaf ears. As this fresh heart-break starts to sink in, Maria's optimism from Saturday crumbles into dust. She feels like she did something wrong when she met Nick in person the week before – that she was too nervous or she did not wear sexy enough shoes – and he is not interested in her and no one else would be either.

Maria clicks on Father's number and he surprisingly answers.

"Thank you for calling me yesterday to wish me a happy birthday."

"It was my pleasure. I wish you many, many happy years and may God bless you with love, peace and joy in your heart. How was your big day?"

"It was really nice, thanks. Krys and Maxim came over and we had chocolate cake at church and then Napoleon torte at the house…"

"Your mama makes the best."

"Yes, she does, but…"

"But what?"

"I was distracted. I wasn't able to let it all in and appreciate my day as fully as I wanted to."

"What happened?"

"Well, I met Nick in person last week…he came over to Victoria and we had a nice time and I told him my 50th birthday was coming up, but he didn't call me at all, and even though everybody else was so wonderful, especially my mother, I felt so sad that Nick didn't bother to do anything," she says in a futile attempt to hold back the tears.

Father Odyn's heart sinks. He truly wishes that Maria would find the love of her life but knows it will not happen if she keeps picking up scraps from guys like Nick, who, for whatever reason, are not available to her.

"Don't let that *shmata* ruin your days!"

"I don't understand why God hasn't introduced me to my husband at all in all of these years. Where is he? Is there someone out there for me? Am I supposed to die a spinster? Why would God keep me hanging on the vine? I just want to share my life with someone and I thought it was him… that I finally met the man for me."

"I know you don't think this right now, but I know for sure that God has someone really special picked out for you. I know many women who have found their first husbands later in life. Don't give up, Marichka."

"Please say a prayer for me, Father. I don't know how I'm going to get through this."

"You are always in my prayers," he says. "And you'll meet a wonderful man soon – I know this without a doubt – and don't be surprised if he's Jewish – which is okay, by the way."

"I was hoping it would be him, though."

"Do you even know how he feels about you?" he asks her.

"No."

"Why don't you just call him up and ask him?"

"I could never do that."

"Why not?" the priest says playing the devil's advocate.

"Because what if he tells me what I don't want to hear. I'd rather…"

"He could say that he doesn't feel the same way about you, but what if he says that he does care about you and wants a relationship with you?"

Maria starts warming up to the idea.

"What do I say to him?" she asks wiping her face from tears.

"Say something like, 'I have a question for you. I need to know this for me. Are you interested in me as a friend or something more significant?' You can also add, 'I was hoping to hear from you over the weekend after we met but I guess you were busy. You are in my thoughts and in my heart.'"

"Thanks, Father. I'll think about it."

"If you ask him, at least you'll know one way or the other. You may be pleasantly surprised."

slide • show

Maria opens the mustard envelope with the green-handled letter opener her father had given her. She reaches in and pulls out a pocket-sized booklet with a hand-drawn logo of a Canadian flag superimposed on a seashell that somehow, oddly resembles a beaver, the Canadian mascot.

Finally, Maria's own green, pilgrim *credencial* from the Canadian Company of Pilgrims has arrived in the mail!

Buying the special passport for $10 is a critical, early step on her journey because it shows she has made a commitment to her goal. As she unfolds the blank pages of the accordion-style booklet, Maria wonders, "Will I ever fill these pages or am I just going to shelf this thing for someday, another day?"

"No," she thinks again, pressing the pages back into a tidy, little square. "I'm going on this Camino this summer come hell or high water!"

Maria is able to count on her fingers and toes how many people she knows who have already walked the Camino in recent years and there is no shortage of experienced advisors and well-wishers she can talk to about her upcoming expedition. Everyone from her hairdresser, to several people from church, to friends from childhood, have blazed the trail before her and Maria is very keen to follow in their footsteps and pass on the torch to others as well.

Daniel is the first person to introduce the whole Camino experience to Maria during one of Lubomyra's famous dinner parties and so it seems fitting to meet with him posthaste. Daniel is an artist and beekeeper.

Shortening his name to "Dan" or "Danny" does not suit him. Lubomyra always looks forward to receiving his abstract Christmas cards and she frames them as part of her art collection. So far, he has never married but has a long-term, female companion, who lives up island, who Maria has never met.

Hearing about Maria's upcoming expedition, Daniel promptly invites Maria to his urban homestead, which is nestled a few streets from Emily Carr's old house, for 4:30 on Thursday afternoon.

They sit in his garden, under the shade of an apple tree, with birds chirping in the leaves above them. Daniel has so much information to share, he can hardly contain himself.

"Here's my copy of Brierley's Camino guidebook," Daniel says as he hands over a rumpled up book to Maria. "You're welcome to read through it and make photocopies. Like here's an elevation map that tells you how steep the inclines are on certain stretches of the trail. When were you planning on going?"

"I was hoping to go this summer, the sooner the better, because I'm off work and have the time," replies Maria.

"The best time to go is from May to mid-June and then again in September. I wouldn't go in July or even August because it will just be too hot. It's also when all of the locals leave and the tourists come. At the peak of summer, it will be much more crowded and possibly quite difficult to find a bed every night."

"About the bed situation. How does that work?"

"Well, you have some options. They have a system of private and public *albergues*, like youth hostels, dotted all along the trails. They're all listed in this guide. You can either pre-book all of your *albergues* before you leave from here, like if you joined a tour group and they can take care of all of that for you – including transporting your backpack between towns – or you can just wing it and try your luck each day – but this is what I did..."

Maria thinks it may be a good idea to take some notes, but decides to just listen and let Daniel's words soak in verbally instead.

"Each morning, I would get up and walk for a couple of hours and then I'd stop somewhere for coffee and breakfast," he continues. "By then, I'd know roughly what town I'd be able to walk to by around 3pm that day and so I'd call ahead and make a reservation and then I was able to relax and walk at my leisure and enjoy the day."

"Yeah, I can't see myself booking before I go, though that would give me peace of mind. How should I know at this stage where I'm going to end up from day to day?"

"You'll eventually find your rhythm, your Camino legs, as they say," remembers Daniel. "I managed to walk somewhere between 18 and 29 kilometres a day and if you follow the recommended itineraries in the guidebook, you should be fine. But you also run the risk of everyone else being on the same pace as you because everyone else has this book, too, which goes back to the bed race scenario. Do you know what route you're taking yet?"

"From my research, I don't think I'll have the four, five, or six weeks it takes to do the 800-kilometre hikes across Spain or France, so I've started looking a shorter sections. There's one called, *El Camino de Invierno* or the "Winter Way" on the *Camino Frances*, which starts in Ponferrada and it's really speaking to me."

"Oh yes, Ponferrada. That's where the Templar Castle is."

"And it's close to Madrid, so I can land there first. It covers a distance of 275 or so kilometres, depending on who you talk to, and I figure I can do this route in just under two weeks, giving me some wiggle room."

"That sounds good to me but I'd recommend going in September, after Labour Day, and even into October, if you can swing it," Daniel says.

"Okay," says Maria. "That's when I'll go. Ponferrada in September, here I come!" and with that decision, she thanks

Daniel and leaves with his tattered Brierley's guidebook and a DVD version of the movie, "The Way," written by Emilio Estevez and starring his father, Martin Sheen.

"Let's make a plan to watch this movie together, soon," suggests Maria, walking toward her car. "I think my mother would enjoy it as well."

"Sure," Daniel says, waving back.

* * *

MY THOUGHTS ON "FOOTPRINTS: THE PATH OF YOUR LIFE" MOVIE

by Maria Ponomarenko, Wellness Coach

I've just realized that in two short months, I'll be flying to Spain to walk the Camino. There's still so much to do to prepare!

Although I'm not yet physically on the trail, I feel I have already started my pilgrimage.

I've been talking with many people who have already walked the Camino and on Monday, one of my friends, Daniel, who was perhaps the first person to plant the seed of going on this journey, came over to watch the movie, "The Way," with me and my mom.

My mother had also invited Vasylyna, who had also walked the Camino, and Matthew and his mother, who were interested in seeing the movie.

Well, somehow, we had gotten off to a rough start. We couldn't get the DVD player to work and once we put the disc into an old laptop, not everybody could hear the dialogue and see the screen.

Our old technology just wasn't working and it was an exercise in frustration!

Finally, we decided to switch gears and watch another movie on the same subject on Netflix called, "Footprints: The Path of Your Life."

"Footprints" is a documentary that follows a group of 10 men while they walk the Camino de Santiago with their Parish Priest. I suppose fighting with the technology and then figuring out that we could watch another movie on another platform was a lesson in not forcing something to go in a certain way and letting another option – a better one – emerge instead.

Once we made that choice, the energy in the room calmed down somewhat. As it turned out, Footprints was actually the better choice for us to watch because it was more "realistic" of what I could expect on my journey, according to Daniel and Vasylyna.

In the beginning, each of the men were really struggling with their own fears and challenges and sadly, a few of the men in the group had to bow out and leave early.

That's what happens with any new, ambitious project – stuff comes up. We all have the best of intentions but somehow, all of this emotional baggage that has been buried deep down over a lifetime, gets stirred up.

That's the struggle! It's how we deal with all our stuff that we've collected over the years that will make our break us.

The fear and the obstacles are saying, "I know you want to get to Santiago de Compostela, [for example] but here's what you have to deal with first, and once you face this garbage head on and clear it out of the way, the world will be your oyster and you can be, do, or have whatever you want!"

For some of the men in the movie, it was too much too soon. The stuff that came up for them was too much to bear. I know they gave it their best and it wasn't an easy decision to make to not finish. I hope they have a chance to try again and succeed.

But after a couple of weeks and many miles under their belts, the remaining men got a rhythm and got stronger. By the end of their 500 mile, 40-day journey, they were laughing and dancing and walking barefoot!

It was beautiful to watch the men go through their spiritual transformation!

I think the turning point occurred for the group after they saw a piece of wood from Jesus' actual cross with their own eyes – which would have been amazing! – and then suddenly the men were inspired to work together as a group, not letting the weakest fall behind.

That's the choice we all have – either we continue to carry our heavy baggage that is weighing us down and give up on our dreams, or we face our challenges and let them go and leave them at the side of the road and move on and help others along their way as well.

Going on a pilgrimage gives us the opportunity to release our rocks and burdens, once for all! And in the same spirit, working with a Wellness Coach like me would also be valuable.

Both coaching and pilgrimages open up new options that we may not have seen before (like watching a different movie at the last minute like we had) and give us the chance to make new choices and start fresh.

If we can make it through that initial turbulence and interference, we'll be stronger for the rest of the journey. That's where the expression, "what doesn't kill you, makes you stronger" comes from!

And with wellness coaching, there's extra support during the rough patches so you don't have to travel alone.

Have you ever noticed that fear is built into the word, "interference"? Some people let the fear interfere and stop them from experiencing a blissful miracle because whatever came up was just too much. The turbulence was too scary and the plane was shaking too hard!

Meanwhile, other people on the same flight will just push through and keep going and make it through with flying colours.

So I ask myself, "What kind of person am I? Will I let fear stop me in my tracks as I'm attempting a challenging leg on my journey? Will I let those excuses block my path and give me an out to turn around and go home? Or will I rise to the challenge and dig deep and keep moving?"

That's why I think the pilgrimage has already started for me. The more emotional baggage I can release before I physically set foot on the Camino, the easier and the lighter the walk will be.

I'm not going to let potential turbulence keep me from getting on that flight or let fear stop me from living my best life! *Buen Camino, Maria*

* * *

Now that Maria is a member of the Victoria chapter of the Canadian Company of Pilgrims, she wants to meet likeminded people who are also on the verge of walking their first Camino.

As luck would have it, long-term members of the club, Charles and Svitlana, have organized a talk at St. Nicholas for anyone who wants to hear an inspiring story about the Camino. They have invited another pilgrim, Finley, to speak about her experience of doing her Camino, not on foot, not on a bicycle, not on a horse, but in her wheelchair!

Maria is keen to attend and Lubomyra comes along for support. When they arrive, the church hall is teeming with *Kamin'chyky*, a punny nickname Maria has come up with for her fellow pilgrims.

In Ukrainian, the word, "камінь" (or kammeen' with a softened "n" sound on the end) means "stone or rock." Adding the chyk makes the word cute and familiar, and the last letter, "y," makes it plural.

She figures that since the Camino is a cobbled, rocky road, both literally and metaphorically, the people who walk on it are also by extension, loose pebbles and rubble themselves. A rolling stone gathers no moss.

With her cookie and cup of tea, Maria sits with Svitlana and Lubomyra at a round table at the front of the room. They have a good view of Finley, her husband Peter, the emcee for the evening, and the slideshow screen.

Finley shares that while she was riding her bike years ago, she was involved in a traffic accident. She was struck by a car, which left one side of her body non-functioning, and has been relying on a wheelchair for mobility ever since.

Fast forward ten years. Finley has grown to accept her situation and decided to take on the challenging goal of travelling the Camino herself.

Going on a pilgrimage should be available to anyone who has heard the call and wants to go, but unfortunately, the ancient trail network that entwines Europe like a connect the dots puzzle, had not been designed with wheelchairs in mind.

During her talk, Finley describes some of the challenges she faced. Just getting to Europe from Victoria, Canada, by airplane, was already a difficult start.

Finley researched her trip for a year. The plan was to launch in Sarria, Spain and travel the last 100 kilometres of el Camino, arriving at the Cathedral of Santiago de Compostela in five days. Finishing this stretch would ensure she and her husband, Peter, would receive their official pilgrim certificates, or *Compostelas,* evidenced by the stamps they collected along the way.

Finley and Peter trained to prepare themselves as best they could for the obstacle course that lay ahead of them by going out every weekend to various parts of the Galloping Goose Trail and then rewarding themselves with a beer afterwards.

Maria is impressed by the warmth and the humour emanating from Finley and Peter as they tell their story. Finley's loving husband did not walk the Camino for his own reasons and only came to help his wife, but without Peter, "her rock," Finley could not have gone at all.

While on the trail, the formidable couple encountered stones the size of watermelons, passages too narrow for Finley's chair to go through, streams blocking the way, mud, stairs, uphills, downhills, tight washrooms, hot sun, and rain. Once Finley even fell at the foot of a stream, but somehow they managed to pick her up again and get through it all and live to tell the tale!

"If it was easy, everyone would do go on a Camino," says Finley.

"Looking back, is there anything you would do differently?" someone asks from the audience.

"Yes, in hindsight, I wish we had practiced on more hills," she replies.

Maria makes a mental note. For the most part, Finley's husband pushed her wheelchair along the dusty, gravelly roads fairly easily but sometimes they also needed to rely on pulleys, friends, and strangers to help them along the way.

In an unexpected bonus, Finley and Peter also enhanced other people's pilgrimages too by giving other travellers the opportunity to give back and be of service to someone who was in need. Helping each other out and interacting with the locals and foreigners who showed up along the way, made the experience that much more colourful for everyone.

"All in all, it was worth it," Finley says.

She and Peter went on an adventure of a lifetime and even became trail celebrities with every new photo that had been taken.

After listening to Finley's talk, Maria concludes that if Finley was able to complete her ambitious, amazing, and extraordinary Camino in a wheelchair, it was certainly possible for Maria to have her own adventure!

nerve • us

"Happy Canada Day," says Lubomyra to Maria as she enters the kitchen. "I'm making us pancakes for breakfast."

"It was nice how we finagled that invitation for dinner last night at Petrovna's and Luke's. Those hamburgers were pretty good."

"I liked playing that train boardgame, too, but we really shouldn't have imposed."

"Nonsense," replies Maria. "They loved having us."

"Do you have any plans for today?"

"Just going to buy my plane ticket to Spain. Air Canada is having their Canada Day seat sale and I think I'll get a good deal."

"Good luck. Now where did I put that maple syrup," says Lubomyra as she shuffles through the fridge.

As much as Maria is excited about her upcoming Camino, she is nervous about actually buying her ticket and making a firm commitment. She types in Air Canada seat sale… departing from Victoria YYJ… arriving in Madrid, Spain… on Tuesday, September 17, 2019… returning Tuesday, October 1st.

"Okay… here we go… what are the options?"

She scans the many flights that pop up in her search.

"I don't want to leave first thing in the morning. I want to go through Calgary. I don't want to spend more than $1500 return."

Maria narrows her search to a flight that leaves Victoria at 11:35am.

"What do you think of this flight?" she asks her mom, the chief benefactor of this whole expedition.

"Looks good," her mother says scanning the page.

"There are tickets for bargain basement, mid-range, and business class, with a difference of a few hundred dollars between each," she says not expecting first class but points to the happy medium prices, remembering it will be a long flight to Europe.

"Good Lord, if you're thinking over $1000 one way, think again. I wouldn't even book that seat for me."

"Okay, I'll book the cheapest," says Maria taking a deep breath, feeling put in her place.

"Here's my credit card."

"Are you sure?"

"Yes, go ahead and remember, I won't be around to drive you to the airport because I'll be in Lourdes then. You'll have to ask a favour from somebody else."

"Right," says Maria under her breath, trying to shake off what her mother said before.

She clicks the button and launches the "book now" sequence.

"Now the return flight. I guess I'll figure out how to get back to Madrid later once I'm there."

She thinks the hard part is over but there are still more decisions to make.

"Would you like to pay extra to book your seat now? How many pieces of baggage are you bringing? Would you like to order a meal with dietary restrictions? Would you like travel insurance? Would you like to book accommodations? Would you like to rent a car?"

"Oh my word! So many questions! Travel has changed so much since last I booked a flight!"

After saying 'no' to all of the bells and whistles and punching in her mother's credit card number, Maria's plane ticket arrives in her email.

"There's no turning back now!"

via • duct

"I've been here before and I deserve a little more," sings Maria as she walks through Rithet's Bog to train for her Camino. Her "20K" playlist has now been synced to her iPhone and the song, "Rain King" by the Counting Crows, is a fun and energizing song for her soundtrack.

When Maria returns home, she finds a text message waiting for her from her coach-friend, Jordan.

> Want to meet for tea or something July 5th or 6th in Victoria? I'm to be there with my husband and daughter and I'd love to see you.

> Yes!

> Yay!

We can do more than tea.
I'd love to meet your
husband and daughter,
if they want. We can go out
for dinner or something.
I have so much to tell you.
Lots of progress.

K. I'll be in touch. We land on
the 4th. Staying in Sooke.
Would you be up to coming
out to our place?
Join us for a meal and you
and I could go for a walk?
That sounds nice!
What day were you thinking?

Either Saturday or Friday.

Saturday is good.

K. How about you come out
about 3:00 and we can walk,
then have dinner?

Great. Let's talk more on
Saturday to finalize
the details. I'm looking
forward to seeing you!

Yes, me too!

Maria puts down her phone and thinks about how she and Jordan first met. They were introduced online via a mutual coaching acquaintance, Michelle, who ended up burning her bridges with both of them.

Michelle is a strong-willed individual, though she is deeply wounded. She is also a Walker graduate and Maria got to know her when they traded coaching to get some extra hours towards their certifications.

Meanwhile, Michelle met Jordan through another network and for a year or so, the three of them met regularly online, each from their home bases of Texas, California and British Columbia, to brainstorm new ideas on how they could each build their coaching businesses.

Coincidentally, they are all Gemini's, and when these chatty twins got together, it often felt like there were six in the meeting, not three.

Seeing that it was harder than they all thought to get their coaching businesses off the ground and in an attempt to help Maria get on her financial feet, Jordan stepped in and gave Maria the opportunity to sell health supplements. Maria reluctantly agreed to try her hand at network marketing and within a few weeks, Jordan flew up to Victoria to help her launch her business.

"The job seemed simple enough."

All Maria had to do was start taking the algae herself so she had her own success story to share and by extension, bring people in for Jordan's upcoming, promotional talks.

* * *

STEM CELL NUTRITION

Supporting our own Stem Cell system is the key to good health and it's a perfect complement to wellness coaching!

By Maria Ponomarenko, Wellness Coach

As Count Tyrone Rugen says in "The Princess Bride" movie, "Get your rest. If you haven't got your health, you haven't got anything."

Being healthy means having the freedom to do whatever you want with your life and that is why I am so passionate about promoting wellness.

In my travels, I have found a new and unique aquatic-botanical product that supports our own release of bone-marrow stem cells. It's a health supplement made from blue-green algae that comes from Klamath Lake, Oregon.

As a wellness coach, I help my clients to get clear on the kind of life they would like to create for themselves and then identify and release any obstacles, challenges and resistance that may be in the way.

Eventually, by making slow, incremental changes over time, my clients make tremendous progress toward their vision.

Well, these stem cell nutrition wellness products do the same on a cellular level in the body!

Let me explain. Stem cells are essential building blocks of a healthy mind and body. They occur naturally in the body and serve to replenish cells that are lost through normal wear and tear or injury.

The magic of stem cells!

Stem cells are master cells. They are like superheroes because they can turn into whatever they want! If they need to become a heart cell, they become a heart cell. If they need to become a skin cell, they become a skin cell!

And on top of that, they make a clone of themselves, too!

Remember your stem cells the next time you would like to make a change in your life!

If we are all made from stem cells and stem cells can turn into whatever they want, then it stands to reason that we can do the same and become whatever we want, too!

The thing is, our stem cells age as we age and our body's ability to self-repair and maintain optimum health decreases because the number of circulating stem cells decreases.

However, with this blue-green algae technology, it is still possible to increase the number of circulating stem cells, no matter how old we are, and allow the body's process of self-repair and self-renewal to continue.

This is literally a cutting-edge, breakthrough product created by a Canadian Scientist. Clinically-tested in double blind studies, this botanical product stimulates, produces and releases millions of adult stem cells from the bone marrow into the blood stream – releasing 30% more adult stem cells into the bloodstream within three hours – with only two capsules a day.

This supplement is a stand-alone product, but just like in a coaching conversation, it is not necessarily smooth sailing all the way. Often times, obstacles and past conditioning keep us from getting to where we want to go, regardless of our best intentions.

The same can be true in our body and the obstacles are called plaque and inflammation.

Sometimes, well-meaning stem cells get blocked from reaching their destination and cannot do their repair work because there is too much stuff in the way.

Sound familiar?

Good news!

The good news is, these health supplements also address this issue and help remove the interfering road blocks as well.

See I told you it's like coaching!

There has never been anything like it. And, it is backed by scientific testing and proof!

There are tons of testimonials out there and I have had my own success after using this product for only a couple of months.

Let's just say, a callous that I've had on my finger since 2010 has all but disappeared! What will your amazing story be?

So, if you'd like to hear more about stem cell nutrition, to boost your health, to support your body's own repair system, and get your hands on these supplements, please contact me, Maria, by email today.

* * *

Both Maria and Jordan surmised, "Surely, Michelle would be interested in buying these supplements," and so they arranged a call with her.

Initially, after sitting through the sales presentation, Michelle enthusiastically bought the product and Maria got the commission. Things seemed to be looking up and Maria started to feel like she could make an income from this new enterprise, but her new hope was fleeting.

Suddenly, Michelle changed her mind and without any further discussion, she sent the following email:

Subject: coaching

Hello Maria, As per our conversation last night, we need to suspend all future coaching sessions so that you may devote your time and efforts of getting the help that you need to move forward with your life and your goals. You are a good person and I wish you nothing, but success. The only way you can move forward is to address the issues we discussed, which are getting in the way of you moving forward with all of your goals. I recommend you talk with your doctor and go on anti-depressants and also go on welfare. Please feel free to drop me an email from time to

time when you are feeling better to let me
know how things are going. All the best!
Michelle

Michelle was referring to Maria's emotional state that lead to the reason why Jordan jumped in to help Maria in the first place. Michelle knew that Nick had met someone else (the real reason for Maria's misery) and could tell from a mile away that things were not going to end well at all for her. It was hard to watch/not watch. Finally, Michelle had to pull the plug on their friendship.

Maria did not respond to the email and never spoke to Michelle again. She felt like she had been kicked in the gut, kicked when she was down, kicked on the battlefield of life while gaping wounds oozed blood from her body, being left only to die in the middle of nowhere, with no help and no compassion – by someone who called themselves a life coach, no less.

"What kind of coach tells someone to go on welfare – especially when they're trying really hard and things are starting to look up?" Maria asked Jordan. "It goes against everything life coaching stands for!"

"You just don't stand by watching someone else drown," said Jordan, who subsequently unfriended Michelle online.

It was no surprise that the health supplement business venture fizzled rather quickly after Michelle had backed out, but somehow Maria and Jordan stayed in contact.

Maria also managed to make it through that extended rough patch without declaring bankruptcy, or going on welfare, or committing to a course of anti-depressant prescriptions, or worse.

"Those days are behind me," thinks Maria as she drives to Sooke, B.C. for the second time that month to see her old friend from California. Once again she turns right on Sooke River Road and finds herself near the Sooke Potholes. "I'm seeing more of this island in the last few weeks, than I have the whole time I've lived here," thinks Maria as she pulls into the driveway of Jordan's cottage.

Maria steps out of her car and heads towards the front door where Jordan is standing, waiting to greet her.

"So nice to see you again," says Maria, handing Jordan a gift of tea.

"Yes, come on in. Let me introduce you to my husband and daughter."

"Hello, she says. "I've heard so much about you over the years and have seen you walk around in the background sometimes during our calls. It's nice to finally meet you. Welcome to Canada."

Maria smiles knowing that Jordan had her fourth child at the age of 46 and loves seeing a real life woman who had a healthy child in her mid-forties (like Sarah, wife of Abraham, and Elizabeth, mother of John the Baptist). Now Jordan's daughter is a teenager, who is looking at her options and is getting ready to fly the nest.

After about an hour of visiting, Maria and Jordan go for a walk in the forest, in a completely different section of the park from her earlier visit with her brother and nephew.

"Have you talked to Michelle at all?" asks Jordan.

"No, I haven't though I'm still connected to her. I've come to realize the role she played in my life's journey."

As an English major, Maria is interested, more than just casually, in how good stories are told. When she had the chance to explore the archetypes of the hero's journey, she was able to understand the deeper meaning behind Michelle's seeming betrayal.

"See, in the hero's journey, certain characters show up in pivotal moments. There's the herald who delivers the call or message," starts Maria counting on her fingers. "The psychic who gives prophetic news, the enemy who stands in the way and makes things really difficult…"

"I'm with you so far." "

The shapeshifter who bounces between worlds and has questionable allegiances, the coach-mentor who gives guidance but cannot go on the journey with their clients… let's see, who else? Oh yes… the trickster who brings comedy relief, the love interest who makes it all worthwhile, and an ally – because everybody needs a friend."

"Wow. That's quite a list. Was Michelle the coach-mentor?" asks Jordan with furrowed brows.

"Sort of, but there's a shadow side that can come into play, too."

"Oh."

"And by firing me from her life, probably in an effort to save herself and not get pulled down with me, she showed me a negative example of coaching. Now I know the hard way that I don't want to be a coach like that."

"Me neither."

"Yes, and I'm a better coach for it because now I have compassion, especially for people who are really struggling. And on top of that, I can ask myself, 'What character am I playing in someone else's life? Am I the enemy? Am I an ally?'"

"I'd like to think I'm the coach, giving guidance and wisdom."

"And you do... from your yurt," says Maria with levity.

"I do love my yurt," says Jordan wistfully. "I'd rather be the soft place for someone to fall than an obstacle and I'm certainly not going to bail on someone in their darkest hour."

As they keep walking along the wide forest path of the Galloping Goose trail, both Maria and Jordan have lost track of time.

Eventually, they come upon the Todd Creek Trestle, a 100 year-old curved, wooden trestle bridge that was originally built for trains. The viaduct spans 113 metres in length across the valley below and stands 21 metres tall at its highest point. The crisscrossing wooden beams look impressive, but the structure is a little worse for wear.

"This is probably a good place to turn around," Jordan says.

Their conversation braids like tree roots along the ground, from Maria quitting her job at the Inn, to Jordan's Buddhist practice, to health supplements and moving to Portland, to Zoryanna understandably preferring to go shopping with her friends rather than do the family thing, to Shirley McLean, to how Maria's plans for her Camino are coming together. They talk about everything under the sun – everything except Maria's recent encounter with Nick a couple of weeks earlier, even though Jordan was all too familiar with the topic.

The wind starts flaring up in unusually strong gusts, as if Maria and Jordan have stumbled onto another path in another dimension.

Up ahead, Maria spots something blue on the ground. Before she has a chance to walk the twenty steps or so to investigate more closely, a guy comes out of nowhere from behind on his bicycle and picks up the parcel as if he is playing Cricket.

He turns around for a second and asks while holding something up in the air, "Does this belong to either of you?"

"No," says Jordan.

"OK, great! This cash is mine then," and he takes off down the path like a bullet.

"I thought that was a five dollar bill," Maria says to clarify her currency for her American friend. "The Canadian fives are blue."

"I couldn't see what it was. It all happened so fast."

"Something tells me that little gift was supposed to be for us. I think I have a belief that when I have my eye on something and really want it, someone else is going to butt in line and beat me to it, just like that guy. I really need to stop that way of thinking because I'm missing out at the last second."

"Yes, that's a topic we can coach on for sure."

mist • tickle

"Does butter, fly? Do bees, be?" Maria fondly recalls David Addison asking on "Moonlighting." When winged creatures like butterflies, bees, birds, owls, and dragonflies light into Maria's awareness, she intuitively knows they are angels in disguise. They often fly overhead, flutter nearby, or call out to try to remind her to look up, cheer up, and keep the faith.

In a seeming contradiction to her own nature, Maria often copes with stress by becoming even more resourceful and creative than usual. The harder she gets pushed beyond her limits, the more her creative juices flow.

Maria knows by studying new age philosophy and following the odd guru, she has to see and feel her hopes, dreams, and desires as done deals in her imagination first, before they can show up in her present reality.

Maria has long used vision boards as tools to help lift her dreams off the ground but instead of cutting and pasting pictures from magazines into old school scrapbooks, she adds inspiring artwork and quotes to her Pinterest boards, a neater and more portable solution.

One of her boards, "Purple Butterflies," is supposed to bring in the love of her life. Her idea for the board comes from reading a blog post about Twin Flames, an esoteric concept that alleges a mystical connection between two people who live in separate bodies, but who share the same soul.

"The whole idea of Twin Flames actually comes from Plato of all people," she remembers reading somewhere. In "Symposium," Plato is the one who introduces the idea that early humans were two people living in one body, with two heads, four arms and four legs.

Apparently, sharing a space made humans blissfully happy and confident. But Zeus would not have it and split the humans in two, flinging them in opposite directions, forcing an eternal quest for a reunion of souls.

Love is born into every human being; it calls back the halves of our original nature together; it tries to make one out of two and heal the wound of human nature
~ Plato, Symposium

Twin Flames are beyond soulmates in the sense that they are not just passengers riding on the same train, who meet each other en route and share a few laughs. Twin Flames are the same passenger, travelling in two bodies, holding the intention of reuniting as one higher self in this physical world, somewhere down the track.

As a Gemini, Maria does not question the idea of having a spiritual twin, a divine masculine complement to her divine feminine form, who is floating out there somewhere in the Universe, entangled to her by ribbons of light and love.

Maria senses her twin is hovering in her orbit and hopes this high-tech vision board will be the magic that brings him full frontal into her life for good.

"And when the twins reunite, it's the greatest love story of all time – that's what I want!" she dreams.

In spite of only receiving breadcrumbs from Nick, Maria is curious if he is indeed her Twin Flame as she hopes, or if he is just a cosmic case of wishful thinking. She searches the internet and finds a blog post where the author gives a "fool proof" method to see if someone is your Twin Flame or not.

The test is based on the premise of believing first and seeing second and it involves noticing signs that can show up suddenly, out of the blue.

"This is like the song, 'Tie A Yellow Ribbon Round The Old Oak Tree,' by Tony Orlando & Dawn," thinks Maria as she reads the post. The yellow ribbon is a secret love note!

The instructions state that in the first step, Maria has to pick a sign that represents her relationship with her heart's desire (in her case, Nick). The sign has to be rare on the one hand and not so preposterous that it is completely out of range, on the other.

Maria chooses "purple butterflies" as her sign because "butterfly" is a code word that has flown between them more than once and purple is her favourite colour.

Metaphorically, butterflies are the epitome of transformation. They are unique beings in nature who are born as caterpillars and crawl along the ground, but eventually, by miracle and spending time alone in a dark, chrysalis, they eventually emerge as butterflies, flying through the air on their own gossamer wings.

"Mother Nature has some pretty cool tricks up her sleeve."

Nick once asked Maria, "What's not safe about being a butterfly?" when she was talking about how wonderful it would be to lightly fly from flower to flower, sharing a joyful connection in the sunshine.

From Nick's deep and powerful question, Maria realized she did not want to lose the work she had already spent so much time on, of uprooting her own, familiar garden, of losing her connection to the past. It was the fear of loss that was not safe. It was the fear of letting go of the old self, the caterpillar self, that was keeping her stuck.

Since that day, Maria developed a new affinity for butterflies and even tested Nick once to see if the next time they spoke, he would use the word "butterfly" at all in their conversation, without any hints, coaxing, or prompting from her.

As it turned out, Nick said "butterfly, butterfly, butterfly" and Maria was thrilled!

The second step in the Twin Flame sign test involves writing an email asking the Universe to send the specific sign three times in the next three days to confirm if the man in question is indeed her own Twin Flame. Quickly, Maria hops to it and sends herself the following email:

Subject: Purple Butterflies

Dear God, I ask for a reminder out of my trust rather than a sign out of my need. If I'm on the right track today, send me a sign of confirmation to let me know that you support my efforts to reunite with my true love. I'm looking forward to your creativity so that I'll be inspired to keep going. The sign I choose is a purple butterfly. Thank you, God, for showing me a purple butterfly three times in the next three days if Nick Walker is my Twin Flame. I trust you will confirm that he is my Twin Flame and that we will be together in this physical dimension shortly! With love and thanks, Maria Ponomarenko

After sending the email to herself, the third and hardest step involves trust. Maria has to trust the sign will show up in Divine

Time without actively looking for it. She has to trust that the Universe wants a Twin Flame reunion just as much as she does, if not more, because Twin Flame couples play an important role in lifting the consciousness of humanity.

Much to Maria's relief and staying true to the song – and without searching for any purple butterflies online yet – the experiment is a success!

Now the whole damned bus is cheerin'
And I can't believe I see
A hundred yellow ribbons
round the ole oak tree!

Maria notices all kinds of purple butterflies in her field! She comes across purple butterfly motifs on stickers, on a throw blanket, and on a shirt. She also finds a necklace with matching earrings her father had given her of butterflies embellished with Amethyst gems.

She steps outside and spots two grey-purple butterflies dancing and spiraling together in her yard and picks up a brochure that was just laying around in her garage from Butterfly Gardens, a tropical jungle for kids and tourists, up near Butchart.

Maria also finds the quote, "You cannot speak butterfly language with caterpillar people," set against a background of blue and purple butterflies.

Also, during this three-day period, Maria's friend, Kvitka, posts an aerial photo by Andrew Makarenko of Synevir Lake in Ukraine on her page. Synevir Lake is one of Ukraine's seven natural wonders and is the largest lake in the Carpathian Mountains. Forests surrounding the lake are 140 to 160 years old, and the water that fills the lake is indeed a blue shade of purple, and the border of the lake itself is unmistakably shaped like a butterfly.

On top of that, after searching the yellow ribbon song for fun, Maria is delighted to find an old video of Tony performing on a purple stage, with his two backup singers swaying on either side of him, wearing glamorous white feathered gowns, and the three of them look very much like a fluttering butterfly!

"I guess that answers that," thinks Maria and although she does not need to expand her scope beyond "purple" or "butterfly" to get her initial three signs, she does eventually include angels, hummingbirds, dragonflies, and abstract art, in a range of colours from pale lavender, to blue, to indigo, to deep violet into her collection of evidence and on to her digital vision board.

* * *

Maria is spending much of her time indoors because so far, July in Victoria has turned out to be unusually rainy. The pouring rain is a welcomed relief from the previous three summers which had been very dry indeed, with tinder conditions leading to forest fires.

Yes, thankfully, this summer, the fires have not cast a disturbing haze of orange across the sky, fooling the brain and tinkering with its natural bio-rhythms. No, this summer is very wet.

On this particularly rainy afternoon, Maria is feeling drained and tired. She decides to take a break from working on her laptop and take a nap like a cat. She also thinks it may be nice to listen to one of Dr. Oscar Boshon's interviews during her quiet time.

"Why not turn on the ol' Himalayan salt lamp, too?" she suggests to herself.

The topic of the interview is about how we create our lives and attract miracles and how everyday people are learning to connect to the quantum field where they are beginning to change their environments, without physical force or manipulation.

The quantum field is described as a field of energy that expands across the universe, that is filled with nothing but possibilities and potentials, like the indigo space between the golden stars in the night sky.

And when a person is able to connect with this field by getting past their false and superficial selves, and peel the layers off their cumbersome packaging, and come from a place of love and gratitude, and open their eyes to the possibilities that are everywhere, their lives will be enriched, their minds and bodies will be healed, their dreams will come true, and even a mystical experience may find them.

"How do I have my own mystical experience?" thinks Maria as she looks outside her bedroom window at the rain.

In that moment, without her knowledge, just by asking that question, Maria sets a chain of events in motion that will create what she wants.

As soon as the interview is over, Maria is inspired to go for a walk outside in the pouring rain. She has to wear her thick purple raincoat because the downpour is that heavy.

"I'm going to train for my Camino," she says to her mother over her shoulder as she steps out the door.

With her hood over her head, Maria tunes into the hollow tapping sound of the rain as it lands on the green leaves, the pavement, and her jacket. The chunky raindrops sound like they are the size of egg yolks and feel cool as they splash down on her hands and face.

As she walks down her familiar street, she keeps her head down and her eyes to the ground to avoid any puddles. The road banks left at the top of the hill where her mother's car had once gotten stuck in the snow, and from this vantage point, she sees two streams of rainwater flowing toward the main street below.

She chooses to stay along the rock wall to the right, admiring the pink flowers tended by her neighbours. On this stretch of road, the tall trees on the steep slope offer some protection from the rain but even within just a few minutes of being outside, Maria's coat is already drenched.

One more step with her left foot and she would have been sorry, but instead, she catches herself at the last second.

There he is, a purple dragonfly, sitting on the side of the road, about a foot from the retaining wall.

He is still moving but is not able to get himself off the driveway to safety. She can see the poor thing is struggling, so she bends down and places her right hand on the cold road next to him. To her surprise, the dragonfly crawls onboard.

"Oh, oh, oh," she says as she stands up, the dragonfly clinging to her wet index finger.

She places her hand on the brown earth, thinking the dragonfly will just march off and she will continue on her walk. But he does not. The purple dragonfly stays on her hand!

She points him towards a pink flower. "Maybe you'll like it better here," she says to him. Still, he does not budge.

"Come on Love. It's okay," she coaxes, but the dragonfly stays put.

"Oh dear… you can't fly, can you? Your wings are soaking wet… too heavy to fly."

So Maria remains there, at the side of the driveway, with a living dragonfly on her hand and rain dripping from her nose, for several long minutes.

"What am I going to do?"

Everything else in her environment has faded away and she is now in a bubble with a dragonfly. No one else is around and no cars pass. All she can do is study him close-up and personal and what a beauty he is!

The dragonfly is the size of a doorknob, fitting neatly into her palm. His tissue paper wings are a soft grey-lavender and have bold, black stripes across the span. Every minute or so, he flutters his wings to try to lift himself up to fly, but his efforts are frustrated. Maria feels a slight tickle from the current from his tiny feet as he steps lightly on her rain-drenched skin.

"I have to get you out of the rain," she thinks. "I'll take you to the mailboxes because at least they're under a little bit of a roof."

So, Maria turns around and heads back towards home, transporting her little friend in tow, keeping her eyes glued on him so he does not fall off. The mailboxes are banked further up the wall and are protected by trees in behind and have a wooden roof overhead. Maria rests her hand on the cabinets to let the dragonfly off but still he does not leave her hand.

Maria keeps repeating, "You'll be okay. Keep going. You're doing great. I love you. You're beautiful and you can fly!" The dragonfly tries to take off but cannot get any lift. "I guess I'm going to have to take you all the way home with me."

Within a few steps down the cul de sac, Maria opens the gate to the courtyard entrance of her home. She pushes the front door open and calls to her mother: "Mam, can you get my phone from my night table? I need you to take a photo for me."

Curious, Lubomyra puts down her sewing project and comes to the front door right away.

"Look," says Maria, gesturing with her hand. "I found a dragonfly."

"Oh, he's beautiful," says Lubomyra. "I'll be right back."

"And a video, too!"

After Lubomyra goes back into the house, Maria sends some healing energy to her dragonfly friend.

"I connect to the Angels of the animal kingdom, especially Archangel Ariel. Please let me be a pure, clear, channel of your loving and healing energy. Please bring this purple dragonfly the loving and healing energy he needs to fly again. Thank you, Amen."

By then the rain has let up somewhat. Lubomyra returns with Maria's phone and zooms in with the camera. She successfully captures the purple dragonfly on video with Maria's purple raincoat in the background.

Maria turns toward the green and yellow Rhododendron shrub that is growing in the corner of the front courtyard. She extends her hand and with the help of her prayer, the dragonfly steps off and lands on one of the leaves that is sheltered under the canopy of the neighbours' roof and the rest of the shrub.

Maria and her mother sigh with relief. They leave the dragonfly to sleep off his big adventure.

Every few hours, Lubomyra asks, "Is the dragonfly still there?"

"Yes," Maria says, glancing at his spot through the French door windows, trying not to worry. "He hasn't moved at all."

The next day, Mary-Jo comes over to meet him. "Oh, he's just drying off," she says. "He'll be okay."

"I hope so," says Maria.

Finally, on the third day, when Maria looks into the leaves first thing in the morning, the dragonfly is gone. He is strong enough to fly again! "Thank you, God! He made it!"

Maria is happy her dragonfly is able to fly again but she is also sad he is gone. On that bittersweet note, she reminds herself of a folk song she learned when she was seven at summer camp, called "Volya," which means "freedom" in Ukrainian (a song that was later recorded by Luba before she became known for "Every Time I See Your Picture I Cry").

I saw a bird who had fallen from her nest
Poor thing was lying there, crying in the snow
A little boy helped her and the little bird was healed
Soon she forgot him and flew into the spring
The boy could not forgive the bird for leaving him
He did not understand the song in the wind
That freedom is the natural song of all birds
And that's how, my darling, I also must live

* * *

Maria is finally ready to take Father Odyn's suggestion and reach out to Nick to ask him how he feels about her. She calls him on the phone and leaves a message.

"Hey, Nick. Just wondering how you're doing. Would you like to talk sometime and catch up?"

On that evening, Lubomyra has gone to Whistler with Krys and his family, so Maria has the house to herself. To pass the time as she waits for Nick to call back, she has her first dance party since Easter.

"June 21st, that's going to be tonight's playlist."

Maria thinks June 21 would be a nice day for a white wedding, so she has a playlist with all of her favourite wedding reception songs that guarantee a packed dance floor. For more than two hours, she dances non-stop in her bedroom as if she is the bride at her wedding and works up such a sweat, that she has to take a second shower that day.

Nick does not return her call that night but the next day, he sends her a text:

> Sorry I missed you.
> How are you?
>
> I'm OK. How are you?
>
> I am good.
> Finally stopped raining here.
> We have had rain almost
> every day since June 1st.

Glad to hear the sun is
shining again.
We had lots of rain too and
I found a dragonfly
who got too wet to fly so
I took him home and
nursed him back to health
and then he flew away.
There's a video on my FB.

That sounds amazing.

It was a very spiritual
experience for me.
I felt like we were
communicating.

We put dragonflies on
our hats now.

Nick sends a picture of his fisherman's cap topped with a pin of a
yellow dragonfly. His pin reminds Maria of her own yellow
dragonfly pin that had been stashed away in one of her jewellery
boxes since childhood.

That's sweet. Why do you
do that?

Dragonflies are very special.
It has been a thing of mine
since I was small.
There is something about
them I don't understand.

That's so lovely. Let me
try to send you my video.

Maria sends Nick the video of her encounter with a dragonfly.

> That's amazing.
> Good for you.
> You are a kind soul.
>
> Thanks. Well, thank you for
> sharing about dragonflies
> with me. I hope you have a
> fun Monday.
>
> Thank you. Getting ready
> to teach a class. Be well.
> Go fly.

Yes. Thank you! I'm smiling.

rock • hound

Maria is pleasantly surprised to see references to the world of crystals in the opening chapter of Dr. Oscar Boshon's new book, "MegaGravity."
"Since the dawn of time, the energy of life has been coursing through the Universe, creating a spectacular and dynamic cacophony for all of us to behold. Yes, even crystals have energy!"

"That's been my experience," she says.

"Rocks are powerful," her favourite geologist and the only one she can name, continues. "And believe it or not, they too have a chance to become enlightened. Depending on their mineral composition and environment, and if they can endure the intense pressure-cooker conditions they are sitting in, it is possible for their molecular structure to change. Their work is hidden behind the scenes, but eventually rocks can transform into crystals and go from solid to transparent, from heavy to light. I like to call them, 'geological beings of enlightenment.'"

Maria pictures orange explosions in outer space turning into twinkling diamonds.

"If rocks can go through a transformation, we can too! Nature is so inspiring!" she says as she slams her book shut and exhales.

The more time Maria spends learning about geology, quantum physics, and spirituality and the more often she goes walking in the great outdoors, the more she becomes interested in the mystery of life on our planet. Suddenly flowers are more delicate, trees are more friendly, oceans are more connecting, mountains are more open, and animals are more curious.

Though they are the latest to arrive to Maria's party, crystals, rocks, minerals and seashells, are no exception – and unexpectedly for Maria, rocks and stones feel alive!

"There's a life force inside that is driving this whole she-bang!" she exclaims. "What makes our planet spin on its axis and along the same track around the sun, day in and day out? What makes mountains move and bunch up? Where do waves start?"

Maria is starting to recognize that rocks are not just solid and chunky pieces of grey earth rolling around in the dirt, they actually have their own stories to tell. Like, for example, Maria is surprised to find out that rocks have the ability to actually move on their own! Sometimes moonlight and ocean waves come into play and help move the rocks along, but after talking with some farmers, she also knows that each spring, they have to clear the fields of heavy rocks that were not there the season before, that have somehow risen to the surface over the winter, against the pull of gravity.

Then the algorithm leads Maria to the Guardian's headline from May, 2017 that reads: "Irish Beach Washed Away 33 Years Ago Reappears Overnight After Freak Tide."

"Whaaat? Let me read that again."

In this case, the miracle did not take tens of thousands of years of incremental changes to be observed — the miracle happened literally overnight after a freak tide rearranged the furniture, so to speak, shortly before Easter, in a little place called, Dooagh, Achill Island, in Ireland.

One morning, the islanders woke up to find the golden sand that had been washed away by storms in 1984 (and had been replaced by rocks and rock pools for the next 33 years), had suddenly returned home, like the Prodigal Son, without the help of human intervention.

"Don't tell me rocks don't have a life force," thinks Maria to herself as she reads the article.

After she closes out the page on her laptop, Maria quickly gravitates to her kaleidoscopic collection of crystals, gemstones, seashells, and rocks. She picks up one of her clear quartz crystals.

As she holds the crystal with the point facing down between her index finger and thumb, and brings it up to the light, she can see right through it, as if looking through a window.Inside the clear cut crystal, she sees lines and angles into a whole new world. Maria closes her eyes. The crystal is vibrating ever so slightly in her palm.

"Yes, it does have a presence, just like Dr. Oscar said."

Maria imagines she is being transported inside the illuminated crystal and walks around, admiring the glassy walls of light surrounding her. She has learned this technique from Jordan, who learned it from the infamous Shirley MacLaine, (another lefty).

"What do you want to tell me, Crystal?" she says while gazing into her mind's eye. "I see an angel with wings outstretched, facing me. How lovely!"

The word "crystal" is a word originally coined by the Greeks who found dazzling, spiked clusters of quartz during their expeditions in the Swiss Alps. They believed these sparkling natural wonders were actually a form of frozen water that would never thaw, so they named them, *krystallos*, which means "ice."

Maria is aware that human beings have been using mesmerizing crystals as practical tools and in metaphysical healing rituals since the Paleolithic Era, (also known as the Stone Age).

Maria also knows she is in good company in regards to her affinity for crystals and gemstones even though there is also a tacit woo-wooness about them.

Deep down, she understands there is a certain universal quality about the mineral kingdom that draws people to pick up rocks or seashells while walking on a path or beach, or wear a piece of gemstone jewellery that holds a special, personal meaning for them.

Then there are the people like Maria who just buy the rocks, that may or may not have been tumbled and smoothed out, for no reason other than, they just 'speak' to them.

"I think I'll do my Patchouli tour today. Maybe I'll find a Double Terminated Quartz Crystal, which will allow me to send and receive energy at the same time in my meditations."

On days when she feels particularly inspired, Maria likes to go on what she calls a "Patchouli Shop Tour" which always leaves her clothes smelling like incense.

She drives downtown and parks in the centrally-located View Street parkade. From there, she walks to Broad Street and pops into the bead shop for a minute. Then she heads down Johnson Street towards the bridge and visits the Avalon Book Store that is tucked in the far corner of the touristy, though haunted, Market Square.

On previous visits, Avalon was the store where Maria bought her red Jasper, orange Sunstone, yellow Citrine, Yellow Butterfly Jasper, Green Aventurine, Blue Quartz, blue and gold Lapis Lazuli, and purple Amethyst.

After reading the write-ups for some selected gemstones and crystals and chatting with the shop keeper about Geodes, (which are much like *Piñatas* once broken open) Maria cuts across to Pandora and finds the 'secret/not so secret' entrance to Fan Tan Alley, Canada's narrowest street, which at its most tapered point, is only 0.9 meters (or 35 inches wide), and is a bridge to Chinatown.

Victoria's Chinatown broke ground in the mid-1850's as a gambling district with restaurants, shops, and Opium dens, accommodating gold rush miners and prospectors from California and beyond.

Walking through Fan Tan Alley with its high, red brick walls is trippy for Maria. The Alley was named after the Chinese gambling game, Fan-Tan, and the energy of the tunnel-like hallway always makes Maria feel uneasy.

Nevertheless, it is a shortcut into Canada's oldest, and North America's second oldest, Chinatown (after San Francisco), so Maria takes her chances and braves through it. Plus, she likes to deke into Triple Spiral Metaphysical while inside. Maria cannot find anything that catches her eye in the crowded, tiny shop in the alley, so she carries on towards Fisgard, a street flagged at Government by the Gate of Harmonious Interest.

When she pops out on the other side of history, she lands on a bustling street that is bulging with fresh vegetable stands and trendy brunch spots. People from all corners of the world are going about their business, speaking in transoceanic languages, and adding their own flavours and spices to the city's soup pot.

Across the street, Maria spots one of her favourite shops, Bamboo Beads & Bling. Bamboo is where she bought her powerful, swirly, green Malachite, which should only be held occasionally because of its potency. On other visits, she bought a cheery, apple green Chrysoprase cabochon that would make a lovely pendant, as well as her creamy blue Angelite that rolled by itself on the tray as if to say, "pick me, pick me!" so of course, she did.

She likes the store because they weigh the gemstones to calculate the price, which is a nice, jeweller's touch. Also, when Maria was buying her pink Morganite in yet another attempt to bring Nick into her life, the shop keeper encouragingly said, "We [men] are starting to awaken."

Unfortunately, this visit to her lucky store does not pan out this time. As she heads back to her car, this time walking back to the parking lot through Centennial Square, she thinks of one more place to visit today.

"Rockhound, near Mayfair Mall is where I'll go next."

The Rockhound Shop is a family-run business that has been selling rocks, crystals, fossils, prospecting supplies, lapidary tools and jewellery-making accessories to the people of Victoria since 1967.

A "rockhound" is a geologist or amateur collector of rocks and minerals and a "lapidary" is a person who cuts, polishes or engraves gems.

Here, over the last couple of years, Maria has found a heart-shaped Green Aventurine pendant that she gave to her mother as well as a piece of blue Sodalite that she gave to Olivia for Christmas. She also found a heavy piece of Pyrite which she gave to Krys, to remind him of the Fool's Gold they used to dig up in their unpaved driveway in Nova Scotia.

Maria also gives credit to Rockhound for teaching her about a local stone called, Dallasite, a black and white stone named after the picturesque beach along Dallas Road in Victoria where the rock was originally discovered. She has her own piece of Dallasite, which is almost shaped like an Italian boot. She likes how on the one hand, it helps release negativity, and on the other hand, it increases and provides "more" to any aspect of life, including abundance, love, and intuition.

As Maria slowly makes her way through the store, peering into every cabinet and not overlooking a single shelf, she spots a real treasure! Although it is not a double-ended arrow like she originally wanted, it does have two points coming from two crystals growing side-by-side together from the same base, a crystal configuration known as a Twin, Tantric Twin or Soulmate crystal. On top of that, it is a beautiful, orange colour.

"This is what I've been looking for today!" says Maria as she heads to the counter to pay the sticker price of $14, which is a little steep for her rock budget, but worth the splurge anyway.

"Where did you find this beauty?" asks the shop owner wondering how he missed this one in the inventory.

"Just over there behind the glass shelf," replies Maria catching the thought that perhaps the orange, twin-peaked crystal had been placed there just for her eyes.

"Can you tell me a little bit about the colour?"

"Yes, it's a Tangerine Quartz most likely from Brazil. It gets its colour from the Iron Oxide – also known as Hematite – in the water.

"Oh, I know Hematite – it's the heavy silver one. I've seen pictures taken with a powerful microscope that show big red dots in its structure," says Maria.

"That's it. Almost like blood or hemoglobin. That's where it gets its name."

"Yes!" says Maria picking up her purchase from the counter. "Thanks!"

When she gets home, she looks up "Tangerine Quartz" on the Internet and is happy to see it works well with the feminine and creative energies of the Sacral Chakra. Maria hopes her newest crystal will help her unite with her twin, build her strength, put the past behind her, and emerge as an entirely new being.

"Just like the butterflies, just like the beach in Ireland, and just like the crystals!" she says while bringing the Tangerine Quartz closer to her heart and looking outside her window at the vast blue sky above the trees.

The Tangerine Quartz has its work cut out for it.

whirl • pool

The intermittent whirling motor of Lubomyra's sewing machine underscores the pitter-patter of the raindrops landing on the roof in an almost complementary way. Maria is sitting at the head of the dining room table with her laptop, trying to write a blog post about Ammolite, a rare treasure that has the unique honour of being both a fossil and a gemstone at the same time.

Ammolite is a flashy, Opal-like organic gemstone, that runs the full range of the visible colour spectrum from red, to yellow, to green, to indigo, and is found primarily along the eastern slopes of the Rocky Mountains of North America, more specifically from a small area along the St. Mary River in southwestern Alberta, Canada.

Ammolite is made of Ammonites, and Ammonites were fossilized sea creatures that lived about 70 to 75 million years ago in their ribbed, spiraling shells, under an enormous body of water, which is now known as the "Western Interior Seaway."

"It's hard to believe that whole area from the Arctic Ocean all the way down to the Gulf of Mexico was once underwater," thinks Maria as she reads more articles online.

In the days when the Rocky Mountains were young and peaking, rains washed sediments that contained many forms of life, including fish and sharks with interior skeletons, mixed in with crustaceans, sea turtles, and ammonites with exterior skeletons, into the seaway. These sediments, along with sandstone and volcanic ash, compressed and eventually formed a dense layer of rock in the earth's crust, known as the "Bearpaw Formation."

People have found spiraling Ammonite fossils as big as one meter in diameter, but most have been measured at about a quarter to half that size.

"That's huge!" says Maria outloud.

The spiral of the Ammonite's tightly-coiled shell, which is similar to the Nautilus, has its own significance in the scientific world. With each turn and notch along their unfolding and expanding pattern, spirals represent the creative nature of the Universe itself – all the way down to the math!

Spirals are the actual living representations of the Fibonacci Sequence of 1, 1, 2, 3, 5, 8, 13, 21, 34, etc., which is calculated by adding the previous two numbers together to determine the next number. Fibonacci's incremental sequence, that curves around a never-ending central point, building on itself into infinity, is a pattern that has been splashing itself all over nature as spinning galaxies, cresting waves, whirlpools, hurricanes, tornadoes, ferns, snakes, snails, seashells, curly hair, and even fingerprints since the moment of the Big Bang!

"Oh, and look, the word, "spiral" is built right into the word, "spiritual," notices Maria, her eyes coming in and out of focus on the words.

Spirals live in the space between science and religion and in a fleeting moment of lucidity, Maria can see it all. A spiralling cycle of creation, from birth… to growth… to destruction and ending… to transformation, transcendence, and taking an evolutionary leap… to rebirth and back to the beginning on a whole new level… and on and on. Her thoughts rub together like clothes in a washing machine.

"I think I'm on to something!"

Maria's blog post is coming along nicely. To accompany her story, Maria wants to take a photo of her Ammolite ring. She grabs a few props from the hutch and heads to her washroom because the natural light coming in from the skylight would be helpful.

She rests her Ammolite ring on to a silver trivet on the counter, but the automatic focus function is not landing on anything. Every time Maria presses the button halfway, the lens keeps zooming in and out, back and forth, without a clear image in sight to capture.

She stands on the toilet seat, she stands on the counter, she stands on one foot and tries to bring the camera closer to the ring, then farther away, then overhead. Nothing is working. She steps back on the floor and while bending at the knee from counter height, she clicks the shutter.

"Finally, the focus locked in!"

Quickly, Maria downloads the image of her Ammolite ring onto her laptop and when she views her photo, she gasps!

"There's an angel living in my ring, clear as day!" says Maria while admiring her photo. "It's a white angel with wings and everything… like a Christmas tree ornament. No wonder I was having such trouble focusing! The angel was too bright and fast for the lens to lock on! So amazing!"

Maria's Ammolite ring is already showing up powerfully on that Sunday afternoon in July but there is another miracle to come. As she puts the finishing touches on her blog post, suddenly, she starts to smell the sulphuric odour of gas. At first, she brushes it off and carries on with her writing, but after a few sniffs, it becomes too distracting.

"Has one of the gas burners on the stove been left on accidently?" thinks Maria as she checks the kitchen. "No… Was the fireplace on? No… Mam…" she calls down the stairs, "Do you smell gas?"

"No," says Lubomyra.

"I think I can smell something."

"Let me check," says Lubomyra as she gets up from her sewing machine and walks toward the gas furnace in the crawl space.

"Yes, I can smell gas, too."

"Oh dear, what do we do?" asks Maria.

"Well, open up the windows and doors…"

"And I'll call the fire department." She picks up the landline and presses 9-1-1.

"Police, ambulance or fire?"

"Um, fire, I guess," says Maria.

"What is your emergency?"

"I smell gas in my house."

"How many people are in your house?"

"Two. Just me and my mom."

"Anyone injured or feeling dizzy?"

"No."

"Fire has been dispatched. Please step outside and leave your doors open and wait for us there."

"Thanks."

The rain lets up. Maria and Lubomyra stand on the driveway in silence. Within a few short minutes, they hear the sirens racing towards their house. Maria wonders how the big red truck will make it up the narrow street, but it does.

"You say you smell gas?"

"Yes," says Lubomyra.

"Do you have a gas fireplace?"

"Yes."

"Is it turned on?"

"Just the pilot light."

"Okay. We'll shut that off. Gas furnace?"

"Yes, it's fairly new. We just had it replaced a couple of Christmases ago."

"We'll check everything out," says the Captain as he enters the house.

"Oh, he was cute," says Lubomyra.

"Of course the firefighters are cute," says Maria. "It's part of their job description. Everybody knows that."

"Remember that Christmas a couple of years ago how the guy who replaced the furnace said it was just a matter of days or hours before it could have blown up and we caught it just in the nick of time?" says Lubomyra.

"And you were the one who noticed it just by chance as you were walking by it."

"Yes, all of that yellow oozy stuff coming out from the top of the tank caught my eye."

"Thank goodness."

"And we almost couldn't get anybody in to fix it because it was December 22, maybe even the 23rd and the weather was bad."

"That was close. Something about that furnace, Mam… another miracle. Maybe this special protection has something to do with Father blessing our house by candlelight and holy water every January."

The Captain returns to give them an update.

"We've shut off the gas. You will need to call someone to check it and turn it back on. It might take a few days so you won't have any hot water for a while. Better use whatever's left in the tank while it's still hot. We've also put an industrial fan in the entry to clear the air. Just leave that on for about a half-hour. Everything seems to be okay and you can go back inside.

"Thank you so much," says Lubomyra. "And thank you for coming so quickly."

"Yes, thanks for your service," says Maria and then asks herself, "Was that the firefighter I interviewed 20 years ago for a story in the *Peninsula News Review?*

"I can hear the fan from here," says Lubomyra as they walk back into the house.

"Wow, that feels really strong… it could fly a jet!"

"Thanks for noticing that smell, Marichka. That could have ended much differently if it happened in the middle of the night or something."

"Thank you, angels," says Maria in her head while admiring her ring.

WHY AMMOLITE INSPIRES ME!

by Maria Ponomarenko, Ammolite Wellness Coach

I am wearing my Ammolite ring as I write this post. I love my Ammolite ring because I feel I was in the flow state when I bought it. I went to a Gem Show a couple of years ago at the Pearkes Recreation Centre in Saanich, BC.

I remember when I first entered the space on the Saturday morning in August, the room was just buzzing! All of the people were in good spirits and it was as if all of the gemstones and crystals were waking up!

I didn't know what I was looking for exactly at the Gem Show so I just kept my mind open to whatever jumped out at me. When I go to these types of shows, I like to start at one end and go through all of the booths, one by one, in order, all around the large room to see everything first before I narrow down my decisions.

Somewhere in the middle of the room, there was a man selling loose, polished Ammolite gemstones for custom jewellery.

I had heard about Ammolites before from my friend, Mary-Jo, who wore her Ammolite necklace one day and I asked her about it because it was so colourful, unique, and lovely. She said "it's from Alberta" and she bought her jewell as a present for herself to celebrate her 50th birthday!

I made a note of the name, "Ammolite," for future reference.

Meanwhile, before I left for the gem show, my mother gave me a gold ring setting that didn't have any stone in it, to see if I could find something for it.

She said it used to have an unknown pink stone inside but when she had it cleaned, sadly, the pink crystal disintegrated! Afterwards, the naked ring sat in her jewellery box for years, waiting for a second chance to shine.

The gold ring itself has its own history. According to my mother, her parents somehow procured the ring while they were living in a displaced persons camp in Austria in the 1940s after WWII, while they were en route to immigrate to Canada.

So, my gold ring is an antique and has an ancestral tie to my family and I am grateful for the sacrifices my grandparents made to ensure future generations (i.e. me) could lead a better life.

By the way, because Ammolite is from pre-historic times, it also symbolizes our ancestors!

Anyway, I showed the gold ring to the Ammolite sales rep/jeweller. He thought he may be able to help me find something suitable. As we were looking at the different configurations and picking our favourite combinations, it seemed like the noise around us in the big room hushed and I lost track of time.

I was in the zone.

We looked for colours, shape and size, and I trusted his recommendations. Together, we found a beautiful square-shaped cut that had all of the colours of the rainbow in a pleasing pattern!

But would it fit? What if it cracks? What if the prongs that hold it in place snap off?

The pressure to marry the two pieces together was on!

I held my breath and stared at the ring and the jeweler's nimble hands as he fastened everything in place!

And then it happened! Everything came together beautifully! The Ammolite jeweller carefully inserted the delicate Ammolite gemstone into to gold ring setting. He gently folded the prongs down to secure the stone in place and voila!

A new ring was born! Exhale!

I put my new Ammolite ring on my finger and beamed with delight!

Not only does my Ammolite ring connect me to my grandparents, it also taught me a valuable lesson about how creativity and manifestation work.

Earlier, I said I felt like I was in the flow state while I was buying this ring and I meant that I just let things unfold in their own way without trying to force my ego, or try to control the details, or insist on my own agenda.

I just played it by ear and followed my nose and let whatever wanted to emerge to show up. Not always easy! I felt like I was trusting my intuition as I followed the metaphorical breadcrumbs, and somehow I managed to create this beautiful and powerful Ammolite ring for myself.

The next time you have an opportunity to bring different worlds together and create something new that never existed before, I hope you feel inspired by my Ammolite ring story.

Ammolite inspires me because it's a natural miracle.

The events that were set in motion millions of years ago, that had to take place in order for me to wear this ring today on my finger, are beyond incalculable. It is literally the impossible becoming possible!

womb • man

"Hello everyone, thank you for joining me today on this feast of Mary Magdalene," says Freya, one of Maria's most cherished mentors, to her online audience in a calming and soothing voice.

Freya's name means, "lady" or "noblewoman" and she was named after the Norse Goddess of Love, Beauty, and Fertility. Maria signed up for her, "How To Be A Mobile Spa Queen" class in 2011 and they have stayed in touch ever since, even though they have yet to meet each other in person.

If it was not for Freya teaching Maria about the concept of spa parties, she would never have provided mini manis, mini pedis, mini massages, and mini facials to people from all generations and walks of life, (including kids as young as three and seniors as young as 102), in homes, offices, schools, community centres, hotels, and hospital rooms across the Greater Victoria area.

Although Maria finds spa work too stressful, she does appreciate the nature of the vocation. She is grateful for the trust her clients have given her and views kneeling on the floor to wash people's feet, and then giving them an extraordinary foot massage, as the most sacred of all her services.

To Maria, Freya is an inspiration; she is everything Maria aspires to be – an innovative thinker, a healer, a published author, a successful entrepreneur, and on top of that, Freya is kind, generous, sweet, smart, happily married, healthy and fit – and she likes cats.

Freya is a living example of Maria's ideal self, showing her it is possible to be who she wants to be.

So when Freya announces she would be holding a guided meditation in honour of Mary Magdalene to celebrate her Feast Day on July 22, Maria makes sure she participates.

Freya opens her live video from her cheery, Caribbean blue, beachfront, home office. "I like her pink satin, keyhole blouse… it's so feminine… she has such a relaxed style," Maria notes.

"We're going to be doing a little meditation to connect with Mary Magdalene… I want us to sink in and connect over the ethers as best we can," Freya says. "Close your eyes and sit up tall. Take some deep breaths, breathing in… and breathing out."

Maria gets comfortable in her chair while Freya places a drum on her knee and begins to beat the drum in a low, slow and steady, one, two, three, and four rhythm. Maria tunes into Freya's drumming. One, two, three and four. She pictures four graceful elephants moving across the tundra under a hazy, orange sky.

"Ground your energy through the base of your spine, your root chakra, all the way to the center of the earth, and imagine a white light emerging, shining up through your spine, lighting up all of your chakras one by one, all the way to your crown chakra, creating length in your pose, so your energy is free and open," says Freya as her drumming echoes in the background.

"Take some deep breaths and exhale, breathing in, breathing out. Again breathing in, breathing out." Once the energy settles down to a steady hum, the drumming fades away.

"Place your left hand over your heart...your right hand on top... and send some loving, healing energy into your heart chakra, your alter of love...

"As we sit here," Freya continues, "imagine Mary Magdalene, sitting in front of you. A soft, white glow surrounding her... What would she say to you right now?... Imagine energy emanating from your heart chakra to hers and hers to yours, feeling the love and the light getting bigger and growing brighter...What would she say to you right now?"

In the space of her heart, Maria hears Mary Magdalene say, "You do not have to be married to be loved." A tear comes to her eye.

"Just hold that wisdom and allow any insights that she is sharing with you to come forth into your consciousness. Allow any visions or knowledge to come to the surface...

> *Holy Mary Magdalene, You, whose name has been battered and bruised and tarnished through the centuries, help me to endure the trials in my own life with courage and dignity.*

You, who have loved Jesus so much that you watched his dying breath, teach me to love truly. You, who were pure of heart, cleanse my own wayward ways of pride, arrogance, bitterness, and hard-heartedness.

"Take a deep breath in and exhale. Breathe in and exhale. Breathe in and exhale. When you are ready, slowly come back to the room, to the space... Wiggle your toes, rub your fingers together, and gently open your eyes," says Freya.

As Maria opens her eyes, her vibration is noticeably lighter than it had been in the beginning of the meditation. "I don't have to be married to be loved," Maria recalls in her mind. "That's comforting. All of my life I thought there was something wrong with me because I wasn't married, that I wasn't chosen by some guy. This is really powerful. Thank you Mary Magdalene."

"So who was Mary Magdalene?" asks Freya. "She was likely a very wealthy woman who supported Jesus on his travels and she clearly was very close to Jesus. She has her own gospel, "the Gospel of Mary Magdalene," though some pages are missing."

"What? She had her own gospel? Why have I not heard of this before?" wonders Maria.

For those who have ears, let them hear; for those who have eyes, let them see ~ Mary Magdalene

＊ ＊ ＊

"Talk about strong women in history!"

Mary Magdalene did not walk an easy road. She was known to describe strange visions and ideas and may have been possessed by seven demons before she was healed by Jesus. She was not identified by a father or a husband, as was the custom in her day, and perhaps had acquired her wealth through the world's oldest profession, but that was unknown. She was not portrayed as reliable or relevant, so she had been reduced to a mere footnote in the Bible stories.

The movers and shakers of the Church, the ones who had carefully crafted the doctrines of Christianity, whose cultural biases leaned on men, had missed Mary Magdalene's brilliance entirely.

But who better than a repentant prostitute (if that was part of her journey) to show how it was possible for someone to redeem themselves? And maybe, given the way women were treated and regarded in Jesus' day and even now, that path may have been all that was available to her, but still, somehow she rose above it.

And now, after centuries of living in the shadows of history, the mysterious and mystical Magdalena is finally coming into her own. Her wisdom has come to light in her own Gospel, that had been lost and then recently found again, showing that she has had a very special place in Jesus' heart all along.

"Maybe they did share a physical intimacy, as some say, but that would only make Jesus more human," thinks Maria. "He had to experience life as a man first in all of its aspects... so He could have empathy... and many of those moments would have happened in private. Maybe that's what was written in the missing pages of Mary Magdalene's Gospel?"

Mary Magdalene was so devoted to Jesus, that she followed Him in His ministry and supported Him financially, and as He was dying on the cross and most everyone had deserted Him for fear of being arrested themselves, she stood by Him, next to Mother Mary, and compassionately washed His wounds.

Three days later, when she went to check His tomb and discovered that Jesus' body had vanished, Jesus appeared to Mary Magdalene in a solid, luminary vision.

Jesus Appears to Mary Magdalene

11 Now Mary stood outside the tomb crying. As she wept, she bent over to look into the tomb 12 and saw two angels in white, seated where Jesus' body had been, one at the head and the other at the foot. 13 They asked her, "Woman, why are you crying?" "They have taken my Lord away," she says, "and I don't know where they have put him." 14 At this, she turned around and saw Jesus standing there, but she did not realize that it was Jesus. 15 He asked her, "Woman, why are you crying? Who is it you are looking for?" Thinking he was the gardener, she says, "Sir, if you have carried him away, tell me where you have put him, and I will

get him." 16 Jesus says to her, "Mary." She turned toward him and cried out in Aramaic, "Rabboni!" (which means "Teacher"). 17 Jesus says, "Do not hold on to me, for I have not yet ascended to the Father. Go instead to my brothers and tell them, 'I am ascending to my Father and your Father, to my God and your God.'" 18 Mary Magdalene went to the disciples with the news: "I have seen the Lord!" And she told them that he had said these things to her. ~ John 20:11-18

"Jesus had chosen Mary Magdalene from all of His disciples and followers as the first person to encounter Him after His physical death!"

"In that moment, as the single witness to the miracle that Jesus rose from the dead, and before she has a chance to tell anyone else about what she'd seen, Mary Magdalene was the Church! Christianity was based on a woman at its very roots!" marvels Maria. "Not so patriarchal after all!"

* * *

"In 2016, Pope Francis, thank goodness, claimed this day as the "Feast of Magdalena" and proclaimed that Magdalena was an example to all Christians," continues Freya in her talk.

So that woman, who is the first to encounter Jesus... now has become an apostle of the new and greatest hope

~ Pope Francis

"Thank you Pope Francis! It has been a long time coming!" says Freya, pausing to hear the message for herself.

"So what are you going to do today to celebrate the wise woman in you? I hope you'll do something to honour that woman in you and to honour all women who have had their voices taken away from them, or have not been allowed to express their sensuality, their wisdom, just because they are a woman, something we are still seeing it today."

"I don't know what I'll do but something fun for sure," thinks Maria.

"But as women gathering in sacred circles, I hope you will remember to love with all of your heart," says Freya. "Happy Feast Day of Mary Magdalene. Thank you so much for joining me. I would love to hear what words of wisdom Mary Magdalene whispered to you in the meditation."

After a big sigh, Maria promptly writes this comment: "Thank you, Freya. That was wonderful. You are wonderful. Mary Magdalene gave me the message, 'You don't have to be married to be loved.' Thank you again. Peace and Blessings to you."

"Your message just gave me goosebumps," replies Freya.

sweet • heart

"So what am I going to do to celebrate the Feast of Mary Magdalene?" asks Maria to herself. "I know, I'll go for a run outside!" Although Maria had been running on Angie's treadmill before their fitness class every Tuesday at 5pm for the past several months, she still cannot run much more than 15 minutes non-stop.

Without giving herself much time to talk herself out of it, Maria changes into her stretchy workout clothes, puts her hair in a ponytail, straps her phone with earbuds to her arm, and laces up her pink running shoes.

"I'm just going to see how far I get and if it's just five minutes, it's just five minutes. No pressure," she tells herself, as she stretches her quads on the driveway.

Maria knows it will take her four minutes to walk to the mailboxes as a warm up, exactly the length of the first song on her "Run for the Cure" playlist.

"It always gets colder and windier around here," she reminds herself as she approaches her landmark starting point. "Here we go!"

Maria picks up her heels to an easy jog. "It's all coming back to me now. How long has it been… seven years since I've done this run? This isn't so bad. I think I can do this. I think I can keep going."

She runs downhill, past the little park and under the bush where all of the bees buzz. She runs uphill and waves to her neighbour who is power-washing his driveway. Soon, she turns right onto another street and follows it, song after song, further and deeper into the neighbourhood.

"Their roses are looking good… that's where the grey cat lives."

She remembers the rainbow that she once saw arching above these houses that appeared just after she had been writing about angels and rainbows in her journal.

"It was like a wink and a smile from the Universe!"

Cyclists pass her from behind. "To your left," they call.

Then she turns right again at the tee, runs past the row of blackberry bushes that hedge the forested path that she normally takes when walking.

"And I'm running," sings Maria out loud to Jully Black's song.

Yes I'm running for the fight now
Won't stop me 'cause I'm running

"I'm just going to keep going," she decides as she turns right again. Her pace is good. She feels strong as she passes the house with the Buddha statue, the swing set, and the wind chimes, and then the Tudor house with the country garden that looks like it has been transplanted straight from England.

"The bench at the park will be a good place to turn around and I'll still have enough steam to get back."

She glances at Mt. Doug and makes a wide left to cross to the other side of the street. She waves at her neighbours who are working in their garden and heads back towards home.

Katy Perry's "Firework" song is perfectly timed. "Make 'em go "eye – eye – eye!" sings Maria as she pounds her fist three times in the air in unison with the lyrics.

Maria keeps running. As she approaches the tee from another direction, she asks herself, "Do I want to go up this way or turn left? Maybe it would be better to turn left even though I'd be running up hill for most of this street. Left it is."

She waves to another runner, a dog walker, and a sauntering couple. She digs deep to climb the hills that are waiting for her to crest.

"Just another half a song until I reach the mailboxes again," she says as she turns left onto the next street and treads over a damp patch of sidewalk where the guy with the power washer lives.

Normally, when Maria gets close to the end of her run, she is breathless and barely hanging on. She normally tells herself, "Don't slow down right before the finish line."

Those last few seconds are often the hardest and it is all she can do to press forward.

"That's funny. I feel like I can keep going. I just want to go one more song on my playlist. Oh, I love this song by Rihanna and unexpectedly finds herself singing, "only girl in the world..." out loud for all of the neighbours to hear.

Suddenly, Maria gets a second wind. Not only does she pass the mailboxes, but she passes the escarpment where the deer like to climb. And then she passes her very own street and keeps going, running down the big hill towards the highway. When she reaches the bottom, she turns left.

"I'll go as far as the bus stop and then I'll call it a run. Just a few more houses...there it is… there's the bus stop… just a few more steps… five, four, three, two, one! Oh my goodness! I did it! I ran farther in my neighbourhood than I ever have before. That must have been about 5K! Oh my goodness! I feel great! Now I just have to walk back up that big hill as a cool down."

Maria is dripping with sweat! She feels energized!

When she walks through the door, her mom asks her, "How far did you go?"

"I don't know – but far!" she says proudly. "Best run ever. I'm going to take a shower now."

* * *

Perhaps not wearing a watch was a blessing but Maria still wants to know her total run time. All she can do is add up the minutes of the songs that played along as her soundtrack. "Oh my gosh, I have to tell Angie," she says picking up her phone to send a text.

> Hi Angie, You'll be so proud
> of me!
> I ran 27 minutes outside today!
>
> I'm SUPER proud of you!!!
> Way to go sweetheart. Wow!
> Thank you so much for sharing.
> We need to measure you again
> so come a little early on
> Tuesday, okay?
>
> I'll be there with bells on!

* * *

Contrary to previous weigh-ins, this time Maria cannot wait to step on the scale. The deal is, Angie records the results but does not share them every time with Maria because that has worked against her progress in the past.

Angie always keeps a poker face while she runs her measuring tape across Maria's neck, upper arm, bustline, waist, hips, thigh, and calf, counting the notches.

Maria takes off her running shoes and steps on the scale. She faces forward and looks through the window as Angie marks the number in her file.

"I just have to calculate the numbers and I'll send you your results later tonight," says Angie.

Maria feels compelled to tell her classmates about her run during warm-up.

"And I just kept going and going!" she tells them. "It was like I was flying!"

"Way to go, Maria, that's awesome!" they say.

"Yeah, you're looking really good these days! Keep it up!"

Maria is pumped. She throws the ropes and swings the cowbells with new vigour.

That evening, after the fun but intense fitness class, Maria receives the following text from Angie:

> Congratulations!!!!
> You've lost over a foot of inches
> off your body since June!!!!!!
> And just shy of 22 pounds!!!!
> You are amazing!
> I'm so proud of you sweetheart.
>
> Oh my gosh! Thank you! I
> had no idea! Wow! Thank you for
> helping me again.
>
> It's my pleasure my beauty.
> I'm soooooo proud of you!
> Time to celebrate!

I'm so glad I'm working out
with you again. You're the best!

Thanks sweetheart.

Big hugs!

Closer to Indigo
Maria Koropecky

PART 3

well • come

E ven though running is exhilarating, Maria prefers walking. As she said to Samantha one day, "learning to walk is our first taste of freedom as babies." By mid-July, Maria is up to walking at least 25 kilometres a week – sometimes around the airport, sometimes to visit her father at the cemetery, and sometimes just going to her favourite pond in her neighbourhood.

She is excited to receive the following email from the Canadian Company of Pilgrims inviting her to a Saint James Day hike around Beaver Lake where she will add yet another trail to her mix:

Subject: St. James Day hike

JOIN US FOR A BEAVER LAKE HIKE AND BBQ TO CELEBRATE SAINT JAMES DAY:

For those wanting to walk 20km, start at 8am on Sunday, July 28, 2019 and go twice around Elk/Beaver Lake for a full 20km. For those interested in only walking 10km, please arrive at 10am and walk once around.

Experienced pilgrims will be on hand to offer advice on the Camino de Santiago.

BBQ OF HAMBURGERS AND HOTDOGS, SALADS, CAKE AND COLD DRINKS WILL BEGIN AT NOON:

There is seating for 50 people at picnic tables. If you have a camp chair to bring along, that would help accommodate everyone.

Registration closes: July 25th

DIRECTIONS: From the Pat Bay highway, turn onto Elk Lake Drive and then right onto Beaver Lake Road. Following the yellow arrows, proceed through the first large parking lot and over the 9 speed bumps, onto the next parking lot to the Filter Beds. You'll see the shelter festooned with balloons and an energetic group of volunteers.

We hope you'll join us!

Saint James (the Greater) is the Patron Saint of Pilgrims; he is also one of Jesus' twelve Apostles. In Iconography, James' portrait illustrates a young man with reddish-brown hair and long beard, who carries a scroll in his left hand and has a reserved expression on his face.

"Jesus chose each of his Apostles for specific reasons but they weren't always obvious," thinks Maria. "I wonder if Jesus saw a certain colour of light in their aura, or some sort of mark, that told Him who would be on the starting line-up of His A-Team."

When Jesus first called James to walk with him, James and his younger brother John (the Evangelist) had just come into shore after a day of fishing on the Sea of Galilee with their father, Zebedee.

In spite of their quick temper and related moniker of the "sons of thunder," both James and John, along with the Apostle Peter, had a special place in Jesus' innermost circle. Jesus gave them the honour of witnessing His Transfiguration, a significant event in His life that gave them a preview of His Divinity.

2 After six days, Jesus took Peter, James and John with him and led them up a high mountain, where they were all alone. There he was transfigured before them. 3 His clothes became dazzling white, whiter than anyone in the world could bleach them. 4 And there appeared before them Elijah and Moses, who were talking with Jesus. 5 Peter said to Jesus, "Rabbi, it is good for us to be here. Let us put up three shelters—one for you, one for Moses and one for Elijah." 6 (He did not know what to say, they were so frightened.) 7 Then a cloud appeared and covered them, and a voice came from the cloud: "This is my Son, whom I love. Listen to him!" 8 Suddenly, when they looked around, they no longer saw anyone with them except Jesus. 9 As they were coming down the mountain, Jesus gave them orders not to tell anyone what they had seen until the Son of Man had risen from the dead. ~ Mark 9:2-9

"Imagine sitting on that for three years," thinks Maria to herself.

After Jesus' crucifixion near Jerusalem, where He transcended death, the Apostles began to venture far and wide to share Jesus' message of light, love, joy, and hope.

According to the "Historia Compostelana," which was published in the 12th Century, the Apostle James preached closer to home in Judea and SaMaria. Eventually, with his fishing and sailing experience, James travelled much farther afield, some three or four thousand kilometres, across the Mediterranean Sea, with possible sojourns in Greece and Italy, all the way to Iberia, now known as Spain!

"Talk about a pilgrimage," says Maria. "He wrote the book!"

Ten or so years later, when James returned to Judea, he was sentenced to death by Herod Agrippa I (as recorded in Acts 12:1-3) and was the first Apostle to be martyred for his faith. After James' death, the remains of his body were transported back to Spain by boat and then carried inland, further West towards the Atlantic Ocean, over the same rugged and steep terrain as what would later become the Camino Frances.

Saint James' relics (authenticated by Pope Leo XIII on November 1, 1884) were later enshrined in the Cathedral of Santiago de Compostela in Galicia, Spain, and became the center of the Camino de Santiago pilgrimage, drawing pilgrims from all corners of the earth to continue the centuries-old tradition of crisscrossing Europe and following the Way of Saint James.

* * *

Participating in Saint James' Feast Day celebrations (normally observed on July 25th) with other pilgrims, gives Maria a small taste of what she can expect during her own expedition. Normally on Sunday mornings, Maria attends Saint Nick's with her mother, but for today, walking outside in "God's Country," is her church.

Thinking back to Krys' comment, "If you want to be married, you need to get on that" speech during Maria's birthday dinner, Lubomyra is convinced Maria will meet someone special on this hike. Unfortunately, Lubomyra's fussing and fluttering is off-putting and so, Maria starts the day on the wrong foot.

Wearing the authentic, blue and yellow Camino t-shirt Vasylyna had given her, Maria arrives a couple of minutes late to Elk Lake Park. Her lateness is uncharacteristic but she got confused by someone else's signs and arrows in the parking lot, and by then, most of the hikers were well out of sight. Meanwhile, the stragglers keep butting ahead of her at the welcoming table.

From the tent, Maria heads along the far-side of the lake. Before long, she comes across a patch of flat rocks that bank along the water's edge and is immediately transported to the afternoon she had spent on this very same spot, twenty years ago, to deal with the news that her boyfriend at that time, Benjamin, decided that he needed two weeks, without any contact whatsoever, to think about their relationship.

"I haven't thought about him in years," says Maria with a long sigh. "How sad I was that day. It's all flooding back to me now. To think I wanted to marry him after he returned from working on the cruise ships. Probably would not have been happy with him though. I can still see myself sitting on that rock, crying, staring into the water, wondering what was going to happen, crying, wondering what his answer would be, crying some more."

Lost in thought, Maria trips on a protruding rock but does not fall.

"And even though he decided he wanted to stay with me after that agonizing two weeks, the damage was done, and he changed his mind shortly thereafter anyway, and my heart was broken again."

She continues along the forested path, making sure to mind her footing and avoiding things like uneven rocks, slippery mud, and road apples left by the horses. Across the lake, she is able to catch glimpses of the Pat Bay Highway.

"I have a long ways to go this morning."

After about an hour or so into the trail and still hiking on the far side of the lake, Maria notices three women coming toward her who had passed her from behind earlier. She figures they are completing their second go-around in the opposite direction and is not concerned.

"Are you on the Camino hike?" they ask Maria politely, knowing her answer would be 'yes.' "We missed the turnoff. We need to backtrack for a bit. That's what we're doing but you can go the longer way around, if you want."

"Oh, I guess I'll come with you, if that's okay," Maria says turning around, trying to catch up to their quick pace.

"Here it is," says one of the ladies as she turns off the main path.

Maria is annoyed that the event organizers did not mark the trail better.

"That's how the Camino works," says another woman seeing the disgruntled expression on Maria's face. "You get off course and somehow, someone steers you in the right direction and you find your way again. Hi, my name's Diane."

"Maria, nice to meet you. Thanks for the tip."

The two other women gain a slight lead and walk a few steps ahead, leaving Maria and Diane to walk together.

"We're from up island," says Diane. Have you been on a Camino before?"

"No, I'm going on my first one in September."

"I've been on five."

"Goodness, that's a lot of walking!" says Maria.

"Will you be taking poles?" she asks Maria, noticing that she is not carrying any.

"No, I don't plan to."

"You're going to regret it."

"I'll take my chances," says Maria thinking she does not feel like carrying poles on the plane or leaving them behind somewhere accidentally.

"How about your boots?"

"I haven't bought mine yet. What kind do you have?" Maria asks eyeing her purple shoes.

"These are called 'Trail Runners' – really light – so much easier to wear than hiking boots."

"Good to know. I didn't want to walk in heavy boots."

"If you get them at MEC, and don't like them for whatever reason, you can return them even if you've worn them outside a few times. I'm going to return a pair later this afternoon."

"Another good thing to know! Thanks!"

They make their way to the highway side of the lake, somewhere around the halfway point. They can see the Canadian Company of Pilgrims' tents flapping kitty corner across the long end of the lake.

"Do you have your Brierley guidebook?"

"Not yet."

"You'd better get one of those, too. When did you say you were going?"

"September."

"Yeah, you need to seriously amp up your training. Do you have your backpack yet – let me guess – not yet?"

Maria winces.

"Get your backpack and start adding more and more weight to it every week."

Maria is feeling overwhelmed by all of Diane's information and how she is nowhere near ready for her Camino. She uses the public bathrooms at the beach as an excuse to break away from their group.

"Thanks, see you at the barbeque. I'm just going to take a little rest here."

Maria makes sure to give some distance to the other women she had been walking with. From there, she hikes by herself the rest of the way, with the wavy lake on her right and the roaring highway to her left.

She makes it back to the pilgrims' tent after close to three hours of hiking. The barbeque is still fired up, but by then, most of the participants have already left the park. Maria fills her paper plate with a hamburger, the last of the Caesar salad, and potato chips, and heads for the picnic tables.

"Is this seat taken?" she asks.

"No, go ahead. Sit down," says the woman across the table. "Would you mind looking after my dog while I get my food? Thanks."

Before Maria is able to say, "sure," the woman has already left the table. Maria holds on to the dog's leash while trying to eat her hamburger and swatting away wasps. Soon, one of the more seasoned members of the group sits next to Maria.

"Hi, I'm Earl."

"Maria."

"Are you getting ready for a Camino or just coming back from one?" he asks.

"Going in September. You?"

"I've gone three times already. I'm just here as a volunteer today."

The first woman comes back to the table with her plate of food.

"Thanks for looking after my dog. I'm Charlene."

"Have you been on a Camino yet?" asks Maria.

"Yes, I was just there in May."

"How did it go?"

"It was great! I'm so glad I went. I'm so glad I was able to take the time off work and do this."

Another woman sits next to Charlene and across from Earl.

"Did you do your Camino as a spiritual experience or for adventure?" asks Maria.

"A little of both," Charlene replies. "And by the way, I'm so glad you asked me that question rather than, "What do you do for a living?" which is what most of the Americans open with."

Earl lifts his finger as if he is about to ask Charlene something and then clams up.

"Was it really hard to find a bed to sleep in every night?" asks the other woman.

"It wasn't too bad, but the closer you get to Santiago de Compostella, the harder it gets. But if you can't find a place, just take a taxi to the next town and then take a taxi back to where you left off the day before and you'll be fine."

Maria does not want to back track with taxis but appreciates the option.

"But the best thing I can tell you…" continues Charlene, "is just have fun."

"I agree," says Earl. "Just have fun."

"Well gotta go," says Charlene picking up her empty plate and the handle end of her dog's leash, her dog following quietly behind her. The other woman makes her excuses and leaves, too.

"So what do you do for work?" asks Earl.

"I'm a Wellness Coach," says Maria.

"Why did you get into that?"

"I like to help people be more proactive about their health."

Finishing up the last of her juice and wiping her hands on her paper napkin, Maria thinks, "Maybe the hot dog would have been the better choice today. It was nice to eat chips though." She scans the tent for an easy exit. "How can I politely leave this conversation?"

"I can see you're single, sensitive and intense," Earl says.

Maria does not take any of these words as compliments at all (even if Earl was perceptive) and on that note, she tries to hint that it is time for her to go home.

"Well, I guess that's that for me today. Thanks for the lunchtime conversation."

"I'll walk with you back to your car."

They head back towards the parking lot.

"If you want, we can exchange emails. I'd love to hear about your trip when you come back," he says trying to find a piece of paper in his car.

"If you can't find something to write on, that's okay," says Maria. "Well, we have a nice dinner in November to welcome everyone back from their Caminos. Maybe I'll see you there."

"Sure," says Maria.

"I'd just like to give you a little gift. Here's a scallop seashell for you," he says removing a heavy, toonie-sized pin from his hat. "I bought a bunch of shells at Michael's and filled them with sand so I could glue the pins to the back. See?"

She nods.

"It's donativo," he says handing the pin to her with a pause.

"Umm."

He notices the confused expression on her face and adds, "a gift… it means 'by donation' in Spanish."

"Oh, I don't have any cash on me, today," she says padding her pockets.

"That's okay – I just like to give these to some of the people I meet."

"Thanks," says Maria accepting the seashell. "That's sweet."

When Maria comes home from her first Camino experience, her mother is eager to hear if anything interesting happened.

"Did you meet someone?" Lubomyra asks.

"No," Maria says, putting Earl's, reddish, scalloped seashell in a Mother of Pearl dish with the other shells she has collected.

shoe • lay • says

"Only five weeks until I leave for Spain," says Maria to Samantha on the phone. "The summer is just flying by."

"I'm so happy you're going. I wish I could come with you."

"As much as I'd love for you to come with me on this big adventure, I think this is something I need to do on my own."

"Yeah, I can see that but if all goes well, maybe you can take groups – like your wellness coaching clients – wouldn't that be amazing? – and I then can come, too!"

"Oh, that would be awesome! That's what I'm hoping for but in the meantime, part of the tradition of going on a pilgrimage is to pray for other people who can't go themselves for whatever reason. My hairstylist did that for me when he went a couple of years ago and he sprayed a tiny vial of *Miracle* perfume – that I sent along with him – somewhere along the trail."

"That's so fun!"

"I know! If you want, you can write out a prayer and I can wrap it around a rock and leave it behind somewhere on the trail for you."

"Yes, I'd like that. Thanks, Maria. What are you going to do when you get back?"

"Well," says Maria as she checks over her shoulder to see if it's okay to say something out loud.

"Can I let you in on a little secret?"

"I'm all ears!"

"Well, all summer long, I've been thinking... or rather feeling... that there's a man coming into my life in September. The summer is just my prep time. It's my chance to get in shape and all of that."

"I feel that too! Maybe you'll meet a younger guy!"

"Oh my goodness, younger? I keep on seeing a clean-shaven man with short, grey curly hair – like the Roger Sterling character on "Mad Men" – have you seen that show?"

"Maybe a long time ago."

"He was the boss at the advertising agency. Anyway, when my brother said on my birthday, 'Go to Spain, meet a guy, we'll ship your stuff...'"

"I remember that."

"And then Joyce at the Lantern Inn said a week later – totally unprompted by me – 'I can see you meeting a wealthy guy and being swept off your feet while you're in Europe, just like my friend did...'"

"When did she say that?"

"When I went back in June to pick up my last tips… I got the idea that I'd be moving somewhere to be in a relationship."

"Oh, that's so exciting!"

"And that might be Nick."

"Oh," says Samantha with a thud.

Maria steps over the change of tone.

"So, I was thinking, maybe I'll move to Calgary and I'll live closer to you, too, and we could drive to see each other on weekends!"

"Oh, I'd like that!"

"That's my plan but I need to head out the door now. I have to go downtown and buy my hiking boots, or shoes, or maybe just a pair of socks, I don't know yet."

"Good luck. I hope you find a good deal!"

"Thanks and with the August long weekend, I think my chances are pretty good!"

* * *

Maria has no idea there are so many stores dedicated to outdoor sports and camping within five blocks of each other in Victoria's downtown core. Today, instead of doing her Patchouli tour, she enters the fresh, green world of the outdoor enthusiast!

Although Maria considers herself a nature lover, she does not appreciate winter sports like ice skating because of the hard landing surface; or camping in the rain because it just makes her feel too cold and uncomfortable; and she has never gone fishing a day in her life because in her family, that is a guy's thing. Still, she is not that delicate.

* * *

CAMPING IS A LIFE SKILL

by Maria Ponomarenko, Wellness Coach

Going camping is part of my childhood and the stuffy smell of the canvass awning from my family's camper trailer (that got pulled behind the blue Marlin and later the gold Buick Riviera across the Rockies) is just a thought away. I spent many summer days and nights camping with my friends from *Plast*, a Ukrainian Scouting organization, that taught me many practical life skills like:

* How to pack your stuff in a backpack (remember to bring a pillow);

* How to set up a tent (not on a slope, over big tree roots);

* How to build a fire (mark the circumference of the pit with cool rocks);

* How to boil water over an open fire (which takes forever) to enjoy a warm cup of *Chang* (a spontaneously invented portmanteau word that combines *chai*, the Ukrainian word for 'tea' plus Tang drink powder, originally for astronauts);

* How to build a latrine (toilet paper must not get wet);

* How to change from your wet bathing suit into your brown, scouting uniform in less than 10 minutes (being able to stand up in the tent would have made that so much easier);

* how to identify Poison Ivy (it has three leaves and a reddish tinge);

* How to identify cow patties (they can be anywhere – even at the side of your tent);

* How to water ski (relax your grip);

* How to paddle a canoe (the Jay Stroke lets backseat drivers really shine); and

* How to perform a skit around the campfire (exaggerate your gestures).

But why they required the scouts to learn the Morse Code in Ukrainian for one of their badges, I will never know.

* * *

"Going on a Camino – where I get to be outside just walking and not having to worry about the camping part – sounds like the best of both worlds for me," thinks Maria as she strolls past the Bay Centre.

She turns onto Broad Street again but on this occasion, she stops inside Robinson's Outdoor Store.

"I wonder if the name is a reference to the classic, Swiss Family Robinson story," thinks Maria as enters the historic building, noticing the backpacks to her left but looking for shoe displays.

Robinson's has its own story and has deep roots in Victoria – since 1929! Starting with Fred, (who opened his bicycle repair and baby carriage rental shop at the onset of the Great Depression, no less), the family-run business eventually evolved into a sporting goods store, and has helped countless people stock up on provisions for their own great adventures, over the next 90 years and beyond.

"Oh, the places they have been…"

Maria has inherited her feet from her father – same wide instep, same high arch – so finding decent footwear is always a challenge.

"Purple trail runners on sale would be best but I'll see what's here."

"Can I help you?" says the young sales clerk, who probably would have preferred to be camping with his friends on this Sunday of a long weekend.

"Yes, I'm looking for a pair of shoes for my upcoming trip," says Maria.

"Where are you headed?"

"I'm going to Spain to walk the Camino. Have you been?"

"No, I'm more interested in going to South America next but I know many people who have hiked that trail and had a blast. How long are you going for?"

"Two weeks."

"What kind of footwear are you looking for?"

"Well, I'd prefer not to wear hiking boots. I heard there's something called trail runners. Do you have any of those – preferably on sale?"

"Yes, we have some over here. Do you want waterproof or not waterproof?"

"Umm."

"Waterproof is heavier and not as flexible but it might be worth it."

"I hear it gets pretty hot in Spain in the summer and I don't think it's supposed to rain that much, so I'll go with not water proof."

"Okay. We have some options. What's your size?"

"Nine – nine and a half, depending."

"Let's measure your feet just to make sure," he says while placing the notched, metal Bannock device with the sliding levers on the floor in front of her.

"Take your shoes off, stand up, and place your right foot in here."

Maria is grateful she is wearing socks that do not have any holes in them.

"Switch feet. Okay, great. I'll be right back."

Maria sits down on the chair and watches some other customers browse through the store. The shoe clerk returns with three shoe boxes in his arms.

"Try these first," he says as he takes the tissue out of the shoes.

"Umm… how am I supposed to tie these?" she asks after she puts the shoes on. "There aren't any laces."

"Yes, these are laceless shoes. They're supposed to save you some time. You just pull the buckle… see… there you go."

"Too high tech for me. I think I'd prefer old school. Is there another pair I could try on?"

The clerk opens the second box. "These have laces," he says while handing another pair of trail runners to Maria.

"This is more like it," she says while loosening the laces and freeing the tongue.

"I like the colour – it's not quite blue and it's not quite purple, sort of a creamy indigo."

"Walk around the store a bit. See how they feel on your feet. Take your time."

"So far they're okay," she says as she walks up their little ramp.

"The left foot feels good but the right foot feels a little odd."

"Yeah, most people's feet aren't exactly the same size."

"But I think I can live with them. They're comfortable enough. I think I'll buy these."

"Okay, great!"

"But can I return them just in case?"

"As long as you don't wear them outside, you can return them within seven days of purchase," he says annoyed with the question.

"Good to know. Thanks for your help," and with her shoes in hand, she goes to the sales counter and buys the vessels that will carry her across Spain on her big adventure.

* * *

"I bought my shoes today," says Maria to her mother as soon as she comes home from the store. "Look! Aren't they nice?"

"Good for you!"

"Oh dear," says Maria as she takes her shoes out of the box and looks at them from all angles. "There's an awful lot of dirt on the soles… see?"

"Oh, I think that's just from the store."

"No, this is more like piney soil, not like grey dust on a floor that hasn't been vacuumed for a while."

"Well, what are you going to do?"

"I'm going to call them right now before they close!" she says while pulling out her cell phone from her purse.

"Yes, hello, I just bought a pair of trail runners from you guys and I just noticed there's quite a lot of debris on the soles – I swear I've just taken them out of the box and haven't had a chance to wear them outside at all!"

"Well, it's probably just from the foot traffic in the store."

"No, they're quite dirty as if someone wore them on the trails and then returned them. Can you give me a discount or something?"

"You'd have to bring them in again and we'll take a look, but no promises."

"Okay, I'll come back tomorrow."

* * *

The next day, on the Monday morning of the August long weekend, Maria drives back downtown to Robinson's to see if she can get a "previously worn" discount on her big shoe investment.

The bell chimes as she walks into the store again. The store clerk looks like he is expecting her even before she says a word.

"May I speak to the manager please?"

"Hang on a second," he says picking up the phone.

"There's a woman here to return some shoes… okay, I'll let her know. Yes, head on upstairs and the manager will meet you there."

"Thanks," says Maria grabbing her shoebox from the sales counter.

Compared to the first floor, the second floor is much more brightly lit and spacious.

"Can I help you?" says the manager from behind the counter.

"Yesterday, I bought this pair of trail runners and when I took them out of the box when I got home, I noticed they looked like they had been worn outside."

The manager looks at the grooves in the fluorescent, greeny-yellow soles.

"Yeah, I see what you mean, but it still might be scuff from the store."

"I don't think so and I swear I didn't wear them outside."

"I know. I can tell you're being sincere. Do you still like them?"

"Yes, I do."

"Tell you what. I'll give you a 10% discount but you can't return them again – because they've been worn. Deal?"

"Deal. Thanks so much."

Maria is happy that she stood up for herself.

"After lunch, I'm going to take my new shoes for a spin around the airport!"

* * *

Maria puts her new shoes on – first the left and then the right. She pulls the laces taught, then double-ties the bows so they will stay. She stands up and plants both feet firmly on the floor.

She walks around for a few steps and feels as if the sock on her right foot is slipping. She decides to take the shoe off, adjusts the sock, and tries again.

"Yeah, that's better."

When she was just learning to tie her shoe laces as a youngster, (a big milestone for kids growing up in the 1970s, but not such a necessary life skill for kids today), her father saw how she was struggling and showed her an easier way.

The trick was to tie the two loops together to make a bow, rather than making one loop and wrapping it with the free end like everybody else. Perhaps this was a lefty thing; perhaps she just could not figure out how to do it in the normal way until much later in life.

Maria ties her hair back into a ponytail, grabs her purple sunglasses and her pink phone, and hits the dusty trail. She parks near the old, Anglican church again.

The path around the airport looks more or less like the continent of Africa, if you look at it from above, the top facing North-West. She starts breaking in her new trail runners in the northern most corner of the airport landing field and heads clockwise, towards the town of Sidney.

She watches a couple of butterflies and dragonflies sailing alongside her, disappearing into the grasses, and then showing up again later, further on down the road.

"You came back," she says gleefully. "Hello again, Dragonfly."

She presses on and says, "hi" to the occasional dog walker and bicyclist coming from the other direction.

"The blackberries look ready to pick," she notices and if it was not for her three-meals-a-day eating schedule with no snacking in between, she would have thoroughly enjoyed eating some juicy, almost wine-flavoured blackberries, that are bursting this month on the edge of the road.

"So far, so good with the shoes," she thinks as she carries on for the rest of the 10 kilometres without issues. "I think I made a good purchase.

Next thing I need to do is buy my backpack."

turn • key

Although Samantha does not have high hopes for Maria and Nick, she is intrigued by the prospect of Maria moving to Alberta after her Camino. Samantha told Maria's story to one of her cleaning helpers, Rica, as they were cleaning a client's house, as a way to pass the time.

Unbeknownst to Samantha, Rica owns a second house in Calgary and is currently renting it out as an AirBnB – "Would Maria be interested in renting it herself?"

"What a great idea!" thinks Theresa and with her big news, calls her friend at the next opportunity. "I have something to share with you but I can't talk tonight. Call me back tomorrow morning," Samantha says frantically on the phone, trying to contain her excitement.

"I wonder what that's about," thinks Maria as she replays Samantha's message. "She never calls with such urgency. How am I going to last till tomorrow?"

The next day, after a restless sleep and after eating her go-to breakfast of black coffee, toast with butter and yogurt with fruit, Maria returns Samantha's call.

"Hi Samantha, what's going on? You said you have something to share?"

"Yes! I was talking with one of my helpers yesterday and I told her about how you were thinking about moving to Calgary and she said she has a house she can rent to you!"

"What? A house in Calgary? Oh my goodness!" says Maria secretly thinking this is too easy.

"She wants to meet with you and have a chat and maybe you can work something out?"

"Yeah, I'd be up for that. Give her my phone number and have her call me. Thanks, Samantha! You're amazing!"

"Okay, I'll get right on it but I have to go to work now – the houses aren't going to clean themselves. We'll talk again soon."

"Have a wonderful day!"

* * *

As Maria sits at the head of the dining room table tinkering on her laptop, her mother sits on the purple couch and watches her talk shows. From her vantage point, Lubomyra is also able to look through the sliding glass doors that lead to the deck, a view that includes a grove of trees, the neighbourhood, and the Pat Bay

Highway. The dome of the telescope at the Centre of the Universe is also within range.

"I just love watching the squirrels jump from tree to tree – they're crazy!" says Lubomyra out loud. "Oh and you have to come and see this, Marichka – four eagles flying overhead."

Maria gets up from her seat and heads towards the back of the house.

"Hey look at that but I don't think they're eagles. They're probably Turkey Vultures. They're smaller than eagles and like to travel in groups, but they're still birds of prey though."

"How do you know about Turkey Vultures?"

"From the neighbours when I go on my walks."

Maria's phone rings and takes her away from the Nature Show. She goes back to the dining room and picks it up.

"Hi, Maria, my name is Rica and Samantha told me you were thinking of moving to Calgary?"

"Yeah, thanks for calling," says Maria as she heads downstairs to her cluttered office.

"Well, if you're looking for a place to rent, I might be able to help you out. But first, I'd like to get to know a little bit about you. You're living in Victoria right now – why do you want to move to Calgary?"

"It's a bit of a story. Yes, I'm living in Victoria with my mom and I just turned 50 in June."

"Oh… you're just a few years younger than me, I'm 54."

"And for my birthday, my mother and family gave me a gift of going on a Camino."

"That's amazing."

"I know! Have you been?"

"No, but I've done some travelling and that's something I might like to do some day."

"Anyway, I feel like this is my chance to start a new chapter in my life. I feel like I've got 20 or 30 years ahead of me and if I don't go for my dreams now, I'll be 60 and still living with my mother, thinking I should have gone to Calgary, or wherever, while I had the chance and now my life has passed me by."

"I get that."

"I don't want to waste any more time and the way I see it, the Camino that I'm going on in September, is the bridge between my old self and my new self and after that, I want to start fresh in a new city!"

"Wow, that's how I feel."

"So, when Samantha mentioned your house in Calgary, I thought, 'it's all coming together. This is a sign that I'm meant to be doing this.'"

"Calgary just might be it for you. Let me tell you a little bit about me. I was married to a man and we lived in a house in Calgary, but he died suddenly a few years ago."

"Oh, I'm sorry."

"And then I met another man and after a few months into the relationship, we moved to Edmonton and bought a house with a

3-car, heated garage to be closer to my family and for his work, but I kept the house in Calgary."

"That's smart."

"But as of this week, my relationship has suddenly ended."

"That's too bad."

"I didn't see it coming and I'm having a hard time dealing with it but I've realized it's also time for me to start over in my life and so I've decided to sell my house and just stay here without him."

"So, you're selling you're house in Calgary?"

"Yes, but you're welcome to stay there for a few months until I sell it – that way you can get to know the city and see if you'd like to find another place and stay, or move back to Victoria, or move somewhere else entirely."

"So, month to month? That sounds like a good idea."

"It'll be like a trial run for you."

"I'd be open to talking about this more. Let's keep in touch."

"Sure, sounds great."

When Maria hangs up the phone, she thinks about Nick.

"Maybe if he and I lived in the same city, we would get to know each other in the real world and we would become a couple. So far, nothing is happening while I'm in Victoria and he's in Calgary. Maybe this move would make all of the difference," she says crossing her fingers.

Scanning the room, her eyes land on some workout clothes she set aside to pack for her trip.

"Wearing my vintage, 2006, turquoise Lululemon yoga top, means I don't have to wear a bra! Speaking of my Camino and places to stay, I think it might be a good idea to book a room in Madrid on my first night when I land. I'll go and do that now."

back • pack

Sunday, August 11, 2019, is a special day on the Ukrainian Catholic liturgical calendar. The church bulletin reads: "Blessing Of The Fruits & Vegetables: as we celebrate the Transfiguration of our Lord right after Divine Liturgy, we will be blessing fresh fruits and vegetables and thus give thanks to God for a good harvest."

"That's neat," thinks Maria, connecting the bonus blessing to what she has recently learned about the new-to-her Apostle James. "I wonder where his icon is," asks Maria to herself as she scans the iconostasis, the screen of icons that separates the nave from the sanctuary in Eastern Christian churches.

"I guess he's the third one from the left on the top row, since he was the third one to be chosen. He does have a long, red beard."

Lubomyra makes sure to bring plums and grapes to church that day and after the blessing, she and Maria go downstairs for coffee. They sit with Petrovna and Luke.

"How is your training going for your Camino?" asks Petrovna.

"Pretty good. Got my shoes last weekend thanks to your birthday gift certificate and they work. Today, I'm planning to look for a backpack."

"Before you do that," says Luke, making eye contact with his wife before proceeding. "Petrovna has a backpack that she's not using… you're welcome to borrow it if you can't find anything else."

"Yeah," says Petrovna, taken by surprise but not objecting to the idea. "You're welcome to come over this afternoon to try it on to see if you like it."

"I'll do that! Thanks!"

"Oh and make sure you talk to Brett before you take off."

"Brett?"

"Yeah, you met him at Petrovna's birthday party in March… remember?" says Luke.

"Oh, yes."

"He's writing a book about his Camino and can give you some last minute pointers. I'll give you his email address so you can contact him directly."

* * *

Maria rings the doorbell of the grey house in James Bay.

"Come on in," says Luke opening the door. "We've got the backpack ready for you."

Maria slips off her shoes and stands in the foyer. Their dog circles around her feet.

Luke hands the grey backpack over to her. She reaches her arms through the padded straps. The backpack dangles loosely from her shoulders.

"It's a 60-litre."

"They recommended a 30 to 40 litre for my two-week hike. Perhaps this is a bit big for me?"

"Well, you can adjust the straps like this," says Luke.

"It's supposed to sit high on your shoulders…"

"This high?"

"Yeah, and above your hips. Make sure the straps are pulled as tight as possible. What do you think?"

"It feels alright. So, it would be okay for me to borrow it?"

"Yes, of course."

"Well, I'm still going to look around for my own one but it would be nice to have this as a backup – get it? – back…up," she says, proud of her pun.

Luke rolls his eyes.

"I really think it's great that you're doing this," says Petrovna.

"Yes, it's way out of my comfort zone but I'm up for the challenge."

"About that," says Luke. "I'm going to give you another challenge."

"What's that?"

"You can't cry at all while you're there."

"I'm not going to accept that challenge. There's no way."

"Seriously, see if you can go that whole two weeks without crying one single tear."

"Not going to happen. Why are you asking me to be someone else?"

"He's just being funny."

"No, I'm not. Think about it, Marichka."

"Thanks for the backpack and the lesson. Gotta go. See you next Sunday."

Maria is livid as she walks back into her car.

"Jerk! What was he talking about? Not cry… I guess it's not okay for me to be me."

She tries to not let Luke get to her but he sure did hit a nerve.

She drives along the touristy part of Government, past Murchies and Munro's Books, and finds a parking spot in her favourite parkade on View.

Maria had never stepped foot into the Mountain Equipment Co-op store until that day.

"Oh, that's what this store is," she says as she approaches the corner of the innocuous tan building. "And that's where the Plaza Hotel used to be before it burned down a couple of months ago. I saw the smoke from Hillside Mall that day. It's all boarded up now."

Even though the MEC store is unassuming from street view, it is packed with shoppers inside. The cashiers' line is long and winding but it is moving fast.

"I'm going to need one of those… and one of those…oh and that's a clever idea," Maria says to herself as she walks up and down the aisles and scans the shelves, trying to imagine the people who will be using all of these neat gadgets in the future.

"Good thing I won't be needing any winter camping stuff," she says as she passes the sub-zero tents. Will I need a sleeping bag? Maybe I can find something at home instead to save some money? Passport wallet? That might be good. Focus, Maria, focus. Right. Backpacks. Here they are."

As Maria stands in front of the wall of backpacks that are neatly arranged by size, colour and price, a young sales clerk approaches her with a casual confidence, as if they are at a party.

"Can I help you find something?" he asks.

"Yeah, I'm looking to buy a backpack for my upcoming Camino in Spain and I haven't done anything quite like this before so am not exactly sure what I'm going to need."

"Camino? Good for you. First of all, how long are you going for?"

"Two weeks, just going to hike the last 250 kilometres or so."

"Okay, so you're probably looking at one that's 30 to 40 litres in size."

"Yes, that's what I've been told."

"You really don't need anything much bigger but try not to carry more than 20 per cent of your body weight."

As someone who goes by the motto, "Better to have it and not need it, than to need it and not have it," that she learned from good ol' Benjamin back in the day, keeping her supplies to a minimum is another one of Maria's challenges.

She spots an orange one that may work. It reminds her of a square backpack she had briefly as a kid, that somehow got lost in the move to Hawaii.

"Let's try this one first," she says. He pulls it off the hook and loosens the straps. "Turn around, put your arm in here. Other arm. Good. Turn back around. How does it feel?"

"Good."

"It's got a place for water bottles here and here," he says as he tightens the waist. "And a loop for your bladder hose, if that's the direction you're heading."

"Oh, I don't think I'll be bringing one of those," she says shyly.

"Okay, cool. That's fine. What do you think?"

"Can we try on another one just to compare?"

"Sure, how about this blue one? It's on clearance, if that helps."

"Yes, that does help. And I like the colour!"

"It's called, 'Intense Blue!'" he says as he reads the tag. "And good, Women's, 40-litre."

Again, he opens all of the tightened straps on the backpack. Maria shuffles in as he holds the backpack behind her.

"Just pull on these to tighten. Here you go. And here and here."

By now they are standing nose to nose and toes to toes in the narrow aisle and Maria is feeling a little heat between them.

"Thanks."

He is very patient with her as she pictures herself backpacking through Spain wearing this model. "I'll take it!" she says looking into his eyes.

"Good choice. I'll ring it up."

in • turn • net

"See you in October," says Maria giving her mother a loose hug at 7am. Maria is off the hook this time for airport drop off duty because Lubomyra's friends, who are also going on the tour to France and Ukraine, are taking her to the airport instead.

"Stay safe, enjoy your trip!"

"Don't forget to turn the water off before you leave…"

"Where is that again?"

"Behind my closet. You just turn the tap all the way so the pipes don't burst."

"Oh, okay," Maria says making herself a mental note.

"And tell the neighbours when you're going so they can keep an eye out on the house while we're both gone."

"Okay, I will, and get some water from Lourdes for us. Love you!"

"Love you, Ciom," her mother says as she waves with one hand and pulls her suitcase through the gate with the other."

Maria sees the car back out on to the street and drive away.

"Ah, freedom," she says stretching. "I have the whole house to myself, even if it's just for a week. If I was a drinker, I'd pull out a bottle to celebrate. But I'm not anymore. What else can I do to start my staycation?"

* * *

"If I'm going to move to Calgary after I come back from this trip, I'd like to have a job in hand before I go," thinks Maria as she scans the Internet for 'spas with wellness centres' and 'wellness retreats with coaches' near Calgary.

She finds a very promising lead to a wellness company called "Cherish" that holds retreats in Kananaskis. She likes how she recognizes one of the names on their team of coaches, nutritionists, personal trainers, meditation leaders, and nature guides.

At the bottom of the contact page, Maria reads, "Send us your resume if you'd like to join our team!"

"Oh my gosh, this is so up my alley!" thinks Maria with a smile. "Coaching, nature hikes… I'm going to reach out to them right away."

> **Subject: Interested in Joining your Team**
>
> Hello! I'm a passionate wellness professional with a background in life coaching, spa therapy and self-care. I've attached my cover

letter, resume and life coaching certificate and I'd love to join your team!

I look forward to the possibility of talking to you soon to further discuss my qualifications, ideas and this great opportunity.

Sincerely, Maria Ponomarenko

based in Victoria, BC

Much to Maria's surprise, she receives an email back first thing on Monday.

Subject: RE: Interested in Joining your Team

Hello Maria, Thank you for reaching out to me. I am currently on vacation until Saturday. I will reach out early next week to discuss. Thank you for your interest. Lisa, Cherish Retreats

Maria follows up with Lisa and sends another email:

Subject: RE: Interested in Joining your Team

Hi Lisa, I hope you had a fun vacation. I'm just following up to see if you're still interested in connecting. I'm around early next week if that works for you.

Thanks, Maria

Subject: RE: Interested in Joining your Team

Hello Maria, I do have time now if you want to give me a call.

Lisa, Cherish Retreats

So, Maria picks up her cell phone, takes a deep breath and enters the numbers.

"Hi Lisa, it's Maria from Victoria. I just got your message. Is it still a good time to chat?"

"Hi, Maria, yes, I have some time now."

"I was excited to see your call for resumes on your website and thanks for replying so quickly."

"Sure. Can you tell me a little bit about yourself?"

"Well, I'm a Certified Wellness Coach from the Walker Coaching Academy in Calgary…"

"Oh, I know them."

"With a background in spa therapy and self-care."

"Cool."

"I'm currently based in Victoria but am planning to move to Calgary after I return from walking the Camino in Spain in October."

"You're doing a Camino? That's great."

"Yes! I've been training all summer and so far I've managed to let go of over 20 pounds and over 12 inches off my body through working with my personal trainer, eating better, and wellness walking. I love how you offer nature hikes during your retreats!"

"Speaking of retreats, we're hosting a Wellness Day in Kananaskis on October 21st."

"Oh my gosh, that sounds amazing."

"If you can make it, you're welcome to come!

"Oh, I'd love that!"

"Then you can experience one of our Wellness Days for yourself and see if there's something you can contribute to the team in the future. How does that sound?"

"That sounds wonderful! Thanks Lisa! I'll let you know when I come back from my trip if I can swing it!"

"Well, we'd love to have you attend. Enjoy your time in Spain!"

"Thanks, I will! I'll be in touch!"

"Yay!" says Maria as she hangs up the phone.

"This gives me a firm deadline to go to Calgary – after that it will probably be too wintery to drive through the Rockies after that anyway. Wouldn't it be amazing if I could lead wellness coaching retreats with them? It's all starting to come together!"

* * *

Subject: Thanks

Thanks, Luke for sending me Brett's email. I'll contact him today. Would you like to join us if we decide to meet? Also, are you still OK with taking me to the airport? My flight leaves at 11:35 am from Victoria to Calgary on Tuesday, September 17. I hope you're enjoying the sunshine, Maria

Subject: RE: Thanks

Hi Maria, yes I will take you to the airport, what time do you want me to pick you up? Brett and Jean are wonderful people, spend as much time with them as you can. Luke

Subject: Hoping to talk to you about the Camino

Hi Brett, I got your email from Luke. We met back in March. He suggested I talk to you about my upcoming Camino. I leave on Tuesday, September 17. Would you have time to give me some tips? Maria

Subject: RE: Hoping to talk to you about the Camino

Sure, Maria, are you going to the Pilgrim Coffee at Cedar Hill Rec Centre tomorrow morning? If so, that'd be a convenient time to chat. Brett

Subject: RE: Hoping to talk to you about the Camino

Hi Brett, Thanks for getting back to me so quickly. I hadn't planned on going to the Pilgrim coffee but that sounds like a good idea. What time does it start?

Subject: RE: Hoping to talk to you about the Camino

10am

Subject: RE: Hoping to talk to you about the Camino

Great, thanks, see you tomorrow!

* * *

The "service air bags" light pings in Maria's car as she pulls out of the driveway to meet Brett, but she does not know what that means exactly, so she chooses to ignore it.

"I'll deal with it when I get back from Spain."

Parking is tight at the Cedar Hill Rec. Centre and it takes Maria a few passes around the track to find a spot, which is unusual because normally the parking gods are good to her.

When she enters the café, she sees Brett sitting at a table but it is clear he does not recognize her from six months ago.

"Brett?"

"Maria?" She nods.

"Have a seat. They're just about to start the pilgrim meeting, but if it's all the same to you, we can just sit here and talk amongst ourselves."

"Sure, that's fine. Thanks for meeting me here."

"I've brought my notes from my most recent Camino. I walked with my daughter a few months ago."

"Oh, that's nice that you had a chance to go on a Camino with your daughter."

"Yes, it was great that she was able to take time off work and go with me. Here's where we stayed. If you want, I can email you our itinerary."

"That would be great, thanks. If you were to offer your daughter any advice before going, what would you have told her?"

"Oh, good question. Bring earplugs and flip flops and here's what I did to avoid getting blisters."

"Hot topic among pilgrims, I'm sure."

"I brought two pairs of double-lined socks which I washed and alternated every day. Do you have good socks yet?"

"Yes."

"Okay, good. Then each night after a long day of hiking and a shower and each morning before I set off, I'd apply a cream on my feet – it's in a green tin…"

"Yes, I think I know the one."

"And put my socks and boots on top and had no issues whatsoever."

"Wow, good for you."

"If you'd like, we can go to Hillside Mall after this and I can show you the cream so you can buy some for yourself."

"You don't have to do that."

"And what else? Do you have a sleeping bag and a liner?"

"No. I thought the albergues provided the basics…"

"Yeah, they often give you a protective, disposable sheet and pillow case and you can ask for a blanket, but that's not enough. If you can't find anything, you can borrow mine."

"That's most generous. I'll see what I can find at home."

"Like I said, it's there if you need it. Do you want to go to Shopper's? I have a few things I need to pick up anyway."

"Yes."

"Well, I walked here so if you want to drive us there, we can go together."

"Sure, that sounds good."

Brett collects all of his papers from the coffee table and Maria follows him outside to the parking lot.

"My car is over this way," she says.

Sure enough, as she turns on the ignition, the "service air bags" chime goes off again. "This pinging sound is brand new," she says to him hoping he may be able to offer some wisdom.

"I don't have any experience with that," he says. "Turn here."

"I didn't know you can get to Hillside from here. I haven't been on this road before."

"It's a short cut."

Within a few minutes, they drive to the mall and enter the well-lit, gleaming white, shiny drug store. Maria follows Brett up and down the aisles.

"Here it is… O'Keefe's Working Hands. Take it with you and apply it to your feet every night and every morning and you'll save yourself from some painful blisters."

Maria is hoping he was going to recommend the Glysomed which is also in a green tin and is a dollar cheaper, but she chooses to go with Brett's pick because he seems to know what he is talking about.

"Well, I'll leave you to it. Email me if you change your mind about the sleeping bag. And if I don't see you before you leave, *Buen Camino!*"

"Thanks, I really appreciate your time."

Brett does not hang around any longer and leaves the store promptly.

"While I'm here, I'm going to see if I can find a hat," says Maria to herself after purchasing the cream. "I'd like to find a cute, pink baseball cap."

But even though she pops into several stores in the mall, there are no pink baseball caps in sight.

"I guess I'll just wear my red bandana for a hat but while I'm here, I'm going to go into Bolen Books. Hopefully, I can find a great book to read on the airplane."

Maria enters the store through the food court entrance.

"I'm looking for an adventure, something like "Eat, Pray, Love" or "Wild" but I don't think I want to read "Wild" while I'm on the road," she thinks to herself as she walks towards the fiction section.

Maria scans the shelves at hip level and picks up a book that looks promising. She reads the synopsis but it is not what she expects.

"No, that's not it," she says putting it back.

She raises her focus up to the second shelf from the top and over to her left. "'The Signature of All Things'... oh yes, I remember when Liz Gilbert talked about this book on Oprah's 'SuperSoul Sunday'... Alma goes on an adventure and falls in love with a man who 'draws her into the realm of the spiritual, the divine, and the magical?' Check, check, check!"

Without looking at any other choices, Maria clutches the book to her chest and heads to the cashier.

"This is the story for my trip," she thinks as she slides the book across the counter.

"Oh, yes, a nice weekend read," says the clerk.

* * *

Maria scrolls down her newsfeed and sees a nice photo of her mother having lunch with her tour group in Lourdes.

"Good to see she's enjoying herself," thinks Maria.

At that moment, a new email notification flies across the top of her screen.

Subject: Hello from Lourdes
Hi Guys, Arrived safe and sound and had a good sleep in Lourdes. Off to discover the town. Love you all XOX Mam

Subject: RE: Hello from Lourdes
Hi Mam, Thanks for the update. I'm glad to hear you arrived safely. Also, I dreamt that I hugged Tato this morning – maybe that has something to do with you visiting Lourdes? XOX Marichka

In the years following the passing of her father in 2001, Maria has had a handful of dreams about him. These dreams seem more lucid and real than her other dreams and when he shows up in the etheric realm of sleep, the story is always a variation on the theme that somehow, through a mysterious reversal of facts, he manages to come back into his old body, after his death and pick up his life where he left off, which becomes awkward and difficult to explain to the other characters in her dream.

Maria thinks that her father returning to visit her in her dreams is a throwback to her childhood when she waited for him to come back home after being away for months at sea with the navy.

In one dream in particular, Maria had the wherewithal to actually ask her late father, "What is death like?"

To her surprise and delight, her father replied, "It's all love."

"What a beautiful message… It's all love. That's what we need to remember each day as we go through our lives…

"Didn't Jesus say, 'Love your neighbour as yourself?' He wasn't talking about loving people's egos, their old self, their false self… Jesus was talking about seeing behind the ego's clunky chainmail suit – and loving someone's essence, and loving your own essence, and recognizing how the essence of all beings are connected as One in this great, big, living sea. Oh, to live from my essence and see love everywhere!"

sake • red

William Shakespeare is considered a master of it, Alanis Morrissett has written a song about it, and Maria Ponomarenko catches a glimpse of it after reading her friend Linda's random post: "Tourist Joins Search Party, Realizes Everyone Was Looking for Her."

The news story begins when a tour group, who is travelling by bus through Eldgjá, a volcanic region in southern Iceland, stops for a short rest and to take in the scenic views.

When it is time to board the bus again and for everyone to sit back in their brightly-coloured, checkered seats, the bus driver has to take a head count.

Unfortunately, the numbers come up short. Someone is missing.

According to the *Reykjavik Grapevine*, the bus driver contacted police after an hour of waiting and described the missing person as an Asian woman, "about 160 centimetres, in dark clothing and speaks English well."

Without further delay, the search party of about 50 people, including all of the tourists on the bus, has been launched. The weary travellers search high and low in the great Icelandic wilderness for hours, without a clue.

Finally, at three o'clock in the morning, fresh news had come to light – the missing woman has been on the bus all along and has even innocently participated in her own search!

"She was hidden in plain sight – right under their noses – and under her own nose – the whole time!" says Maria not knowing whether to laugh or cry.

Somehow, the tourist, who has been on a personal journey of self-discovery (as most travellers are to some degree), did not recognize the description of herself and on top of that, she had taken the rest stop as an opportunity to change her clothes and "freshen up" before re-boarding the bus.

"But aren't we all just looking for ourselves?" Maria comments on Linda's post, realizing this might generate some eye rolls.

Meanwhile, to add to the confusion, the bus driver had also mis-counted the passengers.

"Oops! Maria muses. "Chalk it up to: 'All's Well That Ends Well' and 'Isn't it Ironic.'"

* * *

Linda is a seasoned traveler and has her own stories to tell. She is a divorced mother of 10 children – the first nine of them boys – and a grandmother of eight! Her oldest son works as a pilot for WestJet which allows her the freedom to travel across Canada and beyond to the United States, Europe, Mexico, Central America, and the Caribbean, on a stand-by ticket, and she is happy to explore the world unfettered.

Linda is by far Maria's best client from her mobile spa days. Linda booked her first appointment for a facial and energy healing after she had won a gift certificate in a silent auction at the Aveda store in 2013.

"Homebody" is not a good word to describe Linda but she is good at making the best of whatever living situation she is in. Over the years, Maria has given facials to Linda in four different living rooms, from an apartment building a few blocks from Maria's house, to another one on Dallas Road, to Linda's bungalow in Sooke, to another apartment in Oak Bay – always leaving the spaces 'smelling like Aveda.'

Maria likes how Linda continues to make her health and wellness a priority and is always up to wearing the lavender spa robes, breathing in the essential oils, dunking her feet in the foot baths, and listening to the relaxing playlist that are all part of Maria's spa services.

Linda is always very generous and has even bought gift certificates from Maria for her friend and daughter. She even signed up for Maria's coaching package, too.

For the wellness coaching sessions, Maria met Linda in a coffee shop in Cook Street Village. From those coaching sessions, Linda was able to manifest a beautiful opportunity to live in the South of France for a few months. The clincher was, "since this AirBnb fell into your lap as it did – you're meant to go," said Maria to her client. "Look at all of the things that came together without you even trying – it's yours to do."

Before Linda left for France, Maria leant Linda her copy of Miriam Fisher's book, "Sacred Soul Dimensions" plus her personal set of homemade cards with descriptions of all of the dimensions featured in the book, which Linda poured over with great relish, literally – she spilled coffee on a few of them.

Working with dimensions struck a deep chord with Linda, so a few years later after she returned from France and when Miriam announced she would be speaking in Victoria, Linda said she wanted to go.

"Would you be interested in coming to see Miriam Fisher with me? She will be speaking at UVic and tickets will be going on sale soon."

"I'd really like to go with you, Linda, but the ticket prices are a little steep for me. Let me know if you end up going – I'd love to hear all about it and thanks for the heads up!"

Undaunted, Linda bought herself a ticket to the event. Meanwhile, Maria let the idea go. Weeks passed and on the cool and rainy morning when Miriam was scheduled to speak, Maria received this text from Linda:

> Maria, something has come up
> and I am not going to be able to go
> to Miriam Fisher tonight.
> Would you like to use my ticket?
> No charge.

Even at 7am, this text required more of a 'pick-up-the-phone-and-call' response, so Maria called Linda back right away.

"Are you sure you can't go?"

"Yes, I have a lot of paperwork to do for my son's business and there's a deadline coming up and I just have to get this done. But you take the ticket as my gift to you."

"I wish we could go together but if it means your ticket would go to waste if I don't accept it, then I'll go. Yes, I would love the ticket. Thank you, Linda!!"

"Great. Come to my place in Oak Bay to pick up your ticket and I'll see you then."

Maria marveled at how this ticket to see one of the most influential authors she had ever read, in person, landed in her lap. Even though Maria got lost driving home from Oak Bay after picking up her tickets and had to stand in line in the pouring rain to pay for parking at UVic and thought she was going to be late as a result, her front row balcony seat was the perfect vantage point. Everything unfolded naturally in its own way.

Subject: Thank you!
Hi Linda, Thank you so much for the ticket. It was wonderful. I'm working on a

blog post now that I'll be publishing later today!
Cheers, Maria

Subject: RE: Thank you!
So happy you enjoyed it!

* * *

DON'T LOSE YOUR HEART!

by Maria Ponomarenko, Wellness Coach & Spiritual Teacher

I had the joy of attending, "The Power of Your Voice" presented by Miriam Fisher at the University of Victoria.

When I woke up that morning, I had no idea I was going to be at UVic by the end of the day. It was a completely unexpected and welcomed surprise.

To me, it was a little miracle how everything came together and interestingly enough, Miriam lightly touched on that idea in her talk.

In essence, Miriam said each day is a new day, a new start, a blank slate, and we get to choose our reality, and what we experience, and it starts with the words we use.

We have no idea what the day will bring so why not nudge it in a good direction with our words.

I love how Miriam says, "We cast spells with our words and create new worlds – that's why putting letters together in a specific order is called spelling." We can literally speak things into life!

I must be choosing some pretty good words these days! I'm grateful to my best client and friend Linda for gifting me the ticket! It was a big deal for me to go and I actually wore a dress, heels, and make-up to the event. I also decided to wear my rose quartz heart Christmas tree ornament necklace and rose quartz bracelet.

Seeing Miriam Fisher in person (from the balcony) was significant for me. Her book, "Sacred Soul Dimensions," explained so much to me spiritually and I even made my own set of Dimension cards from her list.

But more than that, I feel like I've been on a deep and profound spiritual journey of awakening and for the last year or so, it has been intense. Lots of crying, lots of letting go, lots of shedding of my old ways.

To help me through this process, I've also been studying the work of Dr. Oscar Boshon, the famous Geologist. I've been searching for answers to the big questions of life and it's been very emotional and some people told me that I was depressed and that I needed to talk to a therapist.

Miriam Fisher explained that people often confuse depression with a spiritual crisis but we don't have the language to express the confusion, so the mental depression gets the attention, not the spirit or soul.

Both depression and spiritual crisis can show up similarly, but if you sense you need to find the meaning and purpose to your life, then that's a clue that you might be having a spiritual crisis this time.

I thought, yes, that's what I've been going through this past year: a spiritual crisis.

That's good news!

Here's my opportunity to push through into a whole new dimension of living life and I'm really excited about this breakthrough! Instead of letting this spiritual heartbreak be my excuse to keep me unconscious, I'm going to use it to help me awaken into consciousness. That's the message I keep hearing from spiritual teachers.

Dr. Oscar says the most important thing we can do for humanity is to be conscious and present. And Miriam explained that as humans create new technologies that often lead to bigger problems which can potentially destroy us, there's a profound darkness in the world that needs to be healed.

Even so, there is also a counter force to the darkness that is also emerging. It's like two sides of the same coin, one balances the other. In the midst of this darkness, there is also light.

This is when Miriam really lit up! I don't know if it was the stage lighting or something else, but I saw violet light surrounding her. It was like a purple, misty shadow trailing behind her movements.

Violet is the most spiritual colour. It's associated with the crown chakra, our connection to the Divine, so I knew she was speaking Spiritual Truth. That's what we're called to do. As generations living in a dark and volatile age, we're called to be the light!

This reminds me of Bruce Cockburn's song, "Lovers in a Dangerous Time," where he says, "You've got to kick at the darkness till it bleeds daylight." We are lovers in a dangerous time — lovers in the sense of bigger-picture lovers of humanity, not necessarily romantic couples, as I once thought.

But how do you fight the good fight and shine your light when you're living in fear and pain? Miriam said there's a new dimension for people who have been wounded but have somehow moved forward, yet have still remained vulnerable. It's an interesting mix — wounded, vulnerable, and strong – and hard to describe, almost like indigo.

We've all been wounded one way or another, on a personal level and on a global level, and we're really good at re-telling our victim stories over and over again. But we can't wallow in the victim role anymore!

Miriam says, "Coddling each other through the pain has to stop today."

I've decided I'm not going to entertain those victim stories, either from myself, or my coaching clients, or my friends, anymore.

The better question is, "what strength is emerging?" or "what is the gift?" It's not about the adversity, or our history, it's about how we respond from here that counts.

And this is what I got from Miriam's talk: It's time to retire those victim stories and poor spelling and step up in this critical time in history.

Crazy world leaders, missile warnings, and natural disasters are the wake up calls! It's time we take our head out of the sand, or put down those distracting devices, or resist those numbing addictions, and instead, be present!

If you feel like you've been going through a spiritual crises, as I have, and you've been called to shine your light in this world and do something really amazing, then do it!

The only one who is stopping you is you. You are in charge of your reality and it's up to you! The words you say to yourself and out loud will create your path. Choose them thoughtfully!

And that's exactly what I'm doing starting today.

Hearing Miriam Fisher speak affirmed in my heart that I'd like to join her and Dr. Oscar Boshon and many others and be a spiritual teacher as well.

And I'd like to put forth a new dimension that represents people who have been through the trenches but have also emerged as conscious and awakened leaders with heart. Just because you've been through it, doesn't give you the excuse to be miserable and mean, or to fall back into unconsciousness.

Let the adversity be your doorway to enlightenment. Let's define this new dimension together so we can enjoy Mother Earth for many, many thousands more generations to come!

The title of this post is, "Don't lose your heart." That's my message for today.

Although things may seem bleak, remember, we're still in the game. Keep the faith. Prayers are always heard and answered and miracles happen every day.

Miriam finished her talk by praying, "May God live in our hearts and help us be generous of spirit."

P.S. As I was leaving the auditorium, I grazed over something with my shoe. I looked behind me and it was my pink quartz heart necklace on the floor.

I quickly retrieved it and as I was picking it up, a woman who saw me said, "Don't lose your heart!" She was stunned a little by what she said, so she said it again, "Don't lose your heart!"

I said, "Noooooo!"

Talk about the "power of words!" I believe this anonymous woman was speaking on behalf of the Universe in that moment. "Don't lose your heart!"

Thank you anonymous woman in the auditorium, and thank you Linda for the ticket, and thank you Miriam Fisher for coming to Victoria! Come back anytime!

thou • sands

"What is Nick doing in England?" asks Maria as she reads his stacked posts on her feed. In quick succession, Nick posts several photos of himself with people he had only known online previously and just met in person recently.

In the first photo, he is with a woman and her two daughters in England, and then he flies over to Greece to see Maria's former classmate, then he jet sets over to Russia to see another woman. Next up is a photo of him and Alice and then finally his photo with Maria that had been taken by Arielle back in June.

Maria likes that she is included in Nick's summer world tour and hopes that sharing her photo is a sign that their meeting is not just a one-off. Still, she cannot help but think that he is either looking for a business partner or a new girlfriend, and in either case, why isn't he choosing her for either?

Annoyed, she switches gears and checks her email. She finds a new one from her mother.

Subject: RE: Hello from Lourdes

Marichka, Just remembered you are leaving next week. While I still have internet I thought I would share. Met a man on the plane from Ottawa who was on his way to do a Camino starting in France. Here in Lourdes we are 40K from the Spanish boarder. He was starting at this end and doing the whole walk. I am doing a lot of walking even though we are close to the centre. Mam XOX

Subject: RE: Hello from Lourdes

Hi Mam, I'm sure there are many people travelling to do the Camino this time of year. Why did you feel you needed to mention this man from Ottawa? XOX Marichka

Subject: RE: Hello from Lourdes

Because he was starting in France I guess. Mam

Subject: RE: Hello from Lourdes

Hi Mam, Lourdes sounds like a nice place to start from. It would be funny if I met him on the trail also. Marichka

Maria spontaneously decides to take advantage of the big, smart TV that has been sitting quiet for the past few days. She is drawn to watch the movie, "Elizabeth the Golden Age: The New World."

She loves the colourful costumes of the period and the lesson in history, "Oh, that was the Spanish Inquisition!" and is particularly enamored with the scene where Sir Walter Raleigh beautifully describes to Queen Elizabeth I what it is like to sail across the ocean – words that also capture the magic of coaching in their rhythm. She feels compelled to write a blog post about it before making herself some dinner.

* * *

COACHING IS A CREATING CONVERSATION

by Maria Ponomarenko, Ammolite Wellness Coach

What do you want to create in your life? When I first discovered that creativity is at the heart of coaching, I lit up!

I like to think of wellness coaching as a forward-thinking conversation where you have the opportunity to paint a vivid picture in your imagination of what you want to experience in your future... And then... somehow... through the magic of the Universe and your own effort and allowing, you're able to watch your idea come to life in your current reality!

It's a truly amazing feeling to step inside a real life version of what you first saw in your mind's eye in your coaching conversation.

To illustrate the coaching process, here's a clip from the movie, "Elizabeth the Golden Age: The New World," where Sir Walter Raleigh describes the New World to Queen Elizabeth I.

SIR WALTER RALEIGH (SWR): Can you imagine what it is to cross an ocean? For weeks you see nothing but the horizon, perfect and empty. You live in the grip of fear, fear of storms, fear of sickness on board, fear of the immensity. So, you must drive that fear down deep into your belly. Study your chart. What's your compass? Pray for a fair wind... and hope. Pure, naked, fragile hope.

[interruption]

QUEEN ELIZABETH I (QE): Let them wait. Go on Mr. Raleigh, you were hoping?

SWR: At first, it is no more than a haze on the horizon... so you watch. You watch. Then it is a smudge, a shadow on the far water for a day, for another day. The stain slowly spreads along the horizon taking form until on the third day, you let yourself believe. You dare to whisper the word, "land." Life, life, resurrection, the true adventure coming out of the vast unknown, out of the immensity into new life. That, your Majesty, is the New World.

QE: I like your immensities. Your ocean is an image of eternity. Such great spaces make us small. Do we discover the new world, Mr. Raleigh, or does the new world discover us?

SWR: You speak like a true Explorer.

Each day brings us a fresh chance to create and discover a new world! So… I'm going to ask you again… "What do you want to create in your life?"

* * *

Maria wants to include a photo taken from the bow of a ship with land in sight to echo Mr. Raleigh's smudge of land but does not have one in her stash. She decides to go with a photo she took of ducks swimming in the ocean off Island View Beach which shows sandy cliffs in the distance that she always calls, "The Cliffs of Dover."

"That's the best I can do for now," she says as she uploads the photo. After one quick skim to make sure everything looks good, Maria publishes her blog post. Within moments, she receives a request to connect from some guy from across the pond whom she does not know, but seems interesting.

> Hi Maria, From one Purpose-Driven Coach to another, I'd love to invite you to join my Network. Look forward to seeing more of you here on this channel! Cheers, Vincent

Then, a few minutes later, Olivia calls out of the blue.

"Hello?"

"Hey, Maria, what are you doing for the long weekend?"

"I don't have any plans yet. Just thought I'd do some last minute walking and packing before my big trip."

"Oh right… when are you going again?"

"The seventeenth!"

"Do you feel ready?"

"Not really, but I'm sure it will all come together."

"Would you like to come to help celebrate Carlos' birthday with us this weekend? Lada has been planning a big party and we can pick you up from the ferries on Saturday morning so you won't have to drive your car on."

"Yes, sure, I'd like to come. It'll be a good chance for me to travel with my backpack."

"Great – and bring your passport too!"

"Why do I need my passport?"

"Because we're going to Point Roberts for the afternoon first and that's in the States."

"What's in Point Roberts and why are we going there?"

"Because Shawn just bought a house there and we've been invited for a visit."

"Oh, well that sounds nice. Sure, I'd like that. See you on Saturday morning! I'll let you know what ferry I'm on. And thanks for inviting me!"

"You're welcome. It will be nice to see you before you leave on your trip."

Subject: RE: Hello from Lourdes

Hi Mam, I think I might be going to visit Krys this weekend for Carlos' 50th birthday. Olivia invited me and it sounds like fun. Marichka

Subject: RE: Hello from Lourdes

Good idea! Go.... XOX Mam

Maria is excited to have the chance to take her new backpack and passport for a test drive. Adding an hour and 40-minute ferry ride through the Active Pass and across the open waters towards Vancouver is the perfect trial run for her upcoming adventure.

She is in good spirits even though she has to wait for over an hour in the BC Ferries' parking lot for Krys and the family to come and pick her up.

"Never mind they had to go through a drive through first," thinks Maria as she eyes their drinks. "Just let it go."

* * *

Point Roberts only covers an area of 12.65 kilometres squared (or 4.884 square miles) but even if Point Roberts is only the size of a postage stamp, it is still highly collectible for its geographical, geological, and historical significance.

Captain George Vancouver (1757-1798) named Point Roberts after his friend Henry Roberts (1756-1796), who was an officer in the British Royal Navy and who served with George and Captain James Cook (1728-1779) on the high seas.

Point Roberts has the rare and unique status of being a pene-enclave and pene-exclave, which means it is a territory within a territory that is only accessible through the territory of another country, either by land, air, or sea.

In Point Roberts' case, although it is located on the southern-most tip of the Tsawwassen Peninsula, a short, 35 kilometres (or 22 miles) south of the Canadian city of Vancouver, and is surrounded by the country of Canada, the Strait of Georgia, and Boundary Bay, and is only reachable from Washington State by road by travelling for 40 kilometres (or 25 miles) through Canada first and two border crossings, it remains American.

Point Roberts is an area that nods to a volatile time in the world's history when countries continued to shore up their empires and "more land, more land, more land" was the name of the game.

The mid-19th Century was all about continental expansion and this era, (from the end of the War of 1812, between the United States and the United Kingdom, to the beginning of the American Civil War in 1860), was also called, "the Age of Manifest Destiny."

In the midst of the melee, Point Roberts was caught up in a boundary dispute, known as the "Oregon Boundary Dispute" or the "Oregon Question," where the Pacific Northwest of North America was up for grabs and both the United States and England had a vested interest.

The hot ticket territory ran West of the Continental Divide of the Americas, North of Mexico's Alta California border at the 42nd Parallel North, and South of Russian America at Parallel 54°40′ North; a region then referred to as the "Columbia District" by the British and the "Oregon Country" by the Americans.

American expansionists urged the newly elected U.S. President James K. Polk to annex the entire Oregon Country up to latitude 54°40′N, shouting the slogan, "Fifty-Four Forty or Fight!"

If the American Northern movement had its way and 54°40′ was the line drawn in the sand, Canada's generous territory would not have expanded to its current size.

Furthermore, British Columbia, including Victoria and Vancouver, would not be on the map of Canada at all, and Telkwa, Moricetown and Hazelton would have been the United States' closest neighbours.

Moreover, places like Nelson, Kamloops, Williams Lake, Quesnel, McBride, Prince George, Vanderhoof, Fort St. James, Burns Lake, Houston, Terrace and Prince Rupert would have landed in the United States, plus Alaska would have stayed in touch with the rest of its country along the coast.

But President Polk was not paying attention and instead focused South, in the opposite direction, towards Texas and Mexico.

However, off the side of his desk, he made an offer to call the border at 49 degrees with the line straight across Vancouver Island from the mainland, but the British rejected the offer.

Had the Americans known that gold would be discovered up in "them there hills" just ten short years later, they would have fought harder for Fifty-Four Forty, but instead they made another offer to continue to draw the line at 49 and even bend the boundary just slightly more South around the tip of Vancouver Island.

From the British point of view, Vancouver Island in general and Fort Victoria specifically, held huge potential for future settlements and commercial trading, and if necessary, they would have given up territory on the Lower Mainland to keep Vancouver Island in the bank.

That was how the Point Roberts' card got played.

"It was a bargaining chip!"

It was the answer to the Oregon Question! By giving up Point Roberts, (even though it was inconvenient for the Americans),

Britain and Canada managed to keep all of the land North of the 49th Parallel, including all of Vancouver Island. It was all signed on the dotted line in 1846.

"Well played, Queen Victoria! Well played!"

* * *

The Ponomarenko's border crossing into Point Roberts, Washington is quick and uneventful, other than stopping at the store for a case of beer. As the Ponomarenko's enter the United States, Maria's gaze pours over the lush, green Cedar forest that lines the edge of the road.

They find the address and park on the gravel shoulder. Shawn, Kelly and their kids greet their visitors warmly and after a quick tour of their vacation home that was built in the Pacific Northwest style, everyone sits outside on the deck with their drinks.

"Welcome to the best gated community in the U.S!" says Shawn with a big smile.

Although grey clouds hover overhead and the winds pick up, Shawn offers to take the Ponomarenko's on a quick hike on the trail that jets through their backyard.

"There's a surprise on the trail that I'd love to show you, if you're up for it," says Shawn.

"Yes, of course we are," says Krys, getting up from his camping chair. Off they go into the wilderness. Shawn's pace is quick as he leads his guests deeper into the woods.

"Everything is so green and alive!" thinks Maria as she steps lightly in her sandals over the logs, branches, and ferns that are strewn along the ground.

The path twists and turns like ball of wool, knots and all. Soon they are able to see blue water peeking through the trees. Shawn slows down and waits for everyone to gather around him.

"Notice how there's white sand on the path?" asks Shawn. "Where do you think it's coming from?"

Nobody has an answer.

Then Shawn pulls back the curtain at the lookout point.

"This is what I wanted to show you!" says Shawn as they all gasp, especially Maria!

"We're up 300 feet and beneath us is all sand!"

"Oh my gosh," says Maria in sheer amazement. "I'm standing on what I've been calling 'the Cliffs of Dover!' I just posted a photo of these cliffs on my blog! I've walked into my own photograph. Thank you so much for inviting me here! I'm absolutely thrilled by how everything has unfolded in this moment!"

"Don't get too close to the edge!" says Olivia as she takes a photo of Maria beaming with delight, with the ocean behind and the steep cliffs beneath.

"Let's keep going," says Shawn. "We have time to go to the beach, right Kelly?"

"If we hurry, but Martín and Tanis might be waiting for us," she says.

"Let's go everyone – we're burning daylight!"

Maria is still trying to catch her breath from her mystical moment. Soon the group spreads out but they can still hear each other's voices echoing through the trees. In some places, stairs have been built to make the climbing easier. Several other groups of hikers pass them along the way.

Finally, they make their way down the cliff to sea level at low tide. Maria stops in her tracks as she looks Northwest – there is Vancouver Island off in the distance! She pictures herself standing on the other beach, looking out across the water and waves back to herself as she takes another photo.

"I just saw lightening!" says Olivia.

"Where? Where?" ask Maxim and Zoryanna.

"Out there in those dark clouds!"

Both Maxim and Zoryanna scan the rumbling horizon for another lightening rod to crack its way across the sky, but the storm is moving too quickly farther and farther West.

"We'd better start heading back," says Kelly. "Just a few more minutes," says Maxim and Zoryanna. "We want to see the lightening!"

Maria is ready to hike back to the house and follows Kelly up the stairs and through the forest. All she sees are flashes of green leaves as she races back along the narrow sandy path.

She feels exhilarated – like something magical and serendipitous just happened. She was hoping to have a mystical experience on her Camino but Point Roberts showed up before she even got on the plane!

Unbeknownst to Maria, she is walking on the sand dunes of East cliff-face at Lily Point, a geological marvel in its own right. Over the course of 60 million years, layers of sediments consisting of silt, sand, sand-gravel, and peat, were deposited beneath Point Roberts and became known as the "Chuckanut Formation."

On top of that, at least four separate ice sheets, one as thick as 7000 feet, crawled over the formation over tens of thousands of years, leaving behind more sediment, as they headed Southeast. The sediments that settled from the melting glaciers had accumulated to 300 feet or so of soft, not-so-tightly compacted, chalky, beige, Glacial Marine Drift.

To Maria, those Napoleonic layers look like the "Cliffs of Dover" when she looks out from Island View Beach on Vancouver Island, across the Strait of Georgia.

When they arrive back at the house, Martín and Tanis are sitting on the deck waiting. Maria is happy to see them! They are like family even though they haven't seen or spoken to each other since Maria visited them in Vancouver during the 2010 Winter Olympic Games.

Maria likes how Krys' classmates had a chance to know her father, Yaromyr, before he died and they all had spent New Year's Eve 1999 together in the Ponomarenko residence with the view of Mount Baker twenty years before.

"You know, I just remembered. I had a dream about my father last night. He hugged me."

"Aw, that's sweet," says Tanis.

"I just thought I'd share."

Quickly changing the subject, Shawn chimes in. "Did you know we've had some celebrities living here in Point Roberts over the years?"

"Yeah, like who?"

"Well, NHL goalie Glen Hanlon is a neighbour and tons of other hockey players... Pavel Bure…"

"Cool. Anyone else."

"Yeah, the writer, Margaret Laurence," says Kelly.

"Nice."

"And let's see who else? Oh yeah, Nancy Wilson and the guitarist from Heart lived here while they were recording their album, "Dreamboat Annie," back in the seventies."

"COME ON HOME, GIRL, he says with a smile…" Maria sings boldy out loud, catching everyone by surprise.

They all look at her with mouths and eyes wide open!

"Well, on that note," says Krys clearing his throat. "We better start heading back. We have another party to go to today."

"Thanks so much for this lovely afternoon," says Maria. "I had an amazing time!"

* * *

MY MYSTICAL MOMENT

by Maria Ponomarenko, Ammolite Wellness Coach

"Into the Mystic" by Van Morrison is one of my favourite songs and I feel like I "sailed into the mystic" myself this past weekend. The strangest thing happened to me after I posted my blog, "Coaching is a Creating Conversation."

In the post, I shared a video clip from the movie, "Elizabeth the Golden Age: The New World," where Sir Walter Raleigh describes the New World to Queen Elizabeth I.

To me, Mr. Raleigh really captures the essence of coaching. It's a creative process that starts as a smudge on the horizon of your imagination and then somehow grows into something you can actually walk into in real life.

Anyway, for my blog post, I chose to include a photo I took a couple of years ago from Island View Beach near Victoria, BC. It was the closest thing I had to seeing land from the sea as in Mr. Raleigh's story.

I like the photo because there's symmetry with the birds, and off in the distance, across the water, you can also see some sandy cliffs on another shore.

In my own head, I've always called those sandy cliffs, "The Cliffs of Dover" because I didn't know their real name.

Minutes after I posted my blog, I got a completely unrelated phone call from my sister-in-law asking if I'd like to come and visit the mainland for her brother's 50th birthday party. She also said for me to bring my passport because they were also planning on going to Point Roberts that day and that's in the States.

I figured this would be a good opportunity for me to do a dry run with my new backpack and my passport, 10 days before I set off to walk the Camino in Spain, so I said, "Sure, I'd like to come."

So, on Saturday, my brother and his family picked me up from the ferries and we headed to the U.S. to visit his friends who had just bought a house in Point Roberts. Until then, I had never even heard of Point Roberts before even though it's just a hop, skip, and a jump from Vancouver Island.

After we crossed the border, it was like we had stepped into a mythical forest – everything was so green and lush!

We arrived in the middle of the afternoon. My brother's friends offered to take us on a short hike from their home to the beach and we all enthusiastically took them up on their invitation.

And that's when I saw the "Cliffs of Dover" up close! I had actually walked into my own photo that I was looking at a few days before!

Also, just by chance, purely for dramatic effect as you'd find in the movies, there was a major thunder storm brewing further South and we saw some lightning strike across the sky, too!

Later at the 50th birthday party, there was a *Mariachi* band — it was quite the day for me!

Just a few short days ago, I had no idea that Point Roberts even existed. It never occurred to me that I'd actually go to those sandy cliffs myself someday.

I just admired the cliffs from afar for the last 22 years. And then through no conscious effort on my part, no force, no ego, and no wheeling and dealing, I went there in person, anyway!

It's the magic of coaching! One day you're staring off into the distance, dreaming about something with no agenda or attachment, and the next day you're experiencing it for real!

I think that's so cool and I just had to share this update with you.

Have you ever had a mystical experience that you can't explain? I'd love to hear about it. Please send me an email and let's make an appointment to chat. In the meantime, embrace the mystic — it's all around us!

* * *

Subject: RE: Hello from Lourdes

Hi Marichka, How was the birthday party? I really hope you had a good time. Tomorrow is our last day in Lourdes. It is great place. This evening we attended the human rosary candlelight procession and I got to sing some Ukrainian songs and lead twice in **Богородице Діво** [prayers to the Virgin Mary] in front of thousands of pilgrims. I will pray for you at Divine Liturgy tomorrow morning. Ciom Ciom Ciom. Z Bohom, Mam [kisses, go with God]

Subject: RE: Hello from Lourdes

Hi Mam, I had such a wonderful visit! I'm so happy I went. First we went to Point Roberts and saw Shawn and Kelly. Martín and Tanis showed up. We took a really nice walk through the forest. We eventually made our way to Carlos' party. They even had a Mariachi band which was perfect for my trip. Everyone was in good spirits. I understand today is Mother Mary's birthday – it must have been really nice to be at Lourdes for that. Glad to hear you're singing! Marichka

air • bag

Maria has been sharing her pre-Camino updates with her friends online all summer, and so many of them are aware that she will be heading to Spain in September. As a way to pay it forward in the pilgrim tradition, she offers to pray for her friends and family while on her spiritual journey with the following post: "5 days until I leave for Spain!"

> If you'd like me to say a prayer for you
> while I'm walking my Camino, please send
> me a message and I'll make sure to include
> your requests.

"Yes, please pray for my son," and "Can you please say a prayer for my friend who is going through a rough patch right now?" and "I'd love it if you could say a prayer for my cat," and "I'd really appreciate a prayer, thank you, Maria," are some of the responses.

Maria gladly writes down everyone's names on a special page in her journal and is honoured to have the opportunity to pray on behalf of others in such a sacred place.

On another note, after weighing herself in full backpacking attire, she also posts,

> Ironically, my backpack and gear weigh
> that exact amount of pounds I lost. I got
> everything down to 19-19.5 pounds and
> am happy with that.

"That is funny! Or interesting! Or cosmic!" comments Jordan.

"Congratulations on both the weight loss and the perfect backpack gain," writes Linda.

But Maria's friend Stanislav, who walked his own Camino in May and June, has a sneaking suspicion that Maria is not as 100 per cent ready to take off on her backpacking adventure as she naively thinks. He sends her a message to gather more information.

> **Subject: Ready for your Camino?**
> Good luck on the Camino! It is an amazing
> experience. I did the French route in 2018
> and the Portuguese one this year. Which
> route are you walking?

Subject: RE: Ready for your Camino?

Thanks, Stanislav, I'll be starting in Ponferrada and will be walking about 175K in Spain. (I believe it's the French way). Marichka

Subject: RE: Ready for your Camino?

According to my book it's about 210km to Santiago from Ponferrada. If you need any info on where to stay or what to take with you or even other places to go, give me a call.

Subject: RE: Ready for your Camino?

OK. I'll call you.

"Hi Stanislav, I'd love to hear about your Caminos."

"Sure, I can send you some links, but maybe it would be better for you to come over to my place. Do you have time this morning?"

"Yes, I can come over this morning. How about 11:30?

"Okay, see you then."

Before Maria leaves to meet Stanislav, she takes a moment to accept Vincent's connection request from the week before and then watches his coaching video.

"Oh, I love his accent! I think I'll take him up on his offer and book a call with him."

> Hi, Vincent, thanks for reaching out. I'd
> really love to book a call with you, but I
> can't until October after I come back home
> from walking the Camino in Spain. I'll
> contact you again next month. Maria

When she drives up to Stanislav's address near the Gorge, she thinks, "I've been here before. This is the same apartment building where Jill lives – and they're both Ukrainian. I think they would make a nice couple. I wonder if they know each other."

Maria presses the buttons at the entrance of the building with the three-digit code and Stanislav buzzes her up.

"I know someone else who lives here," says Maria.

"Yeah, Jill. I found out you two were friends this morning on your page," he replies. "We're on the lobby renovations committee together. How do you know her?"

"She called me once out of the blue regarding my mobile spa and although she never ended up working for me, we stayed friends," says Maria as she follows Stanislav across the living room. "I like the light in this room."

"I've spent the morning writing about my Caminos. Here's where I stayed if you're interested."

"Oh, great. Thanks. Super," she says as she scans his notes.

"I got as far as Triacastella in my memoirs today – just as a heads up, I turned right at the fork here where you have a choice to go either on the traditional route or on the newer one, but you can take either route, if you want."

"I'll probably follow your path."

"I ended up staying in this wonderful *albergue* in Fonfria near some cows. I think that was my favourite place out of all of them."

"That sounds nice. I'll keep my eye out."

"But who knows if you'll have to stay overnight in Fonfria or not. It all depends on your rhythm. How are you going to be finding your albergues each night – are you bringing your cell phone to book ahead?"

"I'm bringing my phone but I don't want to use up my data."

"They have really cheap cell phone rates in Europe."

"I know, but I don't want to risk losing my cell phone chip somewhere on the road while I'm using a temporary one."

"I understand. Did you end up getting a copy of Brierley's book?"

"No. They were sold out at the book store but I bought another guide book instead."

"Oh," he says furrowing his eyebrows. "Why don't you take my copy of Brierley's to the office supply store and make some photo copies of your route. Do you have time to do that today?"

"Yes, I do. Thanks. I'll do that right now."

So, Maria quickly drives over to the store and sets up camp at the colour copying machine.

"Open book to the right page... Ponferrada... here we go. Insert pre-loaded copy card. Select 'make copies.' Select paper size, 8 and a half by 11, reduce to 75 per cent, layout landscape, wait no, portrait, number of copies – one. Okay, press 'print.'"

A sheet comes out that cuts off some of the writing.

"That didn't quite work. Let's try that again. How do I make this double-sided? Okay, that's better. Turn the page. Next."

What should have been a quick, '10-minutes-at-most-job' (and even though Maria ends up with only seven, double-sided pages), the small task turns into a project and takes over an hour for Maria to complete.

"How's it going over there? Did you get all the copies you wanted yet?" asks Stanislav on the phone, thinking she should have returned ages ago.

"Just finishing up."

"I'm going to the grocery store to pick up some food for the week. Would it be possible for you to drop off the book there?"

"Which store are you going to?"

"The one at Tillicum."

"Sure, I can do that," says Maria.

"I'll call you from the parking lot. Thanks a lot by the way. This will really help me out on my trip."

* * *

Linda is also very interested in hearing about how Maria is preparing for her backpacking expedition because, she too, is planning to do her own pilgrimages – the first will be the Camino in Europe, and the second in Japan – in the next couple of years. She is also planning to spend a few weeks in Italy in October to catch up with another world traveller friend.

Linda sends Maria a link to a video, "Hidden Gems on the Camino French Way," which somehow magically fills in a missing piece of the puzzle for Maria.

"Thanks, Linda! That's super. It really gives me an idea of how the Albergue experience works! I've already pre-booked a room in Madrid and then I'll go to Ponferrada by train or something and then take it from there. How are you? Are you in Victoria these days?"

"I'm good. Glad it helped. I'm in Sooke right now."

"I'll be leaving for Spain in less than a week and I just wanted to connect with you before I go."

"I'll be dog sitting again from the 14th on, but I am coming to Victoria on Sunday the 15th. What does your Sunday look like?"

"On Sunday I'm doing some last minute shopping downtown. Will probably go into MEC. Do you want to come with me?"

"Yes, we can do that. Meet you there at 1pm. We can visit and go for tea and do some shopping since you are leaving soon."

"Wonderful, see you then!"

After church on Sunday, Maria stays downtown to meet with Linda. As soon as they walk into the store, she spots Svitlana and Charles in the sock department.

"Fancy meeting you here," says Maria to her church friends. "Where was your mom today? We missed her in the choir," asks Svitlana.

"Oh, she's doing her own pilgrimage right now. She just visited Lourdes with Iryna's tour group and now they're on their way to Ukraina."

"Oh, that's right. We must have just missed her."

"Everybody's zigzagging across the planet right now! How was your Camino?"

"It was amazing! Charles and I are thinking about going again next summer!"

"Already? Wow!"

"Yes, it was so worth it. I hope you get as much from your Camino as we did from ours and I can't see why you wouldn't. It's a real spiritual experience!"

"Oh, thanks. I'm just here with my friend Linda picking up some last minute items. Let's swap notes when I get back!" says Maria wading her way through the waves of shoppers.

"Buen Camino!" says Svitlana into the crowd between them.

"What kinds of last minute items are you looking for, Maria?" asks Linda.

"Well, I already have a quick-drying towel and some bottles for shampoo and I just bought some little things at the drug store… I can't think of anything that I absolutely still need."

"Okay, well, I'm just going to buy a couple of things and after that we can go for tea."

"Sounds good."

And before they know it, they move through the line and are back outside in the sunshine.

"There must be a nice coffee shop around here somewhere."

"Let's just follow our noses."

Within a few blocks, Maria and Linda stumble upon a small café with a black and green door with some empty metal chairs and tables out front.

"How about this place?"

"Sure. Fine by me."

Maria orders a turmeric latte while Linda orders a tea with a homemade granola bar. They sit at a small table near the door while a group of students with their laptops and backpacks lounge in the booth under the window. Linda hands Maria a bag.

"I thought you might need these for your Camino."

"Aw, thanks so much, Linda," Maria says as she unwraps the tissue. "Socks! Perfect!" Every time I wear them, I'll think of you."

"I hope you like the colour."

"Yes, such a nice, cheery blue!"

"And they're double-lined so they're designed to whisk sweat away so you don't get blisters."

"I love them!" says Maria. "If you want, I can give you a lift back to Sooke today."

"Oh, I can take the bus back. It's okay."

"Seriously, I'd be happy to. It's no problem."

"Alright. I'd appreciate that."

After their Sunday visit, Linda and Maria walk back to Maria's car.

"I just have to warn you that the "service air bags" light has recently come on in my car, so I technically don't have any airbags. I'm planning to get them fixed when I get back."

This information does not sit well with Linda.

"Don't worry. I'm a good driver. I'll get you home safe."

"So what are your plans after you come back from Spain?" says Linda adjusting her position in her seat and checking her seatbelt.

"Well, this is really hush, hush at the moment, but I'm thinking of picking up sticks and moving to Calgary."

"Calgary? I love Calgary! As you know I've lived there for years and a few of my sons live there with their wives and kids. If it wasn't for my ex-husband, I might still live there, too! I think that's wonderful! What does your mother think?"

"She doesn't know yet. I haven't told her. I didn't want to ruin her trip to Lourdes and I was planning to make my final decision while I was walking through the Spanish countryside. To tell you the truth, my mother and I haven't been getting along well these days."

"How so?"

"Well, the other day, before she left for Europe, she asked me if she should bring her cell phone and iPad with her and I was wrestling with my own decision about which phone to bring – my old yellow one that was bought and paid for or my brand new rose gold one, so she reminded me of my own question.

"And she kept asking me, 'should I take my phone and not the iPad.' 'Yes,' I said. Again she said, 'so I should take my phone?' 'Yes,' I said. 'You think it's a good idea for me to just take my phone and not both,' she repeated. "And then I lost it. 'Yes, yes, yes. Take your phone! How many yesses do you need?' I yelled in sheer frustration and in that moment, she put her hand on her heart and her facial expression sank and she said, 'What am I going to do with you?' as she ran into her bedroom and shut her door."

"And then what happened?"

"I felt so bad. I had never seen her make that hurt facial expression before. And then I felt some compassion for my mom. I gave her a few minutes of space and then I knocked on her door and said, 'I'm sorry.' 'Okay,' she said and all of a sudden, a window opened up and I was able to tell her why I was being such a bitch lately."

"Why? What was really going on?"

"I basically told her that she kept on taking over and she wouldn't let me do things for myself."

"Yes, her 'what am I going to do with you' comment says a lot."

"And I'm 50-years-old now and she still treats me like I'm still a child and doesn't trust me to make my own choices and decisions."

"She hasn't been able to let you grow up and let go of her mother role."

"Exactly. So when she kept on asking me about the phone, it was like she didn't trust my answer."

"I see," says Linda. "But you know what's interesting and somewhat ironic?"

"What?"

"By giving you this trip, she's actually showing you that she actually does love you and she's setting you free."

"Oh my gosh, yes, you're right, Linda."

"She's not sending you to some resort where you'd be sitting poolside and working on nothing but your tan for the next couple of weeks, now is she?"

"No."

"She's sending you on an adventure where you're going to be challenged in ways you've never been before. What a gift."

"Thank you, Linda. I didn't think of it that way. My mother really does love me."

"Yes, she does."

gem • stone

Having watched the iconic movie, "Eat, Pray, Love," starring Julia Roberts, a left-handed actor, just days before her own trip, Maria is secretly hoping her adventure will turn into a love story as well.

Her top three reasons for going on a Camino include: to have a mystical experience; to find love; and to let go of her past so she can start fresh at fifty. She feels the Camino will be a bridge between her past self and her new self.

On her last night at home before her big trip, Maria is sitting in her bedroom, studying the knickknacks she has collected over the years. She likes the birthday cards her niece and nephew had drawn for her when they were so much younger, she likes the fancy chandelier that hangs from the ceiling above her bed, she likes her Himalayan Salt lamp and all of her crystals.

As she runs her hand across the bedspread with the pink Peonies (which mean romantic love in Feng Shui) she glances up and admires the photograph she took of her first black cat Charlie.

"Oh, he was such a beautiful cat," she sighs.

She wishes the walls were a different shade of purple. The paint colour her mother had picked before Maria moved in is much too grey. She also wishes she did not have so much clutter.

"Why do I insist on keeping all of these things and dragging them around with me over hell's half acre? Like my TV – it's amazing it still works – I watched the O.J. Simpson car chase fiasco on that thing!"

Suddenly, her Lapis Lazuli prosperity bracelet flings itself off her dresser (like books sometimes randomly fly off shelves) and lands on her floor with a twitch.

"How did that happen?" she says looking around the room, a little spooked.

She picks up the crystal bracelet and studies the little orbs one by one, inspecting them for any clues. "They're like deep cobalt blue planets, some have golden streaks – ooh look, this one's closer to indigo."

She holds the gems in the palm of her left hand and tunes into their vibration.

"The royal blue colour is all about authentic self-expression… open communication… using your voice and speaking your truth… and Indigo is an in-between colour… not quite blue, not quite purple, not quite black… so its energy is subtle too… yet it's electric when isolated. It's the place I go when I meditate and it's about the inside world, inner knowing, insight, visualization, and the mystical dimension… also increases psychic awareness… cool… and also, note to self, I need to trust myself more…"

As Maria places her bracelet back on the dresser with a nurturing touch, her gaze gets pulled toward the painting that hangs outside her doorway. It's another significant painting in her mother's collection because for this one, Krys is the artist.

Krys made this work of art to capture a house party that he and his roommates had hosted while they were living in a loft in Toronto in the late 80's. Krys and three of his Ukrainian friends from childhood, Veslo, Kostyantyn and Steve, shared a loft space on College & Spadina, just north of Kensington Market.

Maria decides to walk over to it and give it a good think, as if it's hanging in a museum. As her eyes wander throughout the abstract mosaic scene, they do not land on any of the twelve archetypal party guests for more than a second before jetting off into another perception and direction. There is always something new to discover even after 29 years of walking past the painting, and her eyes never follow the same path twice.

"The shapes edge together like facets on a gemstone. I never thought of it like that before!"

If this painting was a gemstone, it would mostly resemble Turquoise. Krys uses aqua, cobalt blue, rusty orange, and stark white to capture the party scene.

She remembers how her brother scraped the acrylic paint on the eight by three foot canvass with a palette knife, like a tiler, which created a high-contrasting, geometric effect.

First, Maria notices the big, red *Coca Cola* sign which hangs at the top of the painting, just right of centre. Her eyes keep going right to a swinging lamp that shines over a woman wearing a blue and white dress, who is dancing in midair with her arms wide open, her right leg flying out into space with reckless abandon and left hand holding a martini glass.

"I always wanted to be that party guest," and even though she was present on that night, Krys insists that the dancer is somebody else. She is not depicted in this party scene at all, which is still a sore spot for her.

Veslo is the guy in the green shirt standing behind the camera in the bottom right corner of the painting. A palm tree representing the El Mocambo, which is a bar across the street, famous for hosting iconic bands like the Rolling Stones, Blondie, the Ramones, Devo and Joan Jett, waves hello from the far right of the composition.

Next comes Martín. He is the figure in white who is snoozing on the purple couch, beer still in hand. Krys' friend Roy from high school stands front and centre. He is holding a microphone and is bellowing (in Maria's imagination) a song by Matthew Wilder, "Ain't Nothin' Gonna Break-A My Stride." The song perfectly suits Roy's tenor voice.

Meanwhile, the Nylons, a band well-known for performing, "The Lion Sleeps Tonight," who happened to live upstairs, step in as the house band for the party. Curiously, Maria and five of her choral friends performed the Lion Sleeps song in a musical skit under the band name of, "Lapis Lazuli" in their high school's senior talent show five years earlier.

To balance Martín's pose, Kostyantyn is lounging on a hammock. Hints of the black and white tiled floor in the kitchen run beneath them. To the farthest left, a couple share a romantic moment on the deck with the distant CN Tower behind them.

Maria's eyes sweep up from the line in the hammock. She pulls her gaze back towards centre, past the backup singer in the band, and over to Krys' wall of plastic telephones, an installation he had also created, which adds an 'art within art' layer to the painting.

The three light fixtures are actually shower heads – a nod to the shower that was in the kitchen – the perfect place to keep the beer during parties!

"I assume by the style of the shirt and the jeans, that Krys is the guy in the middle of the painting, standing calmly next to Roy and watching this whole scene unfold."

He is holding some sort of instrument but it oddly looks like a skull to her. Party crashers are a sign of a good party and she is able to spot several phantom party guests in the room.

"Something tells me, the ghostly images are unintentional because they fall in the murky, grey spaces of an otherwise lively scene."

There is a guy lying on his side hovering in the top right corner who has a looped earring and a Mohawk hairstyle. In his shadows, Maria is also able to see a woman with an auburn Beaufont hair-do who seems to come from a James Bond movie. There are also white figures splashed together as if they are an audience seated in an auditorium, watching a play or a movie.

"Krys really does have an artistic talent," she admits. When they each drew pictures of airplanes while they visited their Great Aunt Stefa in upstate New York in her colonial mansion by the blue bridge as kids, "his pictures always seemed so much better than mine."

As they grew older, they graduated from drawing simple scenes of suns with smiley faces to painting more elaborate compositions.

It is clear to Maria that Krys has a certain spatial intelligence and has the ability to visualize in three dimensions. She knows he is able to rotate an object in his imagination and see it from all angles, as if he is physically holding it in their hands.

He also has the amazing ability to draw a perfect circle freehand.

In contrast, Maria is much more auditory than visual in her sensibilities but their father once told her that he really liked her drawings also.

Just as she falls deeper into Krys' "Spadina House Party" painting, the phone rings. It is Krys of all people!

"I just wanted to wish you well on your trip!"

"Thanks, Krys," she says, stunned by his timing.

"But I've been thinking about your backpack. When you mentioned you had pockets in the band around your hips, I got a little concerned. Don't put anything in them. Pickpockets will come up to you and say something like, 'Oh, your hair is so nice' and you're just so trusting and before you know it, they've opened the zippers and reached into your pockets and they'll take your money and passport and you won't know what hit you."

"They're that fast?"

"Yes! It's a poor country and they need to fend for themselves and tourists are easy prey. I want you to be very careful and keep your head low and don't talk to anyone – especially when you're in Madrid. Don't let your guard down for one second!"

"Okay, I'll do my best. Thanks for the heads up," she says politely.

"I'm not sure you understand how important this is. When I spent that semester in Barcelona when I was in art school, I got pickpocketed and it's not a walk in the park, believe me."

"I understand…don't worry…I'll be okay."

"Alright, Marich, have a safe trip and post what you can. We'll be watching your progress with great interest from here."

After Maria hangs up the phone with her brother, she feels anxious.

"Will I be able to handle myself out there in a foreign country by myself?"

She turns and looks at the painting one more time. She catches a detail she has never noticed before.

"Wait a minute…that photographer's gaze is quite intimate… it's like he's looking straight inside the dancing girl's soul through his camera lens."

"Come to the party… kick your feet up…let him in your heart…" she hears whispered from the painting. "Your Camino is waiting…"

* * *

Act • now• ledge• mints

Vincent van Gogh's benefactor was his brother, Theodorus, who was an art dealer. My benefactor is my mother, Motria, who is an art lover and collector. I'm truly grateful to my mother who has given me the time, space and financial assistance to tell my stories and for sending me on my Camino in 2019 because without her generosity, this book would not have been written.

I'm also grateful to Yu-Ting "Leticia" Peng and Miguel Angel Cortes Diaz for walking with me on my Camino. We all came from different countries but all started in Ponferrada on the same day and ended our Caminos in Santiago de Compestella together. If you both hadn't called out to me while I was feeling lost and discouraged on our second to last day and helped me find a bed in an albergue that night, I would never have had the idea to write this book in the first place. Buen Camino.

I'm also grateful to my friend from childhood, Marichka Melnyk for reading my first draft and for giving me valuable feedback, including "it's tremendously flawed" but "I like the character because she just keeps going" and "there's something about the painting that intrigues me." I appreciate your encouragement and your sense of humour and I hope you like my edits.

Also, if you're wondering about the title of this book, the original title was, "Who is Donna Tiva?" but one day as I was out for a walk, the song, "Closer to Fine" by the Indigo Girls (1989) came up on my playlist and it has always been one of my favourite songs. So, I played with the words and themes of my book and renamed my story, "Closer to Indigo" and I'd just like to thank Amy Ray and Emily Sailers for sharing their voices with us and for capturing my own spiritual journey in song so eloquently.

And finally, thank you to everyone I've spoken with during the last 3 years (including friends, family, clients and fellow coaches) who have expressed an interest in my book – our conversations helped and encouraged me more than you know.

play • list

"(Ain't Nothin' Gonna) Break My Stride" (1983) Written By: Matthew Wilder, Greg Prestopino Performed By: Matthew Wilder

"All Out of Love" (1980) Written By: Clive Davis, Graham Russell Performed By: Air Supply

"Blackbird" (1968) Written & Performed By: Paul McCartney

"Beautiful Maria of my Soul" (1992) Written & Composed By: Arne Glimcher, Robert Kraft Performed By: Los Lobos

"Bohemian Rhapsody" (1975) Written By: Frederick Mercury Performed By: Queen

"Bus Stop" (1966) Written By: Graham Gouldman Performed By: The Hollies

"Carol of the Bells" (1914) Composed By Mykola Leontovych

"The Climb" (2009) Written By: Jessi Alexander, Jon Mabe Performed By: Miley Cyrus

"Closer to Fine" (1989) Written By: Emily Sailers Performed By: the Indigo Girls

"The Devil Went Down to Georgia" (1979) Written By: Charlie Daniels, Tom Crain "Taz" DiGregorio, Fred Edwards, Charles Hayward, James W Marshall Performed By: Charlie Daniels Band "Every Time I See Your Picture (I Cry)" (1984) Written By: Pierre Marchand Performed By: Luba

"Farewell to Nova Scotia" (1964) Folk song from Nova Scotia, adapted from the Scottish "The Soldier's Adieu" written by Robert Tannahill circa WW1 Performed By: Catherine McKinnon with Singalong Jubilee

"Fire Burning" (2009) Written & Performed By: Sean Kingston

"Firework" (2010) Written By: Esther Dean, Katheryn Hudson, Mikkel Storleer Eriksen, Sandy Julien Wilhelm, Tor Erik Hermansen Performed By: Katy Perry

"Hawaii Five-O Theme" (1968) Composed By: Morton Stevens

"I Believe" (2010) Written By: Stephan Moccio & Alan Frew Performed By: Nikki Yanofsky

"I Never Will Marry" (1979) Written By: Fred Hellerman Performed By: Nana Mouskouri

"Into the Mystic" (1974) Written By: Van Morrison Performed By: Colin James (2005)

"Ironic" (1996) Written By: Morissette and Glen Ballard Performed By: Alanis Morissette

"The Lady of Shallott" (1991) Written By: Alfred Tennyson, Dan Smith, Rose Prince, Steve Smith, Tom Gilbert Performed By: Loreena McKennitt Based On: the poem, The Lady of Shalott by Alfred, Lord Tennyson

"Laverne & Shirley theme song (Making Our Dreams Come True)" (1976) Written & Composed By: Charles Fox, Norman Gimbel Performed By: Cyndi Grecco

"The Lion Sleeps Tonight (Wimoweh)" (1939) Written and Recorded By: Solomon Linda under the title "Mbube" for the South African Gallo Record Company. Linda's original was written in isiZulu, while the English version's lyrics were written by George David Weiss. Performed By: The Nylons (1982)

"Lovers in a Dangerous Time" (1984) Written By: Bruce Cockburn Performed By: Bruce Cockburn

"Magic Man" (1975) Written By: Ann Wilson, Nancy Wilson Performed By: Heart

"Многая літа (Mnohaya Lita)" Ukrainian. Mnohaya Lita means "Many Years" or "wishing you many years of life" and is a traditional Ukrainian celebratory song. The song is based on both the Greek ("Many Years to You") and on the Byzantine Rite. The song is sung on birthdays, name days, weddings, church events and other events.

"Now My Feet Won't Touch the Ground [Prospekt's March Edition]" (2008) Written By: Chris Martin, Will Champion, Jonny Buckland, Guy Berryman Performed By: Coldplay

"Only Girl (In the World)" (2010) Written By: Sandy Julien Wilhelm, Mikkel Eriksen, Tor Erik Hermansen, Crystal Johnson Performed By: Rihanna

"Perfect" (2017) Written By: Ed Sheeran Performed By: Ed Sheeran

"Rain King" (1993) Written By: Adam Duritz, Charles Gillingham, David Bryson, Matthew Malley, Steve Bowman Performed By: Counting Crows

"Right Here, Right Now" (1990) Written By: Mike Edwards Performed By: Jesus Jones

"Rock With You" (1979) Written By: Rodney Lynn Temperton Performed By: Michael Jackson

"Running" (2009) Written By: Gauntlette Alexander, Gauntlette Jr Alexander, Jully Black, Kellis E Jr Parker Performed By: Jully Black

"Should I Stay or Should I Go?" (1981) Written By: Topper Headon, Mick Jones, Paul Simonon, Joe Strummer Performed By: The Clash

"The Sound of Music (How Do You Solve A Problem Like Maria)" (1959) Composed By: Richard Rodgers Lyrics Written By: Oscar Hammerstein II

"Tie a Yellow Ribbon Round the Ole Oak Tree" (1973) Written By: Irwin Levine, Russell Brown Performed By: Tony Orlando and Dawn

"Today Is Your Day" (2011) Written & Performed By: Shania Twain

"Volya (Freedom) or Ya Bachila Ptashku (I Saw a Bird)" Based on: Ukrainian folk song Performed By: Luba Kowalchyk

"White Wedding" (1982) Written & Performed By: Billy Idol

move • ease

"A Wrinkle in Time" (2018) Directed By: Ava DuVernay; Written By: Jennifer Lee, Jeff Stockwell; Based on: Madeleine L'Engle's 1962 novel. Starring: Oprah Winfrey, Reese Witherspoon, Mindy Kaling, Storm Reid

"Antiques Roadshow" (1979-present) TV series Created By: BBC Television

"Big Bang Theory" (2007-19) TV sitcom created by Chuck Lorre, Bill Prady; Written By: Chuck Lorre, Bill Prady, Steven Molaro; Starring: Johnny Galecki, Jim Parsons, Kaley Cuoco, Simon Helberg, Kunal Nayyar, Mayim Bialik, Melissa Rauch, Kevin Sussman

"Bonanza" (1959-73) Western TV series starring: Lorne Greene, Pernell Roberts, Dan Blocker, Michael Landon

"Christmas Bells are Ringing" (2018) Directed By: Pat William; Written By: Nicole Baxter; Starring: Emilie Ullerup, Josh Kelly, Mark Humphrey

"Eat, Pray, Love" (2010) Directed By: Ryan Murphy; Written By: Ryan Murphy, Jennifer Salt; Starring: Julia Roberts, James Franco, Richard Jenkins, Viola Davis, Billy Crudup, Javier Bardem

"Elizabeth: The Golden Age" (2007) Directed By: Shekhar Kapur; Written By: William Nicholson, Michael Hirst; Starring: Cate

Blanchett, Clive Owen, Geoffrey Rush, Shawn Nygaard; YouTube Link: youtu.be/rRgWiV0OHY0

"Father Brown" (2013 to present) TV series loosely based on the Father Brown short stories by G. K. Chesterton; Starring Mark Williams, Sorcha Cusack, Emer Kenny

"Footprints: The Path of Your Life" (2016) Directed By: Juan Manuel Cotelo; Written By: Juan Manuel Cotelo, Alexis Martínez

"Friends" (1994-2004) TV sitcom created by David Crane, Marta Kauffman; Starring: Jennifer Aniston, Courteney Cox, Lisa Kudrow, Matt LeBlanc, Matthew Perry, David Schwimmer

"Gnome Alone" (2017) Directed By: Peter Lepeniotis; Written By: Michael Schwartz, Zina Zaflow; Based on: a story by Robert Moreland; Starring: Becky G, Josh Peck, Olivia Holt, Madison De La Garza, George Lopez

"Gracepoint" (2014) TV series created by Chris Chibnall and is a remake of Chibnall's UK drama series, "Broadchurch," starring: David Tennant, Anna Gunn.

"Groundhog Day" (1993) Directed By: Harold Ramis; Written By: Harold Ramis, Danny Rubin. Starring: Bill Murray, Andie MacDowell, Chris Elliott

"Heart Takes Tumble on Way to Transplant" Lee Powell, The Associated Press, 12 January 2012

"Mad Men" (2007-15) Written By: Matthew Weiner; Starring: Jon Hamm, Elisabeth Moss, John Slattery, January Jones

"Maudie" (2016) Directed By: Aisling Walsh; Written By: Sherry White; Starring: Sally Hawkins, Ethan Hawke

"Moonlighting" (1985-89) dramedy TV series starring: Cybill Shepherd, Bruce Willis, Allyce Beasley

"The Princess Bride" (1987) Directed By: Rob Reiner; Starring: Cary Elwes, Robin Wright, André the Giant, Peter Falk, Fred Savage. Adapted by William Goldman from his 1973 novel of the same name

"Run Lola Run" (1998) Written and Directed By: Tom Tykwer; Starring: Franka Potente, Moritz Bleibtreu

"Super Soul Sunday" TV series on OWN, the Oprah Winfrey Network; Hosted By: Oprah

"Vikings" (2013-20) historical drama TV series; Created & Written By: Michael Hirst; Based on: the sagas of Ragnar Lodbrok

"The Way" (2010) Directed, Produced and Written By: Emilio Estevez. Starring: Martin Sheen, Deborah Kara Unger, James Nesbitt, Yorick van Wageningen

"X-Men: The Last Stand" (2006) Superhero film based on X-Men by Stan Lee, Jack Kirby; filmed at Hatley Castle, Royal Roads University

read • ding • list

$1 Dollar Canadian Loonie Coin for the 50th Anniversary of the Decriminalization of Homosexuality in Canada (2019) by Canadian artist, Joe Average is a celebration of community, equality and inclusion. coinsunlimited.ca

"And she brought forth her firstborn son, and wrapped him in swaddling clothes, and laid him in a manger; because there was no room for them in the inn" ~ Luke 2:7

"Bluenose Ghosts" a book of Nova Scotia ghost stories collected by Canadian folklorist Helen Creighton over a period of 28 years, Ryerson Press, first published in 1957

Brierley, John, "A Pilgrim's Guide to the Camino de Santiago (Camino Frances): St. Jean Pied de Port * Santiago de Compostela," 18th Edition, Kaminn Media Ltd, 2021

Cameron, Julia, "The Artist's Way: A Spiritual Path to Higher Creativity," Jeremy P. Tarcher/Perigee, 1992

Chapman, Gary, "The Five Love Languages: How to Express Heartfelt Commitment to Your Mate," 1992

"Despite Fire, Notre Dame Cross And Altar Still Standing," By Christopher Brito, CBS News, April 16, 2019

"The Divine Liturgy An Anthology for Worship," published by the Metropolitan Andrey Sheptytsky Institute of Eastern Christian Studies, Saint Paul University, Ottawa, 2004

Follett, Ken, "The Pillars of the Earth," Macmillan Publishers, 1989

Gilbert, Elizabeth, "The Signature of All Things," Viking Press, 2013 and "Eat, Pray, Love, One Woman's Search for Everything Across Italy, India and Indonesia," Penguin, 2006

The Gospel According to Mary Magdalene

Homer, Book XIV, "the Odyssey, Hospitality in the Forest," Trans. Fitzgerald (7th-8th Century BC)

"Irish beach washed away 33 years ago reappears overnight after freak tide: Villagers express delight after entire beach that vanished in Achill Island storms in 1984 turns back sands of time" by Henry McDonald, Ireland correspondent, the Guardian, Monday, 8 May, 2017

44 It was now about the sixth hour, and darkness came over all the land until the ninth hour. 45 The sun was darkened, and the veil of the temple was torn down the middle..." Luke 23:44 Berean Study Bible

Jesus appears to Mary Magdalene ~ John 20:11-18

"Notre Dame Altar And Cross Remain Miraculously Untouched After Fire," VT, April 16, 2019

"Notre Dame's Golden Altar Cross Seen Glowing As Images Emerge From Inside, Showing Fire-Ravaged Cathedral," True Pundit, April 16, 2019

"OPEN: New Johnson Street Bridge unveiled today in Victoria" by Anna James, *Victoria News*, March 31, 2018

Pink, Daniel, "A Whole New Mind: Why Right-Brainers Will Rule the Future," Penguin Publishing Group, 2005

Proulx, E. Annie, "The Shipping News," Charles Scribner's Sons, 1993

Redfield, James, "The Celestine Prophecy," Satori Publishing, 1993

"Robin Hood," Created By: Anonymous Balladeers, 13th or 14th Century AD

"Run offers hope for cure" by Katherine Dedyna, Times Colonist, October 1, 2009. Adrian Lam, event photographer (photos not shown).

Strayed, Cheryl, "Wild," Alfred A. Knopf, Inc., 2012

"The Symposium," a philosophical text by Plato, dated c. 385–370 BC

Tennyson, Lord Alfred, "The Lady of Shallot," 1833

The Transfiguration of Jesus ~ Mark 9:2-9

"Then Jesus said to him, "Get up! Pick up your mat and walk." John 5:8

"Woman Takes Part In Search For Herself," by Andie Sophia Fontaine, *Reykjavik Grapevine*, August 27, 2012

Watch Maria's TV Series

Curious to see how some of the locations in *Closer to Indigo* look like in real life and to hear chapters read by the author, Maria Koropecky, herself?

Introducing *Saanich: Emerging Land; Emerging People*, a 9-episode TV series written, filmed, directed, edited and hosted by Maria Koropecky, coming to TELUS Optik TV, VOD and YouTube starting in September, 2022.

Watch as nature lover and emerging author, Maria Koropecky, guides you to some hidden gems that she also features in her novel, *Closer to Indigo*. We'll touch on the mystical and spiritual side of nature, see examples of geological marvels and historic architecture – and possibly even wildlife – and you'll also hear the author herself read from her novel, *Closer to Indigo*, which inspired some of the locations and scenes in the book.

Saanich: Emerging Land; Emerging People Trailer on Youtube:
https://youtu.be/X1Eliq9SsvE

Subscribe to Maria's Youtube Channel:
https://youtube.com/channel/UCV092G2ixBx5MLiMlLpjum

Connect with Maria Koropecky on LinkedIn:
www.linkedin.com/in/mariakoropecky

To work with Maria Koropecky, visit Ammolite Wellness Coaching and book a call: www.ammolitewellnesscoaching.com

About The Author
Maria Koropecky

Maria Koropecky is a Free Spirit Coach, Crystal Mapper, TV Host and author of the novel, *Closer to Indigo*. Maria lives and works out of her home on an island in the Pacific, near Victoria, British Columbia, Canada, and enjoys singing out loud to the songs on her phone while walking through her neighbourhood as she trains for her next Camino. She has an Honours BA in English Literature from Western University and certifications in Life Coaching & Mentoring, Spa Therapy, and Crystal Reading.